Surrender in Scarlet

"I am no soldier," she said, "but I know there is more than one kind of freedom. One that means having music and laughter and waking with joy in your heart."

Becket drew in a sharp breath.

Her touch was cool on his fire-warmed flesh. He rubbed his lips against her palm.

"How can you see so much?" he whispered against her skin. "There is so much caring in you, it fills you with light and warmth. And I'm so cold inside, Kaatje, so cold and dark."

Kaatje felt caught in the web of his touch.

"I am but a man. A man who hungers . . ."

Surrender in Scarlet

Patricia Camden

AVON BOOKS · NEW YORK

SURRENDER IN SCARLET is an original publication of Avon Books. This work has never before appeared in book form. This work is a novel. Any similarity to actual persons or events is purely coincidental.

AVON BOOKS
A division of
The Hearst Corporation
1350 Avenue of the Americas
New York, New York 10019

Copyright © 1991 by Patricia Camden
Inside cover author photograph by Michael Marois
Published by arrangement with the author
Library of Congress Catalog Card Number: 91-91783
ISBN: 0-380-76262-5

First Avon Books Printing: August 1991

AVON TRADEMARK REG. U.S. PAT. OFF. AND IN OTHER COUNTRIES, MARCA REGISTRADA, HECHO EN U.S.A.

Printed in the U.S.A.

RA 10 9 8 7 6 5 4 3 2 1

To my parents
and my husband—

I am blessed.

Acknowledgments

Writing is a solitary craft. A writer spends countless hours sitting alone in a room, staring at a
computer monitor while her mind is far away in the
fictive dream she is creating. I am fortunate in having
family, friends, and professional colleagues who help
me keep mind and body and book together.

I am especially beholden to three talented writers:
Diane Dunaway, Paula Detmer Riggs, and Barbara
Faith. Their unflagging support, advice, criticism, and
praise were invaluable to me during the writing of this
book, and I continue to rely on them.

For the music of the period, I am indebted to master
voice teacher Sarah Fleming, B.S.M., Juilliard, M.A.,
San Diego State University, especially for discovering
lyrics that so perfectly fit my story.

And many thanks to my agent, Nancy Yost, for making the tough parts seem easy, and to my editor, Ellen
Edwards, for adopting me.

Chapter 1

High Summer, 1708
Chateau de St. Benoit, Flanders

Madame Kaatje de St. Benoit, widow of the late chevalier, walked from the chateau's kitchen onto the back terrace and shook the flour from her apron. She'd risen before dawn, weary and unrested, to mix and knead and bake the coming week's bread. Since Philippe's death every sou had had to be hoarded, but now she welcomed the hard work. It alone seemed able to stave off the trembling anxiety about her son that invaded even her dreams.

She leaned against the low stone wall that bordered the terrace and let her gaze travel restlessly over the gently rolling fields of oats and flax. The pale green leaves of a stand of birch trees shimmered in the distance, and the warm midday air was heavy with the smell of freshly baked bread. Kaatje took a deep breath to try and still the apprehension fluttering in her stomach.

A trill of boyish laughter drifted from the sward between the garden and the orchard, causing a smile to lift some of the weariness from her fine-boned face and lighten her gray eyes. It was high summer now, but at the turn of the new year Pietr would go to live with his uncle, the Margrave of Hespaire-Aube, to be raised in the style a six-year-old of his rank deserved.

1

Two years earlier, when Philippe had been killed at the battle of Ramillies, Kaatje had expected his family to embrace, if not her, at least Philippe's son and heir. But nearly a year had passed without even an acknowledgment of their existence.

Kaatje had begun inundating Philippe's brother, the margrave, with letters demanding that he recognize and provide for his nephew. Philippe may have been a fourth son, but Pietr was entitled to a great deal more than he was receiving. Eventually, a liveried servant had appeared, sniffed at the surroundings, and handed her a very belated invitation for her son.

But now the smile on Kaatje's lips faltered. With Pietr living at his uncle's, it would be extremely difficult to keep the boy's falling sickness a secret. Her uneasiness turned to acid fear. If the margrave knew of Pietr's illness, he could declare the boy insane, strip him of his title, confiscate his estate, and confine him to a tiny cell in a remote monastery.

An image from her black dreams rose up before her: her sweet little golden-haired boy shivering in rags on a filth-covered stone floor, whimpering for a few drops of water. "No," she whispered. "No one else will ever learn of Pietr's falling sickness—no one!"

Medicine kept Pietr's sickness at bay, medicine made by her sister's astrologer and sent every three months. As long as it continued to arrive the margrave would never know; nothing must come between her son and his heritage.

The sound of her old servant's murmuring voice came from the kitchen door behind her, and Kaatje let some of the tension drain from her shoulders. Sweet patient Grette—she and her husband, Marten, were the only servants left now.

"Madame," Grette said, "there's someone here from your sister, Madame d'Agenais."

Lece, only a week late. I knew you hadn't forgotten.

Kaatje straightened the skirts of her faded yellow gown as best she could, tucked a stray blond strand back under her linen cap, and lifted her chin. When she turned, she was every inch the chatelaine.

"Yes?" she said, seeing the stocky man dressed in d'Agenais livery glance at her flour-covered hands. When he looked up, she met his derision with a level gaze. He held a letter packet in front of his chest, waving it to and fro as if deciding what to do with it. Kaatje had to struggle not to let dismay creep into her face. *Where was the box of medicine?*

"I'm to put this into the hands of Madame Catherine de St. Benoit," the servant said, not bothering to bow to her. Her lips tightened into a thin line.

"I am Madame *Kaatje* de St. Benoit," she said, then silently added, *As my sister well knows.* How she hated the French names.

The look on her face hardened, and the servant belatedly dipped into a shallow bow and held out the letter to her. "Your pardon, madame. I was only repeating what I was told."

"I do not doubt it," she said, her words clipped. Her fingers itched to snatch the letter from his hands, but she forced herself to take the folded and sealed paper from him graciously. She went to stand back by the low wall and broke the red wax seal. She read the date, then turned to glare at the servant.

"This is a month old!" she said, gesturing angrily. "It takes less than a sennight to ride here from Chateau d'Agenais." She put her hands on her hips, waiting for his excuse.

"D'Agenais?" The servant shrugged, a carefully composed look of innocence on his face. "The war, madame," he said. "It makes travel difficult."

"This is Flanders—there is always war. The other servants were never so late." She turned her back on him and quickly began to scan the letter, then stopped,

panic coiling into a knot in her stomach. *No!* she cried
silently, *Lece, you can't do this to my son!* She started
to read the letter again, this time more slowly.

"My dear sister," Lece had written, beginning as
she usually did, but then all that was familiar fled.

I'm afraid dear little Pierre's medicine will be delayed a bit. Oncelus is being difficult. You see, he
told my husband that he simply must have more
money for supplies and old Constantin almost had a
fit of apoplexy on the spot! He was screeching, I tell
you, positively screeching. "More gold! How can an
astrologer need so much gold? Some paper, ink, a
few astrolabes, a few books . . ." He went on and
on about it, and the result is that Oncelus has
wrapped himself in those black robes of his and is
threatening to leave!

By the way, Oncelus says that that candelabrum
you sent last time wasn't solid silver. He'd like you
to send that gold and enamel clock you had when
you visited here. You know, the one Maman gave
you when you were a little girl and you cried whenever you saw our new steppapa. Just give it to my
servant. Then Oncelus can concentrate on dear little
Pierre's medicine.

Don't worry. I won't let Oncelus leave. He is, after
all, only two score and five—in the very prime of
manhood. And those black eyes of his put me into
such a fever! How I would love for that tottering old
bag of wind I married to just disappear. I tell you,
Kaat, I don't know how much longer I can bear Constantin's feeble pawing when such a *man* is so near.
I ache for his . . .

Kaatje stopped reading, the paper rattling faintly in
her trembling hands. Oncelus wasn't going to send Pietr
his medicine until she'd paid him more! Oh sweet God,

what was she going to do? After the clock, there wasn't much left to send him.

She shuddered and steadied herself against the low stone wall. Pietr had only had one seizure so far, when they'd been visiting Lece. Oncelus had made up the medicine that kept the sickness from returning, and whatever Oncelus required, she would pay. She wouldn't let anything jeopardize her son's chance to claim his birthright.

Kaatje turned and walked briskly back to Lece's servant. "Wait here," she said, her voice firm with resolve. "I'll bring you what you need."

Hidden in a stand of birch a hundred yards away, Colonel Becket, Lord Thorne studied the figures on the terrace of the Chateau St. Benoit through a perspective glass. He shifted his long form in the thick layer of rotting leaves, the branches of the bushes around him snagging on the borrowed dark blue Dutch uniform he wore. His black stallion, Acheron, stood nearby, his occasional snorts lost in the everyday sounds of the countryside.

Becket shrugged to get more comfortable. The coat was a tight fit across his shoulders, but he'd had no choice; in this countryside it was difficult to watch someone unnoticed while dressed in English scarlet.

His deep blue eyes followed the obviously angry woman railing at an insolent servant. She stood sideways to him, putting her profile in sharp relief. Ribbons on her sleeve fluttered as she cut through the air with her hand in a sharp gesture.

The gold curls escaping her cap and the fairness of her full creamy bosom told him that she was a Flemish rather than a French beauty. And her stance told him just as clearly that she was a beauty with hot blood in her veins. He thought he saw her holding something in her far hand, but he couldn't be sure.

He focused on the woman's face. "You look as wild as your faithless sister," Becket murmured, sitting up with his back against the white bark of a tree. He closed his perspective glass with a snap, and his mouth settled into a hard, uncompromising line. "But I'll get you to tell me what I want to know. Your tricks won't work on me."

Kaatje left the terrace and walked slowly through the kitchen and down the hallway to the wide staircase that curved up to the upper floors. Once she was out of sight of Grette and the manservant, she lifted her skirts and tucked the letter into a deep pocket in her petticoat. She would burn it later; she had to, to protect Pietr.

The leather soles of her shoes rasped on the polished mahogany treads as she ascended, each step reminding her of the Turkestan carpet that had once covered the stairs. It had been sold last winter to buy wood for the fire.

She had been shocked to learn that Philippe had had no income of his own, only an allowance from his family that had stopped when she'd sent them word of his death. Kaatje pushed the past from her mind. It didn't matter now. She and Pietr were managing, and soon her son would be among—

A loud crash interrupted her thoughts. "Grette?" she called, running back down the stairs. She halted abruptly at the bottom step, a scream caught in her throat.

The massive front doors had been thrown open. Three French foot soldiers marched past her into the large entry hall. They went to the old fragile chairs that lined the wall and, one after the other, threw them into a pile, the legs splintering loudly on the marble floor.

"*Stop!*" she cried, staring in disbelief. At that moment an exquisitely dressed French officer stepped through the doorway, his disinterested gaze scanning the scene. The long, precise curls of his wig barely moved against his bright blue uniform coat.

"Are you responsible for this? Stop it at once!" Kaatje demanded. From where she stood she heard others rummaging through the kitchen shelves, carelessly knocking off earthenware bowls and anything else that obstructed their search. Crash followed crash, and she could hear pieces of shattered crockery skidding everywhere on the stone floor.

A soldier started up the stairs, and Kaatje rushed to grab his arm, only to be roughly thrown against the banister. Another pushed a heavy wooden armchair onto its side with a loud bang.

Kaatje whirled on the elaborately dressed officer. "Who are you? Why do you do nothing? *Make them stop.*"

"Ah, madame," the French officer said with a practiced courtier's smile, "I am hardly interested in carpentry."

"Then why are you here? Your soldiers are destroying my home!"

His smile hardened and he gestured dismissively toward the soldiers. "You can surely replace a chair or two."

By now the men had finished with the chairs and moved on to the chests and cabinets, smashing their doors and lids back and dumping the contents onto the floor. Outrage bubbled through Kaatje like boiling lye, stripping her nerves bare. "A chair or two? You are leaving us with nothing!"

He didn't bother to hide his sneer at her Flemish-accented French. She clenched her hands into fists, tighter and tighter until she felt the nails bite into her palms. There were too many of them to take on, she told herself, and they all had swords.

The officer looked at her, his small dark eyes pinning her to her place like splinters of black glass. "They do what they must," he said. "We are here to find your sister."

He turned and strode down the hall to the kitchen.

"My sister?" Kaatje cried. That was the last thing she'd expected. She rushed after him. "Lece? Why are you looking here? What do you want with her?"

She brought herself up sharp in the doorway. The kitchen was a disaster, the soldiers' feet grinding shards of broken crockery into the stone floor. Her newly baked loaves had been trampled into dust, with only a few golden bits of crust still intact. There was no sign of Lece's manservant or of Grette.

The officer looked up at her. "Where is Madame d'Agenais?"

Kaatje struggled with her utter dismay. "Who are you?" she demanded.

The man lowered his head in a shallow bow. "I am the Comte de Roulon," he said with an exaggerated drawl. He straightened and absently adjusted his long lace cuffs. A shadow traveled across his sharp-boned face as a soldier cut across the bright midday sunlight that shone through the open doorway.

"What do you want of Lece?" she asked, trying to keep her voice from cracking. She recognized Roulon's name from one of Lece's letters; the two had once been lovers.

A soldier dumped a basket filled with spoons and knives into a heap on the wooden table, and Kaatje jumped. Then he put the three rabbits old Marten had caught early that morning into a basket—rabbits that would have fed them for days.

She moved to stop him, but a hand gripped her elbow and drew her back. "A few rabbits. What does it matter?" the comte asked with a shrug.

She jerked out of his hold. "It matters a great deal. We shall starve!"

"It is unfortunate that your husband, the late chevalier, did not pound some of that Flemish stubbornness out of you," he said.

"You know who I am, and still you . . ." Kaatje's voice trailed off, a chill tightening the flesh on the back of her neck. Anger began pushing out the fear.

Roulon said nothing, only pulled a scented square of silk from his cuff and waved it under his nose.

You contemptible mincing fool, Kaatje wanted to scream. How could Lece have shared this man's bed?

French army officers. She'd had nothing but contempt for the whole useless aristocratic lot of them even before Philippe's death. Their elaborate wigs and exquisitely tailored uniforms made them look more likely to invade Versailles than an enemy encampment.

Another officer entered the kitchen from the back terrace and bowed, then stood next to Kaatje, ignoring her. This one wore a light brown wig, and the cloth of his uniform coat was slightly less fine than Roulon's. The comte raised an eyebrow at the man, and the junior officer shook his head.

Kaatje clenched her hands in the folds of her skirts. "Is this how your king repays the families of those who have died for him?" she asked bitterly.

Roulon's nostrils flared and he didn't bother hiding the coldness in his small eyes. "You whine of starving," he said with contempt, "but your late husband's brother is Margrave of Hespaire-Aube and rules half the lands south of the Ardennes. What would he say if he heard you sniveling like the scurviest peasant?"

A gasp escaped her. The malice glinting in his eyes told her he'd guessed exactly what Philippe's family would say—that she was sniveling like the scurviest *Flemish* peasant.

I will not be bated like a bear on market day, she vowed silently.

Her eyes narrowed to angry slits and she stalked toward Roulon, but the other officer broke in. "Monsieur, we must locate the d'Agenais woman. We could not find her.''

She spun to face the officer. "Of course you did not find her, she is not here. And even if she were, she would scarcely hide in a chair cushion or a chest drawer!" Kaatje wanted to vent the full force of her rage on him, but he casually put his hand on his sword hilt and stared back at her, unruffled.

"Where is Madame d'Agenais?" Roulon demanded again, the nostrils of his narrow nose flaring and his voice flat and cold.

"If she isn't at Chateau d'Agenais, I do not know. Why don't you ask her husband?"

The other officer snickered, then leered at her and said, "Perhaps you have not heard, madame, that your sister has dealt with her husband in a most . . . ah, unequivocal manner."

Kaatje lowered her gaze to the stone floor. *Lece, what have you done?* She raised her eyes and watched the two officers warily. "It's been weeks since I've heard from her. Do you think I have nothing better to do than have my servants combing the countryside for the latest tidbit of gossip?"

The officer laughed lewdly. "Most unequivocal," he said as if she had not spoken. "The Chevalier d'Agenais—an *old* and venerated man—was found by his servants gagged and tied naked to his bed . . ."

"Enough!" Roulon snapped, a muscle at the corner of one eye twitching uncontrollably. "The manner of her going is not important. That she left with her husband's astrologer is. Where is she, madame? We must find her!"

"We? You mean France!" Her temper neared the breaking point, and she paced back and forth on the uneven stone floor. She stopped at the ancient doorway that led to the terrace and pressed her hand to the granite warm from the sun. She looked out over the rolling

farmlands that sloped away from the chateau, and her
fingers curled into a fist at the sight of the lines of
soldiers snaking over the distant oat fields. She could
smell the dust of trampled grain even this far away.
There would be so little left to harvest, so little bread
to get them through the winter.

"Your sister," Roulon's voice hissed from behind
her.

Kaatje turned abruptly and opened her mouth to answer, but a child's scream interrupted her. It came from
the sward beyond the terrace.

"Pietr!" she cried, and rushed outside. She ran to
the wall that separated the terrace from the garden beyond and leaned over, seeing Pietr struggling in the
hands of a rough-looking French soldier while another
one led away a black pony.

Her son's small arms stretched out toward his beloved pet. "Toca, Toca! Come back!" he cried. "Bring
him back. Toca!"

"Release my son!" she screamed to the soldier holding Pietr. She headed toward the steps that led to the
garden, but strong thin fingers stopped her. Kaatje
wrenched her arm out of Roulon's grasp. "What kind
of beasts are you that you steal a little boy's pony? His
father gave it to him! What possible use could you have
for it in this filthy war? Isn't it enough that he lost his
father? Must your slobbering king take all he has left
of his father too?"

The cold, implacable hatred in Roulon's eyes raked
over her. "Take care what you say, madame, or he may
lose his mother as well."

Becket Thorne glanced at the sun. It was just past
noon—that meant he had an hour, maybe an hour and
a half. He studied the group on the terrace again, a
spark of reluctant admiration flaring for the golden-
haired woman wrenching her arm out of Roulon's grip.

The colonel had watched the comte ride up earlier as if he hadn't a care in the world, but now Madame de St. Benoit faced him in a sizzling fury. What a nasty surprise that must be for the Frenchman, Becket thought. Roulon wasn't known for his patience when something or someone stood in his way. His custom was to terrorize his quarry into babbling heaps.

A harsh smile twisted Becket's lips. His gaze traced the line of French soldiers moving across the field, unsuspecting of another nasty surprise that awaited them when they marched over one more hill: the Duke of Marlborough's Allied army. Roulon was not going to be pleased about that either.

Becket shrugged to ease his cramped shoulders and cursed Dutchmen for being so small. A branch jabbed him in his side, and he shifted cautiously, careful not to disturb the foliage screening him. He focused his glass on the chevalier's widow and saw that her face was still alive with anger. His gut tightened. A pity such beauties could never be trusted.

He glanced at the line of French soldiers again. There would be a battle soon, and he had to be at Marlborough's side, leading a charge into the elite cavalry of the Maison du Roi.

"You'll tell me where your treacherous sister is before the sixteen-pounders fire their first shot," he said, his voice low and edged with steel. "I'll be damned if I'll let you keep me from the action."

It was crucial that madame tell him the whereabouts of Lece d'Agenais. Her sister had run off with a Turk who had made his way into Europe posing as the astrologer, Oncelus—but Becket knew him by a different name. A very different name.

The black-gloved fingers of his right hand balled into a fist. He raised it as if to strike an unseen enemy, and the lace cuff fell back, revealing pale cords of tough crosshatched scars that were just visible at his wrist.

That Turkish dog's name was El Müzir, the dark-souled one.

Becket had nearly died from the tortures of that Turkish animal who had held him captive for four hellish years. Every beat of his heart was a vow to get his revenge on the creature who had called himself Becket's master. Muscles bunched in his jaw. *Hür adam, köle olmiyan,* he chanted silently, as he had so many times during his imprisonment. *I am a man, I am one who is not a slave.*

Becket shook his head to dispel the haze of anger that clouded it. He had to keep his mind clear and undistracted; his enemy was cunning, devious, and ruthless.

Good men had died trying to track that wretch and his whore. But Becket knew Oncelus, knew how his devil's brain worked, knew he was a man who deserved no mercy—and Becket would show him none.

And Lece d'Agenais, it seemed, collected dangerous lovers as most women collected gowns. Without the aid of the glass, Becket focused on the distant golden figure and wondered if that beauty could kill as cold-bloodedly as her sister.

A messenger dressed in French blue galloped full tilt toward the group on the terrace. Becket reopened his glass and held it to his eye. The agitated young man pulled his horse up hard, making it dance to maintain its balance, then jumped off and knelt in front of Roulon.

The Frenchman received a folded paper, read it, then cuffed the young man hard with the back of his hand, sending the youth staggering with blood running from his nose. Contempt and disgust warred within Becket at Roulon's cowardly attack on the messenger, though no doubt the comte had his reasons. It was never easy to learn one had underestimated an enemy, and the

French had underestimated the Duke of Marlborough very badly indeed.

Cursing loudly, the soldiers quickly gathered their horses. Becket put a calming hand on Acheron's muzzle to keep him quiet while the French rode past within twenty feet of him. Roulon's face was deformed into sharp angles of pure snarling hate.

Becket rose and went to his horse, then slid the perspective glass into its pouch. The Englishman's tall, hard-muscled body mounted Acheron with a single fluid movement. Madame de St. Benoit was about to give up her secrets.

Kaatje dashed away hot tears of anger as she watched old Marten lead Toca back to the stables with Pietr perched on the pony's back, his face wreathed in smiles. Thank God those thieves had forgotten it in their haste to be off to fight the English. She was sure, though, that the French would be back for the pony—and what could she tell her son then?

She returned to the kitchen and began helping Grette put what little food Roulon's soldiers had left them back on the shelves. The broken crockery would take longer to deal with.

Lord, what a shambles! she thought, rummaging to find another basket. She found one with a loose handle and began throwing the pewter utensils into it with a loud clatter. Damn the French. Damn the English. She threw a knife into the basket so hard it sliced through the side. Damn them all.

Her teeth ached from clenching them so hard to keep from crying, and her eyes stung as she blinked away the tears. She was born a van Staden and they did not cry! Other women might collapse on their beds helpless with dread, but a van Staden took action, a van Staden—

Kaatje shook her head. Lece was also a van Staden. Where had her sister gone? She desperately tried to remember where Lece's letter had been sent from, but all she could recall of it was the threat to Pietr. She wanted to dig out the letter right then, but knew she couldn't leave the old servant to do all the work.

Grette screamed. Kaatje spun around to see a tall, lithe officer standing in the doorway, one broad shoulder propped against the doorjamb and his arms folded in front of him. He was dressed in a dark blue coat, black leather jackboots that reached to his thighs, and black leather riding gloves; his long dark hair was tied back in readiness for battle.

The muscles in her neck tightened, sending a chill of warning spidering down her back. The very stillness of his casual stance made the air almost crackle with danger; he looked more than able to take whatever he'd come for.

Her eyes never leaving him, she said, "Grette, go make sure Pietr is unharmed." When the old woman had gone, Kaatje's gaze narrowed and she addressed him, her anger barely suppressed. "Why have they sent you? You've left us precious little as it is. Do you want to see if we are hiding any rabbits under our beds?" She remained in front of the table, facing him squarely and refusing to cower, her chest heaving with outrage, her hands on her hips.

He said nothing, but she could see those dark blue eyes traveling down her, taking in everything. It was disconcerting, but she held her ground.

"Why do you stay? There is nothing for you here!"

A finely arched black brow quirked as a lazy smile slowly widened his mouth. She felt awkward and apprehensive in her shabby gown and rumpled linen apron.

"But madame," he said in flawless but accented French, "there is everything."

An Englishman! Kaatje froze. Her eyes darted to the door to see if either Grette or Marten was in sight, but she was alone. The uniform had fooled her; now she could see it was much darker than the Frenchmen's had been.

He straightened slowly, deliberately, to his full height, until he nearly filled the doorway. She took a step back and banged into the table behind her, rattling the cutlery.

There was something in the way he stood, full of confidence and so controlled, that made her feel he was a man used to command, a man of good rank, perhaps equal to Philippe's. If he was a gentleman, he might not harm her.

"What do you want?" she asked him. An indigo light flared in those disturbing eyes of his, and she immediately regretted her question.

He shook his head and gestured with a gloved hand as if dismissing something. His smile disappeared, and she saw a muscle tighten along his strong square jaw. He looked very determined.

He started walking toward her, and panic pressed in on her, making it difficult to breathe. But Kaatje had had enough. She would take no more.

"Stay back!" she cried, her voice breaking. Fear rang through her, making her vibrate like a struck bell, but she clamped down on it hard. She half turned away from him, her hand groping desperately to find a knife on the table. Her fingers closed around the smooth horn handle of a long butcher knife.

She raised it high, ready to spin around and stab him in the chest. But in a heartbeat, before she could turn, his arm stole around her waist and roughly pulled her back against his hard-muscled chest while he grabbed her wrist and held it immobile.

"Let me go!" Kaatje kicked and struggled to free herself, but it was like being pinioned against a stone wall with bands of iron. She raised her other arm to slam her elbow into his side, but he squeezed her wrist tightly in warning, stopping just before he did any damage, and she realized that he could snap it as easily as a dry wheatstalk. She lowered her arm slowly.

"So you can kill like your sister," he murmured in her ear.

She stiffened at the mention of Lece, ignoring the sensations his breath was making against her skin. *My God, Lece, what have you done that even the English are looking for you!* The arm around her waist shifted, and she blinked away the images of her sister, catching the last strange lilt of his accent but missing the words.

"I said, drop the knife."

She struggled to free herself again, but his hold was too solid, and she reluctantly released her grip on the horn handle. It fell bladepoint first into the table and swayed back and forth. "Too bad you weren't under it," she said.

He surprised her by chuckling, causing a vibration against her back. "Do you always try to kill people who ask the whereabouts of your sister? You must not be very successful. You aim too high."

Kaatje snorted in disgust. "Aiming for an Englishman is aiming too high? Ha!"

The Englishman laughed again, and the sound of it resonated through her body. He still held her wrist, and now he slid his fingers up and grasped her hand, then forced it down to her waist so that both his arms were around her. "An Englishman or anyone, my beauty. The heart is well-protected, and it takes a great deal of force to stab a man there." She tried to resist his pull, but he drew her hand up to her chest, then slowly settled it to the inside of her left breast, straining the neckline of her gown.

"You see," he said gruffly, "the ribs protect it." The hand around her waist began to stroke the smooth fabric between her bottom rib and hipbone. "Here," he whispered, making a shiver wash over her, "here is a surer deathstroke. There are no bones to turn aside a blade, only soft, soft flesh.'' He was rubbing her stomach now. ''Plunge your blade in here and it will likely prove fatal.''

It was still in the kitchen. Her heart raced under his hand, and she knew he could feel it too. She told herself it was fear that made it beat so fast, fear that made her breath come in ragged gasps—

Lece! she cried silently. *What have you done? Lece, Lece*—

''Lece,'' the Englishman's voice said, no longer a bewitching whisper. Kaatje squirmed against him, and he raised his head, saying, ''Stop struggling! You almost had me there for a minute, didn't you? My God, you could entice a starving wolf from his dinner. Just as your sister enticed how many other men who now lie buried in foreign ground with their throats cut.'' He spun her around and gripped her shoulders, his gloved fingers digging into her bare flesh, then shook her. *''Where is your sister?''*

His sudden change of attitude left her reeling, and she barely heard what he said. ''The French were here before you. Why would I tell you what I couldn't tell them? I have not had a l-l-letter from her for weeks.'' She mentally cursed herself for stumbling over the word ''letter.'' It wasn't easy to lie, even when she had to.

''Where was that last letter from?'' he demanded. ''Where was she when she sent it?''

Kaatje opened her mouth to answer, then snapped it shut. She grimaced as his fingers dug into her shoulders even deeper. She wasn't sure if he was hurting her deliberately or if he had tightened his grip unconsciously to somehow squeeze an answer out of her.

''I don't remember,'' she told him. ''I really don't remember, so breaking my shoulder isn't going to make me recall it.'' His face remained impassive, but the pressure lessened.

She had been so sure that Lece was settling down. What had happened to change that? Dismay lent her words the ring of sincerity. "It never matters where she is. One place is pretty much like another to Lece. And all her stories run together after a while so it's hard to keep track of her."

"If you don't remember, then find it. I want to know where she was when she wrote—" Just then a shout came from the front of the house. A shout in French.

She took a breath to reply to it, but the Englishman covered her mouth with his gloved hand. "Don't answer," he whispered. "Let him find you."

He released her and looked quickly around the kitchen, his eyes stopping at the huge fireplace that took up one wall. An apparatus large enough for turning a whole ox as it roasted stood on the hearth, unused since Philippe's death. The Englishman reached under his dark blue coat and drew a pistol that had been tucked into the back of his breeches. He silently crossed to the cold fireplace and slipped into the shadows behind the giant turnspit.

A noise in the doorway made Kaatje jump. She turned to see a stocky French soldier standing there, his uniform torn and dirty and his grimy face split into a lewd grin as he looked her up and down. She swallowed her fear and looked as stern as she could. "Capitaine le Comte de Roulon left only a short while ago," she told him. "There is nothing for you here."

He chuckled roughly, then made a coarse noise in his throat and spat. "An' I'm sure Capitaine le Comte de Roulon would tell me what he been doin'." He laughed again, the sound making terror rise like bile in her throat. "Oh, we's close, me an' Capitaine le Comte de Roulon, real close. He thought as how you might be holdin' out on him, so he told me to take a look 'round. A good look 'round," he added with a leer.

The man kicked at something on the floor, then bent

over and picked it up. It was a dried rind of cheese, and Kaatje's stomach turned in disgust as he started to gnaw on it like a rat. It took all her willpower not to look at the Englishman. The wide kitchen door partially blocked the French soldier's view of the fireplace, so he did not yet realize they weren't alone.

When the soldier squinted at the table piled with cutlery and the knife still standing with its point in the wood, she darted a furtive glance at the man behind the turnspit and saw that the pistol was now pointed toward the soldier. What would the Englishman do if she betrayed him?

She took a shaky breath. She opened her mouth, not sure what she was going to say, but the only words that came out were, "Why don't you return to Monsieur le Comte and assure him there is nothing left?" She gave him an unsteady smile.

The soldier grunted and looked back at her, then his small dark eyes slid away from her face. He headed for the table. "Roulon can't be bothered with the likes o' you right now. He's . . . he's busy, y' know . . . busy waitin' fer the English dogs to show up and fight."

"But the English—" she began with a puzzled frown, then stopped when she saw the cunning wariness on his face. In a flash she realized what he was—a deserter!

They were animals. Low creatures who preyed on anyone. Kaatje knew he wouldn't hesitate to throw her to the floor and brutalize her until . . . Her mind shied away from the thought. Surely the Englishman would protect her, she told herself, he's a gentleman. Or would he? With a stab of horror, she realized she couldn't be sure.

She heard a faint clink of the turnspit chain as the Englishman came out into the room, and she held her breath, a bubble of fearful anticipation caught in her throat.

The soldier grabbed the knife and spun toward the

fireplace. He hesitated when he saw the pistol, then, with an inhuman growl, heaved the table onto its side and shoved it into the Englishman. He spun and leaped at Kaatje, holding the knife high.

The crack of a pistol shot rent the air. The knife caught a ribbon on her dress and buried itself in the wooden door, so close she could hear the singing of the vibrating blade. The soldier rammed into her, crushing her against the door, then slid down the length of her dress, leaving a bright red trail as he slumped into a heap.

My God, she thought, every limb trembling. My sweet God. She sagged against the door; she wanted to cry, scream, stammer and beg for mercy, until a voice from her past chided her. *You are a van Staden, girl! Always meet life with head held high, back straight and proud* . . . A loud thump of heavy wood against stone brought her back. *A van Staden,* she chanted silently.

Becket pushed the table off him with such force that it slammed into the wall. He rose, checking for broken bones as he did so, and immediately turned to see if Madame de St. Benoit had been harmed. She had collapsed against the door. A tear ran down her face as her head rocked back and forth. She looked so defeated slumped there. But then, unexpectedly, the rocking stopped, and he watched her slowly straighten herself like a puppet being lifted from the floor. She took several deep breaths, then raised her chin and opened her eyes, challenging him with a clear-eyed gaze.

He crushed the bolt of admiration that shot through him. The sister of the Turk's whore couldn't be trusted or admired, he told himself silently.

A savage twist of pleasure turned inside him when her beguiling gray eyes widened in dismay as he neared her. She tried to pull away, but her dress was still caught by the knife buried in the door. Becket deliberately let his gaze lock with hers, then pulled off his gloves slowly, one finger at a time, the look in her eyes almost goading him to taunt her. He tucked the gloves into his sword belt and stared at her for a long moment before kneeling to check for a pulse at the French deserter's neck. The man was dead.

Becket dragged the corpse to one side, then straightened and reached for the knife, but his hand slowed in its path as his eyes met hers again for an instant. His gaze dropped to where the smooth ivory skin at the base of her slender throat pulsed rapidly. Her coral lips were moist and slightly parted in alarm. This close, he could see copper highlights shimmering in her golden hair. How could anyone prefer the brash, overripe charms of Lece d'Agenais when this enticing beauty . . .

Becket grabbed the knife handle and yanked it out of the wood. He threw it aside and saw her wince when it crashed onto the pile of cutlery on the floor.

"Madame," he said, "I believe you have a letter to find."

Chapter 2

"**L**etter?" Kaatje asked, ignoring the jab of stiff paper against her thigh as she backed away from the dead soldier. What was she going to do? She needed time to think.

"What about him?" She gestured toward the body of the deserter without looking at it.

"He can wait. He's hardly going to walk out of here."

"That's not what I meant!"

"Find the letter."

"You can't leave a dead body in my kitchen."

His hand shot out, his long fingers wrapping around her arm to stop her from retreating further. His thumb pressed into the delicate flesh on the inside of her arm and he held her immobile.

"That cur can feed the ravens for all I care," he told her with an intensity that unnerved her. "In a few hours there will be thousands more dead bodies, madame, and mine may be among them. Right now there is only one thing that concerns me—the whereabouts of your sister and her lover. We tracked them to an inn outside Reims nearly a month ago, but the next morning your sister was gone. Her lover was gone. And the man tracking them was dead. *Where is she?*"

"How should I know that?" she all but shouted. "You English are the ones following her!"

"The letter, madame! I waste no more time."

Kaatje licked her lips. Would an old letter of Lece's satisfy him? she wondered. If it wasn't too old, he wouldn't know the difference. She gestured awkwardly toward the hall, and said, "I'll go find it. It's . . . it's most likely in my writing desk . . . in my sitting room."

She slipped out of his grasp and ran from the room. *Your sister and her lover,* he'd said. Oh, Lece, who have you run off with now? On the stairs behind her, she heard the sound of boots on the bare wood in the hall. She stumbled to a stop and turned to see him step on the bottom tread.

"I will bring the letter down to you," she called to him, hoping he couldn't hear the quavering in her voice. He didn't stop. He was watching her carefully with those dark eyes of his, while he climbed ever upward, the breadth of his shoulders and chest and the smooth, easy movements of his legs proclaiming his masculine power.

She whirled and, grabbing her stained dress in two frantic handfuls, ran up the stairs and through the rooms that led to her private retreat. He followed her inexorably, the loud thud of his boot heels suddenly muffled as he crossed one of the few remaining carpets. She lifted the latch to her door and opened it, holding her breath in anticipation of having finally reached refuge. When she stepped inside, the chaos of the room hit her like a blow.

The French had thoroughly ransacked it. Mute with dismay, Kaatje gently righted a delicate chair that had stood in front of her writing table. She heard the Englishman's footsteps stop at the threshold, and she glanced at him. Must he make all her doorways look so small?

A flash of gold caught at the corner of her vision, and a cry escaped her. She slowly knelt beside the broken pieces of the gold and enamel clock her mother had given her as a child, then picked them up with shaking fingers. Anger and frustration and despair threatened to consume her. What could she give Oncelus now to pay for Pietr's medicine?

Slowly, Kaatje drew her head erect and stared at the Englishman. Some emotion that looked like concern flashed across his lean face.

"Your kind did this," she said, setting the pieces on the table and impatiently wiping away a stray tear. "You always carry out your duty, no matter whose fields of flax or wheat you trample. What does it matter to you if there is no linen to weave, no bread to eat."

His deep blue eyes hardened into shards of river ice. There was no softness in him.

He took two long strides into the room. "You hate the French," he said, grabbing her wrist and pulling her around to face him. "I saw the look on your face when you were talking with that cur downstairs." She jerked at his touch, but his grip only tightened. "We fight to keep your land from Louis's grasp."

The touch of his flesh startled her. She remembered vividly when he'd taken off his gloves, purposely being so slow about it, but now she could feel the strength in his long fingers and the hard callused ridges of a swordsman on his palm. Her gaze locked with his, and a tremor rippled through her. Something had thawed the chill in his eyes, turning them opaque and enigmatic.

He dropped her wrist as if it burned him, and turned away. "The letter," he said, his voice flat. His hand flexed, then closed into a fist. "I will know where your sister is."

Or what? Kaatje wondered, yanking open the drawer of the writing table and clumsily rummaging through the papers there. Surely she could find one of Lece's old letters to satisfy him. She remembered the stories

Philippe had told her about Englishmen, how their deceptive smiles hide cold implacable hearts. She stole a glance at the man watching her. This one wasn't smiling.

Her fingers grew damp with approaching panic and she searched the drawer again. *Where are Lece's letters?* She slammed it shut and moved to a nearby chest, half its contents dumped in a pile in front of it. She scrambled through a pile of old letters, her heart leaping at the sight of one from Lece, but the relief quickly faded when she discovered it was nearly two years old.

The Englishman pushed aside a crumpled silk shawl with his booted foot, then bent to pick it up and absently began drawing the delicate material over his hand. A faint smile rounded the creased sides of his mouth, lightening the fierce intensity that shadowed his face.

Kaatje ignored the curious fluttering in her stomach and turned back to the writing table, searching blindly through the few papers on top of it. They were almost all copies of letters she'd sent to the Margrave of Hespaire-Aube, painstakingly copied on the cheapest foolscap. The Englishman wouldn't be deceived by that.

She spun around to face the man whose presence so dominated the room, though she kept her eyes carefully focused on the wall behind his left shoulder. "I can't find it! You'll have to find out where she is from someone else." She let her gaze dart to his face, then away.

"There is no one else, madame." He dropped the shawl and closed the space between them with two quick strides.

Caught between him and the writing table, she instinctively half turned from him, but he pulled her back to face him. There was a ripping sound at her shoulder. "Damn," he said under his breath, holding a ribbon from her gown. He irritably stuffed it into a pocket of his coat.

His long, graceful fingers held her shoulder, his thumb rubbing her skin just above her dress. *"Remember,"* he ground out, "remember where your sister sent her last letter from."

She shifted her weight to hide a sudden shiver that ran through her. "Would you remember?" she challenged with false bravado, then went on before he had a chance to answer. "I doubt it. You'd be more likely to remember what was in the letter than where it was from."

"Then you do remember what it said." His eyes narrowed as he studied her face.

"I-I may recall something of it." She took a deep breath and instantly regretted it as the sharp masculine scent of him entered her nostrils. Her chin lifted in defiance, but she couldn't hold his gaze and dropped her eyes. There was a long stretch of silence.

"Well?" he prompted.

Kaatje swallowed to hide her discomfort. She forced herself to shrug. "She wrote about what she always writes about."

"And what is that?" he asked. He had moved closer, and his head had bent over hers so she could feel his breath on her forehead. Her eyes were level with his chest, and she studied the open vee of his waistcoat and the linen shirt under his steinkirk cravat, the long ends twisted and tucked through a buttonhole.

"She . . . she mentioned her husband's astrologer, and how she liked to . . . ah, visit him in his rooms. She also said that he did charts for her on promising . . . er, potential . . ." Her words straggled to a halt, and she cleared her throat. His shirt stirred slightly with the rise and fall of his breathing. "Potential friends," she finished.

"Friends?" he asked, his rich voice a tone deeper

than usual. His other hand gently settled on the curve of her neck where it met her shoulder, and his thumb traced the line of her collarbone. ''Don't you mean lovers?'' he asked softly, the words more an exhalation against her face than sound.

He drew his thumb along her jawline and she looked up, startled. His head slowly lowered until his face was so close she could see the exquisite sapphire of his eyes. His sensually mobile mouth hovered close to hers, the lower lip slightly larger than the upper one.

He tantalized her, as food in a winter trap tantalized a starving animal. His eyelids half closed, and her mouth parted.

''Where are they, madame?'' he whispered, the breath of his words warm against her lips.

''I don't . . . I can't . . .''

A distant booming intruded and, shuddering like one coming out of a trance, he released her.

He strode to the window and stood there for a long moment watching something in the distance and cursing under his breath. Then he wheeled around and headed for the door, stopping on the threshold to give her a perfunctory bow. ''Pray I do not survive the battle, madame, for if I return, I shall stand for no more of your tricks. I swear I will drag you from chateau to chateau until we find your sister.''

The echo of his steps on the wood floor stayed in her mind long after she knew he'd slammed the wide front doors closed behind him. Kaatje clenched her eyes shut and put trembling fingers to her lips. How could she have forgotten herself so with that horrible Englishman? My sweet Lord, he'd killed a man right in front of her. Tears seeped out from beneath her lashes and trailed down her cheeks.

The booming of the cannon grew louder. She raised her skirts and pulled out the letter hidden in her petticoat. She quickly unfolded it and looked for the head-

ing under the date—but there was none! She prayed
silently as her gaze frantically traveled down the page.
There! In the corner.

"We broke free from Constantin's shackles and left
him behind! The servant will know where to bring the
clock," her sister had scrawled. The note ended, with
no mention of where she was. And since Lece's miserable servant had disappeared the moment the French
had arrived, Kaatje had no way of discovering where
they had gone.

Oh, sweet God, she had to find them—Pietr's medicine would run out in less than a month! She stared
blindly at the paper, thinking of and discarding possibility after possibility. Her thumb rubbed the red wax
seal that had broken neatly in two. *Lece. Lece. How
can you risk Pietr's future this way?*

Her eyes slowly focused on the seal, and she realized
it wasn't the d'Agenais falcon. Kaatje ran to the window and, holding the two halves of the seal together,
let the early afternoon sun illuminate it. In the center,
a small stylized man raised a bow and arrow in his right
hand. A tear-laden laugh escaped her. She didn't have
to read the words in the circle surrounding the man to
know what they said.

"Cerfontaine," she whispered. "Lece, you went
home."

Neither Kaatje nor her sister had been born at Cerfontaine, yet the chateau in the foothills of the Ardennes was the only home they remembered clearly.
She had been six and Lece eight when their widowed
mother had remarried a Walloon and they'd left the
Flemish speaking north for the French speaking Brabant.

She had to get to Cerfontaine. By horse the chateau
was three days away, but it would take her almost a
sennight to get there in the pony cart. She frowned.
She could hardly leave her son with only two aging
servants to protect him, yet with both the French and

English looking for Lece, it would be too dangerous to take Pietr to Cerfontaine.

Her gaze narrowed on the jumbled pile of foolscap on her writing desk. Hespaire-Aube! It would still take a sennight to reach Philippe's brother by pony cart, but then surely he would lend her a fast horse to ride to Cerfontaine to visit her sister. And Pietr would be safe with the margrave.

A distant shriek interrupted her planning, and she ran to the stairs, calling, "Grette! Grette!"

The frail housekeeper staggered into the hall at the bottom of the steps, her hand at her throat. "Madame," she cried, "there's a dead man in the kitchen!"

Kaatje waved away the servant's concern. "Marten can bury him. I need you to pack. And don't forget the clock. I'm taking Pietr to his Uncle Claude's in Hespaire-Aube. We're leaving this war behind." She rubbed the rip in her gown where the Englishman had torn the ribbon off. *This war—and a certain Englishman,* she added silently.

Becket rode past the supply wagons at the end of the long line of soldiers marching five abreast that wound its way down into the lush fields of Oudenaarde like a scarlet serpent. He crossed the Scheldt River, the impact of Acheron's hooves making the tin pontoon bridge ring, and then quickly made for one of the makeshift rope corrals near where the battle lines were forming.

He pulled the big black animal to a halt as one of the horse boys ran up to grab the reins. "Groom him fast, Jemmy," he said. He glanced at the opposite hill where a blue haze of French soldiers was slowly coalescing into fighting position. "I doubt if the enemy is going to wait for an invitation."

Becket walked fast and purposefully between rows of heavy carts loaded with powder and shot, and resounding with the familiar cacophony of men readying themselves for battle. The air was heavy with the smell of men's sweat, horses, and the pungent odor of gunpowder drifting in from the sixteen-pound guns firing a half mile away.

Damn that woman! The St. Benoit widow was playing him for a fool, and he'd nearly fallen for her clever stalling lies. Anger made the too-tight uniform seem even tighter across his shoulders and his boot heels dig deep into the ground with each determined step.

He hated needing anyone—and he needed Kaatje de St. Benoit to lead him to that base devil who was her sister's lover. There probably *was* no letter, he fumed, or if one did exist, the widow knew exactly where it was.

" 'Ware powder," a rough voice called, and Becket sidestepped to miss a lumbering cart filled with kegs of powder on its way to the battle lines. He had to find El Müzir. It didn't matter that he was playing the astrologer and calling himself Oncelus. What mattered was that all the powder in the world wouldn't be enough if the rumors about what that Turkish devil was creating were true.

Lucifer's Fire. It burned its victims slowly, and neither water nor sand could douse it. Whole battalions would die horribly in an auto-da-fé worse than any the Spanish Inquisition had ever held.

And what mattered was Becket's oath to kill him.

A large red banner bearing the Duke of Marlborough's arms snapped in the breeze in front of the field tent of the Captain-General of the Allied Armies. A lackey held the tent flap open for Becket to enter.

"My dear Thorne! Good to see you," said John Churchill, the Duke of Marlborough, straightening from the maps and reports spread out on the campaign table that dominated the small space. "And how did you find Madame de St. Benoit? Cooperative, I trust." Marlborough looked as cool and unflappable as always;

though nearing sixty, he still behaved with the smooth courtesy of the perfectly polished courtier-soldier who had once captured the heart of a king's mistress.

Prince Eugene of Savoy, the only other general in Europe who could match Marlborough's genius, stood next to him, his dusty green uniform looking as if he'd ridden all day and most of the night before; but his eyes were as shrewd as ever.

Becket bowed to them and then straightened, his glance acknowledging the stout Cardonnel, Marlborough's secretary, the only other officer in the room. He was updating the reports of the French positions and absently returned Colonel Thorne's nod from across the table.

"The widow was very cooperative," Becket said, his voice heavily laced with sarcasm. The fingers of his right hand flexed, then curled into a fist. "Madame de St. Benoit swears she does not know where her sister is."

"And she is lying," the duke said.

"Of course, your grace. But at least she appears to be lying to the French as well." He turned to Prince Eugene. "Your old friend Roulon is also interested in locating the d'Agenais woman, but Madame de St. Benoit seems reluctant to give up her secrets to anyone."

The prince smiled at Becket, then chuckled. "She will to you, my young friend. I have the utmost faith in your . . . er, abilities. The rumors I heard in Vienna were very impressive."

Savoy picked up an ornate onion-shaped traveling flask. "Wine, colonel? Courtesy of"—he paused and turned the flask over in his hands to read the name of a French nobleman that had been engraved deep into the finely wrought silver—"Aurignac. A marquis, I believe, with the requisite soupçon of royal blood." He poured the deep ruby wine into three plain cups, then turned to Marlborough, holding out one of them. "At Blenheim?"

The duke smiled and took the proffered wine. "At Ramillies Aurignac delayed paying his ransom as long as he could. It seems an angry mistress at home made him reluctant to end his captivity." He chuckled, then looked thoughtful. "Wasn't Roulon a prisoner of yours after Turin?"

The prince frowned and set the flask on the table with a hard thump. "Roulon paid for his freedom by murdering four good men. There is not a drop of honor in him." He extended the third cup of wine to Becket. "That Roulon is involved with this St. Benoit business concerns me. His greed is well-known. Louis badly wants that abomination Oncelus has created and is dangling a fat purse for its capture. Roulon is not likely to let a sister's reluctance stand in his way."

For a moment Marlborough paced in what little free space there was, then stopped in front of Becket. "It's good that the French—and Roulon—don't have Madame d'Agenais, but then neither do we. What kind of woman is the Chevalier de St. Benoit's widow? Should we send a guard to the chateau to make sure she doesn't bolt?"

Becket set down his cup, the wine untouched, and slowly shook his head. "Madame de St. Benoit is a Fleming, your grace, stubborn and headstrong. She's dug in her heels, so there's no chance of her leaving. I'll return there after the battle and make her tell me where her sister and El Müz— Oncelus have gone."

A hush followed his words and Marlborough rubbed his temple; only the sound of the distant guns intruded on the silence. "Colonel Thorne," Marlborough began, then looked at his secretary. Cardonnel handed him an oiled leather pouch, and the duke pulled a paper from it.

"Colonel," Marlborough began again, speaking

slowly, as if weighing each word carefully, "we understand your reasons for wanting to find the man Oncelus—reasons that go beyond locating this vile creation of his." Becket stiffened at the reference to the horror from his past. The ever-simmering hatred boiled up his throat, making each breath burn and reminding him of the nightmare his life had once been.

Marlborough glanced at the prince. "His highness has brought some news that complicates the matter considerably." He shook the paper. "It seems that Oncelus's iniquitous project, this Lucifer's Fire, is complete. If Louis should get his hands on it . . ." He stopped for a moment, his famous control asserting itself.

"With this war, we have been able to put a halt to a grasping France that has held sway over Europe for half a century. But Spain is without a king, and an empty throne is too great a prize for Louis to lose. He will do anything, use anything, to gain it. And after Spain, who would be strong enough to stop him?

"We must keep Lucifer's Fire out of French hands!" He held the paper out to Becket. "But both Oncelus and Madame d'Agenais have disappeared without a trace. Thorne, you must run them—and this hideous weapon—to ground."

Becket held his body rigid, and his eyes stared blankly at the paper before him. *Hür adam, köle olmiyan.* No, he wasn't going to let this chance escape him. El Müzir was his to kill!

He had sworn to watch the life drip out of that dark-souled devil and be swallowed by the dirt and sand, though he knew that every drop of blood in the Turk's body could not atone for those who had suffered and begged to die.

Becket had given his oath. A face hovered before him, and he could see the eyes that were a shade lighter than his own slowly closing in pain and grief. *I have*

not forgotten my promise, he silently told the memory.
I swear El Müzir will die by my hand.

Becket woodenly took the paper Marlborough held
out to him. The words blurred and he had to blink
rapidly before he could read them. They confirmed that
before the man known as Oncelus had vanished, he had
unlocked the secret of producing his terrible weapon.
And worse, there was still no trace of him; the trail was
stone-cold.

Esir, El Müzir's voice taunted him . . . *slave.*

Becket's lips were white as he folded the sweat-
dampened letter and put it in his pocket. "France will
not gain Lucifer's Fire. And Oncelus's filthy Turkish
bones will not be allowed to defile European soil." His
voice was deep and full and resonated with the only
emotion left to him that could touch his soul—hate. The
prince gripped his shoulder briefly in silent understanding.

Becket closed his eyes for a long moment, then
opened them. "Madame de St. Benoit knows where
they are," Becket said with a note in his voice that
chilled them all. "And she will lead me to them." .

Marlborough nodded to his secretary, and Cardonnel
consulted one of the many lists in front of him, then
picked up a sheet filled with small script. "Sonning's
company will probably see only light action—they can
accompany you."

Becket looked at him sharply. "No."

Concern made heavy furrows in Cardonnel's forehead. "My lord colonel, surely you will require a company of soldiers," he said. "Oncelus is deadly."

Both Marlborough and Prince Eugene nodded, and
Becket's gaze darted between them. His mouth straightened into a grim line.

"There will be no difficulty, your grace," Becket
said, his eyes dark with anticipation of the hunt. Nothing—and no one—would stand in his way now. "My

aide-de-camp and servant will accompany me. And Madame de St. Benoit. That will be sufficient, I assure you.''

The pounding of the guns in the distance grew louder until Becket could feel the tremors through the packed earth. Marlborough put his hand on Becket's shoulder, saying, ''Are you sure that is wise, Thorne? St. Benoit's widow is a lady of good rank and they are notoriously slow travelers. Speed is of the utmost importance.''

''Any woman moves fast enough with the right spur, you grace.''

''Not all women are like those you've dealt with in the past, Thorne,'' Prince Eugene said, his face reflecting a troubled frown. ''Have you never met a woman with honor?''

Becket bowed and walked toward the opening in the tent, then turned back to face the prince. ''No, your highness, never.''

Becket strode toward the tent his aide-de-camp and servant had set up during his ride to the chateau. The path between the newly raised rows of steep-sided tents was hard and the summer afternoon was bright and hot and heavy with dust, a vivid counterpoint to the darkness settling inside him. Before, Madame de St. Benoit had been the *easiest* way to find Oncelus. Now she was the only way.

Near his tent a crowd of grenadiers stood, carefully checking their grenades and hatchets. An occasional crack of a musket misfiring punctuated the din of shouts and curses. Farther away, the same curses could be heard in Dutch, Prussian, or any of the myriad languages spoken by the soldiers who made up the Allied Armies.

''Ho, Thorne,'' someone called. The carefully polished cuirass of an officer flashed in the afternoon sun.

"Z'ounds, man, how'd you manage it? We're slogging through that damned river with mud up to our necks and you've got orders to go nuzzling secrets out of a French widow." He shook his head. "Should o' known you'd get—"

"She's Flemish," Becket growled out in irritation, then entered his tent, letting the flap drop closed over the man's babble.

His lanky aide-de-camp, Lieutenant Niall Elcot, sat on a low stool at the camp table, the red of his hair clashing violently with his scarlet uniform coat, its skirts hanging down behind him almost in the dirt. He was carefully measuring out charges of blackpowder, guncotton, and lead balls, and putting them in a leather pouch that would hang at Becket's hip when he rode into battle. More than nine years separated the twenty-two-year-old lieutenant from the colonel—nine years and a lifetime—but Niall was one of the few men Becket felt able to trust.

"Sir?" Niall said, half rising from the stool.

Becket waved him down. The other man in the tent, Becket's servant, Harry Fludd, welcomed him with a grin, but it only earned him a glare and the smile quickly faded. He was nearly a score of years older than Becket, his hair heavily sprinkled with gray and the lines around his eyes deeply etched. He bent to busy himself again with polishing the buttons on the colonel's uniform, watching Becket out of the corner of his eye. Fludd cast a worried glance at Niall, then cleared his throat.

Becket stood with feet apart and hands on hips in the middle of the tent. He jerked back the tongue of his sword belt and unbuckled it, then threw it on the cot. "I would like to know, Mr. Fludd, why every man in this camp seems to know of my visit to the Chateau de St. Benoit."

Fludd swallowed noisily, guilt making his face ruddy.

"Sorry, kern'l. I thought you was slipping off to see one o' your ladies, but I guess I was wrong. Won't never mention you and madame in the same breath again. No, kern'l, you can be sure—"

"That's enough, Harry."

A wide grin split the heavy boned face. "Yes, kern'l."

"And get this damned Dutch coat off me. I feel like a stuffed sausage." He was quickly stripped of the dark blue coat, and Fludd held out one of English scarlet. The colonel stretched his tensed muscles, then let the red coat settle on his wide shoulders with the snug fit of impeccable tailoring. Fludd then buckled on his cuirass, the sleeveless breastplate that had been polished so bright it could have been used as a looking glass.

Before every battle Becket mentally prepared for the fight to come, letting his mind retreat, leaving only that which would aid him. But now, as all the accoutrements of war were buckled and tied on him, he was having a hard time making his mind let go.

Most men of his station were safely back in England, he thought, snug in their manors and estates, listening to their wives' gentle household prattle or smiling at their children's laughter. Most earls' sons did not choose war over peace, but then most had not lived through hell.

If he had not ridden out from Vienna that day, and never fallen into the evil one's grasp, would a valet now be slipping an embroidered waistcoat on him instead of the gold sash of his sword scabbard? Would the noise of children playing at Ducks and Geese be drifting to him instead of the clatter of weapons and the boom of cannon? And instead of a hard narrow cot, would he have risen that morning from a soft bed and the soft curves of a loving wife, her golden hair spread out beside him on crisp white linen sheets?

Becket swallowed hard and cursed himself for a fool.

Nothing could change the past, and nothing could re-store the heart that had turned to stone within him.

"Harry, pack for light travel. I want to move out as soon as the battle is over. And don't plan on any cele-brating—I may need your help at St. Benoit."

The trumpet sounded and Becket heard a horse boy cursing Acheron outside the tent. He headed out, then stopped with the flap half open, remembering the letter Marlborough had given him. He crossed the tent in three strides, dug into the pocket of the discarded Dutch uniform, and pulled it out.

A soft yellow ribbon fluttered to the ground. He picked it up without thinking and, for a heartbeat, held it suspended in front of him, the cool smooth satin lying against his rough palm. Her subtle scent of jas-mine teased him, and when he inhaled he was standing close to her again, smelling the sweet perfume of her hair, the sunlight from the window behind her touching each strand as if it were gold. She had stared at him, her gray eyes wide, and her lips had been moist and parted in anticipation . . .

"My lord? Is something wrong?" Niall asked, his voice hovering between concern and uncertainty. Becket was suddenly back amid the smell of sweat and horses. He made as if to toss the ribbon away, but when the trumpet sounded again, he tucked it into the folds of the letter and put it in the pocket of his coat.

"To arms, gentlemen," Colonel Becket, Lord Thorne said to the two men and strode out of the tent.

Kaatje dabbed at her forehead with a wisp of a hand-kerchief. It was dusty and warm even though the sun sat squatly on the western horizon, and the clop of To-ca's hooves on the hard dirt sounded lonely on the de-serted road. A few days earlier, when news of the approaching French had reached Odenaarde, the road had been packed with merchants and farm families escaping the coming destruction. But now she and Pietr were alone.

At first she had sat straight and tense on the hard wooden plank in the pony cart, the Englishman's threats still echoing in her ears. Now that she and her son had been safely on their way for over an hour, though, and with the clock for Oncelus safely packed in one of their trunks, she was beginning to put those threats behind her.

Pietr squirmed beside her, still excited about the trip. "Why are we going to Uncle Claude's, Mama? I thought you didn't like him. Why couldn't Marten come with us? I miss him."

Kaatje squeezed her son's shoulders and, ignoring his first question, said, "I miss Marten too, sweeting, but he had to stay at home and take care of things."

A sullen young man walked at Toca's head, leading them at a snail's pace. The wretch was the only person Marten had been able to hire to escort them to Hespaire-Aube, but even Toca took exception to him. The pony tried to pull out of his reach, but the servant roughly jerked Toca's head down.

"Be gentle with him!" Kaatje demanded after Toca stumbled. "He is not used to pulling a cart."

"I knows how to handle brutes," he said, giving the harness another yank. There was a brute in front of the cart, she fumed silently, but it wasn't the pony.

"How long will it take to get to Uncle Claude's?" Pietr piped up again. "Toca won't get jealous if I ride a real horse, will he? Marten says Uncle Claude has lots and lots of horses. Maybe five!"

Kaatje laughed. "I don't think Toca will mind if you ride a big horse, but you'll still have to make sure he's fed and groomed properly."

"Of course, Mama. Marten says a chevalier always sees that his horses are well-treated. Is Uncle Claude a

chevalier? How long will we stay there? Will I get riding lessons? I want you to watch every day.''

She felt a pang of guilt and said gently, ''Mama won't
be there all the time, sweeting. I have to go visit Aunt
Lece.''

He sat and frowned at that for a long while, then
said, ''Why can't Aunt Lece visit Uncle Claude?''

''She needs my help at Cerfontaine. Do you remember me telling you about Cerfontaine? That's where I
was a little girl.''

He wiggled a little closer to her and nodded, then
began playing with a button-and-string toy Grette had
made for him.

The dust stirred up by their passing mixed with the
gunpowder smoke drifting in from the battle, making
the setting sun turn the entire sky a dirty orange. Her
eyes stung from the ash and soot in the air, and her
throat felt as if it had been coated with a fine powder.

The sullen servant looked back up the road and
grunted. Kaatje twisted around to see what he was
looking at, her gaze following the dirt road that
stretched a mile or so behind them until it disappeared
around a hillock. A black speck had just rounded the
hill, and she recognized a horse and rider coming toward them at a dead run. The rider whipped savagely
at his horse, and Kaatje's eyes narrowed; she instinctively pulled Pietr closer to her.

Pietr looked up at her, then swiveled his head back
to look too. ''Is that Marten, Mama?''

''No, my love. I don't know who it is.'' There was
something familiar about that bright blue uniform,
though, and the odd cant to the head . . . Roulon!

Kaatje quickly faced forward and bent her head over
her son to shield them both from his view while her
hand slipped beneath her petticoats for the knife she'd
hidden there. Her fingers wrapped around the thin bone
handle, and she tugged at it, but she couldn't pull it

free of the garter. She yanked frantically, but only succeeded in ripping the lace. The hoofbeats were distinct now, and she huddled down over Pietr even more. The only hope left to her was that Roulon might think they were peasants and ride on by.

In a cloud of curses, Roulon pulled his horse up hard next to her cart, the bit tearing into the animal's mouth, but the comte paid no attention. He jumped off, making the cuirass tied to his saddle clank loudly. "You stupid fool!" he said to the man holding the pony. "I told you to keep them at the crossroads." The servant shrugged absently.

The comte's wig had tangled and slid sideways, and long cuts in his once immaculate uniform revealed the mud-splattered shirt beneath. His narrow face was covered in soot and pinched with fury.

"How dare you give my servants orders, sir!" Kaatje sat erect and glared at him, shaking inside at the thought that Roulon had guessed she'd try to leave the chateau.

"I give orders to whomever I please, madame." He grabbed for his sword hilt, but his hand closed on the space above an empty scabbard. He snarled and reached for the dagger in his boot. In a flash, the long thin blade was pointing at her throat. *"Get down."*

A muscle near his right eye twitched, and he kept looking back up the road as if expecting something. His courtier's manners had evidently gone the way of his elegant attire. "Hurry, you scut, the battle's lost." He glanced up the road again. "Thorne nearly cut off my escape. Cold-blooded bastard. He'll pay for that." His eyes snapped back to her. "But that will have to wait. Get down." He seized her cloak at the throat and started dragging her off the cart. She cried out and struggled to keep her balance, but he succeeded in pulling her down.

"Mama!" Pietr cried, standing up and facing the mad Frenchman, his hands balled into tiny fists.

"No, Pietr!"

"You leave my mama alone!" the little boy said stalwartly, though Kaatje could see he was trying desperately not to cry.

Roulon held the dagger to Pietr's chest and flicked a button off his jacket. Kaatje screamed; the comte twisted his grip on her cloak's collar to cut off her air. "Tell your brat to shut up, or I'll sell him to the Turks." He seemed oblivious to Kaatje's struggles to free herself from his suffocating hold. "And don't think I won't. There's a thriving market for pretty little blond boys in Hungary."

She gestured to Pietr to sit down and the little boy hesitated, then sat down hard on the cart's wooden plank, tears rolling down his cheeks. Roulon eased his grip slightly, letting her breathe a bit easier.

"I knew you would bolt after all those lies you told me this morning. Tell me where you go to meet your sister."

"I told you no lies! And we are not traveling to meet my sister—ask your lackey if you don't believe me," she said. "We are on our way to visit the Margrave of Hospaire-Aube, my husband's brother."

It was a grand title and usually silenced anyone impressed by rank, but Roulon only brought up his dagger and rested it against her cheek. "Where is your whore of a sister? *Where?*" he demanded, twisting the gray fabric at her neck. "She's run to that pile of stones where she grew up. The one she used to babble about. Hasn't she? *Hasn't she?*"

"I d-don't . . ." she began, but his grip was so tight that she couldn't breathe. Kaatje clawed at his arm, but the light seemed to be getting dimmer, making it hard to concentrate.

He spat out a laugh. "That bitch never did know when to shut up."

Far off, she heard a shout, and Roulon snarled a filthy

epithet. He threw her from him and she crumpled to the ground, conscious only of the wonderful sweet air she was gulping into her lungs. The hooves of Roulon's horse struck the ground near her head, then were quickly gone.

Grit from the road scraped her face. As she lifted her head and slowly propped herself up to her knees, she saw Roulon disappear down the road, headed, she could only imagine, for Cerfontaine. There was a scurrying sound behind her, then two small arms wrapped around her. "Mama, Mama! Did he hurt you?"

She hugged her son fiercely and shook her head, sure she would cry if she tried to speak. "Truly, Mama? I would've saved you but Marten said I wouldn't need my sword." He sniffled and then squirmed to be released. With the resiliency of a six-year-old, he asked, "Do you think Uncle Claude will have one I can use?"

"Yes, sweeting, I'm sure he will," she said, her throat tight with unshed tears.

Kaatje rose to her feet and put Pietr into the cart. The pony made a nervous nickering sound and she went to steady it, not surprised to see that the servant had deserted them.

A sound like approaching thunder made her look back. Three English soldiers astride huge war horses were galloping toward her, their coats looking bloodred in the last long rays of the sun.

Chapter 3

For a terrifying instant, Kaatje thought the soldiers were going to run her and her son down, but they pulled up their horses with brisk precision just behind the cart.

Her eyes widened in dismay when the tallest of the group dismounted and strode toward her, his spurs jangling as he walked. The Englishman! Black grime covered his face, putting his blue eyes into startling relief. Her stomach fluttered in alarm when she saw the wildness flaring in his eyes and realized that his battle fury had not yet completely left him.

"Lantern," he ordered, and within a breath the area was flooded with bright orange light. He strode up to her and, thrusting his hands on either side of her, trapped her against the pony's side. His glittering eyes bored down into hers. "What did you tell Roulon?" he asked.

"Nothing," she said in a hoarse whisper. She swallowed, and her throat felt less raw. "Nothing, I swear to you." He smelled of gunpowder and singed wool. She stared back into his eyes, fighting the fear that snaked through her.

"You lie!"

"You sound like Roulon," she said. What could she do to be rid of him? If she could get the knife free . . .

"Why do you shake if you are telling the truth? You have nothing to fear if you do not lie."

45

''Nothing to fear! You ride up here smelling of guns and stained with the blood of God knows how many men, and you say I have nothing to fear. I saw you kill a man! You can just as easily kill me.''

The sheathed knife rubbed against her thigh, and she tried to think of how to reach it. Lecé had told her where a lady should hide a knife, but she had failed to tell her how a lady retrieved it. Kaatje fumed silently. She could hardly just throw up her skirts.

The light in his eyes changed as she spoke, and they stood silent with their bodies close together. He took a deep breath, and she nearly felt the force of his chest against her. A long moment passed before she noticed that his arms had fallen to his sides.

''Don't you hurt my mama!'' Pietr cried, his small hands balled into fists. The boy coughed, and his wavering voice told Kaatje he was about to break into tears.

''Niall,'' the Englishman called over his shoulder, ''this brave little soldier sounds thirsty.''

She turned to take her son in her arms, but Pietr had straightened his shoulders and thrust up his chin, and out of consideration for his pride she stopped. A van Staden indeed, she thought.

A young man with the most extraordinary red hair she'd ever seen dismounted and walked with slightly bowed legs toward her son. He smiled kindly at her and whispered in faltering French as he passed, ''I have twelve brothers and sisters, ma'am.'' That he tried to reassure her startled her, making the knot of fear in her stomach ease a little; but she still watched him warily.

''Here you go, my man, drink up.'' Pietr looked delighted to receive the goatskin bag, and he giggled as the long thin stream of water capered on his tongue. He finished and thanked the young soldier with a graceful bow, and the other Englishman still on his horse laughed.

The redhead grinned. "Colonel Thorne, it looks to me like we got us a little general. I'll be following his orders from now on."

Kaatje watched the black-haired man in front of her; he didn't smile but his body had lost some of its taut readiness. Colonel Thorne, the soldier had called him. She tried to put her tongue behind her teeth to pronounce it. She looked up at him and discovered him watching her intently. In trying to pronounce his name, her mouth had puckered as if for a kiss.

Kaatje flushed and looked away, and saw Pietr chatting merrily with the man named Niall.

Thorne bowed, and suddenly his stained and dusty clothes seemed less disreputable. There were powder burns on his sleeves, but he didn't appear to have been wounded. "Forgive my manners, madame. It has been a long day." She could hear the weariness in his voice, but distrusted it. Why the sudden politeness? she wondered, fearful that it was more dangerous than his earlier incivility. "It hs been a long day for us all."

His eyes darkened, and his gaze compelled her not to look away. "Did you find the letter?"

Kaatje chided herself for not remembering how he could change moods so fast that it made her head spin, and it took her a moment to steady herself. What was she going to tell him? The letter was nothing but ash that the wind had blown away. She walked to the edge of the circle of lantern light to put a few paces between them.

She rubbed her arms, and the idea of escaping fluttered briefly through her head. But she could never leave without Pietr, and the empty farmhouses and abandoned barns looked to be nothing more than lonely black shadows in the gray landscape. She heard shouts in the distance and shivered, knowing that by now the countryside was surely crawling with soldiers.

The Englishman's bootsteps were audible on the hard-

packed earth, and then his head and broad shoulders
blocked out the first stars of the evening.

"You have a dilemma," he said, his voice low so
the others could not hear. "Do you lie and say you
didn't find the letter, or do you lie and say the letter
mentioned nothing of where your sister is?"

Kaatje felt a stab of frustration. She had to find Lece,
and she wasn't going to let this Englishman—or anyone—get in her way. "Or do I say nothing and continue
on my journey?" she said in answer.

"Without any kind of escort?"

Kaatje sighed. She'd forgotten about the wretch who
had deserted them when Roulon appeared. "We'll return to St. Benoit, and Marten can escort us."

"It would be a two-hour trip in the dark, amid"—he
stopped as the sound of shouting in the distance grew
louder, then crescendoed in a single piercing scream—
"the horrors of a battle after it has been won."

She trembled. The night had cooled to a chill since
the sun had set, and she unconsciously stepped closer
to him, feeling the warmth emanating from him. "And
what do you suggest, Colonel Thorne?" She was still
finding it difficult to pronounce his name; if only she
could keep her lips from puckering when she said it.

"Where do you go?" he asked.

She let the silence stretch to two breaths, then three,
before saying, "Did you think it would be that easy to
find out where Lece is?" He shrugged, and Kaatje
shivered as she stepped away from him. "I am taking
my son to Hespaire-Aube. My husband's brother is neutral and the war does not enter his lands. Pietr will be
safe there." She thought she heard a faint derisive
laugh.

"And you?" he asked.

She met his eyes squarely. "I will be safe there, too."

He stared into her eyes and her courage started to

waver—what could he see that she did not want him to know?

Pietr's gleeful laughter broke the spell between them, and she hurried back to the cart and the lantern light. Her son was seated on Toca's back while the red-haired man showed him how to hold the reins for a war horse. The boy looked tired and weary, but his face was no longer pinched with fear and there was a sparkle in his eyes.

"Mama! Lieutenant Niall is taking us to Uncle Claude's. Isn't that wonderful? And he promised to teach me how to ride! Must you go visit Aunt Lece at Cerfontaine? Couldn't you stay and watch me?"

She heard Thorne stop in his tracks and hiss, *"Of course."* Her heart sank. He came up beside her, and his long fingers wrapped around her arm in a steely grip. "Your mother won't be going with you to your Uncle Claude's, Pietr," he said, and Kaatje knew from the low vibrant timbre of his voice that the flare of battle had returned to his eyes. A cold wave of fear washed through her, and she stiffened.

He must've felt the muscles in her arm tense to pull away because his voice was a whisper when he said, "Think, madame, before you act. Look around you carefully before you distress your son. Niall *will* escort him to Hespaire-Aube. You *will* lead me to your sister. I suggest you smile and agree with me before the boy thinks you are in danger. You do not want him to worry, do you?"

"You cur, you use my own son against me?"

"Of course, madame. This is war."

"Mama?" Pietr asked, clearly uneasy at the scene unfolding a few paces away.

"I-I need to show Colonel Thorne something, sweeting," she said, struggling to keep the seething fury from her voice.

"But why can't we go with you to Cerfontaine?" he asked plaintively.

"It—it would be a difficult trip for so many," she replied carefully. How could she possibly leave him in the care of these strangers? Then an idea came to her, and she blurted it out before she could be outmaneuvered. "But Lieutenant Niall will take you back to St. Benoit first to get Grette to come with you. You would like that, wouldn't you?"

The colonel's grip on her tightened.

Pietr's eyes lit up. "Would she make me cream tarts?"

The pressure on her arm lessened. "Agreed," the colonel said quietly. "They can go back."

Under her breath, she said to Thorne, "Let me say goodbye." He hesitated, then released her; she ran to Pietr, still seated on the pony's back, and enveloped him in a trembling embrace. "She'll make you as many cream tarts as you want, my love."

Kaatje fumbled in her cloak pocket and pulled out a small bundle carefully wrapped in oilskin and closed with a long leather thong. She tied the thong around Pietr's neck and tucked the bundle inside his shirt, then hugged him again. "Make sure Grette gives you your cordial every morning. It's very very important."

He nodded. He seemed so frail in her arms. She stroked his soft golden hair, straightened his clothes, and murmured all the motherly admonishments: be a good boy, mind your manners . . . But silently she struggled with her tears and cursed the Englishman standing behind her for forcing her to abandon her son.

She held Pietr at arm's length to look at him one last time. She could see his mouth tremble, and his eyes were wide and bright with unshed tears at the realization that his mother was leaving him.

"Mama?" His little voice wavered.

"It will be all right, my little rock. Just don't forget

about your cordial. The lieutenant will take care of you, but you'll have to take care of Grette, won't you?''

He straightened his small shoulders and nodded. "I'll be a good soldier, Mama."

Unable to speak for a moment, she gave him one last hug, then released him and backed away. "I know you will, sweetheart. I know you will."

"Return to the chateau and collect the woman, Grette. Then take both of them to Hespaire-Aube," the colonel commanded. "Is that clear?"

Niall nodded, lifted Pietr off the pony, and set him back on the plank seat, then secured his horse to the back of the cart and climbed up beside the boy. With a gentle hand on the reins, he turned the cart around and headed back down the road, the other Englishman riding guard and the lantern casting a small pool of orange light.

Fear clutched at her throat. Would they harm her little boy? Would she ever see him again? She began running up the dark road toward the bobbing circle of light. How could she let them do this?

"Madame!" The colonel's voice came from someplace behind her, and she stumbled to a halt in the darkness. What chance did she and Pietr have against battle-hardened soldiers? And Roulon might be waiting for them somewhere on the road ahead. The single glow from the lantern faded in the distance. She shivered and hugged her arms to her; she had never felt so alone.

She heard the pounding of hoofbeats coming up swiftly behind her, and in a heartbeat an arm hooked around her waist. Her startled cry was swallowed up by the night as Thorne hoisted her sideways onto the saddle in front of him. She clutched desperately at his coat to keep from falling off.

"Get comfortable, madame," he said, his voice rumbling over her head, "we have a long ride ahead of us."

She pulled her face out of the scarlet wool. "You devil. If you think I'm going to take thi—" The arm around her waist crushed her to him.

"You'll take it, madame. You'll take whatever I choose to give you." He wheeled the horse around and they plunged into the night.

The bright disk of the moon rose higher and higher in the night sky. Time stretched endlessly in front of her, measured only by the black stallion's hooves thundering on the road, beating a steady rhythm into Kaatje's body like some mad lullaby. Crammed sideways between the high pommel of the war saddle and Thorne's hard body, her heart hammered in her chest, and the buffeting wind stole her breath away.

Miles fled by before her fear began to ebb and she could feel the night air on her skin and smell the half-ripened oats in the fields they passed. She opened her eyes, and saw the trampled fields turned pewter by the moonlight, the long straight lines of hedgerows marked only by shadows, and the narrow ribbon of road ahead of them leading south to Lessines and then Mons, leading her farther and farther away from her son.

Pietr needed her. She remembered his face, his trusting eyes wide and his brave chin trembling as he'd sat next to the English lieutenant, trying so hard to be her good little soldier. When would she see him again?

Her throat tightened. She had to help her son—and to do that, she had to get away from this Englishman.

Kaatje struggled to free herself from the colonel's arm that held her fast against him. "Are you deranged? We can't ride like this all the way to Cerfontaine."

"Hold still, woman," he said, gritting the words through clenched teeth. "Do you want a broken neck?"

"What I want is to be off this horse and with my son." She squirmed, then stopped abruptly when she felt the muscles in his thighs move under her. If he'd had a lap, she'd be sitting on it, but he was straddling the back of the powerful black horse, forcing her to settle in the vee between his hard-muscled thighs. Her right hip was tightly pressed against his stomach and she was grateful for the bunched wool of her cloak that separated them.

"Take care," he said harshly. "A dead French widow is of little use to me or your son."

"I'd be a dead *Flemish* widow," she snapped back. "And don't hold me so tightly. I can scarcely breathe."

Jerked sideways with each long stride of the horse, her hip rubbed painfully on the pommel and her shoulder was jammed into his chest with each rocking motion. She felt like a string man on a stick. "Why couldn't I have ridden the lieutenant's horse?"

"You on a war horse alone? Don't be a fool." His voice came in short bursts, a counterpoint to the rhythm of the black horse's long strides, making it seem that he was somehow connected with the animal in ways she did not understand.

"I was riding before I could walk!" she said. She felt how tense and alert he was, his body reading each subtle movement of the horse, and his muscles making small compensations to adjust. She wanted to get away from him; away from the warmth of his body that enveloped her, and the constant awareness of the powerful muscles that moved beneath her as he controlled the horse. "Another horse, then! Surely we could stop at a farmhouse—"

He lifted her from the saddle and Kaatje instinctively grabbed him around his neck, her stomach flipflopping in panic until he resettled her an instant later.

"What are you trying to do!" she cried. "Throw me off?"

His free arm had slid further around her, and he held her in a close embrace. "Isn't that what you wanted?"

he asked, his voice next to her ear and a tone lower than before.

She pulled back with a start. "No! I mean yes. I mean I want off the horse, but I don't want to be thrown off while it's bounding down the road as if the devil were on its heels."

"You relieve me," he said, then added, "and the devil is ahead of us."

It had been a long time since Kaatje had been so close to a man. Long ago, Philippe . . . No, she mustn't think of the past now. She had to stay watchful, ready to take advantage of any weakness. Lece must remain able to send Pietr's medicine, and that meant this wretched Colonel Thorne had to be left behind.

Kaatje eyed a pair of pistols in a matched set of embroidered holsters that hung on each side of the saddle, temptingly near her hand. Moonlight glinted off their silver handles, and she could just see the outlines of a crest engraved on them. They were a gentleman's guns, superbly made, elegant and deadly. Like the man from whose saddle they hung.

He'd probably used them in the battle, she thought. Had he reloaded them? And if he had, could she use one on him? She shifted, and he pressed her waist in warning. She froze. Had he read her mind? He said nothing.

Kaatje pointedly studied the fields, while out of the corner of her eye she tried to tell if the pistols had been loaded. The force of the colonel's presence enveloped her, and she knew that he was not the kind of man who would meet his enemies with an empty firearm. What would he do when she aimed the barrel of his own gun at his heart? She took a deep breath to steady her wavering courage. She had to try.

"That would not be wise," his voice said from somewhere near the top of her head.

''What do you mean?'' she asked, trying to sound innocent and failing miserably.

Becket felt the woman snugged against his body hesitate. He clenched his jaw so hard he thought the muscles would pop. Perversely, he almost wished she *would* go for the gun. It was torment. To feel her crushed against his chest, her hips undulating in rhythm with . . . He shook his head and tried to concentrate on guiding Acheron.

His bruises and bones ached from the battle, and he envied the men who had just dropped to sleep where they'd stood when the French trumpets had blared in surrender. He grimaced as the muscles in his side strained. He'd been hit so hard there that his plate chest armor had been dented and chafed the bruised area for the rest of the battle. He'd gone too long without sleep, and, Jesu, far too long without a woman.

At the curve of the road ahead, a shadow moved. Becket's eyes narrowed, and with his knees he directed Acheron to slow.

Madame de St. Benoit gave a start of surprise. ''What is it? Why are we stopping?'' she asked, her voice lowered.

''Isn't that what you wanted?'' he whispered. He felt her stiffen, and he wrapped his arm tighter around her small waist. There were deserters or bandits ahead, and he needed to withdraw into himself to fight them, but an awareness of the woman in front of him kept interfering.

''What—'' she began to ask again.

''Quiet,'' he commanded, hoping she had enough presence of mind to obey him. She did.

In as low a whisper as he could manage, he said, ''Up ahead, just at the bend in the road. In the hedgerow.'' He felt her shiver, then heard her hair rustle against him when she nodded.

Kaatje strained her eyes to see the moon-cast shadow

that looked like an unnatural swelling in the hedgerow. A hard knot tightened in her stomach. Would this never end?

"I can't fight with you in front of me," the colonel said, his voice low. "Twist around behind me. I'll hold you."

Her eyes grew wide when she realized what he was asking and she looked at the ground; it was a long way to fall. The colonel brought the horse to a halt.

Acheron stood taut and still, his ears upright and pointing forward, listening to the rustling of the men hiding in the hedges. Thorne patted the side of the big stallion's neck, murmuring encouragement to the weary horse. Ahead, the shadow moved, slithering along the side of the road.

The muscles in his arm tensed and he started to lift her. "All right, all right," she gasped, clutching at him. "Just don't drop me."

Kaatje gathered up her skirts as modestly as she could and Thorne held her tightly as she twisted her hips over his hard thigh and threw her leg onto Acheron's back behind the saddle. She settled against the Englishman, his broad strong shoulders like a wall in front of her and, for the first time during this long insane night, she was thankful that Pietr wasn't with her.

His sword hissed as he pulled it from its scabbard, and a chill stabbed through her. "Hold tight," he said. "Our best chance is to get past them as quickly as possible." He dug his heels into Acheron's sides.

"Them?" she squeaked. The horse leaped forward.

In an instant the shadows swarmed into their path and a short scream of surprise escaped Kaatje. Thorne pulled Acheron hard to the right to keep the stallion from stumbling over one of the attackers. His sword flashed in the moonlight, and he slashed at a figure dragging at the horse's bridle. With a shriek of agony, the man fell away.

Curses in guttural French rang out, and there was a hard yank on her skirt. With a cry rattling in her throat, she gripped the Englishman tighter. Another yank, harder this time. She felt herself slipping. She squeezed her eyes shut and kicked out viciously with her booted foot. The wretch below grunted in pain and fell back into the thorny hedge.

Kaatje hurriedly glanced at the moon. Thick clouds were on the verge of shrouding it. They had to get past these brutes before the silver light was obscured. The cutthroats had nothing to lose—only a hangman's noose waited for them if they were caught.

Modesty be damned, she thought, and dug under her skirts. She tore the small bone-handled knife from her garter. Two men jumped at her and she stabbed out blindly at them. She felt the blade meet resistance, then sink into flesh. The man called her a filthy name and crumbled to the ground, taking the knife buried in his neck with him.

The other man grabbed her hand. With only one arm around Thorne, she couldn't hold herself against the strong pull.

Becket felt her slipping. He twisted to help her, but the angle was wrong for his blade to reach. In frustration, he brought his arm up in a long arching swing and rammed his sword hilt backward into the side of the bastard's head. The deserter collapsed to the ground. The woman's grip tightened firmly around him.

With a swipe of his blade to the left, he made the remaining attackers scuttle back for a few precious heartbeats. He seized a pistol from its holster and held it behind him.

"Use both hands to aim it," he shouted. She took it. Two men rushed him, one from each side. He brought the blade down on his left, slicing into the man's shoulder, then heaved it to the other side and ran the attacker through.

Becket gave a hoarse, wordless roar, and the stallion jumped forward with a shuddering breath, leaving the mayhem behind them.

They sped for miles down the road toward Lessines as fast as the tiring horse could take them. Clouds moved in, making the night even more treacherous, and a light drizzle started to fall. Still Thorne did not halt the stallion. For over an hour Kaatje huddled behind the Englishman, her face all but invisible in the folds of her drab gray hood, and the pistol safe and dry under her cloak. *It was loaded!* The words echoed over and over in her mind.

The darkness grew deeper and the drops came down harder, splashing onto the already wet road with a steady staccato drumbeat. Acheron stumbled and at last the colonel slowed the big black horse.

"We can't go much further," he said, his hand soothing the neck of the great beast.

Kaatje clenched the pistol grip, the chased silver warm from her touch. She had been planning on slipping away from him in Lessines, but a village could serve her purpose just as well. They were on the outskirts of the French-speaking Walloon country, where surely even a Fleming would be helped to escape from an Englishman.

"We should be nearing a village that's about a morning's ride from Lessines," she said, her voice cracking.

A sudden bolt of lightning made her jump and illuminated the fields around them for the length of a pounding heartbeat. There was a small stone bridge just ahead of them, and to its right, off the road, she saw a partially burned farmhouse and a barn that appeared untouched. Thunder rolled in the distance.

Kaatje immediately recognized where they were and her heart sank. The village was still miles away—the weary horse would never make it carrying his double

load. As if to corroborate her thoughts, the horse stumbled again, and the colonel brought them to a halt.

Panic seized her. *No more. No more,* she thought,
and in an instant slid off the horse.

"What are you—" Thorne began, twisting around to
face her. She heard him spit a curse when he saw her
standing in the dim light, aiming the barrel of his pistol
at his heart.

"I'm using both hands, the way you told me," she
said, then swallowed hard to quell the terror that surged
up her throat. The rain was falling lightly, dripping from
her hood onto her eyelashes and down her face. She
blinked to clear her vision. "Now get off the horse.
Slowly."

He didn't immediately obey, but sat there studying
her intently. "Get off!" she repeated and had to clench
her teeth to keep them from chattering in the chill of
the damp night. It was too dark to see the color of his
eyes as they bored into her, but she knew they were a
deep indigo, opaque with anger. She shivered.

Without a word, he swung his leg over Acheron,
kicked his other foot out of the stirrup, and dropped to
the ground.

He stood there just three paces in front of her, feet
firmly apart, his gloved fists on his hips. The horse
behind him was a black unmoving mass. Thorne should
have been cowering, but instead his stance challenged
her.

For an instant, her eyes dropped to the gun, then
flashed back to the Englishman. Her stomach churned.
All you have to do is pull the trigger, she told herself
silently.

Slowly, he lifted his hands from his hips, his fingers
uncurling. They moved toward the front of his uniform
coat, its brilliant scarlet dulled to gray in the feeble
moonlight that shone through a break in the clouds. Her
fingers twitched convulsively, and she felt the spring-

loaded steel trigger move slightly. She choked back a sob.

He opened his coat wide, revealing the waistcoat that narrowed into a vee from his broad chest to his slim hips.

"Here," he said, his voice deep and vibrant. He put a hand on the waistcoat over his flat stomach. "Shoot me here, madame. In the flesh below the ribs. Remember?"

Tears of exhaustion ran down her face, mixing with the rain. She trembled all over, and her throat constricted until she could scarcely breathe. "I don't want to shoot you," she said in a whisper that tore at her throat. I just want the horse. Just to the village. You can stay in that barn till morning. You'll be safe."

"Safe," he said in an undertone, the word barely audible above the sound of the rain. "Madame," he said, then stopped. He released his coat and rubbed his face, then lowered his arms to his sides. He gave a small hand signal and the stallion turned and walked between them, coming to a stop in front of her. For a terrifying heartbeat, she stared down the barrel of the pistol into the beast's huge black eyes.

Kaatje lowered the pistol, her hands shaking uncontrollably, as realization dawned. Gun or no gun, the horse would not have gone with her. A trained war horse obeyed its master and its master alone. How could she have been such a fool?

She heard Thorne's footsteps on the wet road as he walked around the horse to face her. In the darkness, his tall form loomed in front of her like the tallest peak of the Ardennes—immovable and silent. She stood shivering before him, cold from the rain and her defeat. He said nothing as he took the pistol from her and shoved it into the empty holster.

The drizzle increased to a steady light rain, and his gloved hand rose toward her wet face, then stopped in its course. He turned the movement into a gesture. "Down there," he said, motioning to a dirt track that led to the burned house and barn.

Kaatje hesitated, staring at him.

He abruptly went to the horse's head and picked up the reins. He watched her, oblivious of the rain. "You have no choice, madame." He glanced at the pistols, and then his shadowed gaze returned to her.

Kaatje's eyes locked with his. Lightning stabbed the night sky, followed by thunder that rumbled like the devil's laughter. She took a step, then another, and slowly walked toward the dirt track.

As she passed him, he put a hand on her shoulder. "Never aim a pistol at a soldier unless you plan on pulling the trigger," he said, his voice almost a caress.

"I shall remember your words, Colonel Thorne," she replied, her voice deadly serious. She walked out of his touch. "I shall remember."

Chapter 4

Exhaustion stole Kaatje's strength. Only years of training kept her back from stooping as she walked in front of Thorne down the dirt track. A slurry of watery mud soaked through the seams of her boots and she felt a twinge of disgruntled envy at Thorne in his jackboots waterproofed with tar and pitch.

As she neared the farmhouse, Kaatje could hear the faint hiss of the rainwater on hot coals. The smell of the wet burned wood was strong, and it slightly sickened her.

There were no sounds of life anywhere: no shouts of greeting from the house, no snuffling of pigs, only the spatter of the rain. And behind her, the near-silent footfalls of the man, and the beast he led. She clutched at her woolen cloak, wishing for the peace of St. Benoit.

How she missed Pietr. Where was he sleeping tonight? Was he warm and dry and safe? A lump in her throat made it difficult for her to swallow. *Please God, keep him from the horrors I've seen. He's just a little boy.* She stumbled, then regained her footing. Grette would take care of him, she knew, but what of the two Englishmen?

She looked at the half-burned farmhouse to her right, glowing coals staring out like cat's eyes, then squinted into the darkness ahead of her to see the obscure gray bulk of the barn. Lightning burst overhead. She flinched and pulled her sopping cloak tighter around her chin. In the sudden light, she saw the barn door was slightly ajar, a gash of shadow on shadow that teemed with ominous warning. The rumble of thunder faded.

The colonel put a hand on her shoulder, and she started at the unexpected contact. "Wait here," he said in an undertone.

Kaatje halted, not wanting to go any closer to that slice of darkness that sucked in the feeble moonlight struggling past the drifting rain clouds. She could sense him studying the entrance to the barn too, and imagined his body taut with readiness.

Thorne silently passed her, his balance on the balls of his feet and his hands held half open and slightly away from his body. With a slow deliberate movement, he pulled a dagger from his boot.

"Thorne—" she began in an urgent whisper, but he silenced her with an upraised hand. He moved toward the barn door, paused in front of the black doorway, listening, then slipped inside without a sound.

Kaatje felt vulnerable and exposed. She wanted to shout, to call him back, but his name stuck in her throat. *No, no, there is no safety with him!* She rubbed a hand over her wet face. *The world has gone mad. And he is part of the madness.*

The stallion came up behind her and stopped. She shivered, stepped closer to the horse, and nervously patted his neck. The horse snorted and stamped a hoof. She snatched her hand back.

"You are well named, beast. Acheron is the lowest river in Hades." She looked at the barn where Thorne had disappeared. "A place your master no doubt knows very well."

The horse flung his head down, rattling the silver on his bridle. "It doesn't matter. I shall soon be rid of you both. Lessines is teeming with horses."

Lessines. The word reverberated through her head

like a desperate prayer. In Lessines she would be free of the Englishman. Free of this madness. *His* madness.

The darkness of the barn doorway lightened to a steady amber glow, thickening the night around her. Thorne must have found a lantern. *At last!* An unsteady breath gushed out of her. She took the reins and started toward the barn, but found herself anchored to a solid immovable mass.

She threw down the reins. "As you will, you great overgrown brute. I've had enough of this nonsen—" Another flash of lightning startled her. She hunched in reaction, then straightened with a quick snap of her shoulders.

The dripping hood of her cloak slid down over her face. She started to push it back, but her hand stopped in mid-motion as the barn door slowly closed until only a sliver of light outlined it. Her nerves skittered with anxiety.

Thorne was still inside the barn.

Kaatje held her breath. Was he waiting for her? Waiting . . . for what?

The door flew wide open, the blade of light expanding to a wide square glowing orange. Thorne stood backlit in the center, a heavy burden in his arms.

She exhaled in a whoosh and shook the rain from her eyes. "Thorne!" she cried, grabbing her skirts and sprinting over the treacherous, muddy tracks leading to the doorway.

Kaatje reached him and staggered to a halt. He held a woman's body in his arms, a worn horse blanket imperfectly covering her. Long tangled brown hair hung down, nearly dragging in the mud.

"God save me, you've killed her!" Kaatje jumped back, her heart pounding in her throat.

"Don't be a fool," Thorne ground out. He pushed past her. "If you must swoon, do so in the barn." He carried the dead woman toward the burned house.

"Damn you, Englishman," Kaatje choked out, not knowing if he heard her. Not caring. She propped herself against the doorway.

Inside, she could see the blood-covered indentation in the straw where the woman's body had sprawled. Kaatje's neck muscles burned with the effort to keep from looking away. Fragmented images from the attack of the deserters flashed through her mind. *God save me, that could be my body he's carrying. Or Pietr's.* Her breathing grew shallow. Panic bubbled in her throat, and she swallowed convulsively.

"No, no," she gasped and stumbled into the barn, falling to her knees by the place where the woman had lain, her hand dropping to the ground to steady herself. Her fingers clenched, gathering a handful of cold straw into her fist. She felt tight inside, warped and out of true, like wood that has dried too fast. She closed her eyes, scalding tears spilling out as she said a silent prayer for the unknown woman, for her son, for herself. Not only soldiers die in war.

Something hard pressed against her palm. She opened her hand and let the straw fall from her grasp. A button, a brass uniform button. She sucked in a breath. From the murderer's coat?

Kaatje held it up to the light of the lantern. The back was plain except for the shank and a word stamped in the metal. She tipped it better into the light to read it. "London."

An *English* button.

A horse snorted behind her, and she jumped to her feet. Thorne was leading the big wet stallion into the barn.

"An Englishman murdered that woman," she said, holding the button out to him in accusation.

His dark eyes regarded her with impatience. He dropped a rough cloth bag at his feet. "Supper," he said, then backed Acheron into the first stall.

"An Englishman, damn you!" Kaatje shouted.

He strode to her. With a black gloved hand, he grabbed her outstretched wrist and held it tightly. "A button proves nothing, madame," he said, glaring down into her eyes. "In battle, a soldier is lucky if his heart stops beating before he is stripped bare."

He snatched the button from her open palm and threw it away without looking at it. It cracked against the wood of a stall.

She wrenched her wrist from his loosened grip. "What kind of brutes have my son?"

The colonel stepped toward her—and kept on coming. She backed away from him, but he loomed in front of her, inches away. She banged against a post. He took one more step, forcing her body against the rough-hewn wood with his.

His deep, barely controlled breaths blew against her chest as if driven by a bellows. He gripped her head, his hands pressing her skull so hard it seemed he would crush it. He looked directly down at her.

"Do you murder me as well?" she asked in a whisper quavering with sham valor.

"Hear me, madame," he said, his eyes filled with a rage that gleamed dark and untamed. "You are never to question the honor of my men again. You know nothing of honor."

He released her and stepped back.

Kaatje sucked in a full breath. "I question everything that concerns my son," she said, meeting his hard gaze. "You are strangers. Foreigners. And you took my child from me."

"Spin me no tales of woe, madame. The blood that flows through your faithless sister also flows through you."

She pushed off from the post. "I doubt your blood flows at all. It is too cold."

He turned his back on her and returned to the stallion. He loosened the saddle and slid it off, the heavy leather hitting him in his side. Kaatje heard his sharp intake of breath.

"Jesu," he muttered.

Despite herself, she took a step toward him, her hands reaching out to him. She was by nature and training a chatelaine, and the impulse to care was deeply ingrained.

With a snarl, he threw the saddle onto a pile of straw and glared at her. "None of your woman's tricks, madame. If you must busy yourself, tend to supper."

She dropped her outstretched arms. He quickly unstrapped the holsters and saddlebags and threw them next to the saddle, then began grooming the horse in quick angry strokes with a fistful of straw. The blood on his coat from the battle had dried to dark stains, and in the closeness of the barn she could still smell the gunpowder.

"I am a fool, colonel," she said, her voice flat. "I should have known you could not act a gentleman. You are in trade."

He looked at her, eyes narrowed. "I am a soldier, madame."

"Exactly, colonel. What can you know of manners?" She rubbed her arms as if to warm them. "Your trade is death."

He spit out a harsh English curse. "As was your husband's."

She inhaled at the stark truth and turned away. The man was a devil. Apprehension fluttered in her stomach. She was powerless against him. Powerless against his strength, his weapons, his experience.

She shrugged out of her cloak and hung it on a rough-hewn peg, then tugged the bodice of her gown straight.

Lessines, she said to herself, the word a promise and a prayer. When she got there tomorrow, she would regain her freedom.

She was every inch the chatelaine of St. Benoit when she picked up the bag Thorne had dropped on the straw. She pulled it open, then faltered at the thought of eating the dead woman's food. Kaatje swallowed. No, tonight she had to meet the madness. The rain was a steady drone outside.

She looked up and saw Thorne's gaze on her, his hands resting on the horse. She lifted her chin. "I shall busy myself with supper, colonel. As you requested."

She stepped toward the lantern, but when she saw the place where the woman had been, she veered toward the back of the barn. The light was dimmer there, making the shadows in the stalls murky and hostile. Her steps slowed.

"We are alone," Thorne said, answering her unspoken fear.

She nodded but did not look back at him, did not want to think about his indigo eyes watching her. She fanned her courage and finished looking around her.

There was an empty chest in one of the stalls, and she struggled to pull it out into the open area to use as a table. From behind her, she heard a muttered curse.

"What has a chest to do with supper?"

She straightened. "Perhaps you would prefer to eat off the straw like animals?"

"Woman, you try my patience," he said, pulling off his coat with sharp angry movements. He threw it on the saddle and stalked to where she stood.

She was startled to see him in his waistcoat and shirt-sleeves. With Philippe's men, too often the uniform had been the soldier, the body underneath merely animating it. But without his, Thorne was no less implacable—and no less dangerous.

He slammed the chest down in the middle of the barn, then went back to his horse, stopping to kick at the blood-covered straw until the woman's deathbed was indistinguishable.

''Thank you, colonel,'' Kaatje said, the muscles of her jaw straining to keep her teeth from clenching.

She turned her back to him, sank to the ground beside the makeshift table, and yanked open the bag. Her first thought was to set out only her own supper. She itched with spite and indignation. Her fingers closed around the narrow neck of a wine bottle and she pulled it from the bag, ready to bang it down on the chest.

Suddenly shame washed over her, and she set the bottle down gently. *That isn't the way, Kaat. He can't rile you if you don't let him.* She drew out a loaf of bread and placed it on the chest, then a small round of cheese and two chipped crockery cups.

The chatelaine took over now. It would be *her* world that was real tonight. She rose and retrieved a handkerchief from her cloak. The bare wood of the chest disturbed her, and she spread the bit of linen on it.

It helped. The embroidered hyacinths that bordered the linen hid the rough wood of the chest top.

At St. Benoit she'd been firm about maintaining a proper household. The silks were faded and the brocades worn, but bouquets of fresh flowers adorned the cabinets and sideboards, and sweet-smelling posies of herbs hung on doors and inside wardrobes. She looked at the handkerchief again; tonight wild hyacinths would have to be enough.

Kaatje heard the rustle of straw behind her and turned. Thorne stood with his hands on his hips, watching her.

''Colonel Thorne,'' she began, then fell silent. Between them there was only the sound of the droning rain and the horse munching his hay.

A few long wavy strands of Thorne's black hair had pulled free of the queue tied at the nape of his neck. He yanked off the plain ribbon and shook his hair free, like a lion shaking its mane.

She expected him to sweep away her handiwork, but she gestured at the rough chest anyway. "Colonel Thorne, would you join me for this light supper?" She indicated the small round of cheese on the cloth. "There is good Flemish edam—"

Thorne walked toward her, his gaze intense and his brow furrowed. She swallowed to clear away the panic that threatened to close her throat. She went around the end of the chest to put the wood box between them.

He stopped in front of the chest and studied it, then looked up at her standing on the opposite side, mistrust glittering in his eyes. "Embroidered linen?" he asked, not bothering to hide his disgust. "Must I suffer a chatelaine's banal small talk as well? I am a soldier, madame. I need no soft words to aid my digestion."

She stiffened. "Small talk, colonel?" she asked, pasting a smile on her face. "You may be a soldier, Colonel Thorne," she said, "but I am not. You may eat with the horse if you prefer." With that, she sat down in the straw, her back straight, and arranged her skirts as best she could.

The mistrust in his eyes faded to something she couldn't identify. "Madame," he said, and to her surprise, he gave her an elegant courtier's bow. She hadn't even thought he knew how to do it.

He turned to retrieve his coat, but she stayed him with a small gesture.

"I have no objections to your eating in your shirtsleeves, colonel."

He raised an eyebrow. "Indeed. Such consideration."

Kaatje didn't look away. "I prefer shirtsleeves to the smell of gunpowder."

She expected him to sit down. He didn't. He threw his stained gloves to the ground. His gaze locked with hers. With one hand, he unbuttoned his waistcoat with deliberate slowness. He shrugged out of it and unwound the cloth from his neck. She opened her mouth to protest.

"Yes?" he said. She saw an embroidered crest on his shirt as he untied it and let it fall open.

"Embroidered linen, colonel?"

"Do you wish me to remove it as well?" he asked. He shook out the lace at his wrists, revealing dark blotches. "It is stained with other men's blood."

Mute, she shook her head.

With a fluid sensuous grace, Thorne lowered himself to the straw. She looked away from the smooth hard muscles revealed in the open vee of his shirt.

He propped his back against a post and stretched his long legs out in front of him with his knees slightly bent. His boots gleamed in the lantern light.

Her gaze followed his hand as he picked up the loaf of bread. He broke it in half, then into fourths. "You brood, madame," he said, holding out a soft middle piece to her.

"Why did you make me come with you?" she asked, taking the proffered bread. "You know where my sister is."

He pulled the knife from his boot with a violent twist, then regained control and carved a wedge of cheese. "Cerfontaine is south of here, is it not?"

The light put the cords of veins on the backs of his hands into sinuous relief. The intricate pattern fascinated her, and she stared at the long slender fingers that were wrapped around the hilt of the knife, full of restrained power.

"S-South? Yes, beyond the Sambre River," she answered.

He held out a piece of cheese. She took it, careful not to touch his hand. "And why should I stop at every crossroads and inquire *where* beyond the Sambre River when I could have a guide close at hand?"

Kaatje took a bite, then swallowed the lump of edam in her throat without tasting it. "But Pietr—"

"Your boy? He is well cared for," he said, his gaze sliding to her. "Niall Elcot is one of the best lieutenants in the army. He'd be a captain if his family could afford the price of the commission. He will keep your Pietr safe, madame, which is more than you could have done."

"How can you say that!" she cried. "I'm his mother."

"You traveled the Odenaarde road alone. Would your mother's concern have saved the boy from the deserters who attacked us?"

"Perhaps not, Colonel Thorne. But it is never wise to underestimate what a mother will do to save her child."

The colonel gripped the neck of the wine bottle.

Kaatje smiled politely and folded her hands in her lap. "Or what a sister will do."

Broken wax from the seal crumbled to the straw. "I shall deal with your sister as she deserves," he said, yanking out the cork.

"My God, what has she done?" Kaatje gasped, then froze as a thought came unbidden to her mind. "Were you—?"

"Lovers?" the colonel finished, pouring the dark red wine into their cups. His dark midnight eyes studied her, making her stomach tighten. "No, madame. Women such as she are not to my taste."

Kaatje flushed and took a sip of the wine. It was tart and had a bite to it, like the man sitting across from her.

His gaze met hers across the cloth-covered chest, the dim light from the lantern making his eyes seem black. "Her crimes are much worse than spurning a lover."

His air of danger returned, as if a clock spring that had wound down was now coiling back up again. "And now, Madame Chatelaine, it is your duty to turn the conversation. Your sister is not a fit topic for supper, however mean the food.''

Anger surged through her. "Turn it to what?'' she asked, gathering her skirts to stand. He reached out, as if to stop her, but she stood quickly. A jagged peg caught her on the shoulder and gouged a tear into her skin. A cry of pain escaped her.

"Turn it to what, Colonel Thorne?'' she cried, backing away from him, her hand on the wound. "Your wife? Your children? Your horses?'' She shook her head, not knowing why it was suddenly so hard for her to keep her mouth from trembling. "Tell me, Colonel Thorne, tell me what you wish to discuss!''

Thorne surged to his feet, his eyes dark. "I am unmarried, madame.'' He stepped over the chest. She backed away, her head rocking from side to side.

"I have no children,'' he said. She stumbled backward into an empty stall. "The horse you are acquainted with.''

He came toward her, the shadow of the wood post falling across his face. "What else do you wish to know?''

Her breath came in shallow gasps. "Nothing,'' she whispered. "Don't hurt me. You need me.''

"Is that what you wish to discuss, madame? My *need?*''

She took another step backward. The straw was slippery. Her heels slid out from under her. She cried out in surprise as she landed in the yielding pile of fresh straw, the smell enveloping her.

His eyes were unreadable in the shadows. His face was lit from the side by the lantern light, the strong firm jaw limned in a golden glow, the arched black brows sharply etched against his skin. Her stomach pitched with a sudden tremor, and her struggle to sit up ceased.

He slowly lowered himself to his knees beside her, the intensity of his gaze increasing to an almost physical force pressing against her the closer he came.

"And what of your need?" he asked, his voice a deep thread of sound. He wrapped his fingers around her upper arms, his head bending toward her shoulder.

"What are you doing?" she asked in a whisper, her voice tremulous. His hold on her arms tightened, but not enough to hurt her.

"In prison, I saw men die from wounds less than this," he murmured, lowering his mouth to her shoulder.

Kaatje gasped when she felt the moist warmth on her skin. He sucked her flesh lightly. She bit her lower lip, then turned her head away and closed her eyes. She wanted to struggle and feel pain, sharp distracting pain. But she didn't struggle. And there was no pain. Only the heat of his mouth, and the moistness of his tongue as it traced the thin line of the cut.

Her body tingled, like winter-chilled flesh warming too fast. His mouth slid from the gash, up her arm to the hollow of her shoulder, then followed the ribbon of her pulse up her neck, leaving behind a paralyzing heat.

"Colonel . . ." The rasp of her breath drowned out the pelting of the rain.

"Chatelaine," he answered, letting the word trail off into a sound of hunger. "Riding with you in front of me is such sweet torture." He flicked his tongue on the soft flesh just below her ear. "Say 'Thorne.' "

She gasped and arched her neck away. "Let me go."

"I do not hold you."

She rolled her head back to face him, and found his lips almost touching hers. She inhaled his warm breath.

"Thor—"

He nipped at her lips. His fingers buried themselves in her hair. He drew his open mouth over her face. "What you do to a man," he said with a growl.

Oh, God, she should run far away. She should ignore the anticipation that pounded in her veins. But she'd been alone for so long. So very long. "Don't hurt me," she whispered.

"No," he breathed against her lips. "Oh, no."

His mouth took hers with exquisite slowness. He tasted her bottom lip with his tongue, and her gasp escaped into his warm mouth. Her lips tingled as he drew his own back and forth across them. His tongue dipped in to caress the soft inner flesh of her mouth, then thrust in further, spiraling around her tongue, stroking it, drawing forth a luxurious hunger from deep within her body.

He pulled back and tugged at her lower lip, then his mouth recaptured hers with a sweeping thrust. His tongue teased hers with insistent strokes, pulling her further and further into the heated mystery of his mouth. A delicious languor spread through her body.

His mouth demanded that she return his kiss. She tentatively flicked her tongue over the moistness just inside his lips. His groan vibrated through her.

She reached out to him, reveling in the feel of the linen on her fingertips as she slowly drew them over his back. Her hands stroked the taut bands of muscle moving under his shirt. The yearning building within her intensified. How she ached to feel the length of him against her.

His hands swept down over her breasts and waist to her hips. She was lost in a strange new urgency. She arched up from the straw, pressing into him. Her body had become separate from her, responding to his touch of its own volition, demanding that she follow where he led. A sensuous cloud was filling her mind, unknown pleasures whispered just out of reach . . . frightening her with what they promised.

Frightening her. *Sweet God.* She rocked her head

back and forth to free her mouth from his compelling lips. She twisted under him, pushing at him.

He pulled back, rolling onto his side. "What do you . . ."

"No," she gasped, tumbling away from him. "Please no." She sat curled up next to the side of the stall, tightly holding her knees to her chest and rocking back and forth on the straw.

Becket sat back on his heels, taking deep shuddering breaths to calm the pounding insistence in his blood. She had been so willing, her lips and tongue so tantalizing that in a few heartbeats he knew he would have tasted the sweet wine of her womanhood. It was all he could do to keep from trembling at the sudden withdrawal of that enticing promise.

He shook his head to clear it. Jesu, but he was a fool to let her slide through his control so easily. How could he have forgotten she was sister to a murderous whore. El Müzir's whore.

The lamplight shimmered on the golden hair falling around her shoulders. "How could I—" she began, closing her eyes. "How could I trust you. You force me away from my son, hunt my sister as if she were your prey—" She broke off, stumbling over the words as if they choked her. "Those are the acts of a madman. An English madman."

He sprung up off his heels to hover over her, his hands imprisoning her face. "Indeed, madame," he said, his voice steel-hard. "I must've been mad to think you would not use your trickery on me. Your sister has taught you well."

He could feel a shiver run through her when she loosened her arms from around her knees, and he thought she would fight him as she had when he'd put her on his horse.

He *wanted* her to fight him. There was something about the way her body moved that enticed him, that burned away his tiredness and the aches of battle. He remembered her twisting against his chest when they were in the saddle; most women would've screamed or swooned, but she'd used her whole body to oppose him—and it had been glorious.

His thumbs caressed the soft delicate flesh at her temples. But she didn't fight him now. "Release me," she said with only the slightest shake in her voice. Her gray-eyed gaze did not waver. She wrapped a trembling hand around his wrist, but her grip quickly steadied and became firm. "Release me," she said again. The strength of her hand was nothing against his, but the strength of her will surprised him. He let her go and looked away.

"Your tricks are subtler than I had expected," he said, rising to his feet. "But I'll not be so easily gulled the next time. I am not one to forget."

His weariness had returned, and he felt the weight of the long day in his bones. He went to retrieve his sword and coat, then threw the coat onto the straw beside her.

He blew out the lantern and heard her gasp at the sudden darkness. He lay down across the opening of the stall, his arms folded and his head pillowed on a cushion of straw. The sword was in front of him, ready to come to his hand to ward off any attack.

The straw rustled behind him as Madame de St. Benoit pulled his coat over her and settled into sleep. In the dark, he ran his thumb over the braided silver wire that was wound around the sword's hilt. It was wrought of the finest Toledo steel and had served him well through seven years of this miserable war. But no weapon could defend him against what he'd seen in the woman's eyes tonight. He'd seen a will that matched his own.

Chapter 5

The heavy gray light of an overcast dawn seeped into the barn, and Kaatje woke but did not open her eyes. She didn't want to. Daylight had a horrible habit of making everything *real*. She didn't want to hear the everyday sounds outside the barn—a wooden bucket thumping against stone and water splashing as it was being drawn from a well, a horse nickering and a low masculine voice answering it. Even through her closed lids, the morning light melted away the soft haze of dream and forced her to remember.

The three red-coated horsemen . . . Pietr taken from her . . . the madness of a night ride . . . the folly of pointing a pistol at a soldier's heart . . . the feel of a demanding masculine mouth on hers . . .

Her eyes snapped open. His coat covered her, and she threw it off. How could she have— Her hand went to the cut on her shoulder. The colonel's eyes, black in the dim light, had pierced through her reason.

Kaatje bit her lip hard in shame. He'd been so close, and the promise of his nearness so compelling. Her will had balanced on a precipice. And she had fallen.

She closed her eyes and rubbed her arms, reluctant to leave the solitude of the barn. Her body felt restless, the way Philippe had always left her after one of his short conjugal visits. She'd asked him to stay once,

78

when the restlessness had begun to change into tantalizing whispers of something unnamed, unknowable . . . but he had mocked her.

And now, with but a kiss, Thorne had made the restlessness return, and had reawakened the whispers, made them grow louder so that she had heard their terrifying promise. Stay in his arms, the whispers had said, and the unknowable would become known.

Afterward her sleep had been light, her mind twisting with schemes. She had considered slipping past him and taking her chances alone in the darkness. But though in a deep sleep, his breaths had hesitated at her slightest movements, as if even asleep he was listening and on guard.

She rose and walked to the doorway, brushing the straw from her gown. The movement helped her to gather the threads of her courage. At the doorway, she paused. The Englishman was there, bent over a bucket of water set on a stump.

He had stripped to his waist to wash, a sheen of dampness on his muscular torso. She could see angry bruises from the battle the day before on his arms and back, and a large, badly scraped one on his left side. And under the bruises—

White slashes of scars crisscrossed his back and chest; when he turned slightly she saw one that puckered the skin just above his heart. "My God, Colonel Thorne! You've been . . ." She choked off her words and screamed silently, *Sweet God, he's been whipped.*

The breath caught in her throat at the evidence of such pain. A poultice of elder flowers, valerian, and plantain would ease the injuries he'd sustained yesterday, but none of her skills could heal those older wounds that looked as if they'd been deep enough to cut to his very soul.

" 'Tis but a bruise, madame. A soldier gets such in

battle.'' He straightened with a swift clean motion, his long wet black hair sending droplets of water flying. A shaft of sunlight broke through the clouds at that moment, making each drop sparkle like crystal.

Their eyes met and held for a long moment before he turned away. She looked down, suddenly aware that her hands had reached out to him, as if she were ready to soothe a balm over his battered flesh. Embarrassed, she dropped them to her sides.

He sleeked his hair back to squeeze out the water and she could see, in profile, the structure of his face. High cheekbones prominent above slight hollows that defined the sides of his face. The straight nose and strong chin. Last night, so close in the lantern light, she'd seen tiny faint lines at the corners of his eyes, lines that in others would have been caused by laughter, but in this Englishman . . .

She searched for something to say, and found nothing but polite banalities. *''Bon matin,* colonel.''

''Bon matin, madame.''

He threw out the bucket of water with a splash, refilled it from the well, then set it on the stump with a solid thud. ''Fresh water,'' he said.

He shrugged into his shirt, then strode toward her, leaving it untied. There was a tightly reined energy to his actions that made her stomach knot. One of his hands grabbed the door above her head and he hovered over her, his face inches from hers.

''I am an impatient man, madame,'' he said. ''Finish your ablutions quickly.'' He removed his hand from the door and walked past her into the darkness of the barn.

Some of her tenseness eased at her momentary privacy. An urge to dash into the oat fields and run away tugged at her. *Don't be a fool,* she chided herself, straightening her skirts. The dead woman last night proved that alone she wasn't safe; on a horse she might've had a chance, but on foot she would have been as vulnerable as a black hare in a snowbank. She smiled to herself. But in Lessines . . .

She stared at the bucket of cold well water, trying not to think of the warm water that had greeted her—had it been only yesterday morning? And sweet little Pietr, was he too having to face cold water on a cold dawn?

Her spirit faltered, nonetheless she dipped her handkerchief into the water and dabbed at her face and neck. She glanced at the empty barn doorway, then drew the damp cloth inside the neckline of her gown.

"Have you finished?" The Englishman now stood in the doorway, completely dressed, one hand holding the black stallion's reins. "I want to reach the Sambre before nightfall," he said, leading Acheron into the sunlight.

Kaatje plucked the handkerchief from her bodice and willed herself not to turn red. "You've given me but a few moments," she protested. "My hair," she said, "my dress. It needs mending."

Becket strode toward her, impatience jarring up his spine with each step. She had artfully wound her hair at the top of her head, letting some of it spill from its pins.

"You stall," he said.

"No, I—"

He reached her and his hands went to her hair. Fear flashed through her eyes. With swift precision, he plucked out her hairpins. He had to will himself not to feel the silkiness of the golden strands as her unbound hair slid over his ungloved hands. When he had done, he held out the pins to her.

"A simple knot will do," he said, his voice brusque. She looked up at him, the wariness in her gray eyes warming to anger.

"As you wish, colonel," she said, snatching the pins.

She turned away and smoothed her hair into a coil at the base of her neck.

He pulled his gaze away from the elegant grace of her neck and shoulders. Damn her tricks! First he'd seen her posed in front of the water bucket, her head tilted back, her eyes closed, and her hand drawing the damp handkerchief along the bodice of her gown. And now she'd turned the simple act of pinning up her hair into an enticement.

She tugged at the torn shoulder of her gown, reminding him of his efforts to suck the cut clean. He felt an unwelcome tightness in his loins. Contempt for his own weakness bit at him like a rabid fox. He should never have kissed her. He cursed himself for having wanted to.

"You are done, madame," he said, and kicked the bucket off the stump. The crash of water and wood made her jump. She inhaled to protest, but it quickly turned into a cry of surprise when he swept her off her feet and set her on the saddle with an undignified thump.

He drew on his gloves and swung into the saddle behind her. With his knees, he commanded the horse to head back out to the road, and the animal obeyed instantly.

"No! Wait," she said, her voice breathless. "My cloak—"

"—is tied behind the saddle." He wrapped an arm around her waist and lifted her to resettle her. He both felt and heard her gasp of surprise. "Resign yourself, madame. The ride will be a long one."

Redcoats. Scores of them. Kaatje clutched at the horse's mane to steady herself. There were redcoats riding north on the road from Lessines and redcoats riding south. In groups of two or three they came, some dusty, exhausted, others trotting jauntily, fresh and lively in the warm summer morning and obviously celebrating their recent victory.

Her gaze followed the fourth group to lift their hats in salute to Thorne as they passed. They saluted the colonel before he even looked in their direction, respect and awe filling their eyes. They looked at her with intense speculation, several smiling boldly. A flush heated her cheeks.

"I thought . . ." she began, but paused to swallow flutterings of uneasiness. "I thought the French held Lessines."

"They thought so as well," Thorne answered. "But they erred." She felt the muscles tighten in the arm across her back and she tried to shift away. "Disappointed, madame? Did you think I would let you run away? *You* erred. There is too much at stake."

She said nothing, but her heart sank. She'd pinned all her hopes on eluding the Englishman in Lessines.

Acheron crested a hill and began the descent into a wide valley. Kaatje felt the colonel's legs flex as he kneed the stallion into the fast gait she remembered from the night before. Neat fields of flax and oats bordered the road, and far ahead Lessines shone in a shaft of sunlight, like a beckoning angel in an old monk's tale.

"Do we have to ride at this pace?" she asked, her voice jouncing with each step. Her fingers curled into the black mane to hold on.

"It is how a British regiment of horse rides into battle," Thorne said, an undercurrent of pride in his words. "Steady. Fast. Controlled. The sight of a regiment of red-coated cavalry riding knee to knee in a long deadly line, swords at the ready, can throw an entire enemy brigade into chaos."

"You aren't riding into battle now!" Kaatje said, the muscles along her spine tightening as she unconsciously tried to ease her body away from him. A prickle of sympathy for Thorne's enemies danced through her.

"No?" he said.

Anxiety caught at her. Awkwardly, she turned and looked up at his hard, set face. His gaze was focused on the road ahead.

"What do you mean? You said the Allies hold Lessines," she said.

"And the Meuse Valley to the gates of Namur," he added. "But Cerfontaine . . ." She grabbed at the turned-back facings on his coat. "What of Lece? Is my sister in danger?"

He did not answer her immediately, nor did he lower his gaze.

"Thorne."

"Your sister . . . is in a great deal of danger."

Now it was Kaatje's turn to be silent. She licked her lips, then swallowed.

"From you?" she asked.

He did not answer.

Kaatje released his coat facings. "Why?" she demanded. "Tell me the why of all of this!" She rubbed her arms, her fingers catching on the bedraggled lace at the end of her half sleeves. She wanted to tear it off. "Why do you want my sister? What has she done to you?"

"I am impressed, madame. I almost believe you don't know."

"I don't." *Damn you, Thorne.* "Tell me! I deserve that much."

He grasped the back of her neck and held it immobile. "What you *deserve,* madame, is the same fate that awaits your sister, though the fact that you are assisting me may tilt the scales of justice somewhat." He released her.

"I am not English. I will not be tried by English

justice." She sat stiffly in front of him, refusing to settle back into the crook of his shoulder.

"Not English justice," he said. "Mine."

Becket itched to force her rigid body back against
him, to feel her soft supple form molding itself to him
as they rode. He had expected her to swoon, not ar-
gue. Seduce him, not hold herself rigidly away. He
wanted to throttle her. He watched the quicksilver
flashes in her eyes. His gaze dropped to her lips. He
wanted . . .

One kiss, he thought, one long slow kiss would burn
away the chill in those gray eyes of hers. He wanted to
crush her to him, and feel her responding under him,
feel the force of her will focused on him.

Jesu, don't be a fool. Think who she is.

She was a beautiful woman, yes, and he, a man with
hot blood in his veins. But if he wasn't careful, that
blood could be draining away into the ground.

But he wanted . . . and the intensity of that want
disturbed him. He was known for his self-control, and
he'd be damned before he'd let a golden-haired Frenchman's widow make him lose it.

Hür adam, köla olmiyan, he chanted silently. His
hand closed into a fist. Jesu, what did it matter. He was
already damned.

Lessines was crowded. They rode in on the main
road, past the ancient stone guildhouses and the spired
church—and more Allied soldiers. Where the French
had plundered, the Allies spent. The day had turned
into a market day, everyone bringing out goods that
had successfully been hidden during the French oc-
cupation. Discarded bouquets and ribbons were trampled underneath the stallion's hooves, the last vestiges
of the welcome the Allies had received from the pop-
ulace.

A group of hussars road by, shouting their greeting.

Kaatje's throat tightened; her father had been a hussar. She felt like a hare during a hunt, but she was a van Staden. The blood of the van Stadens went back to the beginning of Flanders itself.

She would escape the colonel here, in Lessines, and she would get to Cerfontaine to warn Lece. No Englishman would stop her.

But she hadn't counted on the Allies being here: Englishmen, Prussians, Dutchmen, Austrians . . . There were enemies in every street, every back alley—enemies Thorne could command at a word.

She didn't just have to escape one man now, but an army.

The colonel slowed Acheron in the crush of people. Kaatje bolstered her courage. She had to be alert, ready. But she was used to the walled city of Oudenaarde, and the sprawling chaos around her made her head spin. The market streets were all a jumble, one row of stalls running smack into another. Two farm wives squabbled over a choice corner spot, one keeping tight hold of a bleating goat. A few steps away a red-faced baker loudly defended the quality of his heavy-looking loaves—*No! He did not cut his flour with alum. How dare he be insulted* . . .

Thorne headed down a narrow street, the high walls of the buildings on either side shutting out the noise. Kaatje's eyes darted from doorways to windows, hoping to discover an escape route, but the doors were bolted and the windows too high from the ground. They came out in a wide city square and her heart dropped—the place was bustling with soldiers.

"Ho, Thorne!" a bellowing voice called out across the square. Behind her, the colonel's body tensed. The arm around her solidified into an unbreakable iron band.

A thick-necked English colonel with elaborate gold braiding on his coat forced his horse through the crowd of soldiers. He swatted at a couple of the men who cursed him as he pushed past. "Blighted devils," the man muttered as he came up to Thorne.

"Commercy," Thorne said levelly.

The man squinted at Kaatje, and his thick sandy eyebrows shot up. He sucked in his breath through his teeth. "Damned fine woman. There a sister?"

Kaatje held her breath. Thorne's body tensed, and Acheron stamped his foot and blew air out his nose in annoyance.

"Just askin' old man. No need to look thunder at me."

"She is the wife of a chevalier, Commercy. I am escorting her. The battle confounded her travel plans."

The man snorted. "Chevalier, eh? Which one?"

"That is my concern."

"You look ready to go for your sword, man. I'm just askin'." Commercy's horse nervously pranced around, forcing him to struggle to control it. "Too much hot blood in you, Thorne. Courier rode in a couple of hours ago. Heard about your charge into the whole cavalry of the French left wing. Wild stunt. Did the business, though. Damned sorry I missed it."

Commercy shook his head. "Gotta tend to some piddlin' hangings. That Bergheyck fellow seems to have had quite a following here. You wouldn't think these Brabanters would be all that fired up about a count from Flanders, but there it is."

The thick-necked colonel's glance swept over Kaatje again and he sucked his teeth. "Damned fine woman." He reined his horse hard to the right and began swatting and bellowing curses as he pushed his way back through the crowd.

Acheron moved forward, toward the opposite side of the square. "Who's Bergheyck?" Kaatje asked.

"No doubt you know nothing of that as well," Thorne said, his arm still tight around her.

A blond man spit in the dirt in front of Acheron. *"Verrader,"* he snarled in Flemish. Traitor. Kaatje stiffened, blanching at the thought that her own countrymen could so easily assume her an Englishman's whore. Still, she followed the blond man with her eyes. He met up with a man dressed in a blue bricklayer's smock who stood idly in front of a goldsmith shop. The blond man nudged him and jerked his head in her direction. The bricklayer frowned and nodded, then slipped into the goldsmith's shop.

As they neared the corner, Kaatje tried to memorize the location of the shop. There were Flemings there; they might help her when she got away from Thorne.

"Bergheyck, colonel?" Kaatje prodded, attempting to mask her interest in the shop with idle questions.

"A Flemish count who conspired against the Allies, madame. No doubt you've had him to dinner any number of times."

"What if I have, colonel?" She looked up and saw his eyes studying the goldsmith's shop. Dismay crept up her spine. Had he guessed her intentions so quickly?

His gaze dropped to hers. "What if you have, madame. A few days ago, Bergheyck delivered up Ghent and Bruges to the French."

A sharp clang made her start. Behind her, to the horse's left, the man in the blue smock was banging a stick against the metal reinforced sides of the hod at his feet. Acheron's head arched up in surprise. Thorne's arm around her waist loosened to get greater control of the reins. He cursed fluently.

She sucked in a quick breath for courage. She twisted. The crowd was a blur. She pushed herself down the side of the horse.

She hit the ground hard and staggered. Thorne roared his fury, turning Acheron around to circle back to her. She ran forward since the way to the goldsmith's shop was blocked, the stones slippery under her feet. Panic bubbled in her throat. Iron-shod hooves struck hard on the cobblestones behind her.

The crowd closed around her, cheering her on as if it were a race at a fair. Kaatje half feared Thorne would use his battle-trained war horse to clear the way. The smells suffocated her. She pushed her way in the pressing mob. "Let me through . . ."

"Madame!" she heard Thorne bellow.

She fled around a corner, then another and another until she felt like a weaver's shuttlecock. Where was the goldsmith's shop? Surely the Fleming she'd seen there would lend her a horse.

At last she stumbled into an alley and slumped, gasping, against the back wall of a bakery, the smell of baking bread a painful reminder of her last morning at St. Benoit. Her ears rang from the shouts of the crowd, but she still strained to hear the sound of hooves striking the cobblestones.

The back door to the bakery creaked open and a stocky English foot soldier stepped out, wiping greasy fingers on his heavily stained uniform coat. There was a bright red streak down the side of his face. He'd been scratched.

He looked startled when he saw her, but his expression quickly changed to bold assessment as his gaze roved over her.

Kaatje stared at him wide-eyed, not knowing which way to run. A horse. All she needed was a horse. She had to get to the goldsmith shop.

"Come lookin' for a little rogerin'?" the soldier asked in rough French, an impudent grin on his broad face. His hand went to his breeches flap. "All the ladies come ta Nic now or later. Word gets out." He took a step toward her, his eyes devouring her. His grin widened. "Oooo. Don't it though."

Something was missing. At her back. Something

she'd come to expect to be there. Kaatje shook her head to chase out the longing for a strong arm and the reassuring radiance of power.

"Leave me alone," she said, forcing her voice not to quaver. "Around that corner is a man who could slice off your head with one blow."

The soldier stopped in his tracks, a look of slyness washing over his face. "He gonna come save you, huh? I saw you jump off that black mountain of a horse. You's runnin' from him. Maybe I'll save you from him, eh? Then maybe you'll be mighty grateful to ole Nic."

"Then maybe not," Thorne said from behind him, punctuating his words with the deadly rasp of his sword being pulled from its scabbard. The soldier spun around. The Englishman stood in the mouth of the alley. Kaatje backed up against the wall with a thump.

"Sweet Jesus," the soldier said. "She's yours. She's yours." He held his hands away from his body, palms out. "Sweet Jesus. Don't look at me like that. I didn't touch 'er. I swear!"

Thorne came toward him.

"Nic-o-deeeem-mas!" a voice shouted from inside the bakery, bringing the soldier up sharply. He suddenly looked like a boy caught peppering the chicken feed. The back door slammed open and a large red-faced woman stood there, hands on hips, flour drifting from her apron like summer snow. "Nicodemas! There you are! Get your randy arse back in here." She put her body between Thorne and the soldier, then glared at Kaatje.

"And you leave my man alone! He isn't much, and he's English, but he's mine. I got enough trouble without the likes o' you sneakin' round here." She jerked her chin toward Thorne. "Use that big strapping redcoat o' yours to cool your fever." The door closed with a slam.

Kaatje stared wide-eyed at Thorne in the sudden silence. He stood there, his feet apart, sword in hand, his breaths deep and ragged.

"Madame," he said, his voice deadly quiet.

She backed along the wall, scraping her arms and gown.

"Damn you, woman. Commeryou found the goldsmith's shop, and it was a nest of Flemish traitors, Bergheyck's supporters. If you had been there, you would have been hanged."

"I had nothing to do with Bergheyck, colonel," she told him, still inching away from him along the wall. "I met him only once, when Philippe and I first moved to St. Benoit. All I wanted from the Flemings was a horse."

Thorne whistled. From behind her came the steady beat of a horse's hooves. She spun around. Acheron rounded the corner.

"Your horse." Becket slammed his sword back in its scabbard.

He didn't relax his stance. Fury gnawed at him, fury at himself for the uneasiness that had haunted him as he'd looked for the Flemish widow. If Commerсy had found her first . . . He crossed his arms over his chest.

He braced himself for more of her tricks. Would she now coyly cling to him and plead for him to forget Cerfontaine and her poor innocent sister? But all she did was step away from the wall.

Damn her. Where are her artful glances and careful posturings? But perhaps that was the trick of it, to make him wait, to keep him off guard with anticipation.

"My horse?" Madame de St. Benoit straightened her shoulders and walked toward him, her gait firm and unhesitating. She stopped in front of him. "For now, colonel. *For now.*"

Her chin was up, but he saw her hide her trembling hands in her skirts. He knew what it was costing her to show such courage, and he had to ruthlessly suppress a flash of admiration.

Becket signaled to Acheron, and the great beast came to him. "We waste time," he said. He put his hands around her to lift her to the horse. He paused. His thumbs rested just below her breasts, and he could feel the pounding of her heart through the satin. He looked into her great quicksilver eyes.

"Damn you, woman," he whispered, and pulled her to him. He took her mouth with a deep sweeping kiss. She stiffened in surprise and put her hands lightly on his shoulders, then her lips softened as her body responded to him. The touch on his shoulders became a caress.

He slid his fingers into her hair and cradled her head. For an instant, he remembered how his gut had tightened when he'd thought he'd lost her. He reveled in the taste of her, in the moist hot mystery of her mouth, and kept kissing, as if he wanted the taste of her to linger on his tongue forever.

At last, he lifted his mouth from hers. "Jesu, woman. You would have been hanged." His hold on her head tensed into a vise. "Do not disobey me again."

She looked deep into his eyes, her lips still glistening from his kiss. "What kind of madness have you dragged me into?" she asked, her voice scarcely a murmur.

Becket dropped his hands from her. Something surged through him at the look in her eyes. He slammed it down. He'd been willing, too damned willing, to fight for the Flemish widow.

"My madness," he said evenly.

He set her on the horse and mounted behind her, his arm instinctively going around her waist to steady her.

He headed them toward the southeastern road to Haine and the Sambre River.

"Remember, madame, I am a soldier. I ask no quarter. And I give none."

Chapter 6

The ride south to the Sambre took most of the afternoon. Not trusting the loyalty of the Brabanters this close to France, Thorne circled the town of Haine and stopped only briefly at streams to refresh the horse.

The sun slowly arced through the blueness above them. And with each hour spent in the saddle in front of him, Kaatje's body absorbed the way Thorne subtly shifted his weight to ease the fatigue and flexed his powerful thigh muscles to guide the stallion. Gradually, her own muscles began to act in concert with his, responding, reacting in a thousand different ways.

Thorne's arm rested around her waist, encircling but not rigidly restraining. He perplexed her. He frightened her. Yet the fear did not consume her, only settled in like a low fever that couldn't be shaken.

The sun was an hour above the horizon when they crested the last hill and began descending into the Sambre River valley. A tiny shack perched on the bank, and nearby a flat-bottomed boat bobbed in the river on the end of its rope.

Ahead of them were the greens of beech, birch, and oak, all blending together in a dappled, lush landscape. On the opposite side of the river, the ground leveled off briefly, then rose to a high ridge that showed the white outcroppings of limestone near the top.

Kaatje smiled. The scene was deceptively simple. She

94

would wager Thorne didn't realize that Cerfontaine was just on the other side of that ridge. Few did unless they'd visited before. And even fewer realized that the ridge itself was laced with tunnels and caverns; tunnels and caverns that she had mapped into her memory in childhood. There were dead ends and false passageways that led nowhere, but one ran the entire width of the ridge and came out on the hillside just above Cerfontaine. It would be child's play to escape him now.

"We'll make camp on the other side of the river," Thorne told her.

"Whatever you wish, colonel," she answered spritely, nearly light-headed with confidence. He looked at her for a long moment, then kneed Acheron toward the ferry crossing.

Kaatje watched Beckct make camp. He kicked fist-sized rocks to the center of the small clearing and then tossed in dry sticks and branches. Larger branches he broke across his thigh. Each movement was quick and efficient and appeared almost effortless—at least to someone not trained since childhood to search for signs of pain.

But Kaatje knew what the blankness that came over his face whenever he lifted a heavy rock meant. She guessed it was his side causing it, the large, angry red bruise she'd seen that morning. He needed to be careful, have it seen to, before the muscles cramped on him permanently.

She turned away and began picking up small rocks and throwing them into the woods in an effort to clean the campsite. Why should it matter to her? She would be gone by morning, escaping through the ridge to Cerfontaine. Then she'd never have to concern herself with him again. Lece would be warned, Pietr would have his medicine, all would be as it was.

She reached for a rock, and the shadows from the

tall beeches fell across her arm in long thin lines. Her gaze followed the lines of darkness to where Becket was unloading the supplies he'd purchased from a farmer outside Haine. The shadows pointed to him. *As it was?* the shadows seemed to mock. *It will never again be as it was.* She snatched her hand back.

He walked toward her, his footsteps silent on the grass that covered the clearing. "Can you cook a poorly dressed rabbit?" he asked, holding out the farmer's sack to her.

"With a good fire and a sharp stick," she said, "anyone can." She threw the rock in her hand and heard it crack against a tree trunk. The sharply defined shadows of a moment ago were muddling into the dark grays of twilight. It needled her that she would let a few shadows disturb her so. Things *would* be as they were—she just had to get away from this Englishman. She took the bag.

Less than an hour later, a gibbous moon sat squat on the treetops, vying with the fire for brightness. Kaatje sat across the stone fire circle from Thorne, watching him eat. She'd found some wild thyme growing just beyond the edge of the clearing and had rubbed it over the meat. It was a simple enhancement, but he appeared to be savoring it.

She took small bites of her own piece and chewed slowly. She'd seen him grimace when he'd sat down, and her conscience niggled.

Thorne pulled off another piece of rabbit. "This is good," he said, holding the golden-brown meat in front of him. "Amazing what one can do with a stick and fire."

"I am pleased you like it," she said, and realized, with a twinge of surprise, that she *was* pleased. It was an uncomfortable feeling.

One dark eyebrow arched as he studied her across the fire. "So there is more to the chatelaine than posturings and artifice," he said. "I had not expected that." His tone was low, musing. "I am intrigued by the unexpected."

"I do not posture, colonel," she told him. "And I do not care what intrigues you."

His eyes met hers and held them. The shimmering curtain of fire separated them, distorting the lines and angles of his face until he looked like a being just ascended from the Inferno. He had taken off his coat and rolled up his shirt sleeves before he'd sat down. The firelight played over his corded forearms, making the flesh as tempting and inviting as a forbidden dream.

She rose and turned away, discarding her half-eaten piece of meat. He was a man, like any other. A man who felt hunger, who felt pain. Her breathing arrested for a moment, then continued. *A pain I could ease.*

Genuine caring was as much a part of her as her heart, but the past years, first with Philippe and then without him, had taught her pragmatism as well. And Thorne, with his bruises soothed, would sleep soundly, letting her easily slip away at the first light of dawn. The idea, at first just a small seedling, quickly took root and grew.

She turned back to him. "As for artifice—I am a chatelaine and I use my skills where I choose." She gingerly reached into the fire and pulled out a just-caught branch to serve as a torch. Thorne's gaze was intent on each movement, but she forced herself not to react. The trees loomed dark as she headed for the edge of the clearing.

"Madame."

She hesitated, but kept her back to him.

"If you do not return within a reasonable time, I will retrieve you."

She stepped into the woods.

"And you will spend the rest of the night tied to a tree."

She stalked into the underbrush. Spiny leaves of a shrub caught at her dress, and the spindly fingers of low-growing tree branches grabbed at her hair.

Thorne and the light from the campfire were soon obscured by foliage. Her torch crackled and hissed as it burned. She was careful to mark her way, her eyes constantly studying the plants revealed in the small circle of orange light. The ground was soft and spongy, and the damp air was heavy with musty odors mingling with the sweet scents of night-blooming flowers.

A small white flower caught her eye, and she stopped and leaned closer to it. "Elder flowers," she murmured to herself. She broke off a leaf and rubbed it, holding it to her nose. She lifted the hem of her skirts and tucked it into the waistband to form a large pocket, then began pulling leaves off the plant by the handsful.

When she was done, she walked on a bit farther and discovered a tiny grotto filled with plantain, its large leaves spreading close to the ground, and the fragrant lavender flowers of valerian, whose roots could soothe. She wedged the torch into a crack in a large rock, her mouth softening at the bittersweet memories the place conjured.

She remembered giggling with her sister as she and Lece had laid out funny faces with the leaves and roots and seeds their mother had so carefully gathered. Their tricks inevitably earned them a gentle scolding and an afternoon spent in patient drills as they bundled the herbs and hung them to dry in the big cavern in the hills just east of Cerfontaine.

Of all her memories of her sister, Kaatje thought she loved those long afternoons the best. And with the folk medicine she'd learned, she'd been able to mend scythe cuts, soothe the aches and bruises of a harvest made urgent by a sudden frost, settle a little boy's—

Bitterness surged through her as if she'd bitten into rue. What use was all her training when she could not make the one medicine Pietr so desperately needed? She violently began to snap leaves off the plantain.

Pietr's cordial had proven too complex for her to unravel. She'd consulted chirurgeons, apothecaries, and old wise women living miserably in fens to try and discover the secrets in that leather bundle she'd so lovingly tied around Pietr's neck. But none of them had been able to help her. She remained forever dependent on Oncelus to make the medicine, and on Lece to provide it.

The image of a smiling devil in a red coat rose up out of the shadows of her mind. But how long would Lece be able to provide Pietr's medicine? And what if Lece couldn't be warned in time?

The sharp crack of a branch rang out like a pistol shot. Kaatje spun around.

Becket loomed out of the dark, looking like a nightmare come to life. His eyes were cast in deep shadow. The orange light from the sputtering torch played over his red waistcoat. Her stomach clenched, but she forced her lips into a smile to cover her uneasiness.

"How much father did you expect to travel tonight?" he asked, his mouth hard with anger.

Kaatje gestured at the thick brush around her, her smile stiff. "With all this clear ground? A good league, at least."

"You underestimate your talents," he said, cutting through her sarcasm. "And you know the land well."

She threw the plantain leaves she had just plucked to the ground. "And no doubt my 'talents' include having a pot of chocolate with the wolves and wild boar in the dead of night as I make my way, hopping and skipping and tra-la-ing to Cerfontaine." She yanked the torch from the rock. "Just what kind of addle-brain do you think I am, Thorne?"

He leaned against a tree. "What kind? What *kinds,* rather," he said and opened his hand as if to begin counting off on his fingers. "One, the kind who contemplates jumping off a fast-moving horse. Two, the kind who points a man's pistol at his own heart. Three, the kind who thinks she can 'borrow' a horse from traitors and live to tell about it." He looked directly at her, his eyes dancing in the torchlight with a gleam that made her catch her breath. He counted off another finger. "Four, the kind who kisses a man and then calls him mad—"

"Stop it! I wasn't running from you," she cried, gripping the torch tighter still. *Not yet anyway,* she added silently.

"Fifth, the kind who flouts a man's orders after he has threatened to tie her up if she disobeys." He spread his hands wide. "What is a man to think?"

"The wretch can think what he will," she ground out. She pushed past him, but he caught at her wrist and took the torch from her grasp.

"So you want to return, chatelaine?" he asked her, pulling her close to him. "I shall guide you—and keep the wolves and wild boar from nipping at your skirts." He turned and began dragging her back through the trees toward their camp.

"Thorne—" she began, then stumbled on an exposed root. His iron grip kept her from falling. He kept walking, branches cracking underfoot, his strides long and swift and unhesitating, forging through the woods like a cavalry charge. To keep up with him and avoid being pulled off balance, she had to adopt a staggering run. "Thorne! I don't want to be tied up. Listen to me, for God's sake. I wasn't running from you. I swear!"

Thorne swept a curtain of oak leaves from his path and they broke into the clearing. He stopped and pulled her around in front of him, their bodies just inches apart. "Do not move," he said, his eyes boring down into hers.

Her heart hammering in her chest, it took all her

willpower not to look away from the light in his eyes. "I won't let you bind me, Thorne," she said breathlessly. "I've done nothing wrong!"

"Do not move." He released her. With a snap of his wrist, he threw the burning torch stub into the fire and headed for Acheron, who watched them from the edge of the clearing with black enigmatic eyes.

Kaatje let Thorne take four, then five strides before she spun around and headed for the opposite side of the clearing.

"Madame."

She stooped to pick up the biggest, flattest rock she could find, then a long oval-shaped one. She turned to face him, a rock in each hand.

"Colonel."

They stood there for several pounding heartbeats, gazes locked, the fire a wall of flame between them. Her fingers itched to throw the rocks at him.

She took a step toward him, then another. His eyes narrowed and filled with a light of anticipation, but he did not move. She neared the fire, his gaze riveted to her. A fallen tree cut through one side of the clearing, and she stopped at it. She dropped the flat rock on it, the half-rotted wood muffling the sound, then dropped the other one beside it.

"You disappoint me, chatelaine."

She broke their gaze and knelt by the log. "Do I, colonel?" she said, untucking the hem of her skirts from her waistband. "I'm so sor—" She broke off, biting her tongue to keep from groaning with embarrassment. She'd been confronting him with her skirts up.

"Not as sorry as I, madame, to see you get yourself properly clothed."

Her embarrassment curdled into anger. She rummaged in the pile of herbs, roots, leaves, and flowers she'd picked, and chose a valerian root. She broke it in half with a pop. She tossed the root onto the flat rock and then picked up the oval stone and struck the root with a satisfying whack.

Over the crackle of the fire, she heard the faint tread of his footsteps on the grass. The muscles along her neck burned to raise her head and see what he was doing, but she kept her head down. She strained to see him out of the corner of her eye. He stood four paces away, and she could see him only from the waist down. His snug red breeches rose from his thigh-high black boots and disappeared under his long waistcoat. In his right hand he held a coiled rein, his thumb rubbing its smoothness as he snapped it against his leg. Kaatje swallowed hard.

"What are you doing?" he asked.

"Don't you recognize a chatelaine's artifice, colonel?"

"I recognize a great many things, madame. But the sight of a beautiful woman kneeling does . . . intrigue me."

Her hands stilled. *Beautiful* . . . She grimaced at her foolishness, then met his gaze. "Colonel Thorne, you've ignored your cuts and bruises for two days now. If not properly seen to, that bruise on your side could cramp on you permanently."

Her words seemed to catch him off guard, and he withdrew into himself. "Keep your balms for those who wish them, madame. I do not." The reins resumed their *slap, slap* against his boot.

She deliberately lowered her gaze back to her work. With intense concentration, she was able to keep her hands from trembling as she scraped the milky pulp from the root onto a broad plantain leaf she'd laid next to the flat rock.

"I did not *wish* to be parted from my son, colonel," she said softly. "Yet I was. I did not wish to accompany you on this journey. Yet here I am." She threw a handful of herbs onto the rock and began grinding, letting the steady rhythm dissipate her anger. When she mixed them with the pulp she'd ground earlier, it would make a soothing balm for his bruises.

But why was she doing this? Her back tingled, knowing his eyes were on her, studying her movements. Why did it matter to her that he was in pain? Look what he had done to her. Even now they were at odds, with no real truce possible between them. She scraped up the herb paste and threw it onto pulp on the leaf; it hit with a plop.

Accept it, Kaatje. You are hopeless with men. She stared at her green-stained fingernails. *Stepfather, Philippe . . .* She shook her head. If she couldn't cope with them, how could she possibly deal with a man like Colonel Thorne? Lece was the only one who could ever deal with Stepfather, and then she'd had all those beaux. How would Lece approach this Englishman?

Kaatje used a stick to stir the salve she'd made. Stupid question. Lece had only one way of approaching a man—but it was remarkably effective. Maybe it was worth trying to convince Thorne to give up his search one last time.

She struggled to put a soft smile on her lips. She picked up the leaf with the salve on it and faced him, smiling, her stomach tumbling end over end.

"Let me do my duty, Colonel Thorne," she said, her voice a tone deeper, a bit breathier. There was a sudden wariness on his face, which quickly coalesced into surprise, then dissolved into an unemotional mask. The teasing Thorne was gone.

"I do not require tending."

"This will ease the soreness, colonel," she answered, letting the melody of her soft words linger in the air. "Please. Lie down on the grass by the fire and remove your shirt."

"No tricks, madame." His voice held an unmistakable note of warning.

"Colonel Thorne," she began, and he raised an eyebrow in a mocking question. "Please. I want . . . I need . . ." Her courage failed her. She couldn't make her lips form the words. She wasn't Lece. She could never play the teasing courtesan.

"You try my forbearance."

Finally Kaatje simply held out the salve. "I want but to soothe your wounds, colonel. There can be nothing to fear in that."

"Fear, madame? You taunt me to do as you bid?" With a sharp, angry movement, he unbuttoned his waistcoat and threw it to the ground. He gritted his teeth to keep from wincing at the stab of pain in his side. Holding her gaze locked with his, he pulled his shirt over his head and dropped it to the ground.

"Madame," he said, his fists on his hips and his breeches riding low on his naked torso. He raised an eyebrow in challenge. "Tend me." He saw her neck muscles move in a convulsive swallow before she gestured to the grass.

He dropped to the ground in one easy motion. A stab in his side caught him unawares again, and he breathed in sharply. Jesu. It must be worse than he'd thought. It had been a long time since his body had not instantly met his demands on it. He stretched prone on the soft patch of grass, crossing his arms under his head. Seven years. Since his escape from hell. A long time—but still only yesterday.

The brush of petticoats against his skin made his muscles tense, and he closed his eyes to ward off the sensation.

"Relax, Colonel Thorne," a gentle voice told him. "I'll not hurt you."

Something cool and silky was being smoothed on his back. With long steady strokes, Madame de St. Benoit's hands rubbed the balm into his skin. At first she concentrated on his back, avoiding the tender bruise on his side. He forced his breathing into a steady rhythm. Her touch was firm and sure, easing the weariness from his muscles, then lightening to little more than the brush of a feather whenever she encountered a bruise.

To his surprise, the dull aches he'd been ignoring all day began to lessen, letting him feel the touch of her fingers on his flesh, spreading the cool balm. When she reached the bruise on his side, the balm stung only slightly before the coolness overtook the heat of the pain. He started to drowse. Sweet Lord, he would've offered up his soul to the devil to have felt this touch of heaven in that black hell in Temesvár.

A cinder hissed in the fire, bringing Becket back from his reverie. There was an unexpected tightness in his body, and he inhaled deeply to dissipate it. That only served to clear his head, making him realize how well the balm had done its work. Now her hands were engendering a new kind of heat.

Kaatje was vividly aware of the man and the heavily muscled torso beneath her hands. His skin was warm, and the coolness of the balm on her fingers heated as it slid across his back. Her hands tingled from the friction.

Long faint strapmarks made her shudder at the pain he must have suffered. She traced one of the scars that could only have been caused by a whip. He tensed, the muscles under her hands becoming like a sheet of iron, and she quickly resumed letting her palms slide over his back.

As she did, an unfamiliar warmth began to spread up her arms, then into her chest and stomach. She frowned and shifted her position, thinking she was too close to the fire.

Without warning, Thorne rolled onto his back, and for a moment, she was spreading the salve on his hard, flat stomach instead of his side. Her hands stopped.

The heat pounding through Becket intensified at the

sight of the golden woman leaning over him. He lightly caught her wrists when he felt her start to pull away. Though he barely touched her, she stopped, her great gray eyes wide and luminous.

His hands slid up her arms, and he pulled her to him. The sleeves of her gown were warm from her body. His hands stopped at her shoulders and his thumbs traced the delicate bones that ringed the base of her neck. She bent toward him, her body pressing against his.

He drew his hand up along her neck and slipped his fingers into her golden hair. The beauty of her face, limned by the firelight, burned into his mind. With the lightest of pressure, he coaxed her head lower. Her eyelids fluttered, and her lips parted with a sigh.

Kaatje felt suspended between one breath and the next. No thoughts, no images intruded, just the beguiling ribbons of heat that twined around her. When his fingers slid into her hair, she lowered her head.

Their lips touched. Lightly, softly. He pulled away a hair's breadth, and through her closed lids she sensed his eyes traveling over her face. She didn't move, held in the spell of the sweet summer night.

She heard him drag in a breath. His arms enveloped her and his mouth returned to hers, full and demanding. The pressure of his lips sent heated eddies swirling through her like the air above the fire. His tongue dipped into her mouth and spiraled around hers, then withdrew, only to return with greater urgency. His hands caressed her bodice, his fingertips slipping inside the neckline and tracing the soft flesh there.

A sweet lethargy filled her veins. His lips left hers and trailed light sucking kisses along her jawline. With each kiss, he drew out more and more of her will. She felt it leaving, rising from her like the scent of a flower in the hot sun. She was succumbing to the power of his kiss, his touch.

His tongue swirled around her ear and he tugged lightly at her earlobe with his teeth. Lightning arced through her and a sigh of surprise, of surrender, escaped her.

Her hands kneaded his shoulders, then slid down to caress the sharply delineated muscles of his arms. She kissed his neck, then the soft flesh below his ear, flicking her tongue over where her lips had been. She had never *tasted* a man before. She drew in a long slow breath, savoring the taste of him on her tongue like an exquisite wine.

A deep rumbling moan of elemental hunger reverberated in his chest and his long-fingered hands began stroking her back, sliding below her waist then back up in a slow caress, as if he was memorizing the feel of her. She tasted him again and again, her mouth descending from his neck to his chest.

Her fingertips traced the outline of his muscles. A pulsing urgency burned inside her, driving her hands and her lips. Just a few inches away from his heart, a vicious white scar reminded her of his pain, and with no conscious thought other than to give him ease, she kissed it.

"Jesu!" he cried out, his voice raw. In a heartbeat, he lifted Kaatje from him and rolled away, leaving her facedown in the grass. Disoriented, she raised herself to her elbows and shook her head.

"Did I hurt y—" The words froze in her throat. His eyes were as cold as a winter sky at midnight.

Becket shook his head, and rubbed the heel of his hand over the deep scar on his chest. Blackness hovered at the edge of his vision.

"So you *are* like your sister," he spit out between deep gulps of breath. His body was in a battle with itself. The fire in his loins demanded to be quenched, while the cold black memories her touch had just summoned threatened to engulf him.

He sucked in another breath. "S'blood, how could I have let you . . ." The heat of her tongue had caught him completely off guard. Suddenly, instead of passion all he felt was the blade of that sword. At the time it had actually pierced his flesh, he had thought it was the last sensation he would ever feel.

"Damn you . . ." He shook his head. "No, sweet Jesu, it is *I* who am damned." *Hür adam,* Becket began silently. Then the image of another man's face rose up in his memory. It was pain-wracked; the man's breaths were rough and uneven, and as Becket had held him, he'd begun coughing up blood. The man touched Becket's arm with the back of his hand, all the fingers having been broken. "Swear," he'd said, his voice a thread of a whisper. *"Swear you will kill him."*

"I swear," Becket had answered, his throat choked with unshed tears. "By the blood of God, I swear I will."

With that, the body had gone limp in his arms, the breath seeping out in a rattle.

Becket opened his eyes, expecting the black hell of Temesvár to surround him, but he smelled the fresh night air and saw the golden woman lit by firelight. His eyes narrowed and his fingers closed into a fist. He'd given his oath, and this woman would help him fulfill it.

Kaatje watched him standing there, terror flooding her veins. His hair had come out of its queue and fallen around his face, keeping his expression in shadow.

Becket's voice came from that shadow, menacing. "You will lead me to your sister—and the devil, El Müzir—and that will be the end of it. Nothing more. *Ever.*" He turned and strode toward the darkness of the forest.

"Colonel Thorne," Kaatje called out to him, rising to her feet. He halted at the edge of the clearing, though he kept his back to her. The light from the fire was dim; it didn't illuminate, only suggested the shadows of movement on his naked back as he struggled to control his anger.

"Who is El Müzir?" she asked.

His body went still.

The silence between them was heavy. The hiss and pop of burning sap, the rustle of a night breeze in the treetops, the distant cry of a small animal succumbing to a nocturnal predator—these were the only sounds Kaatje heard over the whisper of her own breathing. She waited.

Thorne turned. "Now is not the time to act the innocent."

Kaatje shook her head. "I am not acting, colonel. I do not know this—"

"El Müzir," he finished. The name hung in the air between them, tainting it. "The dark-souled one. Your sister's lover."

"Thorne, no! Lece would not—"

He was in front of her in a few long strides. He grabbed her shoulders. "Lece would, madame. Power is seductive. And power is this devil's sustenance," the colonel said, his own power burning into Kaatje's shoulders. "He preys on those whose lives he holds in his hands, squeezing until their souls run out with their blood."

"How can you think my sister would be with such a man?" Kaatje asked. Her stomach trembled, but she went on. "Lece is very beautiful. Men have always"— Kaatje looked away—"been drawn to her. But she is my *sister*—"

"She is the devil's whore."

Kaatje wrenched out of his hold. "You go too far! I hear your words, colonel—your talk of devils and darkness. But they are words used to scare children and simpletons on All Hallows' Eve. I would not have guessed you were a man given to believing in phantasms.''

Becket held out his fist to her, the strap scars on his wrist sharply delineated by the firelight, the muscles along his arm standing out in relief. ''These are not from a phantasm. These are signatures of a slave's shackles. Turks have seven different words for slave. Mine was *esir*. Prisoner of war.

''I and . . . someone else . . . rode out too far from Vienna one day. I was a fool then, a boy colonel whose father had bought him a regiment. I played soldier, not on any battlefield, but in the salons of Paris and Rome and then Vienna, thinking I held the reins on all the world. But Turks were never far from the gates of Vienna, and they took us fast, without warning, and sold us to the sultan of Temesvár.

''*Owned*, madame. I was owned, like a brute animal, by one who, even among his own people, has no honor. He is an infidel.''

The firelight shimmered over his naked chest and glistened on his side and taut stomach where she'd rubbed the slippery balm.

Kaatje looked away, crossing her arms in front of her, trying to mask her reactions to his tale. ''How can you think any woman would consort with such a man! You have mistaken Lece's inconstancy for—''

''I mistake nothing, madame. Such things are in her blood—as they are in yours.''

''*You* are the devil, Thorne! Lece would not consort—''

''Deny that your sister has warmed the beds of Auriac, Roulon, Maraillat, Guillon, Neuvialle—''

''Stop. Stop!'' she cried out, and put her hand over his mouth to halt his words. She recognized name after name from her sister's letters. The warmth of his flesh permeated her fingers and she quickly pulled them away.

"I will not stop," he said. "And I have reasons aside from my own dark memories to find El Müzir." He slid his hand around her neck, his fingers stroking the hollow at the base of her skull. "Understand this, madame. The devil has developed a weapon that only a creature as steeped in evil as he is could've created." He pressed his thumb over her hammering pulse.

"Lucifer's Fire. It burns, but there is no quenching it. Neither water nor sand can put it out. If it was fired from a cannon, entire battalions would meet their deaths without ever seeing their enemy."

Kaatje moved her head from side to side to deny his words. "No, I don't believe it—"

His fingers spread into her hair and stilled her denial. "All of Europe could be in his devil's grip. Even kings would not be spared."

"Thorne, I swear to you. Lece has never been with any El Müzir. I know she isn't the best wife, but she's been getting better! She used to visit chateaux all over France on the slimmest pretext, leaving Constantin behind at Chateau d'Agenais. But for the last twelvemonth or more she hasn't left him."

"She is at Cerfontaine," Thorne reminded her.

"Yes," Kaatje answered slowly, "but not with this El Müzir!"

His hold on her neck tightened. "She is with him."

"No!" Kaatje cried. "Lece took only her astrologer with her."

Thorne remained silent. Incriminatingly silent.

"Her astrologer?" Kaatje asked in disbelief. "Oncelus is an old man."

"Oncelus is El Müzir."

"You're wrong. He can't be," she began. Oncelus made Pietr's medicine! She twisted out of his hold, and he let her go. "No, you have to be wrong." She backed away from him, gesturing wildly. "You're mistaken, Thorne! You must be. I've seen him! He's an old man."

"Have you seen him? Have you seen his face?" Thorne asked, his voice, deep and grim, sliding under her near-hysteria.

"Of course I have," she answered, then with a shock realized she hadn't. Eyes wide, she stared at him. "No," she said, the word slipping out on a thread of sound.

"He is El Müzir."

"No! He's just a man. A man, not a devil," she said, the hysteria starting to build anew. "Lece wouldn't . . . no, no . . ."

"Why do you defend him?"

"You're mistaken." This can't be! she wanted to scream. "Thorne, no! You *lie."*

Thorne's head jerked back as if she'd slapped him. His hands clenched into fists. She heard his breath expel in a hiss.

"It doesn't matter what you say, madame," he told her. "You shall lead me to him tomorrow. You shall lead me to El Müzir."

Chapter 7

Becket woke near dawn in a foul mood. The leaves cushioning his head rustled as he rolled onto his side. The exhaustion from battle that had kept his sleep undisturbed the previous night had left him, letting his dreams fill with a confusing mixture of images from his past—and a certain gray-eyed beauty.

He remembered his response to her the night before and drew in deep, steadying breaths. It had been a long time since any woman had stroked him in just that way. Contempt at his hunger for her hovered at the edge of his mind, but he brushed it away. He was a man and had responded like one. Her body alone would entice a eunuch, but add her spirit and . . .

He turned to look at her and his stomach wrenched. She was gone. He jumped to his feet and stamped into his boots, then went to inspect the patch of thick grass where she had slept.

"Damn her." He laid his hand where she had been. The blades were still flattened from the weight of her body, but the ground was cool. He guessed she had half an hour lead on him. He pulled a handful of grass out by the roots and tossed it aside. "Madame, we will see an end to this."

He searched the perimeter of the clearing and easily found her footprints in the underbrush. A bitter smile curved his lips. Betrayal ate at him—the betrayal of his own senses. He snapped off a twig and broke it into smaller and smaller bits as he studied where her path led.

Moments later, he brushed his hands clean and strode back to the fire circle. He dressed with quick angry movements, broke camp, and saddled Acheron. He mounted, his eyes sweeping the clearing one last time for missed clues, then turned the horse and headed out. The treacherous beauty would pay for her betrayal in full.

Kaatje's breath exhaled in a hiss as she yanked at yet another twisted vine that had grown over the cavern entrance. The sky had lightened to a bright blue; time was getting short. She glanced over her shoulder, half expecting to see a red-coated Englishman glowering at her from atop a huge black war horse.

She tugged at a long root that had anchored itself to the limestone. Years of growth had changed the landscape. It had taken her longer than she'd expected to locate the large goose-shaped rock marking the entrance to the caverns. She'd been fifteen and in the closing days of childhood when she'd last explored these caves, but she knew them well. They led through the ridge to Cerfontaine, a trail Thorne couldn't follow.

She tore the last vine away, then with a whoop of satisfaction, ducked through the hole in the limestone. Just inside the entrance was an old oil lamp, a pile of tallow candle stubs, and a striker. But the lamp proved empty, most of the candles had been gnawed down to the wicks, and the striker had rusted. She choked back a curse of frustration.

She picked up what was left of one of the candle stubs. It smelled of old tallow, but in her memory, she heard the giggles of her and her sister the last time they'd been here.

The candlelight had glittered off tiny diamond chips

that had circled the pearls in Lece's new earrings. *Do you like them, Kaat?* Lece had asked with a breathless laugh, shaking her head to make the earrings dance. *Steppapa gave them to me. What did he give you?*

The younger Kaatje had stared at her sister and the pretty earrings, then looked down at the ground. *I didn't want anything.*

Lece giggled again. *Poor Kaatje. No beaux, no presents. You'll never understand what a man wants, will you?*

Kaatje felt her nails digging into her palm. The bite of the memories hadn't lessened with time. She unclenched her hand and saw the lump of tallow that she had squeezed into a ball. The caverns were silent, except for her ragged breathing. She swallowed hard. There was no time. No time to let those haunting whispers in her memory distract her now.

She started to throw the ball of tallow away, then stopped, an idea coming to her. She knelt and began squeezing all the bits of candle into one ball around a wick, and then pressed it into the small bowl.

She picked up the striker. The crude vise holding the flat piece of flint had weakened over the years, making the flint wobble, and the ridged iron strike plate was orange with rust. She struck them together. Nothing. Her hands shook. It had to light. It had to. She had to get away from Thorne.

It took her a while to get the striker to spark, and then even longer for the spark to catch on the wick. Finally it caught, though she nearly blew out the feeble light with her sigh of relief. At her feet, pink dice-sized crystals glittered. The trail was still there.

Outside the cavern entrance, a horse snorted. Kaatje strangled her scream silent. How could Thorne have found her so fast? In a heartbeat, she spun toward the dark tunnels, pebbles grinding beneath her boot, and began following the trail of crystals she and Lece had

laid as children to keep from getting lost in the labyrinth.

"Ride on, Thorne," she whispered into the flickering darkness. "You can't follow me here." It would
take him hours to ride around the ridge. She turned a
corner, and the glow of the morning sun disappeared
from sight.

Becket reined in Acheron hard. The tangle of freshly
torn roots and vines was an unmistakable wound in the
side of the ridge. An unpleasant smile of triumph curved
his lips. Did she think she could hide from him there?
He dismounted and quickly climbed to the goose-
necked rock. He swept aside the broken vines, expecting to find a cowering Flemish beauty. He found a hole
in the rock.

"Damn the woman," he said under his breath, his
gut tightening. She truly *had* escaped him. He bent to
get through the opening, but even when he was through,
he couldn't straighten up all the way.

Black memories crowded in on him in the sudden
darkness. *Pain . . . burning stripes of agony on his back
. . . the coppery smell of his own blood . . . the metallic taste of it making his throat spasm as it dripped
down the back of his mouth . . . the cold clammy air
thick with the stink of bodies rotting even before they
were dead . . . and ink-dark blackness consuming his
soul, sucking out the light until not even an ember remained of the man he had been.*

He cursed and shook his head, willing the waking
nightmare away. His hand dragged along the rough
stone.

He picked up the striker, noted the fresh scrapes, and
threw it away in disgust. It clattered against the wall
before falling silently to the dirt floor. The tunnels were
discernible only by a blacker darkness and he peered

into them, hoping to find a trace of the woman he sought. Nothing.

Anger warred with admiration. *S'Blood, but she's good.* The fingers of his hands flexed, a plan of battle forming in his mind. The cave system was clearly extensive and he had no light, but his loins stirred at the chase. And he'd thought her a swooning court pet. He saluted into the darkness.

"You've just upped the stakes, chatelaine."

He decided to cut his losses. He could never find her in here. He crawled back out into the sunlight and studied the ridge that rose above him. He dropped his gaze back to the tunnel entrance.

Did the tunnel lead directly to the other side of the ridge? His jaw clenched and his mouth settled into a hard straight line. That baggage had lied to him. He'd bet his last stiver that Cerfontaine was just on the other side of the ridge.

He mounted Acheron, his hands tight on the reins. His eyes followed the jagged line of the ridge to the southwest. Going around would take hours; he'd lose her forever that way. He should have tied her to a tree.

He dug his heels into the stallion's sides and headed the strong, surefooted horse directly up the side of the ridge through the brush. He would play out the battle. And he would win.

Less than an hour later, Kaatje ducked through the cavern opening on the other side of the ridge and walked into the sunlight. Overgrown shrubbery surrounded her, but the path down the hill was still discernible. Below her, the morning light played over the gray stone of Cerfontaine, making it look like a magnificent palace in miniature. She gazed at it, fighting the memories.

Two wings jutted out from either side of the central building, framing the courtyard in a squared-off U. Poplars lined the steep winding approach, giving the small chateau a grand air. Her stepfather had preened himself on that as he had on how easily Cerfontaine had survived the endless recent wars—though Kaatje knew it was because his loyalty had been as maneuverable as a cavalry regiment.

She descended the hillside, keeping to the shadows. Once on level ground, she easily stole from shrub to bush dotting the unkempt grounds. Closer now, she could see that small broken panes in the windows had remained unmended and deep ruts in the gravel had gone unraked.

Two men walked across the courtyard, and she quickly ducked out of sight. The nursery was on the second floor in the far wing, and she'd spent years hearing the crunch of coach wheels on that gravel approach . . . *Stop,* she scolded herself silently. It was an ordinary manor house, put together with ordinary mortar, not the cause of a little girl's nameless fears or a young woman's broken dreams and lost hopes.

Kaatje frowned. The men crossing the courtyard looked like soldiers. She peeped around the bush and studied them. When her mother and stepfather had died, Cerfontaine had been left to one of her stepfather's nephews, who lived on his own estates in southern France. A steward was supposed to be seeing to the upkeep of the chateau. She had planned on convincing him of who she was and being admitted.

But why the soldiers?

The men went through a door into the eastern wing. She moved closer to the house, keeping low. Were they quartered there? It would be just her luck to go sneaking up on a barracks. Her stomach tightened with a sudden fear. *And what if Lece isn't here?*

The crash of a door slamming open made her jump. Above her, a balcony looped out from a second-story room. She crouched behind an overgrown rose bush, a thorn jabbing into the cut on her shoulder. She sucked in her breath to keep from crying out.

A man walked out onto the balcony, followed by three others. *French army officers.* Kaatje would've laughed at the irony of that if her nerves weren't already jangling. The studied elegance of the first man to walk out made her uneasy. She rubbed her stinging shoulder. The haughty angle of his head seemed familiar. One of the men spoke to him.

"They are not here, monsieur. We have searched everywhere."

"If you cannot find them, you have not searched everywhere!"

Kaatje went cold inside. The voice was unmistakable—*Roulon.* My God, she thought, he must have ridden his horse to death to get here. And those men—where had they come from? They looked scruffy and unkempt and made her think of the deserter that Thorne had killed. She shuddered, her eyes on Roulon. Only a misbegotten wretch like the comte would lead such men.

Roulon stamped his foot, his face mottled. "They are here, I tell you!" he shouted. "That d'Agenais whore and her poseur of an astrologer are at this chateau." His voice rose and cracked. "Search the attics again if you have to. *Find them.*"

Relief that Roulon had not yet found Lece helped settle Kaatje's barely suppressed trembling. At the mention of the attics, she looked up to the roof line at the row of tiny windows—and smiled.

Of course. One set of windows lined a secret room that could only be reached one way.

Roulon pranced back into the chateau, trailing obscenities behind him. Kaatje rose cautiously from her hiding place and darted to a window below the balcony. It sagged loose from its hinges. Heart pounding, she pulled it open and scurried through.

Once inside, she pressed her back against the wall and held herself immobile. The room was empty. It had once been a tiny servant's bedroom, but the rough furniture had been removed. She hurried through the rest of the stripped servants' quarters, alert for any sound, until she came upon the servants' stairs.

She ascended the narrow wooden staircase until she came to a door on her left. She wasn't sure it was the right one, but the walls around her were dark and damp and seemed to be closing in on her.

"Lece," she whispered to herself. "Warn Lece. That's all that matters right now."

She put her ear to the door and listened, slowing her breathing so she could hear. She pressed on the door and opened it a crack to peer in.

It was the library. No, she corrected herself, it *had been* the library; now it was a collection of empty shelves and bare floors. She stepped into the room, her eyes darting frantically about. It had been her favorite room. There'd been a table by the window, and she'd spent hours reading her mother's herb books and studying their carefully drawn pictures.

But everything was gone. The books, cabinets, chairs, and tables . . . all except a faded threadbare carpet in front of the huge marble fireplace that had evidently not been worth the taking. Tall graceful caryatids, half women, half creatures of myth, supported the corners of the fireplace. They seemed to be the only familiar faces left at Cerfontaine.

A filthy French oath burst out from the other side of the main door, and she darted back out the servants' entry. She glanced behind her and saw where her skirts had stirred up the dust on the floor, every footprint as clear as if she'd walked on newly fallen snow.

She bit back a groan. "Easy," she murmured to herself. *You have to keep your head about you, Kaat! God save you if you blunder away Pietr's future.* She quickly swept off her cloak and began brushing it back and forth on the floor to disguise her footprints. The noises grew louder.

She dashed through the servants' door and silently closed it behind her. In seconds, sounds of scuffling feet filled the room.

Her heart tripped heavily in her chest at her narrow escape. She leaned against a wall and tried to steady her nerves. *Don't faint!* she commanded herself. *Pietr needs you.* A loud thump against the panel made her jump. She jammed her fist into her mouth to keep from crying out. Long minutes passed, filled with curses and shrieking wood and the crash of stone. Something scraped on the door. She held her breath.

There was more scuffling of feet, then the steady beat of boot heels on a wood floor gradually fading to silence. Were they gone? She listened so hard she could hear the sound of the blood rushing through her ears.

Every nerve jangling, she lightly pressed against the panel door. It opened with a pop. She gasped and jumped back, but no ravaging wolf threw back the door and slavered at her. She opened the panel and scanned the empty room.

The shelves had been toppled and broken up. The men had even tried to pull the paneling from the wall. Her heart thudded, and she spun to face the fireplace. One of the caryatids had had its face and an arm smashed off.

''No,'' she gasped, and hurried to the fireplace. The rug on the hearth was gone. She stepped onto the bare stones and quickly inspected the caryatids. The one on the right was unharmed. She expelled her held breath in relief.

She stuck her finger into the stone creature's mouth. The hidden button clicked when she pushed it, and a wooden panel beside the fireplace opened.

The tension in her shoulders snaked up her neck. She

licked her lips, suddenly hesitant to climb the narrow stairs that led up to the secret attic room. Her fingers clenched the edge of the panel door, holding it open. What was wrong with her? she wondered, looking up into the dusty gray stairwell. What was she afraid of finding up there? She took a few deep breaths to force her shoulders to relax.

She put a foot on the first step, then the second. "Lece," she murmured, thinking to practice what she would say. The panel door behind her closed with a muffled click, giving Kaatje a start.

She made it to the third step. "There's a man trying to find you." Fourth step. A breath of ironic laughter caught in her throat. Describing Thorne as "a man" was like describing the ocean as a handful of water. "An Englishman, Lece. A very tall, strong, powerful English army officer."

Fifth step. "Lece, he wants information from you." *But don't look too deeply into his eyes, Lece, or you'll see them in your dreams forever.*

She stopped climbing, her hand splayed against the wall to steady herself. *Stop this.* Think of Oncelus. One look at the battle fury in Thorne's eyes and that poor old man would collapse. He *was* old. She may not have seen his face clearly when she'd visited Lece at d'Agenais—he'd been wrapped in his robes the whole time—but she had seen a strand of long white hair. How could such a man be Thorne's El Müzir?

She resumed climbing, forcing herself to keep to a steady pace. The stairs were steep and she had to climb two floors before reaching the door to the attic room. She could hear muffled sounds behind the door. She swallowed, then raised her hand and knocked softly.

The door didn't open, but Kaatje heard a woman's throaty laugh that was quickly stifled, then a low masculine command. She knocked again. "Lece," she whispered, "Lece, it's Kaatje."

The latch rattled and the door snapped open. A disheveled Lece stood there, dressed in only a transparent lawn chemise and lace petticoats. She brazenly wore no stays, and her rich brown hair fell loose down her back. She laughed when she saw who it was, and negligently leaned against the doorjamb.

"Well, well. A pale little mouse comes knocking at the door," Lece said, her brown eyes carelessly studying Kaatje. "Why have you come, little sister? And why haven't you brought the clock?"

Becket led Acheron into a tree-shaded glen behind Cerfontaine's gatekeeper's cottage, careful to keep the horse on the grass at the edge of the gravel walk to muffle the sound of their approach. By the sun, it had taken him little more than an hour to travel over the ridge.

A trickle of cool water burbled out of the limestone into an old terracotta bowl that looked as if it had been there for centuries. The horse drank deeply. Becket stroked the stallion's neck, proud of his courage and heart. The ridge had been a treacherous climb and descent, but Acheron had made excellent time and had balked only when the next steps would have cost them their lives. The stallion would never betray him—unlike a woman.

Becket was on edge. But he was close to El Müzir, and he couldn't risk so much with one false move.

The gray stone of Cerfontaine gleamed almost white in the morning sun. Becket guessed that it had been built about a century before; it didn't yet have that mellowed look that truly old buildings acquire through the wars and weather of centuries. The panes of its windows had not yet turned amber, and he could imagine all of them polished and sparkling, making the chateau a sight to dazzle the eye. An unexpected diamond set in the lush hillside.

He wondered what it must have been like to grow up here, and to have left this pompous grandeur for the very modest chateau at St. Benoit. His own home had been a rabbit warren of ancient timbers and worn stone and he'd loved it, from every bolt hole down to its crumbling mortar.

He cupped his hand and dipped out a handful of water, then rubbed it over his face to clear away the memories.

He tied the ends of the reins into a loose knot and draped it over his horse's neck, then took one of the long loops and snagged it on a nearby pomegranate bush. The light hold would keep Acheron in place unless—or until—Becket had urgent need for him; then he could easily break free.

A murmur of voices drifted on the morning breeze, and Becket crouched behind a crumbling stone wall to listen. The rabble of mongrel French soldiers had made no secret of their presence, and now two of them sauntered along the road that bordered the front of the cottage, speaking in their rough soldier's patois.

The mix of slang and dialect was difficult to understand, but Becket deciphered enough of it to learn what he needed to know. His gut tightened with a melange of emotions. No one had been discovered at the chateau; in fact, it seemed as if the only one in residence was the Comte de Roulon.

Had madame known Roulon was at Cerfontaine? Becket studied the chateau more intently. An earlier idle thought had triggered an idea. The last century had been filled with wars, wars no owners were likely to survive without a few bolt holes and secret rooms. A smile of anticipation lifted the corners of his mouth. Roulon may think he's in charge, but Becket was about to pay a call on the *real* residents of Cerfontaine.

He gave the stallion one last affectionate pat and began walking to the chateau. He still hadn't decided whether madame relied more on luck or cunning—but she was nigh to running out of both.

Kaatje stood unmoving in front of the doorway, looking up at her sister. Lece was clearly disheveled, her eyes still slightly unfocused, her lips full and rosy . . . Kaatje realized what she had probably interrupted, and a flush of embarrassment crept up her cheeks.

A few days earlier she would not have recognized or understood the state her sister was in. But now, after Thorne had kissed her, after she had touched his body and felt that strange hunger . . . Her flush deepened.

"Have you been struck dumb? I asked you what you're doing here, Kaat," Lece said, not hiding her irritation.

"Lece," Kaatje began, confusion making her words come in fits and starts. "I came to warn you. The English . . . the French are all over Cerfontaine! Why are they here? They trampled my bread. Why do they all want you, Lece? How can you be so calm? For God's sake, *Roulon* is here."

Kaatje stopped and forced herself to take a long deep breath to bring some coherence to her speech. "Lece, there's this Englishman—"

Someone moved in the shadows behind Lece. Kaatje's words died on her tongue. A man walked away from a long oak table that filled one end of the room. He crossed the bands of sunlight piercing the shuttered window. A cry lodged in Kaatje's throat like a barb.

He wore only black silk trousers. He came toward her, sliding a long black robe over his naked muscular torso, his straight white waist-length hair whipping sinuously over the silk. His skin was the color of age-darkened oak, and it seemed to glow in the arrows of sunlight.

Oncelus.

Words from Lece's letter hit Kaatje like a blow. *In*

the very prime of manhood her sister had written. *Two score and five.*

He nipped Lece on the neck, then behind her ear, his eyes on Kaatje as his tongue licked her sister's creamy flesh. Kaatje flushed and looked at her boots.

"How long has it been since a man suckled your flesh, little sister?" a deep exotic voice asked, his accent like dark music. She gasped and her head shot up. A slight smile lifted the corners of his thin mouth. He pushed Lece aside.

His hand tightened around Kaatje's arm, and he pulled her into the room. She stumbled, but he caught her in his bruising grip. He brought her to a halt in front of the shuttered window.

"Tell me of your *anglais,* little sister," he said, caressing the last two words into an endearment that made Kaatje want to back away.

El Müzir, Thorne's voice whispered in her head.

"No," she gasped, answering the accusation in her head. "It can't be." *Pietr!* She desperately wanted the old astrologer who made Pietr's medicine to step out of the shadows. But she knew that "old" man and the man who held her immobile were one and the same.

The grip on her arm tightened, cutting off the feeling in her hand. "Your *anglais,*" Oncelus demanded. His obsidian gaze impaled her where she stood.

"You're hurting me," she said, trying to pull out of his hold.

"Not yet."

She stopped. She blinked up at him, her stomach knotting. She had felt the thrill go through him when he'd spoken. His nostrils flared with anticipation. Her knees felt weak.

El Müzir. She swallowed a bubble of panic, knowing she faced the Englishman's hated Turk. She had expected such a devil to be ugly and misshapen, a physical abomination.

But he wasn't. He was nearly as handsome as Thorne, a match for the colonel in height, and in strength . . .

Suddenly Kaatje felt apprehensive for the Englishman. She took a steadying breath.

"There is an Englishman," she said hesitantly, "but the Comte de Roulon—he's right here in the house!"

"Roulon?" Lece laughed, the sound unpleasant and full of unspoken insinuations. She came up to Oncelus's side and slipped her hand inside his robe, rubbing his chest. Her eyes were sultry when she looked into his. "Oncelus, dear Kaat, will take care of him." Lece cast an amused glance at her sister.

With a stab of pain, Kaatje realized Lece was deliberately taunting her, and she forced herself not to look away from her older sister.

Had she and Lece really once huddled in this very room, pledging their eternal loyalty to each other, vowing to keep each other safe? How had those little girls become so lost?

Oncelus put his free hand around Lece. He curled his arm, lifting her from the floor, and kissed her quick and deep. Then he released her abruptly and pushed her away.

Kaatje closed her eyes and turned her head. She felt his thumb on her lips and jerked away. She looked at him and went cold inside at his smile.

Oncelus's eyes slid to Lece, and he studied her for a moment, a look of malice washing over his deep amber features. "It has been some time since I have had sisters," he said. He rubbed strands of Kaatje's hair between his fingers. "Gold and sable. The treasure of kings." His laughter was low and disturbing.

Kaatje gasped when the meaning of his words hit her. "No, no, I'm not like—" She glanced at Lece and bit off her words. "I came for Pietr's medicine," she said, panic rippling at the edge of her voice.

Kaatje could feel Lece's eyes on them. "Poor man's gold," Lece said. Oncelus smiled.

Disgust filled Kaatje. *I'd wave a flag to help Thorne find the both of you if I could.* Then she trembled to think of what would happen to Pietr if she did.

Oncelus's fingers gripped her chin, and he drew her head back to face him. "You are reluctant to tell me of this Englishman," he said. He lifted her head, forcing her to stand on her toes.

He put his face a hand's breadth from hers. "Tell me, little sister." His hot breath buffeted her skin.

Kaatje forced herself to shrug. "Aren't all Englishmen alike?" she asked, her voice weak and quavering like Grette's. She could feel his piercing black eyes studying her. Her stomach tightened.

"Please . . ." she whispered. She slid her eyes sideways to her sister. Lece was idly inspecting one of the flasks on the oak table. Kaatje's fear was curdling into dread.

"Your sister will not answer for you."

Kaatje kept her gaze averted from the dark face so close to hers. "What would you have me say? He looked like an Englishman. I-I saw him. In a red uniform coat. Gold braid. Not—not as much as Philippe used to have.

"I thought you'd be worried," Kaatje added. "I wanted to help you. All I need is Pietr's medicine."

"And the clock?" Lece asked, not taking her eyes off the flask.

"The clock? It was . . . ah, accidentally sent on to Hespaire-Aube with Pietr. I'll send it as soon as I arrive there."

Oncelus pulled his face back and stroked Kaatje's face. "Of course you shall have dear little Pierre's medicine." She tried to smile her thanks, but her mouth wouldn't cooperate.

Oncelus's fingers pressed deeply into the soft flesh

under her jaw, hurting her more. "I shall send the medicine to Hespaire-Aube," he said. "When I have received the clock."

Fear coiled inside her. She needed the medicine now. She opened her mouth to bargain.

"Enough!" He seized the hair at the back of her neck. Involuntary tears tumbled from her eyes. "Enough about your precious little wretch. Tell me of this Englishman." He tightened his hold, and she had to tilt her head back to keep from crying out in pain. "And do not lie. I do not take kindly to lies."

"Tall," she choked out. "He's tall."

" 'Tall' means nothing. Is he as tall as a Prussian grenadier?"

Prussian grenadiers rarely stood under six feet. Kaatje tried to nod, but his grip was too tight. "Yes."

"You are too slow, little sister." The dark eyes widened with manic intensity. "Is his face haughty and proud? Is his hair so dark it looks black except in the brightest sunlight? Do his eyes mock you and challenge you and turn from the blue of new steel to the pure black of hate when he wants to plunge a dagger into your heart?"

His voice lowered to a caress. "Do scars lace his body like threads of white silk on a weaver's loom?" His voice lowered even more. "A very skilled weaver."

Kaatje was breathless with fear. An infidel, Thorne had said. A devil. Patches of gray clouded her sight and she felt her mind drifting away as if in sleep. Images flickered before her eyes—of the crosshatched lines on Thorne's back and the cords of white scars at his wrist. The pain. The pain he must've been put through.

At this man's hands.

Sweet God, Pietr's life is held in thrall by Thorne's El Müzir! But even though her son was as dear as life to her, she knew she could not betray the Englishman to his enemy, whatever it cost her.

She shook her head as much as Oncelus's hold would allow. "No," she said, "that's not the one. This one has . . . red hair and his legs are slightly bowed. I think his eyes are green."

Oncelus threw her from him. She staggered against the table. An onion-shaped flask rocked from the impact. Lece hissed at her and jumped to steady it.

"It must be him! He follows me. I know it!"

Kaatje shook her head again, staring at the flask, too frightened to speak. *Lucifer's Fire. Sweet God, sweet God.*

He swirled, his robe billowing out around him, and grabbed the flask from Lece's hold. He caressed the flaring bulb as if it were a lover, and it seemed to calm him. Kaatje wanted to look away, but his words stopped her.

"There is only one man I wish to kill, little sister," he said, his tone low and dangerously matter-of-fact. "And I will annihilate an army to do it."

He looked at Kaatje, a knowing smile on his mouth. She shivered. "He is out there. I know he is. And he is *mine*. I want the truth, do you hear? Or I may forget to send your son's medicine."

Lece smiled and snuggled her body next to his, one hand slipping inside his robes to stroke the hard muscles at his waist.

"Lece, you do nothing?" Kaatje asked.

Lece laughed. "I do a great deal, little sister. Perhaps you want to watch?" Her sister licked her lips slowly, then bent and kissed Oncelus low on the waist. "Your Englishman . . . would thank me . . . for teaching you how to please a man . . ." Oblivious to Kaatje, Lece let her eyelids flutter closed, and her lips parted slightly.

A flush of embarrassment stained Kaatje's cheeks.

She spun, ready to flee, then forced herself to leave the room with a steady tread. She stepped down onto the first stair and, behind her, the door clicked closed.

Tears welled in Kaatje's eyes, and she had to slide her hands along the walls to feel her way down the steep stairs. Her body shook with anguish and terror.

Sweet Pietr! She wanted desperately to deny it all. Her son's life in that devil's hands. She stumbled and had to stop a moment before the weakness in her passed. Her son's life subject to a devil's whim—and she was helpless to change it.

And Lece. Her sister had fallen farther than Kaatje could believe. She had seen stark desire in Lece's eyes—but no joy.

How had they all come to this?

She began making her way back to the library. *El Müzir.* The name resounded in her head, vibrating with all the hate and pain with which Thorne had said it. It was a name of darkness. A darkness that enveloped her son, her sweet Pietr . . .

She stumbled through room after room. The bare wood of sun-faded paneling mocked her. She had expected to find refuge at Cerfontaine, but she had found nothing but a nightmare. Thorne's nightmare.

From close by, Roulon shouted a shrill command, quickly followed by the bellowing of an officer. Heart thudding, she ducked through a servant's entrance and leaned against the closed door. Through the soles of her boots she could feel the floor shaking as soldiers ran past her hiding place.

She found herself in the servants' stairs that led down to the kitchens at the back of the chateau. She turned and hurried down, not caring where Roulon and his men were. All she needed was time to reach the stables and steal a horse. There was nothing left for her to do but to go to Claude's and wait.

At the entrance to the kitchen, she paused, listening.

There was only silence. She took a step into the large room, her eyes darting from corner to corner, looking for peril. Her memories of the room were clouded with heat and smoke and shouts from the cook when Lece had dared to snatch marchpane right off a banquet tray. The huge fireplace still lined one wall, but it was empty and cold now, the turnspit toppled on its side.

Kaatje glanced at the back door, still apprehensive. Sunlight danced through the uneven glazing and beckoned to her. Outside she could see an indistinct gray building—the stables. She picked up her skirts and began making her way past the turnspit.

A flash of movement at the corner of her eye sent a surge of panic through her. She inhaled to scream. A gloved hand clamped over her mouth, stopping her breath. Pulled backward, she lost her balance and fell back hard against a muscular body. An arm clamped around her, pinioning her arms to her side.

"You spend a great deal of time in the kitchens, Madame Chatelaine," a deep male voice said, the accent unmistakable. All too unmistakable.

Thorne.

Chapter 8

Kaatje squirmed, her back against Thorne's chest. He tightened his hold on her, the pressure of his hand over her mouth pushing her head onto his shoulder. She tried to shake free of his grip, but he held her fast.

"Let me go," she cried against his leather glove, but the words were only a stifled mumble. The taste of the black leather was bitter.

He bent his head and put his lips next to her ear. "Fight me, chatelaine, fight me," he whispered, his mouth moving against her skin. "I'm not letting you escape me. Not this time."

She tried to elbow him in his side, but his arms held her too tightly. Her struggles weren't even shaking his balance. His footing remained solid, as if he were rooted to the floor.

"Your family excels in betrayal." The resonance of his words, of his conviction, drummed against her back. "What other tricks did you learn at your mother's knee?"

Fury whipped through her like a cord suddenly pulled taut. Kaatje twisted and turned, but his strength was too great. She forced her body to go motionless, but her anger still surged. The sound of her quick angry breaths was loud in the empty kitchen. *What tricks, colonel? Wait and discover.*

Slowly, almost imperceptibly, his hold on her loosened. She waited. She wanted to swallow, to rid her mouth of the taste of the bitter leather. The side of his face pressed against her ear, and her pulse fluttered against his cheek.

"I knew you would betray me," Thorne said.

Kaatje's stomach was a tangle of knots. She'd only get one chance. She bit his hand.

"Viper," he spat, his hold loosening only slightly. But it was enough. She slipped out of his grasp.

"Betrayal!" Kaatje shouted. "I owe you no allegiance. I owe you nothing."

"You miserable little piece." He shook his hand with a snap.

She glowered at him. "What do you want of me now, Thorne?" She waved her arm to take in the kitchens. "You're *in* Cerfontaine. That's what you dragged me here for!"

The haze of her anger faded, letting her see him clearly in the light streaming in through the window. A trickle of blood oozed from his right temple.

"My God, you're hurt!" she cried out before she could stop the words.

He wiped negligently at the seeping blood. "I needed information, but the wretch proved reluctant." He glanced up the stairway she'd come down, then his eyes returned to her. "This house is old enough to have a hundred priest holes," he said, his voice unexpectedly low and quiet. Deadly quiet. "And I'll wager you know every one."

"Pr-priest hole?"

His eyes narrowed. "A bolt hole. A place to hide and not be found." Thorne watched her. He flexed the fingers on the hand she'd bit, and she realized it was his sword hand. "He's in one of them, isn't he? El Müzir."

The breath went out of Kaatje. Her body felt like a

pillar of stone that had grown from the floor. Her heart thudded. She heard rumbling in the distance, and it took her a long moment to recognize it. Soldiers' voices. At the top of the stairs.

"*We* need a hiding place," she choked out.

"I wait, madame."

"Thorne!" He did not move.

She turned around and ran her fingertips along the edge of the wood paneling that lined the wall opposite the fireplace until a door clicked open. Behind her, she heard the whisper of a sword being drawn from its scabbard. Her back stiffened in terror.

"Here!" she cried, pushing the door open wider. Cobwebs and dust and the smell of musty damp filled the doorway. "In here. It leads to the biggest of the caverns." Panic flooded through her, making her words quaver. "Hurry, Thorne! We'll be safe there. They'll never find us. There are scores of dead-end tunnels with only one way in and out—if you know it."

From outside the kitchen came a muffled scrape of steel against stone. "They're in the garden, too! *Thorne—*"

He grabbed her around the waist and pulled her from the panel opening. "No one's been in there for years," he said with a snarl.

He hauled her to the kitchen door, flicked up the latch with the point of his sword, and kicked it open. The blue of soldiers' uniforms flashed amid the green of the overgrown kitchen garden.

"Damn me for a fool," he said, and stepped over the threshold, Kaatje in one arm, sword raised in the other.

In an instant, two soldiers rushed him. He parried and thrusted and one went down. Thorne lunged, and the remaining soldier scurried backward. He took the spare instant to set Kaatje on her feet, facing west.

"Run, woman.*"* Blood from the wound at his temple dripped into his eyes, and he swiped at it with the back of his glove. Behind him two more soldiers leaped over the garden wall. She inhaled to warn him, but he forestalled her. "I know, damn it. *Run.*"

She ran.

She bunched up her skirts and petticoats and bound down the gravel path that led out of the kitchen garden toward the woods beyond. Terror swelled up her throat. The gravel was slippery under the soles of her boots. Brambles snagged her skirts, but she kept running. Behind her she could hear the grunts and curses of fighting men, then a desperate moment of silence.

Someone was running after her. Her breaths came in gasps. She glanced back.

Thorne ran toward her, gravel spitting out from each bootstep. She glimpsed four inert mounds of blue in the garden.

"Keep running," he shouted at her, then let out an ear-piercing whistle.

He caught up with her, and they ran into the woods side by side. Tree branches whipped past. His arm shot out and squeezed around her shoulders. Breathless, she found herself half running, half flying over the rough ground.

She heard crashing off to her right and had to swallow a scream. Thorne whistled again. Behind them, muffled by the trees, came the shouts of the Frenchmen. The crashing grew louder and a pounding heartbeat later, Kaatje saw a huge black shadow coming toward them.

Suddenly, Acheron was in front of them. Without missing a step, Thorne scooped her up and set her on the horse, then mounted behind her. The stallion plunged forward.

They fled for miles through the forest, alert for the sound of pursuit. Thorne held her tightly to him as the black war horse drove onward, but all too soon, in the distance they heard the unmistakable cries of pursuing soldiers. Acheron, though strong and able, was slowed down by his double load.

"We can't outrun them," Thorne told her. "We'll have to hide."

"There's no place to hide," Kaatje said. "There's nothing but trees for miles."

"Then we'll hide in trees."

She looked up at him in surprise. "You can't be seri—*aaaa.*" She slipped on the saddle and grabbed at Thorne. He'd kneed the horse hard to the right, aiming them toward the darkest part of the forest.

They were moving fast, but their passage was eerily silent, the thudding of the horse's hooves muffled by the layer of rotting leaves that covered the ground. The air was thick and musty. Around them were beech and birch trees that let in bright shafts of dappling sunlight. But ahead, the stallion's straining gait led them toward a grove of oaks so ancient that their canopies had grown into one thick, impenetrable roof. Only an occasional spear of sunlight pierced the darkness.

"Duck," he said, pushing her head down until she was nearly doubled over. He bent over her as a low branch scraped his back. Fingers of wood caught at her hair. She huddled closer into the protection of his body, swallowing her screams. The sight of the ground moving so swiftly beneath them made her stomach twist. She closed her eyes, but the sensation only intensified.

Sure and true, Thorne guided the horse through the trees. They entered the grove, and the gloom fell around them like a cloak. Acheron's hooves thudded louder. The ground was harder here, the sparse undergrowth struggling in the dimness.

She felt Thorne straighten. "Get ready," he said. The muscles in his thighs tensed, and the horse slowed instantly.

Kaatje sat up warily. "Ready for what?" she asked in a hoarse whisper. They halted under one of the largest oaks. "No, you don't mean for me to—"

Thorne's hands tightened around her waist and, in a heartbeat, lifted her toward the bottom limb. *"My God. Thorne!"*

She grabbed onto the thick branch, the bark tearing into her hands. The Englishman's hand cupped her behind and gave her an unceremonious push. She nearly choked on a shriek of indignation.

"Climb, woman." He smacked her behind to get her moving.

Kaatje kicked out at him. "Stop that! I'm climbing. I'm climbing." She scurried upward as best she could, grappling with skirts and petticoats and slippery-soled boots.

The leaves were thick and intertwined and she could see only directly below her. She saw Thorne dismount in one smooth jump. He grabbed the reins and led the horse out of her range of vision. She had to clench her teeth to keep from calling out after him.

In the distance, she could hear the jingle and rattle of the bridles and swords of Roulon's men as they rode nearer. *Where was Thorne?* She settled cautiously on a limb and twisted around, but could see nothing through the leaves.

A thin trickle of sunlight splashed over the branches to her left. Below her, a flash of red caught her eye.

"It's about time," she snapped. Thorne leaped up and easily caught the tree limb that had been a struggle for her to reach even from the back of the horse. He swung himself up, and with a few lithe movements, climbed up and sat on a branch at a right angle to her.

His knees pressed against hers. "What have you done with the horse?" she asked, forcing herself not to squirm sideways.

"He will be behind Roulon and his men. Men rarely search ground they have just passed over." He struck his right foot against her branch to brace himself, the blow making the leaves rustle. "It is a failing men often have. I do not." His boot was less than an inch from where she sat.

The rhythmic clatter of Roulon's men was closer now. Kaatje stared wide-eyed at Thorne, her breaths rasping in her throat, choked closed with fear. She saw him silently slide the hilt of his sword an inch out of its scabbard, then slip it back. It was a habit she'd seen in some of Philippe's men, the habit of a man comfortable with not only wearing a sword, but with using one.

"They're riding right to us," Kaatje whispered. Fear made the words little more than a squeak. Her knuckles were white where they gripped the branch she sat on.

"They could have tracked us all the way to Hespaire-Aube on that soft ground," Thorne said, his voice low but even. "Our only chance to lose them is on this hard ground." His gaze locked with hers. "If you wish to lose them."

"Of course I do! But won't they know where we . . ." she began, but her words trailed off.

The sound of horses' hooves was suddenly louder, crisper. Hard ground. Roulon's men had entered the oak grove. Kaatje held her breath. Thorne's sword hilt slid in and out. A trickle of sunlight caught on the silver wire wound around the hilt and reflected back onto Thorne's scarlet uniform. She exhaled in a gasp.

"Your uniform," she whispered without sound. The only bit of sunlight in the grove played over the scarlet of his coat, making it as bright as holly berries against new snow.

Roulon's men came closer, sounding as if they were

heading directly for the tree she and Thorne were in. *Sweet God,* she thought, *if they look up . . .*

Thorne's gaze darted up at the bit of blue sky just visible through the leaves. His eyes lowered to hers, then quickly traveled over her gray cloak.

"Cover me," he commanded on a thread of sound.

Wide-eyed with astonishment, she shook her head.

He silently leaned toward her. "Choose, Madame Chatelaine. Me, or Roulon. *Cover me.*"

She licked her lips, her breathing suspended. She looked down, then closed her eyes. She nodded, and her hand went to the clasp at her throat.

Without warning, he grabbed her arm and pulled.

For an instant, she felt herself weightless in the air, then his fingers closed firmly around her other arm and he leaned back against another branch, pulling her up his hard body. Her chin scraped against his chest, the ribbons and bits of lace that decorated the front of her gown catching and tearing on his buttons.

"Thor—" she began, but the sound of the approaching horses made her swallow the words. He tucked the skirts of her cloak around him with swift efficiency.

Hands on his shoulders, Kaatje tried to hold herself rigidly from him, letting the indignation in her eyes speak for her. His hands closed over hers and, seemingly without effort, drew them away from his shoulders. With no support, her body lowered to his until they were in contact from knee to shoulder, her face nestled against his neck. She counted the seconds until Roulon's men would pass.

They approached the tree, slowing. *No. Don't stop,* Kaatje cried out in her head. Her counting trailed off.

"Halt!" she heard Roulon say directly beneath the tree she and Thorne were in. "Well, you little weasel, can't you find the trail? *Imbecile.*" The last word was punctuated with the sound of a sharp slap. "Sieriac, have your men search the area."

Kaatje tried to lift her head, but Thorne's hand prevented her from moving. She could feel his alertness in every taut muscle beneath her. Little by little—and with her mind blank—she let her body fall slack against his. His heartbeat held steady, but she knew the pulse of his soldier's heart had quickened with anticipation. If they were discovered, he would fight, even against such great odds.

"Monsieur," a whiny voice said, "why do we waste time searching for the English cur and his wanton? Oncelus and his whore are at Cerfontaine, and they're the ones Louis will pay gold for."

Thorne's heartbeat accelerated. His fingers slowly curled into her hair, tightening his hold.

"If they are at Cerfontaine, then why haven't you found them?" Roulon asked, then hissed as if dismissing the man's answer. Absently, he said, "The two whores are sisters, Sieriac. They've both shared the Turk's bed. Maybe the pale one knows something the dark one doesn't."

Kaatje jerked with indignation, but Thorne's arms pinned her to him. She tried to shake her head in denial, but the Englishman held her fast.

"Where're those stinking wretches of yours?" Roulon went on. "Those swine couldn't find a cart track in thick mud. How am I to find this Colonel Becket, Lord Thorne with such dullards?"

"Why have you never mentioned this Colonel Thorne before, monsieur?" Sieriac asked. Kaatje could hear the creak of saddle leather as Roulon resettled himself.

"You ask a great many questions, Sieriac, for a man who spent the last battle in bed with a farmer's wife."

"That farmer's wife must've fought harder than St.

Benoit's relic. You were quick to return from foraging, I hear.''

"Bah!" Roulon said. Kaatje heard him spit. "I did not have a mind to follow where a filthy Turk had been.''

Thorne's muscles hardened beneath her like ice forming on a pond, and a trickle of fear dripped down Kaatje's spine.

Kaatje squeezed her eyes shut. *Roulon lies, he lies,* she cried silently. The Englishman's pulse beat against her forehead.

Below them, a man ran up to Roulon, out of breath, and gasped out, "There's no sign of them, monsieur.''

"Why would an Englishman be this far south?'' Sieriac asked. "Marlborough's still gloating up in Odenaarde.''

Roulon hissed. "Cease babbling, Sieriac.'' His words were punctuated by the rattle of a bridle and a horse's neigh of protest. "We return to Cerfontaine.''

A thin voice shrieked out commands. Muttered curses answered him. Kaatje held her breath. Were the soldiers going to disobey and not return? Sieriac cursed back, and soon she could hear the sound of horses' hooves moving away from them, toward Cerfontaine.

For a long minute after the clatter of Roulon's men had faded, Kaatje lay frozen above Thorne, afraid to move. "Roulon lied,'' she whispered. "He lied.''

Thorne gripped her upper arms and lifted her up, holding her suspended above him. He brought them both upright with one smooth motion, locking his legs around hers. She tried to meet his cold hard eyes, but couldn't.

"Down,'' he said. He released her legs and thrust a booted foot against the other branch to balance himself. The powerful muscles of his thigh stood out as he shifted his weight to lower her to a branch below them.

She teetered for a moment, then steadied herself. She looked back up at him, sitting in the cup of the tree limb like a prince on a throne. Anger swirled around him, disturbing the air. He seemed to inhale it with fiercely controlled breaths. His eyes were hard and opaque, giving away nothing; his mouth formed a straight, uncompromising line.

Her grip fumbled on the limb in front of her. His gaze locked with hers. "Down, madame." She obeyed.

At the lowest limb, she hesitated, not able to summon the courage to jump to the ground. Leaves rustled above her, and she looked up to see Thorne dropping from branch to branch as if he were descending a familiar staircase. He landed next to her, the branch shuddering beneath her with the sudden weight. He leaped, caught himself with his hands, and swung once, then dropped to the ground.

He whistled a single sharp note before turning around to look up at her. "Jump," he said. His hands were at his side.

"Are—are you going to catch me?" she stammered.

He flexed his right hand. "Jump."

With a gulp and a quick prayer, she threw herself off the branch, and his hands snapped up to catch her. But he released her just as quickly, thrusting her from him. She reeled before catching her balance.

Acheron trotted up and halted in front of Thorne. "We return to Cerfontaine," he said, his words tearing at her like shards of knife-thin ice, "and your infidel lover."

"No! Lece. It's Lece . . ."

His gaze raked over her. "He knew I would find you, didn't he? That part was easy. You were the only one he left alive who could know where he was." He gave his head a sharp shake and looked away from her, then pulled off his right glove and began checking Acheron's saddle with quick brusque movements.

She stepped closer to him. "Thorne, it was Lece! It was Lece who ran off with him . . ."

"I should have smelled the taint on you. El Müzir cannot . . . touch a woman without causing her decay." He gestured at the horse without turning around. "Mount."

"Thorne!" Kaatje screamed, raising her fist to beat on his back. He spun and caught her wrist, but she didn't unclench her hand. His fury threatened to smother her, but her own anger bolstered her. She glared at him. "Listen to me, you thickheaded Englishman. He is not my lover. He has never been my lover. I am not a part of his schemes."

She could feel the imprint of each of his fingers on her wrist. The grip tightened.

"What are your words worth, chatelaine?" Thorne's voice was low, but its timbre rumbled. "Tell me how much I can *trust* you. Tell me how you *did not* try to stab me in your kitchen. Tell me how you *did not* hold a pistol on me. Tell me how you *did not* run to your lover this morning and warn him of me."

He pulled her closer until there were but inches between them. His voice lowered to a dangerous whisper. "Tell me, madame."

The eyes that bored into hers had darkened to the deepest indigo. She opened her mouth to answer, but the words choked in her throat. The memory of a devil's voice murmured in her mind. *Do his eyes mock you and challenge you and turn from the blue of new steel to the pure black of hate . . .*

Thorne released her. "We ride for Cerfontaine."

The sinuous voice in her memory coiled around her courage. *There is only one man I wish to kill . . .*

"No!" Kaatje cried out, nearly shaking with fear.

"No, my sister and El Mü—and Oncelus . . . They aren't there. They aren't at Cerfontaine."

Thorne went still, only his eyes moved to study her.

"They had been there," she babbled. "I-I could tell. But they were gone by the time I . . . I mean, that's why Roulon couldn't find them—they weren't there."

The energy, the rage that had radiated from him abruptly disappeared; it was as if it had been drawn back inside him.

"Where have they gone?" Thorne asked, the strain nicking the edge of his voice telling her just how tightly he held himself under control. *"Tell me,* madame."

Every muscle in Kaatje's body quivered with fear. By sheer force of will, she shored up her courage. She had to keep him from going back to Cerfontaine; she had to save him, and Pietr.

Thorne grabbed her shoulder and pulled her to him. His eyes were black. "Where have they gone?"

Kaatje dropped her eyes to the hand that gripped her so tightly. The lace at his wrist had fallen back, revealing the scars. She swallowed the bubble of panic that rose up her throat.

"Hespaire-Aube," she whispered. "They've gone to Hespaire-Aube."

"Why?" Thorne demanded. "Why would they go there?"

"My sister once . . . knew . . . the margrave, Claude. That's how I met Philippe. He was Claude's brother."

"A convenient tale." Without warning, he picked her up and threw her across Acheron's back like a bag of grain. "We ride for Cerfontaine."

Kaatje's panic scattered with a *whoosh* as she hit the back of the horse stomach-first and had the air knocked out of her. By the time she'd regained her breath, only her anger remained.

"I am not a sack of millet!" She grabbed on to the saddle and twisted her body until she slid off the other side of the horse. "Lece and Oncelus are in Hespaire-Aube!" she shouted.

Thorne slipped under the horse's neck and caught her by the arms, holding her in the air at eye level. "You will ride with me to Cerfontaine—in front of me as before or behind me trussed up *exactly* like a sack of millet."

She struggled to free herself, but his hold was too powerful. She kicked at him, but her foot slid over the side of his boot. "Hespaire-Aube, you damnable Englishman," she cried, one hot angry tear slipping down her face. "Hespaire-Aube."

Thorne still held her off the ground, her feet dangling. His breaths were deep and controlled, his jaw muscle taut, and his eyes . . . his eyes were like the shadows cast by moonlight. Kaatje stared into those eyes, unable to look away, even though she knew he searched her face for signs of the lie he suspected she was telling.

She shook her head slightly and parted her lips to deny his unvoiced accusation, but with a swift sudden movement he pulled her to his chest and covered her mouth with his.

His lips were hard, demanding, as if he sought to find the truth without words. Caught off guard, she floundered in the sensations that sluiced through her body, unable to resist the pressure of the kiss as he forced her lips to open. His tongue plunged in, wrapped around hers, then withdrew, only to plunge in again. Rhythmically, he tasted her mouth again and again.

One arm encircled her, crushing her breasts against his hard chest, while the fingers of his other hand twined into her hair to support her head. The pressure of his lips increased, challenging her to return his kiss, and her body eagerly followed his lead.

She felt him stir against her. Her arms were around his neck, but it was his strength that held her against him, not hers. The muscles of her body had loosened; conscious control had been replaced with a sweet hot lethargy. Her movements against Thorne were primal, elemental, as if she were a storm that he, the rain-maker, had called forth. Such a thirst . . . such a thirst she had for him that only he could slake.

With a twist of his head, he broke off the kiss, and she slid down his body until her feet touched the earth. Kaatje stumbled. She could hear his breaths, ragged and uneven, but before she could get her bearings, he swooped down and took two, three, four exquisite sucking kisses from her lips.

Unbalanced all over again, she put a hand on the horse next to her to steady herself, but in a heartbeat she found herself sitting on the saddle, looking down at the Englishman. His face had lost its harsh edge, but there was still a set look about him. He mounted behind her and heeled Acheron toward Cerfontaine.

Heartsick at her failure to convince him, Kaatje felt her body slumping against him, but she caught herself and stiffened her back.

They crossed the edge of the grove and rode into a shaft of sunlight that dazzled her eyes. Thorne brought the stallion to a halt. He sat behind her silent and unmoving. She glanced up at him and saw him studying her with intent, narrowed eyes.

"You risk a great deal," he said, his voice low, almost a caress. "I wonder if you know how much." A chill of fear slithered down her back and coiled into a knot in her stomach.

"There is always risk," she said, her voice nearly a whisper. She *had* to convince him. "We're only about a mile from the Meuse River. We could be in Hespaire-Aube in two days if we took a boat.''

"Look across the Meuse this far south, madame, and you see France. Traveling by river would be a fast route to a French prison." The words came from deep in his chest, and the sound rumbled against her shoulder. "Do you yet scheme?''

She clenched her eyes closed. *"No,"* she whispered. "I would not want that."

Thorne was silent for a long moment, and she could feel his eyes on her. "No, perhaps you do not," he said at last, his tone neutral. "For your fate would be worse than mine.''

"Worse?" Kaatje looked up at him in surprise. His face was inches from hers. She looked away. "I-I would not be harmed. Philippe fought—and died—for France!"

"Indeed. And his widow is now traveling unescorted in the company of an attaché to the Captain-General of the Allied Armies.''

"You abducted me!"

His hand tightened on the reins. "Madame," Thorne said, his mouth close to her ear, "that is ended. You are with me now by choice."

"No," she cried. "No. How can you say that?" She squirmed, but his iron grip held her fast. "You tore me from my son and forced me to go with you. You dragged me back to the camp last night." She hit at his shoulder. "You hunted me down.''

He grabbed her fist, their fingers intertwining. "And you ended it in that ancient oak. You could have called out. You had a choice, madame. Roulon or me. *France* or me." He held their clenched hands in front of her face and tightened his hold. "You chose me, madame. Irrevocably, you chose *me.*''

"No," she whispered, closing her eyes and turning her head away. *Yes,* her mind shouted. *Yes, your words are true. But I had to. Don't you see? I had to. To save you. To save Pietr.*

He released her. With a flick of his hand, he turned Acheron off the path to Cerfontaine and headed them south through the forest. South. Toward Hespaire-Aube. Kaatje closed her eyes. She had won. Unshed tears burned in her eyes. But how much had she lost?

Lece d'Agenais rested her forehead against the shutters of the attic room window, feeling a slight breeze drifting in between the wooden slats. She'd stopped listening to the battle of wills raging between Oncelus and Roulon behind her, a battle of wills that was no contest at all.

"You were not to return until you found him." Oncelus's voice was calm, and all the more deadly because of it. "Yet you are here."

Silly man, Lece thought, pivoting her head to look at Roulon. But her gaze was drawn to Oncelus, like iron toward a lodestone. Sharp blades of sunlight that sliced through the window slats highlighted each powerful muscle of his naked chest and arms. He had discarded his robe and now stood, feet spread apart, his fists resting on his hips, his long white hair flicking back and forth over the small of his back.

She smiled a secret smile. *No, not a silly man. A silly cretin. There is only one man in the room.*

Roulon shrugged in answer to Oncelus's accusation. "After I found you . . . when we came to our agreement, I thought—"

"I *let* you find me, Frenchman. While your men blundered around the chateau, I let you find me. Remember that. All is as *I* wish it. You work for me now and do as *I say,* not as you would *think.*" Oncelus raised his hand to strike. Roulon stared at the Turk's upraised hand, looking stunned.

"You would dare to strike m—"

Oncelus's other hand clamped around Roulon's throat and squeezed. "You are nothing but what I wish you to be."

Lece ignored Roulon's choked gurgling. Didn't the fool realize that Oncelus forever came and went like smoke? No one ever found him unless he wished it. Even she had to wait for him to come to her.

Roulon's struggles grew louder. He clawed impotently at Oncelus's hold. An itch of desire began burning in Lece at that testament of her lover's power. She went to the table and gazed lovingly at the onion-shaped flask. She picked it up and caressed it. Oncelus's power would grow a thousandfold once he used the flaming death that swirled inside.

"Heed what you do, pleasure of my loins," Oncelus told her. Her gaze slid sideways to him, and his knowing eyes smoldered over the unconfined curves of her body. She set the flask down and picked up his discarded robe, trickling the silken smoothness through her fingers.

Oncelus loosened his hold on Roulon but did not release him. "The Frenchman has displeased me. His body could easily be added to the carnage of the battlefield."

"No—" Roulon cried, Oncelus's grip choking off the word.

"No? But you have disobeyed me," Oncelus said, his voice silky. "Will you do so again?"

Roulon clutched at the powerful hand around his throat and tried to shake his head. "I won't— I'll do exactly as you say."

"Excellent, Monsieur le Comte." Oncelus smiled. "Do as you are told and I will pay you a far greater price than Louis. Disobey, and I will hunt you down. And then it is you who will pay."

Roulon tried to nod his understanding, but Oncelus shook him. "Now—where is the *anglais?*"

Lece smiled again. She held the robe to her face, breathing in the potent masculine scent. "Kaat is no doubt taking him to Claude, my dæmon. My dear little sister has nowhere else to run but to Hespaire-Aube."

Oncelus's gaze slid over her body. Their eyes met, and she licked the silk draped over the palm of her hand. Oncelus's nostrils flared.

He threw Roulon against the door.

"Take your men by river," he told the Frenchman without taking his gaze from Lece.

Her eyes gleamed. "There's an inn outside the capital city, on the north road," she said. "They'll have to pass there. Wait for them there—and take them."

"Bring the Englishman to me," Oncelus said. "Do what you will with the woman."

"No," Lece said, disturbed by an unfamiliar twinge. "No, she is not to be harmed."

Oncelus studied her thoughtfully. He glanced at Roulon. "It will be as she wills it," Oncelus commanded. "Leave us."

Roulon gulped and nodded, and began creeping along the wall sideways like a crab. He reached the door and scurried through. It closed behind him with a snap.

Ashamed of her weakness toward her sister, Lece looked quickly at the closed door, then lowered her gaze to the floor. Head down, she turned her back to Oncelus. She heard the whisper of his black slippers on the wood floor as he approached her. He gripped her shoulders, pulling her back against his chest, then slid his hands down her body.

"It seems I have not yet banished all others from your thoughts," he murmured against her hair. He cupped her breasts through the thin lawn of her chemise. He rubbed her nipples with the palms of his hands. She moaned at the sensations flooding her and slumped against him.

"You see how wise it is to think only of me?" he said. He released her breasts and reached for the flask, his body pressing hard against hers.

He picked up the flask, his fingers curling around the bulb the way they had around her breast. With his other hand, he grabbed her hair and pulled her head back. He kissed her hard, sucking her tongue into his mouth. When he released her, his eyes were once again on the flask.

"She lied to me, your Kaat." He drew the flask up her body, then circled her breasts with the bulbous container. His grip in her hair tightened, and pain plucked at her scalp. "She lied to me."

He took Lece's mouth again, pressing the flask into the hollow between her thighs. She could hear the sloshing of the deadly liquid inside, and she gasped into his mouth.

Oncelus lifted his mouth from hers and pulled the flask away, laughing at her fear. He grabbed her chin and held her head immobile. "I should never have let her leave this room alive," he whispered, his mouth against her ear.

Lece felt him study her profile, then he pushed her chin up and forced her head back against his shoulder.

He drew his tongue along the inside of her top lip, slowly as if tasting her. His fingers clenched in her hair and she winced. "My little *roulure*. My little whore. Do you care that I may be close to my Colonel Becket, Lord Thorne? He was the only one I could never break. The only one to have escaped me.

"But soon my *esir* will kneel before me." His voice caressed the word "kneel." He licked her bottom lip, then suckled it.

She shivered. The passion, the desire he could command in her was clouding her mind. She knew the last shreds of her conscious will were drifting away. She knew—but he made her not care.

"He will kneel," Oncelus said, forcing her to her knees. The black silk robe she held slipped from her fingers and pooled at her feet. He looked down at her, his broad chest and muscular upper arms delineated by the sunlight.

"This time," he whispered, "this time, he will give me what he denied me before."

Lece drew her hands up the back of his legs, her fingers rubbing and caressing the hard flesh through his silk trousers. Her fingertips explored the back of his knees, then rose higher, stroking the backs of his thighs, then slid higher still to cup his buttocks.

"He will kneel and *beg* for his life."

Lece rubbed her face against the inside of his thigh, her tongue leaving a wet trail on the silk. Oncelus let his head fall back. She drew her face upward, rubbing, licking, to his sleek hip, then along his hardened phallus, outlined by the silken Turkish trousers pulled taut across it. He pressed her head into him, and his hips began a slow rhythmic rocking.

"And then," he said, his voice a low growl. He looked down at her. "And then I shall deny him."

Lece drew the tip of her tongue along the silk covering the hard cylinder of flesh. She gently pulled the trousers up tighter, to outline him clearly. She licked one masculine pouch, then the other. The feeling of the smooth silk moving over the rock-hard flesh added to the desire burning at the apex of her thighs. The heat of him warmed her cheek as he moved against her face. She nuzzled him, her lips outlining his arousal.

His hands gripped her shoulders and he pulled her up his body until his desire probed her through her petticoats. He kissed her again, his mouth twisting onto hers, then he flicked her lips with his tongue.

"Have you ever seen a man die?" he whispered, breathing his words into her mouth. Lece shuddered. He cupped her buttocks and pulled her against him, rocking, the rasp of silk on linen sounding like breathing in the attic room. His fingers explored and rubbed the cleft between the globes of her behind. He bit her bottom lip lightly and then slowly drew the flesh through his teeth.

"If one is skillful, a man can die slowly. So slowly," he said into her mouth, then pulled on her lip again. "So exquisitely slowly." Her eyelids fluttered and she sucked the warm moisture of his breath deep into her body. "I shall lct you watch," he said, "when I finally pluck out this Thorne."

She moaned at his promise, lost in his power, in his command of her. He slid his hands up her body to her shoulders, then along her arms to her hands. Their fingers intertwined and he took control of her touches, splaying her hands over his hips, then slowly bringing them to his loins. His hands over hers, he guided her to touch him, to hold him as he moved against her. She nipped and bit softly at his chest.

He released his hold on her and pulled up her petticoats. His fingers played with her moist sable fleece, while his other hand plucked at a taut nipple.

"It is easy to make them beg," Oncelus said. "Hold out the promise of freedom, of release." His finger dipped fleetingly into her womanhood, and she whimpered. "And even as you tighten your grip around their necks, their last heartbeats throbbing against your hand, they think you can be swayed by their pathetic pleas for mercy." His touch roughened and he kneaded her breast.

The pulsing heat inside her intensified, sparked by the friction of his touch on her breast, coalescing just beyond the reach of the teasing fingers under her petticoats.

His fingers taunted her, dipping into her just long enough for her to feel the agony of the pleasure he withheld. "Please . . ." she whispered. She lunged forward on his hand, but he was too quick. She groaned. "Please . . ."

Somewhere in the heated chaos of her mind, Lece knew he watched her, knew he waited to see her shivering torment as time and again, he kept her from the ecstasy she knew was so close.

Her head fell forward onto his chest. She panted and moaned at the exquisite sensations that hovered just at the edge of pain. Her hands clenched and unclenched against his shoulders. His skin was wet and shiny.

With quick efficiency, he unlaced his trousers and let them fall to his feet. He pushed her backward onto the table, her legs spread to either side of him. The fingers of one hand closed around the neck of the onion-shaped flask while with the other he stroked her stomach. Her eyes widened and her head rocked back and forth on the hard oak table.

"No," she whimpered. She tried to squirm away, but Oncelus held her fast.

"I feel your fear, my *roulure*. It flutters just beneath the surface like a heartbeat."

He slowly swirled the flask, drawing the cool bottle over her skin. Through the roaring of her insistent hunger, she could hear the liquid swirling. He drew the flask lower and lower. For an instant, his fingers renewed their teasing, and she closed her eyes and arched against him with a moan of triumph. His touch disappeared, replaced by a smooth roundness rubbing against her.

"No! My God. Nooooo!" she screamed, but it was too late. The first shudderings of her rapture overcame her and she was swept away into ecstasy.

Long minutes later, Lece came to feeling the pressure of Oncelus inside her. He was thrusting hard and fast, his hold on her hips bruising. She opened her eyes and saw little but a dark haze. A bubble of panic stuck in her throat until she realized Oncelus had thrown his black silk robe over her face. Her hips began answering his thrusts, and he urged her on with harsh snippets of Turkish.

Soon the delicious spiral toward ecstasy began coiling again, taking her to where only he could take her. He kissed her through the silk, his tongue stabbing into her mouth, and she answered it. Their thrusting grew frenzied, the table creaking beneath them.

He clenched her shoulders and plunged into her. "Die *esir!* Die *slave . . .*" His body shuddered.

Lece screamed in release. "Die! Diiiiiie!"

Oncelus drew away, leaving her limp on the table. He pulled his trousers back on and laced them.

"Cleanse yourself," Oncelus told her. "You will accompany that French rat to Hespaire-Aube to greet your sister." He went to the shuttered window and flipped up a slat.

Still dazed, Lece had difficulty focusing on his words. "What?" she asked, pulling the robe from her face and rising to one elbow. "You're sending me away? With *Roulon?*" She looked away, blinking back sudden bitter tears. "You have tired of me. I had hoped it would not be so soon."

He watched her from the window. He smelled the tips of his fingers, then rubbed them with his thumb. He locked her gaze with his. "The scent of your passion clings to my flesh," he said. He put two fingers into his mouth and slowly drew them out. "I have not yet tired of you, my pleasure."

"Do not send me away," she whispered.

"I wish it."

"Why must I? Kaat is hardly going to be ready bait for your trap."

Oncelus laughed and turned back to the window. "No, my *roulure*, your little sister isn't bait. She is only a lure to train the dog to obey. Take her to the margrave's castle. If my *esir* follows, I may join you there."

"Oncelus . . ."

He closed the shutter with a snap. "You will go."

Chapter 9

They traveled for hours through the forests that covered the foothills of the Ardennes, slowly climbing upward toward the summer pass that marked the border between Brabant and Hespaire-Aube. Kaatje was weary and sore, though the pain was nothing to the aching of her conscience. Around her swirled the heady scent of summer, but it did little to calm her as she rode sideways in front of the Englishman.

She had lied to him about what she'd found at Cerfontaine, and about Lece's whereabouts. But what else could she have done? She could hardly have let the colonel find her sister and El Müzir. He wanted to kill the Turk. What of Pietr's medicine then? What of Pietr?

So she'd lied, and, amazingly, he'd believed her. And now she didn't even want to think about what would happen when they reached Hespaire-Aube.

She tried to resettle herself so her shoulder wasn't rubbing against his chest, but the arm across her back was unyielding. Feeling caught and defeated, Kaatje let herself sway with the movement of the horse, oblivious to the world around her, exhaustion tugging at her body and her mind.

A jay swooped and scolded the pair on horseback,

and a hare, all mottled brown, scurried away with long, bounding leaps.

Kaatje blinked into awareness and found that she had slumped against Thorne's shoulder. The lightweight wool of his coat was faintly scratchy beneath her cheek. A warm solid arm protectively encircled her waist.

She straightened, and Thorne's arm quickly resumed its impersonal support of her back. A slight breeze cooled her face. She looked around as if missing something, then flushed when she realized she was missing the soothing rhythm of his heartbeat.

Late in the afternoon, the wind picked up, and rain clouds began blowing in from the west. The air smelled heavy and damp.

They came upon a meadow full of grazing sheep, and a boy of about nine sauntered over to them. He studied them with a half-hidden sneer on his face, the blustery wind snatching at his unkempt hair.

"Take your ease, gentles?" he asked. There was a sly look in his eyes as he belatedly bowed to them, then gestured toward a crude hut behind him.

"I think not," Thorne said. He dug out three stivers and tossed them to the boy. "A round of cheese and some bread will suffice."

The shepherd snatched the coins from the air and held them in a tightly closed fist. He mumbled something again and dashed into the hut.

A burly man stepped out of it, a bow and cocked arrow pointing at them. Kaatje gasped and Thorne pressed her tight against him. She could feel every muscle in his body ready to spring.

The man eyed Acheron, then the Englishman. He pulled the bowstring taut.

"Cheese and bread," Thorne said, his voice low but vibrant with command. "We already paid the boy."

Kaatje tucked in her skirts to make sure the pistols

were clearly visible, and the man's eyes widened. With a rude curse, he threw his bow and arrow to the ground.

"Boy!" he yelled. *"Boy."* The young shepherd appeared in the doorway, his mouth in a sulky pout.

"They give you coin, boy?" The shepherd shot Kaatje and Thorne a look of hate, then nodded, once. The man cuffed him, knocking him against the side of the hut. "You got no wits, boy. Give 'em their buggerin' cheese and bread."

Kaatje took the bread and cheese the boy carried out to her. An instant later, Thorne's arm tight around her, they bounded away across the meadow and were quickly among the trees again, heading south.

The rain began in early evening. Kaatje hunched over the saddle and clung to the horse's mane as Thorne ran ahead, leading Acheron by the reins through the treacherous rocky ground. Lightning flashed, followed quickly by a crack of thunder. The scene in front of her danced before her eyes in an afterimage.

"There!" Kaatje called down to Thorne. "Up there in that ridge. I'm sure I saw a cave."

Thorne tugged Acheron's reins to the right and began leading him up the muddy deer track to the rocky outcropping. The cave proved to be a wide half circle worn deep into the rock. A miniature waterfall tumbled through a crack in the rock at one end, forming a pool little bigger than a basin; from it, a tiny stream flowed out of the cave to splash onto the path below.

They dashed in, and the deluge falling on them abruptly stopped. In the last of the fading light, the colonel lifted her off the horse and set her down in front of him.

"It was all so sudden," she said, blinking wetly up at him. To her surprise, he pulled off a glove and brushed the water droplets from her face. His fingers wiped down her cheek and settled against her throat, as if he were feeling the sound of her words. "One . . . One minute it was cloudy and the next I felt as if I'd walked under a waterfall."

With his thumb, he traced the delicate flesh under her eyes. "You've been crying," he said.

She turned her back on him, dashing at her cheeks. "No, of course not. It's just the rain." She brushed at the sodden sleeves of her gown, but it was useless. She was soaked through. The light-colored material of her gown had turned dark from the rain, and under her gown she could feel the thin lawn of her chemise sticking to her skin like a plaster.

"Madame . . ." he began, putting his hand on her shoulder. She shivered and stepped out of his touch.

"I'm sorry, colonel," she said, looking down at her dress, her voice shaky. "I nearly swooned when I saw that shepherd's arrow pointed at us. I must not be as intrepid as I thought."

"You are a woman who meets the moment," he said. He wanted to touch her cheek and smooth the damp curls of her hair, but his hand remained at his side. "You would not swoon, I think."

She darted a glance at him over her shoulder. The look in her luminous wide eyes made an unfamiliar sensation chase through him, a distant lightness, like the sun glimpsed through a fog. But it passed before he could grab hold of it.

"You are chilled," he said. "There is a clean shirt in my bag. You can wear it while your gown dries. Dry linen would surely be more comfortable than wet satin."

"No, I'm fine," Kaatje said. "I'm fine. I will be dry in a moment. Truly." She shivered again and glanced at him with an odd look in her eyes. "But thank you. You are most kind."

It took him a moment to recognize the odd look she

had given him. Surprise. Surprise at his kindness. He
jerked on the buckle of his saddlebag and dug into the
worn leather pocket to retrieve his shirt.

Surprise at his kindness.

He thought of his familiar chant, *Hür adam, köle
olmiyan.* I am a man, I am one who is not a slave. But
my God, what kind of man had he become?

He grasped her shoulder with gentle but unrelenting
pressure and turned her to face him. He held his shirt
in his other hand. "I am many things, madame, but
rarely kind." His voice held a hint of self-mockery.
"You would do me little good raving from a fevered
ague."

Kaatje stared up at him, not knowing how to refuse.
A flush bloomed up her throat and cheeks at the thought
of having his shirt next to her skin, clinging to her the
way her chemise was.

The rain fell loud and hard outside their shelter, a
solid roaring curtain of water sheeting across the entrance to the cave. A bolt of lightning flashed, bringing
a second of daylight to the cave, then vanished, leaving
them in deeper twilight than before.

The moment of violent brightness had caught him off
guard, and she had seen what he normally kept hidden;
she had seen torment deep in his eyes—torment that
was always with him. She had but glimpsed it at the
camp the night before, when he'd spoken of his El Müzir, but now she knew just how deep his wound was.
The scars from the whips and shackles were physical
wounds that had closed, but they were nothing to the
unhealed suffering inside him.

Shaken, she took the shirt with murmured thanks
and went to the far end of the cave by the pool. She
tugged at the wet bodice lacings with trembling hands.

Thorne began wiping the horse off with a handful
of dried leaves from the mound of debris that had been
blown into the cave over long seasons. He stood with

his legs slightly apart, his height and the breadth of his shoulders a perfect match for the magnificent horse.

Kaatje held out the shirt in front of her, and her courage faltered. It was made of the finest linen, embroidered with a crest. She ran the pad of her thumb over the raised threads. It matched the one etched into the pistol handles.

Had someone who loved him done that? His mother? A sister? The linen draped over her arm was cool and warm at the same time. Someone had seen that the shirt was washed many times to make it soft and comfortable.

She looked at Thorne, grooming the stallion. The rain had brought out the natural wave in the thick strands of his long black hair, softening his proud profile.

She saw a glimmer of the lord rather than the colonel, and it startled her. She tried imagining him in court dress, the way she'd first seen Philippe at his brother's court in Hespaire-Aube, but she could only picture the Englishman dressed in scarlet.

"Have you finished, madame?" he asked, keeping his back to her. There was an impatient edge to his voice.

"One moment, colonel," she answered, and hastily tugged at the wet laces. After a long, frustrating minute, they loosened enough for her to pull the stomacher free and slip out of the bodice. She hesitated at the laces of her stays, but water had seeped through, making the boning chafe her skin, and she quickly unlaced it and tugged it off.

She slipped the shirt over her thin damp chemise. To her dismay, it only came to mid-thigh. She glanced at the colonel's back—she couldn't let him see her like this! Even Philippe had never seen her so unclothed. She tugged uselessly at the shirt's hem as if she could stretch it down over her limbs, then gave up with a silent oath of frustration.

Think! she commanded herself. This was just another difficulty that could be overcome. She'd managed to do that at St. Benoit, keeping hearth and home together.

Kaatje fingered her sodden petticoat. It was of muslin, not linen, and handkerchief-thin, but she had no choice. She wrung it out as best she could and dropped the wet weight of it over her head, then tied it around her waist. It would do, she thought, holding the plain material out in front of her.

"Just a moment more, colonel," she said, and knelt down by the pool of water and dipped her handkerchief in to clean the stains of travel the rain hadn't washed away.

Becket drew his hand over the already dry horse, listening to the rustling of her changing behind him. All day he had wanted to savor his coming revenge, to plan his assault on El Müzir and rehearse his fatal sword thrust. But this woman . . . He squeezed his eyes shut. This woman had kept intruding on his bloodlust.

In some distant part of his mind, he knew that this journey could not be easy for her; she was a lady, no matter that her life had turned hard. With a jolt every bit as sudden as a stab of lightning, Becket realized that it was almost impossible for him to conceive of what she might be feeling.

And he wanted to feel . . . anything. Now, in this rain-drenched night, he wanted her anger to wash over him again. Her outrage. Her passion.

The feelings unsettled him, and he turned abruptly to be rid of them. "Really, madame, it is but a shirt . . ." he began.

She was kneeling by the pool, her head bent forward, exposing her long slender neck and the delicate golden tendrils that had slipped from their pins. The linen shirt clung to her body where her skin was still damp, the material almost sheer. She still wore her petticoat, wet and as transparent as oiled paper. The delicate pink of her long legs shone through, a tantalizing promise of shapely ankles and soft thighs. A sweet-hot sensation surged through his blood.

"Sweet Jesu," he whispered.

Her head came up and she stared at him, as if transfixed. She blinked once, twice, then seemed to collect herself.

She turned her back to him and rinsed out her handkerchief in the pool. "I will be done in a moment, colonel," she said. Her voice was calm, but Becket could see her hand shaking in the water.

"Your pardon, madame," he said, and turned back to face Acheron.

There was an unwelcome tightness in him, and he closed his eyes and ran his hands through his hair. "Sweet Jesu," he said again, convinced that madness danced at the edge of his mind. In the past, the needs of his body had been simple to satisfy—with courtesans or camp followers. But he thought of those women now and recoiled. A deeper need was igniting inside him, a stronger hunger heating his blood.

In his mind, he called up the words with which he had cursed her: *liar, betrayer* . . . but they were weak things now, without flesh or bone. He clenched his fist and began the chant that stirred up the hate that had fed him for so long. *Hür adam* . . . But the hate did not come. The anger did not come. All he saw was the golden image of Kaatje. The image . . . and the madness.

"I am ready, colonel."

He turned.

She sat on a pile of leaves, her arms wrapped around her knees, the thin wet petticoat carefully tucked around

her feet. Becket ruthlessly clamped down on the urgent
heat that pulsed in his blood, withdrawing into himself
as if he were preparing for battle.

"Madame," he said with a bow, then shrugged out
of his coat and waistcoat and threw them aside.

Her eyes narrowed as he came toward her, carrying
the cheese and bread they had bought from the shep-
herds. It was nearly dark now, but he could still see
her. She seemed uneasy, as if the abruptness of his
movements disturbed her, and she tightened her hold
around her knees.

He dropped the food next to her. "Supper," he said.
He gathered a bundle of small dry branches and a handful of leaves, then knelt beside her. He could feel her
watching him, and he forced himself to concentrate on
the placement of the wood.

He retrieved a flint and striker from his saddlebag
and soon a tiny flame flickered among the dry leaves.
He looked at her, sweeping back a lock of his hair that
had fallen forward.

"It won't give off much heat, but perhaps it will keep
some of the damp at bay."

"It's a lovely fire, Colonel Thorne," she said, keeping her eyes on the flames. "Perfect for a wet summer
night."

Her gaze met his, and she smiled. Gold curls tumbled enticingly around her face, and her gray eyes were
trusting and unshadowed. The linen of the shirt, unused
to feminine curves, clung to the swell of her breasts
and glistened with dampness.

Her eyes abruptly turned serious. "The cut on your
temple has opened again," she said, and rose to her
knees and began dabbing at it with her damp handkerchief. She gently brushed his hair back from his face,
a faint frown of concentration marring her forehead.
"One of the branches must've caught you. I should have
seen to it earlier."

The soft caressing touch of her hand nearly undid him. There was no coyness in it, only caring. No one had ever touched him in that way before. He let his breath out in a long controlled exhalation, then gently grasped her hand and pulled it away from his face.

"I am not an invalid, madame," he said, the usual hard edge absent from his voice.

She looked into his eyes. "I know, colonel," she whispered. "I know."

She sat back on her heels and hugged herself, feeling the damp shirt move against her back. "Forgive me, colonel," she whispered, the words nearly drowned out by the roar of the rain. "I should have remembered from last night that you do not like . . . your wounds . . . to be touched."

His eyes turned opaque, and his face still. "I have been long in the company of soldiers, madame. I am unused to—"

"To what, colonel?" she asked, then held out her hands to stop his answer. "No. I don't want to know." She was tired and sore, yet something between them nourished her. But it was new and unknown—and it made her restless.

She picked up the bag that contained their supper. "I will see to our meal." She began fussing with arranging dry leaves and stones.

"Madame," he said. Her hands stopped.

"Do not concern yourself," Thorne said. "There is little to know."

She resumed her work without answering, but for the first time in her life, she couldn't quite make the chatelaine in her take over. She kept her back straight, careful to not let Thorne see her clumsy attempts at clearing the ground for their "table." She had to make their supper right; she had to. She was a lady. At St. Benoit, that had shielded her from her fear like a firescreen. She wanted it to shield her from Thorne.

"Why do you labor so?" he asked, an undercurrent of tension in his words that she couldn't name. "The stones and leaves will not turn into a gilt table, nor the cheese into a roast capon." He watched her intently. "It is but a plain shepherd's supper."

She turned to him, a stone unconsciously gripped in her hand. "I labor so because I am *not* a shepherd, Colonel Thorne. My mother's line is descended from the Dukes of Burgundy. My father was a van Staden— a family as old as Flanders itself! My son is a chevalier. He will grow to be a gentleman. He is nothing like that wretched little boy in the meadow. Nothing! He wakes to the perfume of newly picked flowers— not sheep. Sweet herbs are tucked under his pillow. His shirts are linen as yours are—and washed and washed until they're soft. And they're always mended. Always."

Her words choked off, caught in her throat. She looked at the rock in her hand, not knowing why it was there.

Thorne rose in one swift movement and gently pried the rock away. He let it roll out of his fingers and drop to the ground.

"And now, Madame Chatelaine, do I know you? Do I know the chevalier's wife? The widow? The mother?" He grasped her shoulder, his thumb stroking her skin through the linen. "Do I know the woman?"

Kaatje's emotions rioted inside her. His touch was warm, warm in a slow, calming way, like a cordial sipped by a fire.

"I no longer know the woman," she said softly. She met his eyes. "You frighten me, colonel. You make me frightened of myself. I don't know what to do, how to act. I have never been so long in the company of a man. Not even Philippe."

"He was your husband. Surely—"

"Surely what? He *wintered* at St. Benoit." She pulled out of his hold and knelt back on the ground, her unsteady hands setting out the cheese and bread. "He was not the sort of man who sat in front of a fire with his wife and son in a picturesque tableau." She rearranged the crockery cups for the third time.

"I saw to his needs, Colonel Thorne. His household, his breakfast, his dinner, his clothes, his—" She broke off and shook her head, a slight flush growing up her cheeks. "I saw to his needs. It is what a wife does."

Lightning flashed outside, then the crack and rumble of thunder. He knelt beside her, covering her hand with his to still her work.

"Is it what a woman does?" he asked.

It was a simple touch, but it made the long years at St. Benoit seem far in the past. "Woman, wife, widow, mother . . . They are the same."

"Are they, madame?"

When she didn't answer, he removed his hand. "We have both fought battles, it seems."

The warmth of his touch lingered on her skin. "We are weary, colonel," she said softly.

"Body and soul," Thorne said, rising. He went to the basin and splashed water on his face, then ran his hands through his hair.

The image of him made her body feel flushed in the damp night air. What would it be like to wake with his long black hair draped over her? Philippe had kept his hair bristle-short and, without his wig, he had always looked like a peeved hair brush. His hair had always jabbed her the few times he'd fallen asleep after one of his conjugal visits.

But the colonel's hair would fall like black velvet across her skin if he nuzzled close to her ear and whispered, *Sweet . . . betrayer.* She flushed again and shook her head. If he discovered she'd lied to him, there would be no chevalier's wife, no widow, no mother—no woman. Only betrayer. Then his touch would not warm her, his arms would not offer shelter, and his lips would not kiss away her lies.

The fire popped, jerking her back to the task at hand. This was just another night to be gotten through, she told herself, dismayed at the musings of her muddled mind.

She remembered their night in the barn—and his kiss. The night by the campfire—and the feel of his skin sliding beneath her hand. *No, Kaat. Earlier. Before Thorne. Before your dreams had turned from simple things.*

The firewood had run out during a frigid winter storm. She and Pietr had huddled by the fireplace in his bedroom, pretending the ashes were really glowing coals, and singing every song her father had ever taught her.

She smoothed her petticoat and began humming a rousing martial air, wishing it were only the cold she needed to keep at bay.

Becket looked up from where he'd been kneeling, feeding the paltry fire. He couldn't quite believe his ears. Was she singing? He felt an unfamiliar tickle in his throat. Laughter.

"A lullaby, madame?"

She glanced at him, her eyes wide as if she was surprised at the genial irony in his voice. "Of a sort," she answered with a hesitant smile. "My father sang it to me when I was little more than a babe."

He raised his eyebrow skeptically. "The Chevalier de Cerfontaine sang to his daughter?"

"Cerfontaine? No! He was my mother's second husband," she said, her voice full of dislike. *"My* father was Kapitein Pietr van Staden. He fought under Prince George Frederick of Waldeck. He came home so seldom, but when he did, oh, how I loved to hear his tales."

She looked at Becket, her eyes bright with reminiscence. "Such stories he used to tell! Lece never liked them, but I'd sit on his lap and listen for hours. Kapitein Kaat, he called me."

"Kapitein Kaat," he repeated. He said the words straight out, not mocking her. "I would have made you at least a major."

She smiled. "It was long ago, colonel. The memories seem but faded dreams now."

"Hold on to them," he told her. "Sometimes they are all that's left you."

For an instant, he let her see the sadness in his eyes, then he shuttered it away. He gestured at the bread and cheese and crockery cups filled with clear cold water.

"I see the roast capon is done to a succulent turn," he said. "And the wine the finest from his lordship's cellars."

Becket saw the corners of her mouth lift with an answering smile. He stood and bowed deeply, like a courtier. "A supper fit for a . . . perhaps not a prince, but surely a colonel and a lady." He rose from the bow and saw her smile falter. She busied herself with the bread.

He sat down next to her and watched her pull the soft white middle out of the bread and pop it into her mouth. Kaat, he thought to himself. Kaatje. Catherine. No— Kaatje. His mouth silently formed her name.

Becket looked into her eyes. Enticing eyes. Eyes that he could look into forever.

He shook his head, trying to divert his thoughts. Once, long ago, he had known how to amuse a lady with clever conversation, but now all he knew was the army—and revenge. He clung to that.

"Your father," Becket said, cutting off a slice of cheese, "was he a hussar?"

"Yes! How did you know?"

"That song," he said. "I've heard Austrian hussars sing it. They tell me they learned it at the battle of Zenta."

"Zenta?" she said, mulling over the word. She shook her head. "I don't recall Papa or Philippe ever mentioning that battle. Did you fight there?"

"No," Becket said, leaning back on his elbow and drinking in her features lit by the firelight. "I was still playing in Vienna." The rain was a soothing drumming in his ears, and he felt curiously at ease inside.

It was tempting to imaging her sitting across a splendid gilt table from him, supping tête-à-tête, the light from a hundred candles sparkling off her hair, a large single jewel nestled between the mounds of her lovely breasts—a ruby, to set off the blushing alabaster of her skin.

"Zenta," he said, reminding himself of what they'd been discussing. "Once, the Turks had been camped at the gates of Vienna. But at Zenta, Eugene of Savoy defeated them in one crushing blow. After that, there were few strongholds left for them." His eyes focused on the sheet of rain that fell across the cave opening. The gilt table and candles had disappeared from his mind, replaced by darkness.

"And over the years, those strongholds proved not so strong, though the Turks still haunted the area around Vienna—as I discovered to my cost." Almost to himself, he added, "Men kept deserting, running to the east and safety. Prisoners kept escaping, running to the west . . ."

"And safety?" she asked quietly.

Becket glanced at her, surprised at the question, and surprised at himself for considering it instead of pushing it away. He looked out into the wet dark world. "It is the sky," he said, "the sky that's the first thing I truly remember seeing. Before that is hazy, like a bad dream that's difficult to remember. I'd been nearly—" He broke off speaking and finished the sentence silently in his head. *I'd been nearly mad with grief.* The darkness had become one long night to him—the sun did not rise, the sun did not set. He did not wake and he did not sleep.

Becket didn't remember when he'd realized that the guard had come into the hellhole El Müzir had had dug especially for him, or that, for the first time, the man had been alone. Alone except for his clanging keys.

Becket was aware of the woman watching him, her breath slow and even, her lips slightly parted as if waiting, suspended, for him to continue. He stared at her, hard, as if it was his awareness of her that let him remember the past without reliving it.

It had been a simple matter to slip the chain of his shackles around the guard's neck and silence his mocking taunts. An instant later, Becket had ripped the shackles off his wrists, tearing the flesh as he'd done so.

He inhaled deeply, letting the night's damp air fill him. "I staggered into the sunlight, blinded by the sudden brightness. I crept along a wall by touch and sound, edging my way until my eyesight returned. And then I'd seen the sky, wide and intensely blue, with wisps of white clouds."

It had been an easy matter, then, he remembered, to slip through the undermanned western gate. Then the alarm had sounded. He'd stolen a horse and fled into the swamps that had surrounded Temesvár, slogging through the bogs and the sucking mud, barely evading the searching janissaries.

"Escape to safety?" he finally said, exhaling slowly. He rubbed the heel of his hand over the place the terrible scar marred his chest. He shook his head. "No. Escape to freedom. Escape to sunlight and untainted air . . ."

"And did you find it, Colonel Thorne? Did you find your freedom?" Her voice was soft and reflective.

He said nothing.

"I am no soldier," she said slowly, as if she were weighing her words, "but I know there is more than one kind of freedom. One that means having unspoiled food, and enough of it, a bed to sleep in, a fire to keep away the cold . . . and another, the kind with music and laughter and waking with joy in your heart."

Becket drew in a sharp breath, caught off guard by her words. How did she know? He rose off his elbow and cupped her face.

"Madame Chatelaine, you see too much with those great gray eyes of yours." He brushed her cheek with his thumb. "The air is pure and scented with flowers, the water is fresh and cold and quenches my thirst. It is enough." *It has to be.*

She shook her head slightly in his hold. "It is not enough," she whispered, and reached out, slowly, tentatively, and lightly brushed his forehead. "At times, your face goes so still and your eyes shutter themselves from the world. Your freedom will never be enough until whatever haunts you, whatever demons are loose inside you, are banished forever. Then will the scent of flowers soothe you and the taste of water ease your thirst."

Her touch was cool on his fire-warmed flesh. He closed his eyes and drew her hand down over his face. He rubbed his lips against her palm, then kissed the pads at the base of each finger.

"How can you see so much?" he whispered against her skin. "You must be a spirit of the air. A golden sylph set to lure the gods." He kissed her wrist and traced the line of her pulse with his tongue. He saw her eyelids flutter and her breath quicken.

"Colonel . . ."

"Do you know how beautiful you are?" he asked, his voice a hoarse whisper. He slid his hand up her arm inside the loose sleeve of the linen shirt, and lightly grasped her elbow, his thumb caressing the soft inner flesh at the crease.

"There is so much caring in you, it fills you with light and warmth. And I'm so cold inside, Kaatje, so cold and dark."

Kaatje felt caught in the web of his touch. Achingly sweet sensations shimmered through her. His hand slid down her body, cupping her breast through the soft linen, his thumb brushing the peak.

She gasped at the fever rising in her blood. His hand went lower to trace the curve of her waist and the swell of her hip. He caressed the undulations of her bottom with a hot, possessive touch.

"I am but a man. A man who hungers . . ." His hand massaged the small of her back in exquisitely slow circles.

He kissed her. He buried his hands in her hair, holding her head while he explored her mouth with deep thrusting strokes of his tongue. He rubbed her back and roughly caressed her behind. She felt his quick arousal growing against her.

His mouth took hers again, his tongue plunging in. A desperate urgency began growing low in her body. Her bones were dissolving. She tried to answer his kiss, but her passion was a soft thing next to his.

"Colonel," she said breathlessly, her body fevered, every nerve exploding to life. "Colonel, please . . ." Her voice trailed off, as if she had forgotten how to speak. She was too near the flame and she was melting.

"Such a hunger," he said huskily, and trailed fierce wet kisses down her neck.

How easy it would be to let herself fall into the warm promise of his caresses, and of his long hard kisses that made her limbs tremble, burning away every last wisp of thought.

And she wanted to. Everywhere he touched her, her body was coming alive with a need she'd never felt before.

"Come to me," he whispered.

Kaatje opened her eyes and saw him watching her, waiting, aware of her body's responses. His hunger for her was a wild thing straining to be free, a fierceness barely held under control.

She was caught. The darkness in him terrified her, but she was caught. Even in a lifetime she could never know all the convolutions of his soul, but God, sweet God, she wanted him, the darkness and the light. He terrified her, but she wanted him.

"Thorne," she said softly, the word a whisper of surrender, then let herself fall toward him.

His eyes widened. "No!" he cried out and grabbed her shoulders, holding her away from him. "Jesu, no." His grip tightened painfully.

"Madame," Becket said, then squeezed his eyes shut. God, how he hurt inside. He felt unstable, dizzy, as if he'd just spun around and around in a child's foolish game. But what had almost been unleashed inside him was no game. He wanted to take her, take her hard, full on.

He wanted to possess her, to consume her. It was as if he suddenly found himself half empty and he needed to be filled up. Deep inside him, something he had thought solid and fixed had rumbled in warning, like the ground trembling under a barrage of cannon fire. He was terrified. Of himself. Of the hunger that still pulsed in his blood. Of what she was coming to mean to him. When he had felt her coming to him, never had his control teetered so precariously. Not on the battle-field. Jesu, not even in Temesvár.

He loosened his hold on her shoulders, fighting a reluctance to let her go. "Madame, forgive me. I am but a . . . a brutish soldier too long alone with a beautiful woman."

"Colonel Thorne, I . . ." Kaatje covered her mouth with a trembling hand and closed her eyes, mortified. "What you must think of me," she gasped out. She felt sick to her stomach, and the air had suddenly turned thick and clammy. "I . . . Oh, God, oh, God." She plucked at her petticoats. Lece had dressed this way for her devil lover. "I am not like Lece. I'm not Lece." She tried to pull the shirt tighter around her.

"No," Becket said, his voice unsteady. "Sweet Jesu, no." Those eyes that could see so much were bright with unshed tears, making them seem like quicksilver in the dim light. It tore at him to see the self-blame, the self-doubt that filled them.

He turned away from her and ran his hand through his hair. He breathed in deeply, filling his lungs with suffocating dampness.

"My demons are too great, madame. You soothe my wounds, and your caring drains my hate."

"Is that so wrong?" she asked.

A thin wisp of coldness curled in his stomach, like an expelled breath on a winter morning. Deep inside him, the coldness was growing, a film of black ice that always formed over his pain, to hide it away.

"I need my wounds, my hate. It is all I have to control what is inside me . . ."

"So it is rage that flows through your veins—not blood?" she said, the van Staden fire coming back into her voice. He almost smiled, but the ice was too thick. "And it is hate that animates your spirit like some paltry witch's poppet. No! I do not believe it."

He spun around, grabbing her shoulders and pulling her to him, her face inches from his.

"By God, yes! Believe it, madame. That rage and hate are all I *am*. I died within the walls of Temesvár. Take away my rage and hate and thirst for revenge, and there is nothing left but the bits of straw and cloth of your witch's doll."

"No," she said, pushing away from him. "You are a man—you can be free of those demons."

"You speak of freedom, madame. My freedom will come when El Müzir is dead." Becket knew his eyes were shuttered and face still, but it didn't matter. The sadness in the woman's eyes didn't matter. "My demon awaits in Hespaire-Aube, and that is enough. That is *all.*"

Chapter 10

Becket recognized the too bright colors around him as the colors of a dream. He grimaced in his sleep. His fingers scraped on the cave floor as his hand balled into a fist, but he didn't feel them. He smelled only that long-ago wet spring forest outside of Vienna.

"Beck, c'mon," Kester called to him, his fast little horse dashing into a clearing. Becket watched his younger brother wheel the horse around. "C'mon, you two!"

Becket laughed, a deep, rich, full-of-life sound. "Kester, you wretch! How can we track a wolf with you shouting like a banshee?" He laughed again, just for the feel of it. It was wondrous to be young, full of blood and lust. He grabbed the dark-haired woman who rode beside him and pulled her to him to kiss her, but she pushed his arm away.

"You discarded me, remember, Becket?" she said, spitting out the final "t" of his name between her clenched teeth. "Everyone has heard that the proud English boy discarded the Marquise de Viaur."

"I may have lapsed in my attentions," he said, pulling her to him again, "but perhaps there's still more you can teach me."

She yanked herself away and glared at him. She was a decade and a half older than his twenty years, but

179

when that bitterness came over her face, she added nearly a score of years to her age.

"It is too late, you fool, for anything but your last lesson," she ground out, her mouth twisting into a line of hate. She lifted her riding whip. "And this one you will remember for the rest of your life!"

He grabbed the wrist that held the whip just as they rode into the sunlit clearing. Her dark brown hair suddenly gleamed golden and her brown eyes changed to quicksilver gray. Her features softened to finer, more delicate lines, and her skin paled to the color of a blushing pearl.

Her beauty dazzled him, cutting through his irritation at her old crone's words. His blood seethed through him, hot, insistent. He nearly pulled the golden beauty off her horse, holding her against his thigh, his mouth taking hers before she could speak.

They rode on into shadow, and the marquise reappeared in his arms. Startled, he loosened his grip, and she ripped herself away. "You search for a wolf, Becket Thorne." She cracked the whip. "You've found the devil!"

Unearthly cries echoed from the right and left of him. The marquise laughed, ruthlessly spun her horse around, spurred it back the way they'd come. The cries around him resolved into words. Turkish words . . .

Kaatje woke with a start. She kept still in the darkness, one arm under her head for a pillow, the other stretched out toward Thorne sleeping a few feet away. The fire had gone out, and the damp air was heavy against her skin.

It was deep in the night. Outside the rain had lightened to a heavy drizzle. From a few feet away, she heard a hoarse cry and felt her hand being clenched as if someone were hanging on to her for safety.

Thorne exhaled sharply, as if he'd been hit, and she

felt him clench her hand again. They had deliberately lain apart, but he must have reached out to her in his sleep.

"Colonel Thorne," she whispered, "wake up." His fingers felt chilled, and she rubbed some warmth back into them.

"Kester!" Thorne cried out. "Ride back! It's an ambush."

"Colonel!" Kaatje said, frightened by the despair she heard in his voice. She crawled to him and shook his shoulder. His skin was bare and damp with perspiration. "Wake up. Colonel, wake up. It is but a dream."

Fingers clamped around her wrist and pulled her down on top of him, crushing her breasts into his chest and twisting her arm behind her back.

"Colonel! It is Kaatje. I was trying to wake you from a dream."

Becket sat up abruptly, braced for the black ice to encase him. He felt its chill, but it was a distant thing, like a memory of winter. "You have succeeded," he said, his voice harsh from sleep.

He released her twisted arm and buried his hands in her hair. "Perhaps I yet dream," he said, rubbing his face slowly on hers. Her skin was so soft. His breaths quickened.

"Colonel Thorne," Kaatje said breathlessly. "Are you . . . Are you all right? Your dream . . ."

He wanted to kiss her, hard and deep, he wanted to bury himself in her, in her softness and her caring, he wanted to . . . He pulled back, then rested his forehead against hers. "What you do to a man, sylph," he murmured, then released her.

She sensed him standing up. For a fleeting moment, she felt a light touch on her hair, then it was gone.

"My name is Becket." The name lingered in the air,

and she breathed in deeply as if she could draw it inside her. *Becket.*

Water splashed in the corner, and she heard him dowsing himself. Inside, she still shook from the sudden onslaught of passion and the effort to hold it at bay. She put her hand low on her stomach, her fingers clutching the linen shirt into a wrinkled ball. What was this aching so deep inside her? There was such a tension there, an anticipation of something new and unknown.

"You frighten me," she whispered into the darkness. His movements stilled in the corner. "Everything about you frightens me." She wrapped her arms tightly around her knees. "And yet . . . Sometimes, when we're riding through the forest and I feel your arm across my back, steadying, protecting, and your chest against my shoulder, solid and constant, then . . . God help me. Then I'm not afraid."

Kaatje shook her head to clear it. Before, she'd thought it was the darkness she saw in his eyes that frightened her. Or the soldier in him. Or the Englishman, who was so different. But this evening . . . here, now . . . she realized it was none of those things.

It was the man.

In the deep gray of the night, she could just discern him moving toward her. He went down on one knee in front of her, his hand cupping her chin. He ran his thumb over her lips.

"You were a man's wife," he said. "What is between us cannot be new to you."

She gently pulled his hand away from her face. . . . *cannot be new to you.* His words rang in her mind. Their fingers twined and he kissed the soft web between her thumb and finger.

It is the sky, she wanted to say. *What is in me is like the sky to a man who has lived in darkness.*

"I was a man's wife, Colonel Thorne. But . . ."

"But your husband was gentle and easy," he said, dropping her hand. "And it was soft on your linen sheets, warm under your counterpane." His voice grew louder, bitter. He held her head tightly between his hands, and she could feel his quick breaths on her face. "And I am none of those things, madame. I am not gentle. Easy. Soft. Warm."

He nipped at the delicate flesh over her cheekbone. She held her breath, her flesh tingling, expectant, sparking like the air just before a storm.

"I said I was a man. A lie, madame. I am a beast. Sweet Jesu. You make me *burn*. When I kiss you—no, when my mouth takes yours—I can feel the hunger rippling through you. I can feel your flesh—" He ran his hands down her arms, then back up, rough and quick. "Just below the surface—shimmering with need, with desire. And kisses are but a shadow of what I burn for. But you were a chevalier's wife. Used to gentle, soft, easy."

He wrapped his arms around her and held her tight. "I want to take you. My head pounds with it. I want to take you full on—not gently. Not soft. Not easy."

He released her and rocked back on his heels, and stood. He strode to the entrance of the cave, stopping inches from the cascading water, his head thrown back. "No. I will not let the beast win. *Hür adam* . . . I am a man. Sweet Jesu, a man."

The words came out raw and jagged. Lightning flashed. She saw him looking at her across the cave, the sudden flare making a mask of his face, the agony of his haunted soul carved deep. He turned from her and strode out into the rain.

Kaatje curled up next to the cold ashes, her knees pressed into her chest, her eyes wide and staring into the night. Where was dawn? Where was the sun? Light, light would make this rending despair go away.

"Becket," she whispered, the word a dry sob in

her throat. How long had it been since Becket had
vanished into the rain? An hour? Two? Acheron nickered in the darkness, the sound lonely and lost in the
cave.

She wanted Becket here, silent, withdrawn, or crack-
ling the air with his rage—it didn't matter. She wanted
him here. He could say or do anything, anything, to
take her mind from the confusion that gnawed at her.
She hugged her knees tighter. Was that why a soldier
longed for battle? To fight and let the heartaches fade
into sweet oblivion.

She wanted to scream aloud into the darkness.
*Becket, help me. Help me! My son's life is in the hands
of a madman. Go back! Go back to Cerfontaine! What
does it matter that you would know I'd met your El
Müzir and knew him for what he was and still lied to
you? What would it matter that your devil would kill
you? What would it matter that your body would lay
lifeless on the ground, your wounds forever unhealed?*

She whimpered. *No, no.* All that power and turbulent
energy extinguished. Those deep indigo eyes unseeing . . . ''No,'' she cried out.

Water dripped on her arm and she gasped.

''It seems we both suffer from dark dreams,'' Thorne
said, his voice deep and calm. She could sense that the
fierceness had gone from him. He touched her, stroking
her shoulder, then lifted her into his arms and held her
close to his wet chest. ''You will find more comfort
here,'' he said, and gently lowered her onto a soft cushion of leaves.

To her astonishment, he lowered himself next to her
and pulled her to him, settling her head in the hollow of
his shoulder, his arm comfortably around her. ''Dawn
will arrive in a couple of hours, dry and bright, and our
ride will be easier.'' He stroked her hair. ''Sleep until
then, Madame Chatelaine.''

* * *

She awoke alone. The morning was dry and bright, as Thorne had promised. He had saddled the horse while she still slept, and he now stood outside the cave by Acheron, ready to depart. He gave her a slight bow.

"Bon matin, madame," he said, his tone neutral. "We will depart as soon as you have finished." He gestured toward the basin. Her still-damp gown had been laid next to it.

Kaatje flushed. The intimacy that had grown between them the night before had been packed away like the crockery cups. *"Bon matin,* Colonel Thorne," she said, picking up her limp satin skirts. "I shall be ready in a moment."

The sun had scarcely cleared the hills when they set out. Too soon, she settled into the rhythm of the ride, the power of the man behind her a familiar strength. She forced her mind away from it, and instead made herself study the land around them. The forest was beautiful after the rain; the intense green leaves on the beeches sparkled when the sun surprised droplets of water hidden in the veins and curls.

They stopped and drank from a cool mountain stream, and ate the rest of the shepherd's bread and cheese, then continued their ride. The landscape changed as they neared the border of Hespaire-Aube; the trees grew sparser, less lush, and the undulating hills flattened into rocky plateaus, though tiny waterfalls and impromptu streams still gushed after the night's storm.

Late that evening, they stopped under a rocky outcropping sheltered by a lone oak. Kaatje huddled deep in her cloak, not wanting to remember Roulon's biting lies under another ancient tree. Not wanting to remember her own.

Neither she nor Thorne spoke much, and when they did it was in courteous, polite banalities. They slept apart, not even close enough to touch if one should reach out toward the other in sleep.

The next morning, they set out before dawn, Thorne's arm steady across her back and his hard-muscled chest firm against her shoulder.

The faint path they followed led close to a small waterfall splashing onto flat rocks below. "Careful," he said, pulling her closer into the fold of his arm.

She brushed off the water droplets that cascaded onto her dress as they passed. "There is always water everywhere! Is England like this?" she asked.

"Damp, certainly," he answered, then added, "At least I remember it that way."

"Remember?" Kaatje said, a half smile on her face. "You make winter sound as if it were a very long time ago to have weakened your memory so. Or don't you return home when the fighting stops during the cold weather?"

"Return home," he said, repeating the words as if they carried an odd notion he hadn't thought of before. He shook his head. "No, I do not return home. I wintered at the Hague with my regiment until I sold it. Now I winter where winter finds me."

"And winter never finds you in England?"

"No."

She looked up at him, wondering at the stillness that came over his face. "Why?" she asked.

His gaze lowered from studying the path ahead to her upturned face. The blue of his eyes was lighter in the sunlight, yet still opaque and unreadable. She felt the muscles in the arm tighten, as if he'd clenched his fist, and wisps of unease began growing inside her.

"Why, indeed, madame. I am a soldier. It is not for me to wake in a great stone pile, one servant hovering with a cup of chocolate, another breathlessly holding a letter with the latest gossip, fresh from a London coffeehouse.

"I ride into battle, not down bucolic lanes, assessing the toils of tenant farmers."

"Many men covet the life you condemn," she said. It was the life Philippe had struggled to maintain, though he was at heart a courtier, too full of posturing learned at his brother's court to be happy as a country gentleman.

"I do not condemn it, madame. Merely reject it for myself."

"But what of your family? Surely your family—"

The words screamed in Becket's head. *Surely your family . . .*

Beck! a voice cried out in his mind, a voice from the blackness of his past. *Beck. The pain'll be gone soon. I can feel it . . . leaving. Beck. Tell Father I won't be bringing him that stallion. Orkney wouldn't sell. It doesn't hurt anymore, Beck. There's light. I can see it. Beautiful light. Kill the devil for me, Beck. Promise me. Promise me you'll kill the devil. Beck? Where have you gone?*

Kaatje saw the mask fall over Thorne's face. He wrapped his hand around her neck, his thumb pressing painfully in the soft flesh under her chin. "You ask a great many questions, madame."

Deep in his eyes, she saw a bright flash, like a sapphire held up to the sun, or the eyes of a stalking beast caught in torchlight. She shivered.

"Tell me of *your* family," he said, his voice low and full. "Tell me of your husband. Did he wake beside you demanding his chocolate—and his wife?"

The insult bit into her.

"Release me now," she hissed, her hand closing around his wrist, feeling the rough tissue of his scars against her palm. She pulled, knowing her strength could never match his, but showing him she was willing to try. "Release me, *anglais.* You ask what is not yours to know."

"As do you, *Fleming*."

"No wonder you can't go home," she spit out. "You *are* a soldier, fit only for the battlefield, forever smelling of gunpowder and other men's blood."

He crushed her to him, forcing her face into his shoulder. "Smell the gunpowder, madame, and the blood. Breathe it in deep. And take care to remember that you are on *my* battlefield."

Becket spurred Acheron to a dead run, still holding her crushed to him. Rocks flew out from under the stallion hooves with splintering cracks. The plateau was flat, covered with short stunted grasses, made for traveling fast.

Surely your family . . . She hadn't known what she'd said. He'd lashed out when he knew there was no malice in her—anger at him, fear of him, but no talons to purposely tear into him. She was not like her sister, or those court-weaned women, whose claws were always out.

"Forgive me," he whispered, the wind carrying his words away before she could hear them.

The sun was at its highest point when they crested the last ridge and looked down across the wide valley that marked the northwest region of Hespaire-Aube. In the far distance, high on a hill above the brown speck of the capital city and the two rivers that joined there, stood the castle of the Margrave of Hespaire-Aube, the old gray stones looking white in the midday sun. It had been begun when Charlemagne had been crowned emperor, the land a gift to one of his faithful paladins.

There were no paladins now, no heroes of the faithful to keep the infidel at bay, only Claude and his court, concerned more with the intrigues of the bedroom . . .

"Pietr," Kaatje whispered, leaning over the horse's

mane, her eyes narrowed against the bright sunlight. She tried to gauge how much farther they had to go.

"Rest easy, madame. Your son is no doubt safe." There was a fleeting touch on her shoulder.

She didn't want his reassuring words, but she drank them in all the same; they were a balm to her worries. "How can you sound so certain?"

"Niall and Harry would've taken the northeast road. Its entire length is under Allied control. Your son awaits you. As does my enemy."

Kaatje went still. She retreated inside, huddling inside her skin like a mummer in a costume at a fair. Her lies would soon be exposed. She felt squeezed, trapped.

The ridge sloped down into a forest thick with trees. There were yet more streams to cross and more hills to ride around. The journey was too long; she wanted to be done with it. And yet . . . With a flutter of panic—and relief she didn't want to acknowledge—she realized they could not reach the castle in the half day left to them. They would have to spend one last night together . . .

He signaled to the stallion to begin the descent.

The lengthening shadows of dusk forced Thorne to slow Acheron to a walk. They were still a couple of hours from the city, following the Aube River that ran through the western half of the country. Ahead, a waterfall roared, and perched above it was an old stone mill, what was left of its wooden waterwheel canting to one side, the paddles long ago rotted through.

When the horse reached it, Kaatje readied herself to dismount, but the arm around her tightened.

"Wait," Thorne said, his eyes studying the surrounding forest. He dismounted in one smooth silent motion, then pulled his sword from its scabbard.

"Colonel . . ." she began, but had no idea what to

say. He looked at her, then frowned and turned away. She watched him give the stallion's nose a quick rub with the back of his gloved hand, then walk to the door of the mill.

Sword at the ready, he pushed open the decaying wooden door, pieces of the rotting leather hinges crumbling to the ground. He entered.

Her world became silent, except for the water thundering over the falls. She leaned over the horse's neck, hands buried in the black mane, and listened as hard as she could. The shriek of a jay made her jerk upright, and Acheron nickered at the sudden movement.

Kaatje swallowed to ease the tightness in her throat. "St-steady," she whispered, giving the horse an experimental pat on his neck. Acheron shook his head, then seemed to settle down. She rubbed his neck again.

A crack of splintering wood made her sit bolt upright. *"Becket!"* she screamed. There was a loud splash in the river. *"Becket!"* She tore a pistol from its holster and jumped to the ground, hitting the hard dirt at a stumbling run.

She ran through the open door into the dim interior. "Becket, answer me!" An arm caught her around her waist and pulled her back against a hard-muscled chest.

"I am unharmed, madame," a voice said calmly in her ear, as he slipped the pistol from her grasp.

She twisted out of his hold and spun to face him.

"Why didn't you answer me, damn you. I thought you'd fallen into the river."

"No doubt I would fall like a stone," he said, still in that infuriatingly calm voice. "But in this case, it *was* a stone." He gestured behind her, toward the river side of the mill.

She turned and saw a ragged hole in the floor, big enough for a man even the size of Thorne to fall through.

"The floor gave way under an old grinding stone when I stepped on it," he said. He walked past a stone firepit in the middle of the room, and stopped, pointing at a wide black crack in the floor with the pistol. "It seems solid enough to here. Past this, and you're suspended above the river."

"Why didn't you answer?" She had thought him dead, gone from her forever. Needles of pain stabbed her stomach, and it made her angry. He *would* be gone soon, but only from her, and she hated the empty feeling inside her.

He looked straight in front of him. The sculptured planes of his profile seemed cast in bronze by the last rays of sunlight. He was still for a long moment, then turned to face her.

Damn the woman, Becket thought, squeezing the handle of the pistol, then jamming it into the waistband of his breeches.

"I did not mean to distress you, madame," he said. "I am unused to . . ." *Your caring.* ". . . to someone being dependent on me."

"Dependent on you . . ." Her eyes narrowed to smoky gray slashes, and her hands balled into fists. "Damn you, Becket Thorne, damn you to hell. Not everyone is so buried in their own black hearts that they can't manage a little common civility!"

She paced back and forth in front of the open doorway, the soft soles of her boots making the decades of grain dust whisper under her feet. The material of her gown had gone limp after being drenched and her skirts no longer stood away from her legs. Becket liked the fashion, he realized, watching the satin delineate her thighs with each step. His blood quickened.

"I am *not* dependent on you! I could *walk* to the castle from here."

She was magnificent in her anger. She was like no other woman. He watched her taking deep agitated breaths, her breasts swelling above the bodice of her gown with each inhalation, and an exquisite tension began to tighten in his loins.

Becket clamped down on the urgency that had begun its subtle beat in his blood. He bowed to her. "As you wish, madame, though I should advise waiting until morning before setting out."

Thorne strode past her and out of the mill. Kaatje looked around her, only then realizing how dark it had become. She paced back and forth, waiting for him to return. When he did not, she followed him outside.

"Thorne . . ." she began.

"Here," he said, dumping her cloak in her arms, then piling on one of his saddlebags and a pistol holster. "There's some hard tack in the bag. Soak it in water for half a day before you try to eat it. And some dried beef. It'll break your front teeth—chew on it with only your back teeth." He gave her a look. "You have nice solid back teeth."

"Thorne!" She flamed red in embarrassment and tried to back away from him, but he looped a cord on the holster around her shoulders and stopped her. The pistol handle jabbed her under her chin and she had to hold her head back. "What are you doing? Stop this nonsense!"

His eyes traveled up and down her, as if assessing her to see what she lacked. His gaze lingered around her skirts, and she tried to look over the pile in her arms to see what was wrong.

In disgust, she turned and marched into the mill and dumped everything onto the floor. She dug into the saddlebag, her hand closing around the hardtack, then went and stood in the doorway.

"Here, *anglais,* soak your own hardtack!" she called and threw it at him. He swerved, and it hit the tree behind him with a loud crack, gouging the bark.

He reached her in two leaping strides, grabbed her

wrist, and pulled her to him. His fingers buried themselves in her hair, and his head bent to within inches
of hers.

"*My* battlefield, Fleming," he said, the words ending with a growl. The light in his eyes was reckless.
He used the solid mass of his body to force her back
up against the doorjamb, pressing himself into her.

Wood dug into her back, but she felt only the hard
masculine pressure forcing her body to mold itself to
his. Her stomach tightened, but it was with a tension
of anticipation.

"You smell of gunpowder, my lord colonel."

His eyes glinted with appreciation. "I unloaded the
pistol. I didn't want you to faint if you tried to shoot
some bandit." He released his hold and took a step
back, a twig cracking under his boot heel. The weariness from the day's journey that had lined his face
was gone. "Fainting around bandits is never a good
idea."

"You wretched man!" She snapped her head out of
his reach, ignoring the tiny stings of protest from her
hair that had caught on the wood.

She grabbed her skirts in two handfuls and stomped
through the doorway into the cool musty interior. The
pistol in its holster was still piled on top of her cloak
on the dusty floor. She kicked it aside. "You wretched
man," she said again. "No doubt that's why I've never
fainted around you."

"Not yet," he said from the doorway.

Kaatje had snatched up her cloak and held it out in
front of her to shake it when the provocative meaning
of his words hit her. She twirled around to face him,
eyes wide and the cloak clutched to her chest, trying to
still the sudden shaking inside.

Thorne stood in the doorway, his hands gripping the
doorjamb high on both sides, like Samson holding up
the pillars of the temple. He stared at her, the silence

growing long, then he pushed himself back. His fists
hit the wood frame, the force of the blow making the
door shudder.

"I will return with supper," he said with a growl,
then walked away.

Trembling, Kaatje buried her fingers in the old soft
wool, clenching and unclenching them, the words, the
promise, curling around her like drifting smoke. She
had reconciled herself to the journey on horseback with
this tall English colonel, but now he held out the promise of a new journey, one of the heart that would take
her farther than she'd ever been, one Philippe had only
started . . .

"No," she whispered into the empty room. "Not
yet. Not ever." She kicked at a clump of straw, then
ground it to dust with her boot. "There is only one
journey I make and that is to save my son. My heart
remains . . ." Her words faltered, and she gripped the
cloak tight in her balled fists. ". . . as it was."

While Thorne was away, she cleaned as thoroughly
as she could, trying to dissipate the disturbing mist that
floated through her. Once, she accidentally stepped on
one of the loose floorboards, but caught herself, trembling.

Twilight was fading when she heard a soft noise
over the roar of the falls and glanced at the doorway.
He stood there, watching her, a black outline in front
of the newly risen moon that still kissed the hills.

He entered, a new tension around his eyes, and
handed her a cleaned and dressed grouse. He removed
his coat and unbuttoned his waistcoat, then knelt on the
edge of the firepit and began making a fire. She saw
him brush his fingers over the wood where she'd carefully swept away the dry bits of grain and straw. "You
have been busy, Madame Chatelaine," he said. She
thought he smiled, but it was too dark to be sure.

In a few minutes, Kaatje sat watching the fire, her chin resting on her knees, while the smell of the hot roasting bird made her stomach rumble.

"I wish I could hurry it along," she said, her eyes intent on the fowl laced on a makeshift turnspit. She curled her legs under her and leaned forward. "It's going to taste like heaven after days of cheese and bread."

He squatted near the edge of the stone pit, tending the fire, the flames making bright orange light dance over his features. "Such impatience," he said with a smile. "And in a chatelaine, too."

"I'm starving!"

He reached behind him with his long arms, the motion one of fluid power, and retrieved his saddlebag. He dug inside and pulled out what looked like a gray-white rock, then threw it onto the floor by her hand. It landed with a thump.

"That should tide you over," he said, the hint of a smile lurking at the corners of his mouth.

A laugh burst out of her. She picked it up and put it on her open palm to judge its weight. "Why anyone would *purposely* make anything that looks like a rock, feels like a rock—"

"—tastes like a rock." Thorne took it from her hand, his fingers curling against her palm. "But foragers rarely come back empty-handed when they know this is what they'll eat if they do." He tossed it to the other side of the room and it disappeared through the hole in the floor and into the river.

Kaatje closed her hand, still feeling a phantom warmth on her skin where he'd touched her.

Night had settled in completely by the time Kaatje stared at the grouse carcass with a satisfyingly full stomach. The roasted bird had tasted so wonderful, she'd even licked her fingers to clean them. Now she sat musing by the fire, her arms wrapped around her knees. Thorne sat a few paces away, staring into the flames, his expression enigmatic.

"How many years have you been in the army?" she asked, watching him carefully for signs that his mood had changed.

He glanced at her, his face suddenly still, then he returned to studying the fire. "It depends on how you count them," he said, his voice carefully even. He opened his fist. "I am the second of three sons, and my father bought me a regiment when I was eighteen. But I did not feel . . . destined . . . for the army and played in London, then Paris until war became inevitable. Then Vienna."

He dragged the fingers of both hands through his hair, impatiently yanking off the black ribbon that held the queue. The long dark strands fell in waves past his shoulders. Watching him, Kaatje breathed in the air warmed by the fire, and the warmth seemed to stay inside her.

"Vienna," she said softly. "Lece says it is a beautiful city."

He studied Kaatje out of the side of his eyes, and she squirmed under his scrutiny. "No doubt your sister felt quite at home in Vienna," he said. "There are many women like her there." He clenched his fist. "Many women."

The roar of the river below them was a curtain of sound cutting off the outside world, but inside, Kaatje felt the sting of chagrin, of . . . jealousy. *Many women.* Why had she mentioned Lece?

"You were speaking of the army," Kaatje whispered.

He frowned and absently touched the healing cut on his temple. "You cannot heal all wounds, chatelaine," he said. "It is foolish to try."

His words slid under her pride and bit her. She flew

to her feet. "Perhaps I am a fool, colonel," she said, pacing the floor, her arms wrapped around her. "A fool to care when someone is in pain and a fool to respond to this tug inside me that wants to ease that pain. Perhaps I was a fool when I put sweet herbs under my husband's pillow to make his sleep easier. What good did that do him? Was I there when he needed me at Ramillies?"

Her pacing grew faster, more frantic. "I was a fool, indeed! I had his linen washed in rose water, his meats smoked with apple wood. I used only wax candles when he was at home. I sent him oats for his horses when he was in Italy and five twists of pepper when he was in Bavaria and the meat was not fresh."

She squeezed her eyes shut and clenched her skirt in her hands. "And still . . . *And still* that cannonball found him at Ramillies. I failed him."

Thorne loomed in front of her, his hands on her shoulders, stopping her frantic pacing. "Madame," he said, "I did not mean . . ." The pressure on her shoulders increased. "You must have loved your husband a great deal." The words sounded as if they had been torn out of him.

"No!" Kaatje pushed away from him, stumbling out of his hold. "No. Don't you see? I didn't love him at all! Even when he gave me my son, I did not love him. It was all just foolish trying."

"Madame, he was a soldier. He knew what his fate could be. You did not fail him. You could've done nothing."

"A soldier like you, is that it? And do you know your fate, Colonel Thorne? A c-cannonball? Someone washed your shirt till it was soft. Did you ever notice? Is that your fate? A cannonball through your soft linen shirt? And I can do nothing."

"Kaatje! Stop this."

"Why? Are these more wounds that can't be

healed?'' Anger pounded in her head. Anger at him for being a soldier, for shutting her out when she wanted to do the only thing she knew how to do—tend the deep wounds on his soul.

"What do you know of healing?" she shouted. "You can't even heal yourself. You don't *want* to heal yourself!"

"Madame . . ." he said, the words heavy with warning, but she ignored it.

"I did not love him—but I *cared*. He was the father of my son, my sweet Pietr.

"But what do you know of caring? What do you know of anyone's pain but your own? You brood dark and long on the sins of your El Müzir and my sister . . . What of *your* sins, Becket Thorne?"

Becket stepped toward her. It was too much. Her passion, her fire, her quick enticing movements. Something lunged inside him. And broke free.

He grabbed her arms and pulled her to him, her breasts crushed against him. "What of my sins, madame?" He slowly lifted her from her feet, bringing her eyes level with his. "Do you want to heal me? Is that it? Do you want to heal me of my *sins?*"

He nipped at her jawline, then bit her earlobe. "I give you fair warning, madame, of my *sins,*" he whispered into her ear, his breath hot against her skin.

Becket suckled the soft flesh beneath her ear and felt her gasp, the slight pressure against his chest making the beat in his veins faster, louder. Feeling her respond, feeling the tiny muscles contract under her soft warm flesh sent his blood rushing.

"And you *care* for me," he murmured against her skin. "I can feel it. But I do not want herbs under my pillow."

He dragged his open mouth down her neck and over the delicious curve where it met her shoulder. He nipped her skin where it disappeared under the fabric of her gown. It impeded him. He tore it off her shoulder and tasted her sweet soft flesh.

She turned her head from him, her eyes closed, her mouth parted. "Becket, I don't . . . I . . ." she began to whisper, but her words trailed off.

"You could still leave, be free of me," he said. "The moon is full. Follow the river. You would reach the castle near dawn." He turned her face toward him. "The margrave is a harsh lord—there would be no bandits. You would be safe.

"But if you stay—"

His gaze burned into her, the bold indigo dazzling her with its inner fire. He ran his hand over her hip. A thread of sound escaped her, but no words.

"Do not mistake me, madame. Tonight there will be no soldier, no chatelaine. A man. A woman." His voice was a low caress, filled with all the unsaid meaning that stretched taut between them.

Becket could feel his need for her pulsing into every part of him, like the drums at the beginning of battle, pounding, insistent, calling him to war.

He kissed her hard and deep, his tongue thrusting into her mouth, then twining around her tongue. Her hands went to his shoulders, then slid into his hair. He felt her body pulse with response, and a shudder went through him. The beat of her passion merged into the rhythm of his desire. His lips moved over hers in a long sensuous slide.

He pulled his mouth from her flesh, then let her body skim down his until her feet touched the floor. His fingers dug into her shoulders.

He tried to bring his will to bear. He should call back the challenge, but the sweet wet taste of her mouth was still on his tongue. He should tell her she didn't have to leave; she would be safe with him tonight.

Lies.

"Choose, madame. Safety—or my sins."

Chapter 11

The mill was silent, but for the rush of the river. They were alone, they were together, perhaps for the last time.

Kaatje touched Becket's hand where it held her shoulder, a warm insistent heat thrumming in her veins. "You are cruel," she whispered.

"Am I?" he asked, drawing the simple words out in a long seductive thread. He licked the soft flesh at her temple, then traced the glistening wetness with tiny sucking kisses. "Yet you do not leave."

He nipped at the hollow at the base of her neck. "Your face is beautiful in the moonlight," he said, his mouth tasting her where the swell of her breast began, "but it is not enough. Your hair turns to spun silver . . ." His tongue dipped into the valley between her breasts. ". . . but it is not enough."

"I know every subtle curve of your back, the feel of your hip pressed against my thigh as we ride, this soft roundness that entices . . ." He broke off his words and cupped her breasts through the material of her gown, then his hands slid around to her back and he drew his hands up her spine in one long stroke. "But it is not enough.

"Choose. I am not a man who is satisfied with part of a woman." He kissed her deeply, sucking her tongue into his mouth. His fingers slid into her hair and then he lifted his mouth only slightly from hers so when he spoke she felt the words coming from his lips.

"I want all of you, Kaatje van Staden. *All* of you. Full on."

Heated desire shimmered low in her body, mixing with a quivering fear. She slipped a trembling hand inside his unbuttoned waistcoat and felt his warm hard flesh through his linen shirt. His heart beat against her palm. A feeling of *rightness*, that she was destined for this moment, bloomed inside her.

"It is your battlefield, my lord colonel," she said, her voice husky. Some instinct made her lightly draw her fingernails over his torso. He drew in a quick breath, and the feel of it reverberated up her arm. "I do not leave."

Something flared in his eyes, and she stepped backward without being aware of it. Her shoulders smacked against the wall. He closed the distance between them, his muscular legs at either side of her, trapping her between them.

He pressed his hips, his swollen desire, against her stomach. His mouth took hers with a fierceness she had only glimpsed before, his tongue thorough and probing. Wood pressed against her back, but it was all part of the sensation that swirled around her.

With impatient fingers, he pulled the pins from her hair and scattered them over the floor. His mouth lowered, trailing hot wet kisses down her neck to the shadowed valley between her breasts. He buried his face there, a low growl rumbling deep in his throat.

With a violent tug, he pulled the lacing of her bodice from its bow, and then with quick deft fingers undid the lacings from their eyelets, the ends snapping as he pulled them free. He opened the front and pushed the sleeves of the bodice halfway down her arms, trapping them at her sides. The luscious swell of her breasts rose above the confinement of her stays.

The blood ran molten in his veins, hot, demanding. He ripped open the thin material of her chemise and tore off the ribbons that kept the sweet treasures of her body hidden from him. In a heartbeat her breasts were freed and he slipped his hands over the soft flesh, the rosebuds of her nipples hardening as his fingers rippled over them.

Kaatje gasped at the spark that shot through her, her back arching out into his hold. A groan came from deep inside him, and his head fell forward. He buried his face in her hair.

"Yes. Sweet God, yes, come to me." He rocked his hips against her stomach, his hands kneading her breasts and plucking the pink buds. Her head dropped to his chest, her eyelashes fluttering, and a soft mewing coming from her.

"The touch of you . . ." he said, his voice hoarse. "The touch of you makes me burn." He felt the exquisite tightening in his loins and he groaned against her hair.

She kissed his chest and felt the linen against her lips. It was in her way, and she tried to raise her hand to brush it away, but her sleeves still held her arms to her sides. She whimpered. "I want to touch you."

He slid his palms over her nipples, then down her arms to push the bodice completely off. He impatiently tossed it aside. Kaatje tugged at his open waistcoat.

"I want to touch you," she said again, her great gray eyes smoky with passion as she watched him shrug out of his waistcoat. "I want to feel your skin under my hands like the night I spread balm on your wounds." She looked at her hand in wonder and ran her thumb over her fingertips. "Does skin remember? Is there memory in our hands? My hand tingles as it did that night. I feel the heat, the slippery heat . . ."

She didn't wait for him to remove his shirt, but slipped her hands under it, sliding her fingers along the hard-muscled landscape of his stomach and chest. She felt him untie the waistband of her skirts, the limp material falling to the floor from its own weight.

She pulled his shirt off him with a hunger that she'd never felt before. She leaned against him, wearing only her petticoats, and drew her teeth along the high tight muscles of his chest.

He pushed her head back and kissed her. His hands gripped her bottom and he lifted her against him, her breath exhaled in a long wondrous gasp as her breasts slid up his chest.

Holding her to him, he kicked out her cloak and then knelt on it, taking her with him. He pushed her onto her back and balanced on his knees, towering over her, his eyes devouring her with a hot sweeping gaze. She rose to her elbow and touched him on the large hard swelling of his breeches, molding her hand around him.

"I feel a wanton," she whispered, "but I'm shaking inside to touch you, to . . . know . . . you."

He lightly covered her hand with his and drew it up the swollen length. "Touch me," he said, his voice uneven.

She met his hot gaze, her breath caught in her throat. Deep within her, the reckless thrumming urgency grew more insistent. Her eyes locked with his, she rose to her knees and pulled her hand from his hold. Her fingers unbuttoned the flap of his breeches. He stared into her eyes, breathing with quick shallow breaths. She slipped her hand inside the wool. The heat from his desire warmed her skin even before she touched him. His eyes were still, midnight pools. His breath was held, suspended.

She fit her hand around his phallus and he slowly closed his eyes and exhaled in a long sigh. She stroked him, the flesh of him hotter than any fever, and smooth, like seasoned oak.

"Sweet God, sweet God," he said. He put his hand in her hair and hugged her to him. His head fell back and his hips began moving against her caressing hand.

"What you do to a man, sylph," he said, the words a rumble in his throat. He stopped her hand and pulled it from his breeches, shaking his head as if to banish dizziness.

He pushed her onto her back and threw up her petticoat. He bit at her knee and licked the soft flesh behind it, his tongue hot and wet. His mouth raced up her thigh with soft biting kisses. He ran his fingers through the curls that grew at the crest of her thighs. "My golden sylph," he murmured.

She shivered and drew her knee up as if to protect herself. He kissed the woman-plump flesh between her legs. She gasped and put a fluttering hand on his head.

"No . . . what are you doing?" Her voice was thick from her passion, but he could hear fear trilling at the edges.

He kissed her again, dipping his tongue inside the glade of her womanhood and flicking the fountain of her pleasure.

Kaatje cried out, her hand clenching in his hair. "Becket . . . what are you doing? You're . . . you're . . . hurting me."

"Am I, sweet sylph?" he whispered against her, stroking her stomach to soothe her. "Am I?"

"I don't . . . know . . ."

Becket kissed her womanhood hard and deep, thrusting his tongue inside her as his loins burned to do. He flicked her source of pleasure.

"Oh, God! Becket! Oh, God. What . . . is . . . happening . . . to me?"

Her hand tightened in his hair. Her stomach shimmered against his hand. "Becket! Oh, God. Becket.

I'm scared . . . Please . . . Oh, God." Her hips rose to meet his tongue. "What are you . . . ? Oh, God. Oh, God." Her words trailed off on a long moan as she came closer and closer to her ecstasy. The moan strengthened and her body undulated against him, its long reined-in passion finally free, straining for the first crest of that soul-stealing pleasure.

He heard her sharp cry, a cry that exploded from deep inside her, just before he felt the sweet spasms of her pleasure. A sheet of white light filled Becket for an instant, as if her pleasure had fulfilled a kind of passion in his heart, while his loins still strove to claim their ecstasy.

He covered her body with his, his control fracturing. The tip of him entered her, and he sucked in his breath. It was exquisite. "Sweet sylph," he murmured, his voice thick.

He held himself on his elbows, his arms shaking, and rocked his hips to bring himself slowly inside her. She moaned a delicious moan and said, "Yes, oh, yes."

Kaatje swam in a silken sea. She felt the pressure of Becket's body and thought it the pressure of heaven. Her body throbbed with the echoes of the luxurious waves Becket had made wash over and through her.

She felt him entering her and sighed with the splendor of that sweet invasion. Ragged breaths buffeted her ear, and the smile on her face widened as she recognized the desperate want of his body. She embraced him and felt his muscles straining for release, her hands on the small of his back reveling in the movement of his hips.

Never again could there be such glory as what he'd just given her. Her hips began meeting the movement of his. Mmmmm, this felt good, so good. She stroked her fingers downward, exploring, caressing, her palms settling in the concave valleys at the sides of his bottom that tensed with each barely controlled thrust.

Could Becket ever feel what she had just experienced? Could she give him that? She heard his breaths growing more ragged, felt his arms trembling.

"Full on," she whispered.

He stilled, only his eyes looking, probing into hers. She thrust up her hips, seating him deeper in her. She gasped at the sensation, but he sucked in a deep, ragged breath.

"Sweet God." He thrust into her in one stroke and filled her completely.

A moan turned into a melody of tiny *ahs* that came from her lips as he thrust into her, then nearly withdrew, only to plunge in again. The glory was starting again, deeper, stronger, closer. She wrapped her arms around him and held on tightly as if he could keep her from falling off the edge of the world. Her hips rose and met his with each thrust, the rhythm of her body singing its own song of desire and passion.

He pounded into her. She dug her nails into his back. "Yes, oh, yes, oh, yes, oh yes . . ."

The rushing was in her ears, roaring, gushing, plummeting. "Oh, God. Becket . . . Becket . . ." She held on tighter, letting his body rock her higher and higher. Faster and faster his body plunged into hers.

"Sweet God. Sylph . . . Sweet God . . . Kaatje . . ." Becket shuddered, a primal groan ripping from his throat.

Her bones melted and the world exploded.

Kaatje slowly woke to the warmth of the early morning sun on her face. She smiled without opening her eyes, not wanting to let go of the delicious sweetness that oozed through her like honeyed wine. Her dreams had all been of Becket. That should bother her, she thought lazily, but it didn't. How foolish the dreams had been, though! No one could soar so high and touch the heavens or have such a soul-easing warmth radiating from the center of her heart and her body. No woman could have felt such glory from the steel-hard velvet of a man . . .

There was warmth too beneath her ear, accompanied by a strong steady beat that sounded like the heartbeat of the morning. She yawned and wriggled to stretch like a cat, and the warmth that enveloped her solidified into the body of a man.

Becket.

Her eyes snapped open. She saw a tanned landscape of sculpted muscle as she looked across his bare chest. The awakening awareness of sensation told her that her breasts were also bare and pressed into his side as she lay with her head cradled in the hollow of his shoulder. Wonder bloomed inside her, then increased tenfold, a hundredfold. The dreams had not been dreams.

She inhaled a thread of breath. How could such bliss be real? Fully awake, she let the memories of the night rush in on her. She remembered touching him, and his intimate kiss that flung her senses to heaven, her own luxurious abandon to the man who slept beside her, and the mind-shattering force when he filled her so completely.

She remembered the desire, the hunger that had driven her the night before. She closed her eyes to try and catch the memory of it, but it was elusive. The feelings were so new, so unknown, yet when they'd broken through the surface, she'd known they'd been there, deep inside her, like the bulb of a flower deep underground waiting for the warmth of spring.

She slowly pulled away from Becket's lean frame, careful not to rouse him. He moved in his sleep, his hand running down her arm.

"Sylph," he murmured. A delicate flush tinted her cheeks at the memory of his calling her that in the heat of their passion. She smiled all the same, unable to regret her wantonness, and she rose with her heart feeling light. She gathered the torn shreds of her chemise and stays, and the hastily discarded parts of her gown, and began to dress.

The chemise was beyond repair, even by a talented seamstress, and she tucked it inside the saddlebag Becket had given her. She fitted her torn stays around her and tied the ribbons closed as best she could.

She watched Becket sleeping as she laced her bodice, her fingers fumbling when she remembered the maelstrom of passion in his eyes and the strength of his hands as he'd pulled the laces free.

The power of the man, even in sleep, seemed to fill the room. She breathed it in, and a kind of lightheadedness overtook her. She gave up on trying to lace the bodice and quickly pulled on her skirt and tied it.

Kaatje struggled to clear her head. She had to get some fresh air. She slipped outside the old mill and twirled around in the fresh green grass, her feet dancing almost of their own accord. Acheron watched her with his huge black eyes as he slowly munched on the grasses that lay piled at his feet.

She curtsied her best curtsy to him, pulling her skirts out wide and sinking clear to her heels. "My lord stallion," she said with a soft laugh. The horse remained indifferent to her, but seemed to tolerate her silliness all the same. She ventured closer, holding out the back of her hand to him.

He sniffed it, then went back to munching. With a wide grin, she rubbed his soft black nose with the backs of her fingers.

"What a clever fellow you are," she said to him, her voice a soft croon. "I've seen draft horses bigger than you, but I don't think I'd want to put a saddle on one." She rubbed him with her fingernails. When she stopped, he nudged her, wanting more. "Yes, you like this don't you?" She laughed again and added in a whisper, "So does your master."

She felt giddy, all back and forth inside, like a wonderful blustery spring day, when the new leaves rustle on the trees and one minute the air smells sharp and crisp and the next luxuriant with the heady perfume of a damask rose. She wanted to hold on to it, not let it sink into melancholy.

Acheron nudged the hand that had stilled. "I know it feels good," she said, "but it can't go on forever." She paused, then gently rubbed his nose. "Nothing ever does."

Becket woke and knew he was alone in the mill, knew it with that deep knowing that slips by awareness and into that part of the mind where dreams come from. He rubbed his face and ran his hands through his hair.

The warmth of sated desire was still in his blood. He looked at his hands, hands that had held Kaatje's softness, felt the shimmer of her responding to his touch. Her naïveté had surprised him, and he'd had to slow his hunger. She was like a woman who had never been made love to.

What kind of fool had her husband been? Passion ran deep in her. It had made him shake with his need for her. He had tried not to hurt her, but when she had moaned her pleasure at his first entering her, he had nearly lost all control.

He rose with one smooth motion and strode to the door, buttoning his breeches as he went. Kaatje was there, with Acheron. A tension unknotted in his stomach, and he leaned against the jamb, watching the early morning sun turn her hair into a crown of gold richer than any king's.

She looked up at him with eyes filled with all her caring and passion and spirit. His chest tightened.

The sun sparkled with its morning newness. What does life feel like in the sun, he wondered. Does it become dry and brittle like a leaf in autumn? Or does each day, each season, bring new delights?

Kaatje watched Becket walking slowly, silently toward her. Every part of her tingled with awareness of him. He came up behind her, and his hands caressed her shoulders. He kissed her hair, then turned her slowly toward him, his lips nipping her flesh along the neckline of her gown. His fingers pulled out the few laces she'd managed to tie and she fell back against his arm as he stroked her breasts swelling above the loose stays.

He picked her up and carried her back into the mill. He kissed her as he gently lowered her to the tousled cloak, the kiss hard and deep and filled with the promise of glory.

The sun was near its zenith when they finally started out for the capital city. They followed a track along the river that soon widened into a road. Acheron was fresh and eager, but Becket held him back to a walk. Kaatje settled herself in the protected lee of Becket's arm and shoulder.

There was comfort there; the arm across her back was no longer stiff, the strong muscles molding to her as if he wished to be in contact with as much of her as he could. Beneath her, she could feel Becket's absolute command of the stallion, and a thrill went through her at the memory of that power commanding her pleasure.

The bliss of his lovemaking still pulsed in her veins. The day grew warm, and a capricious breeze cooled them at its whim, but none of it, not even time, could take away the delicious hot haze that shimmered just under her skin. She drowsed against Becket's chest, musing dreamily that things would work out. Somehow.

They crested a hill and Becket brought Acheron to a stop. Below them, to the east, spread the wide Aube valley, rich farmland thick with grain and neatly bisected by hedgerows. Cloud shadows chased each other in the light wind. In the distance stood the city of Hespaire-Aube, sparkling like a jewel held in an open palm, the castle high on the steep bluffs that overlooked the meeting of the two rivers.

Nearby, an inn nestled at the edge of the western woods.

"I did not realize how close we were," Kaatje murmured. "I wish it were on the other side of the world."

"In Cathay?" Becket asked, feeling a lightness inside that seemed unfamiliar and new. He tilted up her chin and kissed her gently, then rubbed his lips against hers. "The minute a mandarin saw you, he would lock you away with his other treasures. The only sight of the sun you would see would be your own reflection in a mirror of polished bronze." He let a loose tendril of her hair curl around his gloved finger, then he kissed the golden strands.

He wanted to laugh, just for the sheer joy of it. For the sheer *life* of it. He drew his thumb over Kaatje's lower lip and saw her eyelids flutter half closed. "What you have done to me, sylph," he whispered, and kissed her. It was thorough and deep, full of his thanksgiving for the light she had poured into his soul, full of his hunger for the woman who had heated his blood without anger or hate. And full of his goodbye, for they would soon part, and soon after he would be parted from her and from this earth forever.

The kiss ended slowly, with an exquisite bittersweetness. He raised his head from hers, but she stopped him with her hands on his face. Her fingers touched him, caressed him, as if she were blind and her memory was in her fingertips. A tear fell down her cheek.

He stopped her hands, kissing the palms, then said, hoarsely, "At that inn, I'll hire you a carriage and a maid so you can arrive at the castle as the lady you are." He kissed the palms of her hands again. "Madame," he said softly, making the word a long slow caress.

She gripped his hand tightly, then held it to her cheek. "My lord colonel," she began, but her voice failed her.

Becket kneed Acheron to a walk. Absorbed in the woman in front of him, he led them to the inn's hitching post and, with his arm around her waist, helped her slip off the horse onto the mounting block. He released her—and noticed the strange stillness for the first time.

The door to the inn slammed open, and Lece stood framed in the doorway, hands on her hips. "Well done, little sister," she said.

"Damn you," Becket growled at Lece, drawing his sword. She gave a negligent wave of her hand.

A dozen soldiers swarmed out of the woods and from behind the inn.

"No!" Kaatje screamed. "Lece, stop them!"

"Get the English dog!"

"Damn your blood!" Thorne roared in English at Kaatje, his eyes shards of blue-black ice. He wheeled Acheron around, kicking up dirt and dust. Shouts and curses rang in the air. The stallion reared at the wretches who attacked. His front legs kicked out, making the once-confident soldiers scamper back waving their swords.

Kaatje jumped off the mounting block and ran to her sister. "Order them to stop!" she shouted. She grabbed Lece's shoulder. "For God's sake, Lece." Her sister sneered at her and pushed her hand away.

A rash attacker darted toward the colonel. Kaatje screamed a warning. Thorne sliced his sword through him. The horse leaped toward the woods with a powerful push of his hind legs. The push ended with a deadly kick. Another attacker fell, his head kicked in.

The stallion neared the safety of the forest. A soldier took aim with a pistol. Kaatje threw herself at him. He toppled just as a shot ripped through the air. She saw Becket jerk, then shake his head.

"Becket!" Kaatje screamed and began running after him.

He looked back. At her. A dark stain spread on his left arm.

He slammed his sword into its scabbard, then took the reins with his sword hand. He turned his head away and kneed Acheron hard. The horse leaped into the thick underbrush.

"Catch the fool," Lece ordered, gesturing toward Kaatje.

Two men roughly grabbed Kaatje by the arms. "No! Let me go! He's been hurt!" They dragged her backward to her sister.

"These pale ones ain't worth the trouble," one of the men who held Kaatje said. "They's all weak and mewing."

"Release her," Lece said, ignoring their talk.

Kaatje spun around. Her head throbbed with both anger and anguish, but she looked at her sister with hate in her eyes. "What have you done?" she demanded. "What are you doing here?"

Lece glared into her sister's eyes. "Saving you, you little wretch. Don't count on me doing it again." She shook Kaatje. "You made us lose him, you fool. Oncelus will be enraged."

Kaatje took an involuntary step backwards. When Lece spoke of Oncelus, a light came into her sister's brown eyes that startled her, sickened her. "Lece . . . I . . ."

"I saw you kissing your black-haired Apollo on the hilltop. Red hair and bowed legs! Really, Kaat. Oncelus knew. Oncelus knew you'd lied to him. But I had to see it with my own eyes. Such duplicity from *sweet* little Kaatje. I should have known all that virtue was a sham."

Lece glanced at a nearby soldier. "Get the carriage," she ordered. The man ran toward the back of the inn.

She looked back at Kaatje. "You stupid child," Lece said and grabbed Kaatje's arm. A carriage rumbled around the corner of the inn, and Lece pulled her toward it. "You lied to Oncelus. That was futile. Did you think you could deceive *him?* He wants his property back."

"Property!" Kaatje's stomach knotted. The carriage door creaked open, but she resisted Lece's tug. "You disgust me," Kaatje spat. "What has become of you? We are talking of a man, Lece. An English colonel. He is owned by no one!"

"Get in! Claude is expecting us," Lece ordered, pushing Kaatje toward the carriage steps. "Oncelus wants his property back. That is all that matters to me."

"Oncelus won't get it," Kaatje snapped, but the force of her words was lost as she stumbled into the carriage. She fell into the forward seat and Lece sat opposite her. Kaatje pushed herself upright and straightened her skirts with a violent tug. "Oncelus won't get it," she said again. "And don't tell me Oncelus does not like to lose."

"I won't, sister," Lece said with a dark laugh. She leaned forward. *"Oncelus does not lose."*

Chapter 12

He's hurt. He needs me. She threw up the leather flap and leaned out the carriage window, straining for a glimpse back into the forest. She could see nothing but dark green shadows.

The carriage was old, and every rut it bounced over sent a jolt up Kaatje's spine. It was a torturous ride, but it was nothing compared to the pain that squeezed her chest.

He would hate her now. It felt as if a knife stabbed into the soft flesh of her stomach. *He would hate her forever.* She clenched her teeth, not wanting Lece to see her pain. Her lies had brought her to this. And she had only wanted to save him.

"Why, Lece?" Kaatje pulled her head back in. "Why did you come here? Why did you do this?" Kaatje watched her sister, sprawled in the seat opposite her.

Lece shrugged. "Oncelus wanted me to."

El Müzir, Kaatje corrected silently. She crossed her arms in front of her to keep from shuddering. How long had he and Lece been lovers? Could anyone be near him and not be tainted? Could Pietr?

Could Becket? A cloud moved across the sun, suddenly darkening the inside of the carriage. Kaatje rubbed her arms to ward off the omen. *Becket, I didn't know of this. I swear I didn't know.* How she hurt inside! She felt bereft, missing the power and strength at her back.

"What took you so long, little sister?" Lece asked her. Her tone was idly curious, but Kaatje saw the sharp look her sister gave her. "It only took us a day and a half to come by river. But then, we had no reason to dawdle."

Lece laughed when Kaatje did not answer. "Did you and your lover lose your way?"

"He's not my—" Kaatje began, then broke off, feeling her face flush.

"Not your lover? Of course he is. I know men, little sister. And I know you. You were kissing your *lover* on that hilltop." Lece laughed again.

Kaatje remained silent, watching smugness and arrogance flicker across Lece's face the way light reflected on the surface of a pond.

"You have much to learn about lovers, Kaat. If your next one ever kisses you like that, for God's sake pull him off his horse and into the bushes."

Kaatje clenched her hands together in her lap. "There will be no 'next one,' Lece," she said quietly.

Lece looked at her, surprised. "Fool," she said. "Do you suppose it's possible not to take lovers now? Do you suppose your body will let you? You're no longer the pinched-up widow you were a year and a half ago. You're a fool, Kaat. Your 'red-haired' lover took more than he gave you. He took the peace from your sleep."

Lece yanked down the leather shade to cover the carriage window. "Bah, you bore me," she went on. "Tell me why you said your lover had red hair. Did you *want* to give him away?"

"No!"

"You must work harder at deceit, then. To make us *not* believe you, you should have told the truth. If you wanted us to think he's short, you should have said he fills a doorway.''

"Lece . . ." Kaatje's cheeks flushed with anger at her sister's teasing. Had nothing changed between them?

"And if you wanted us to think he has spindly, underdeveloped legs that have a definite bow to them, what you should have said is that his thighs are like the trunks of an oak.''

"Stop this! I'm not fifteen anymore," Kaatje ground out.

"And if you wanted us to think he is French or Italian, why didn't you say he cursed you in English before he rode away?'' Lece threw herself back in the seat, laughing.

Kaatje looked away, shaking inside. Her sister's instincts had not dulled with the years. Kaatje bit her lip to keep the tears inside. She bit hard till she drew blood. Lece must know how it cut through her to know Becket's last words to her had been a curse. That the hate and rage in his eyes had been for her, for her betrayal.

Kaatje watched her laughing sister. Lece knew her too well. Her sister's aim at Kaatje's weak spots was always true; even as children, Lece's guesses about Kaatje's feeble little-girl secrets had always been right. But now there was more at stake than carefully bundled herbs strewn about or attempts to make a silly, worthless love potion.

Now they had grown. Now Kaatje had a woman's secrets. And Lece had a devil for a lover.

The wheels of the carriage clattered loud and rough over the cobblestones of the city streets. Kaatje clung tightly to the seat and clamped her jaw shut to keep her teeth from rattling out of her head. The way to the castle was steep, and slippery in the shadows of buildings where the slurry of mud seemed to eternally resist the sun.

The din abruptly stopped as they rolled onto the smooth stone bridge that led to the front entrance of the ancient castle. A half-dozen green-liveried servants swarmed down the wide front stairs to the carriage, opened the door, and snapped down the steps.

"Madame," one said, holding out a white-gloved hand. The word startled Kaatje. Curt, efficient, indifferent, not the warm caress it had been when Becket . . . She stifled the thought and took the servant's hand.

"I want to see Pietr," Kaatje told Lece as they were being led up the wide stone stairway.

"Little Pierre is fine. You have to see Claude first."

"I want to see Pietr."

Lece's brown eyes flashed in irritation. "Want all you want, Catherine. This is Claude's domain. He told me to bring you to him first."

Lece entered the castle with her face suffused with haughtiness. Imperious and demanding, she scattered servants to obey her orders and within minutes they were escorted to one of Claude's private rooms. The chamber was as big as the largest cavern at Cerfontaine. Lit wax candles in huge many-fingered candelabra glittered in front of gigantic gilt mirrors.

There were others there, three women and two men, all languid strangers with polished manners and cold eyes lounging in front of a large unlit marble fireplace. Lece went to join them, leaving Kaatje standing alone near a group of gold brocade couches and chairs that faced rich hangings by de Vos and Vouet.

Kaatje kept her eyes averted from the cavorting nymphs on the hangings and fought the urge to straighten her skirts and smooth her hair. Apparent indifference was the key, she remembered Philippe once telling her. "Never seem to care what others think of you," he'd said, then added, "when really, of course, that's *all* that matters."

Kaatje could feel the people by the fireplace studying her, though half a room separated them. One of the men glanced at the oldest of the three women, then at the double doors to his right. The woman nodded and stood, the others following suit.

The doors swung open, and two immaculately dressed servants bowed till their backs were parallel to the floor. Claude, Margrave of Hespaire-Aube, walked in, ignoring the bows of the servants and the obeisances of the group by the fireplace.

He came directly toward Kaatje. Dazed, she stared at him, unprepared for his resemblance to Philippe. With a start, she remembered to curtsy.

It was unsettling. A decade had separated the two brothers, but Claude, at forty-one, wore his brown periwig long and full, as Philippe had done. And his brown and green brocade coat was draped just so, the wide cuffs of the sleeves buttoned back with gold buttons the size of gaming pieces. But while Philippe had only begun to have lines etched around his eyes and mouth, Claude's cut deep from dissipation.

"Ah, sister," he said, flicking Kaatje under the chin. "I hear you've been traveling extensively of late."

"There was a battle at Odenaarde," she said, forcing herself to speak, "only a few miles from St. Benoit. We had to leave."

"Of course, my dear. Of course." Claude's manner was as languid as the others, but his amber eyes were sharp, searching, aware.

Two of the other women in the room snickered and put their heads together. "Would you look at that dress! At least we don't have to worry about *her*," one said in a loud whisper that was meant to be heard.

The other giggled. "I hear she only slept with her husband!"

"Or that only her husband would sleep with her!"

Lece glanced at her sister, then at the woman who'd spoken. *"When* did you hear that?" Lece said. Kaatje flushed.

The man snorted a laugh. "Say what you will, darlings. At least we know she's the only woman in the room Claude *hasn't* dallied with."

Claude bowed to him. "In the room? In the castle, I daresay."

The three women gasped with outraged laughter.

Claude gave a signal to a servant, "Now I wish to greet my sister-in-law in private." The lackey opened the doors and the five glided out, drifting wisps of laughter and giggles behind them. Claude cocked an eyebrow at Lece, who glared at him, but in the end, she too left. The doors shut with a snap.

When the margrave turned back to Kaatje, his languidness had gone. His gestures were brisk. "I am appalled by your conduct, madame. Your sister came to me, saying you were in some danger from an Englishman. Then my nephew arrives escorted by two redcoats.

"Really, Catherine, how tawdry. You are still my brother's wife and the mother of my nephew. How can I maintain neutrality if my own family seeks English protection? Think again if you believe I'll let you jeopardize my country."

He went to a delicate crystal decanter and poured a glass of dark red wine. He gulped it down in a swallow, then poured out another glassful. "Hespaire-Aube is but a dwarf's footstep in Europe. It takes skill, Catherine, and cunning to maintain a balance between the giants of France, Austria, England, and a dozen more that surround me. I will sacrifice anything—and anyone—that might upset that balance. Remember that, Catherine.

"Bah, how can I expect you to understand? You are

but a woman. The complexities are beyond you." He set down the empty wineglass. "But I did expect you to behave with more decorum, sister-in-law. How could you allow yourself to be abducted by a common soldier?"

"A common soldier?" Kaatje said, seething from his insults and now outraged at his attack. She was tired and thirsty and she wanted to see her son. "By your leave, sir, you heard wrong. No, he was far more than that! I could hardly *let* myself be abducted by anyone less than an English lord, now could I?"

"Ah, a title," answered Claude. "It does help fade the stain of a soiled reputation, doesn't it?"

"Soiled! And what of those *exemplary* women who were here earlier?"

Claude closed the gap between them and grabbed her chin, forcing her to look into his eyes. "You must learn the difference between indiscretion and wit, my dear. I have let you remain alone at St. Benoit for too long. Freedom gives a woman such foolish notions."

Kaatje pulled her head out of his hold and walked a few paces away. "I want to see my son."

Claude watched her, eyes narrowed, assessing. "Pierre has settled in nicely. He'll be rid of his provincial air in no time."

Inside, Kaatje seethed, but she felt relief all the same. "I'm glad to hear he arrived safely," she said calmly, while silently she screamed, *I want to see my son!* "And Grette?"

Claude looked puzzled for a moment, then comprehension dawned. "Ah, the crone who was with him. I suppose she's here." His gaze trapped Kaatje's. "I had forgotten her. That makes two women in the castle with whom I haven't . . . dallied."

Kaatje turned away. "What of the men who escorted Pietr?"

"What of them? They were dismissed immediately,

of course. No doubt your redcoats have run back to Odenaarde to share in the spoils of their victory. Should I have imprisoned them for you? Philippe never mentioned that your tastes ran to such things.''

Kaatje dug her fingernails into her palm and fought the anger that was choking her. She glared at the man who was the absolute lord of all the lands drained by the Hespaire and the Aube rivers. Absolute lord of this castle and all who were in it. Including Pietr.

''My tastes do not,'' she said evenly. ''I wanted to thank them.''

Claude shrugged. ''Pity. Perhaps Philippe wouldn't have complained of you so much if you had been more adventuresome.''

Kaatje looked away. ''May I see Pietr now?''

Claude chuckled as he reached for a small bell, but he stopped his hand and looked at her, his gaze traveling from the hem of her skirts to her face. ''I remembered you as a pale, trembling Flemish mouse.'' He rang the bell. ''I remembered wrong, it seems.''

A servant silently opened the doors and bowed to Claude. ''See to her,'' the margrave told him, his languid manner back in place. ''And see that she is given suitable clothing for this evening's ball.''

''Ball!'' Kaatje said with a gasp. ''I can't . . .''

''Really, my dear, this penchant of yours for peasant clothing goes too far. It is affecting your manners.'' He waved a hand in dismissal.

Rage made Becket's sight shimmer black at the edges. Merchant stalls to either side of him flickered in and out of his vision as he walked up the main trading street of the capital. He felt nothing inside, not even the niggling sting of the flesh wound on his arm. He felt nothing—but cold dark fury.

She'd betrayed him.

He led Acheron by the reins, walking with long

forceful strides, his boot heels clipping on the cobblestones. The merchants of Hespaire-Aube were growing fat and rich off the war, selling supplies to both sides. On seeing a redcoat approaching, they beamed and opened their mouths to call out their wares. But when they saw his face, their mouths snapped shut and they bustled their womenfolk into the shadows at the back of their stalls. Becket ignored them.

A tall gangling youth tried to skip backward out of Becket's way, but the boy stumbled and fell. Becket halted.

"You there," he called. The boy stared up at Becket from the cobblestones, terror making his eyes seem to pop. "Boy!"

The merchants fell silent and the few customers they had gawked with slack jaws. The youth dipped a single nod.

"S-s-sir?"

Becket knelt in front of him and the boy tried to scamper backward. "Tell me where there are any abandoned buildings. Any places not used anymore."

The boy's eyes caromed from side to side in panic. "D-d-don't know of none, s-s-sir."

"None?" Becket dug into his pocket and held out a Dutch gulden, more money than the boy was likely to see in a year. "None?" Becket repeated.

The youth's eyes abruptly focused on the gold shining against the black suede of the colonel's glove. "They'd think I napped it," the boy whispered.

"With all these witnesses?"

The boy glanced at the watching crowd, and the gold disappeared into his breeches. "Maybe down by the Hes," he said, jerking his head toward the eastern river. "Or Crisp's."

The boy scurried away and Becket headed for the barge docks along the Hespaire River. It was taking too long to find Niall Elcot and Harry Fludd. Becket seethed inside, and it darkened his face and made his eyes flash with rage. People saw him and backed away.

Keep searching, keep walking, he told himself, leading Acheron up to one occupied building after another. But the search served only as a bellows for his anger.

Betrayal.

The word stabbed him. It is ended. She is nothing. El Müzir's heart waited to be spitted on his sword, that was all that mattered.

But her betrayal ate deep. She had slid in through his defenses, deeper than the marquise had ever done. Kaatje! The crisp-soft name echoed in his head, like passing bells ringing at a death. He squeezed his eyes closed to concentrate on blocking out the image of her. He wanted to get on with his fight, to finish what he'd started. He growled, a long, fierce, wordless sound.

A thin old man jumped out of Becket's way and smacked against a dray cart.

"I ain't done nothing, sir! I swear!"

Becket looked up, eyes narrowing as he focused on the old man shivering in the warm sun.

"Crisp's," Becket said. "Tell me where to find a place named Crisp's."

The man scrambled to back up further, as if he wanted to melt into the cart.

"Crisp's," Becket hissed, taking a step toward the man. "Why don't you answer? I won't harm you."

"No, sir. No, sir," the old man said. He gulped, making his Adam's apple bob. " 'Course not, sir."

Becket saw the man's eyes start to roll up, as if he were about to pass out. He took a step back. "Old man," he said, sheer will making the tone of his words less threatening. "I will not harm you."

Large, frightened rabbit eyes blinked at him.

"I seek two friends." Becket wanted to lunge at the man and choke the answers out of him, but he held back. Before, he would have just demanded the directions, a dagger at the man's throat if need be. But that was before he'd met a certain chatelaine.

Get out of my blood. Rage at her suffocated him. He clenched his fist. It took every dram of his control not to vent his fury on the hapless man.

"I was to meet my friends in an abandoned building." Becket shook his head as if trying to break something free inside. "There are none. It seems that Claude doesn't allow unused lumber and bricks to sit idle. My only hope is a place called Crisp's."

"C-C-Claude, sir? You mean his highness?" Becket nodded once in answer, and the man's gaze slid to the castle on the hill behind Becket, then back to the colonel. "Crisp's be an abbey, sir. St. Crispin's o' the Vale."

"I've seen no abbey here."

"It be mostly tore down, sir. His highness's great grandfather caught the abbot with his wife." The man laced his fingers together and wiggled them. "They was together, sir. If'n you get my meaning. 'Tain't nothin' up there holy no more. The bishop came and took away the blessings on it."

"Where?"

"East o' the castle, sir, just up the hill from a little stream that runs in the spring and summer."

Becket flipped him a gulden, and the old man caught it out of the air with surprising agility.

"Blessings on you, sir," the man said and scuttled away.

Becket stood there after the man had gone, alone and silent, snapping Acheron's reins against his riding boots.

"Blessings on me, old man," he said bitterly. He led the stallion to a water trough and let him drink. Becket studied the castle high on a bluff where the two rivers met, pain leaping up inside him like a flame catching on dry wood. He clenched his jaw against it. Anger. Anger, that's what he wanted to feel. Bury the pain.

She was an artist, that one. He'd thought her a lady. Her gentle voice and gracious manners had fooled him. And her touch. Her caring. Her innocence. He remembered how little she'd known of loving, and yet how she had made his body quicken.

But her touch was false. Her caring was a lie. And her innocence . . .

Damn your blood, woman. Anguish throbbed through his veins. *Damn you.* She had given him hope, hope that the beast inside him could be quelled. But now it raged strong. *Damn you.*

He stared at the castle, eyes squinting against the bright sun. Was she up there laughing with Lece? With El Müzir? The thought stabbed into his mind like a cold knife.

Becket pushed away from the wall. Sweet Jesu, was she with El Müzir? Becket began walking toward the castle. His hand went to his sword hilt, fingers tightening around it until the silver bit into his palm. Acheron nickered behind him and he halted, his gaze still intent on the castle.

No, he vowed silently, crushing the pain that ate through him like the bite of a viper at the thought of Kaatje with . . . No, he'd been this close before to that night-souled devil and had lost him.

Becket's eyes narrowed. *She* was a weakness in him, a weakness that had to be purged. In that castle, he vowed, in there she would meet her fate at his hands.

"Blessings," he hissed out, the word a curse. "Pray to God for his blessings, Kaatje van Staden de St. Benoit, because only He can save you from your betrayer's fate. Only He can save you from *me.*" Becket willed the black ice to come, to armor him. He mounted Acheron and headed toward the abbey, the coldness and darkness settling in him as if they had never gone.

* * *

   "Mama!" Pietr shrieked and ran across his bedroom toward Kaatje, leaving his valet frowning by the window, holding a pale blue brocade coat behind him. "Niall said you'd come. He did! He did!"

   Kaatje knelt down with arms wide open, and Pietr flew into them, wrapping his slender arms tightly around her neck. She hugged her wriggling son to her, unable to speak. Pietr was safe. Tears streamed down her face.

   "Niall said Kern Torn was the bestest for my mama." Pietr pushed back slightly to look up at her. "Niall was right, wasn't he, Mama? Kern Torn was the bestest for you, wasn't he?"

   "Kern Torn?" Kaatje asked with a laugh, then immediately knew the answer. "Oh. Colonel Thorne." Her laughter evaporated, leaving her with a lump in her throat. She smoothed her son's hair. "Of course, sweetheart. The bestest."

   The valet clicked his tongue in disapproval. "Monsieur Pierre! Have *all* your lessons been forgotten, sir?"

   Kaatje felt her son's small body stiffen. He wiggled out of her hold and bowed to her from the waist, his shoulders pushed back and his neck unbending. His forehead was puckered in a frown as he said, in a monotone, as if by rote, "I am pleased to see you have arrived safely, Mama."

   "Madame my mama," the valet corrected.

   Pietr's chin trembled slightly as he repeated the valet's words. "Madame my mama."

   "Really, this isn't necessary," Kaatje said.

   The valet looked shocked. "Madame. Monsieur Pierre is a chevalier. His dignity must be maintained."

   "But he's only six . . ."

   "I know, I know, madame, already six and so far behind," the valet said, shaking his head and pursing his lips. He straightened his narrow shoulders. "But his highness has the utmost faith in me to work miracles.''

Kaatje stepped between her son and the valet. ''Pietr is not behind!'' she told him, trying to keep a rein on her temper. If Claude was involved, she had to tread carefully.

The valet winced at the boy's Flemish name. ''Madame, please. His highness gave me specific instructions. You are only his mother.'' He gave the little blue coat a shake. ''Now, if you please, we must return to our lesson. Proper grooming is vital to a person of his station.'' He looked at her tattered, bedraggled clothes and sniffed, then lowered his eyes to Pietr. ''Monsieur Pierre,'' he said, ''attend.''

Pietr's sweet face, which had been so open and bright when he'd seen her, now looked sad. Without thinking, Kaatje swooped him off his feet and swung him around. ''I'm so proud of you, my little rock,'' she whispered in his ear, her throat tight.

''Madame!''

She kissed Pietr's forehead. ''Colonel Thorne said you were very very brave.''

''He did?'' Pietr asked her with a squeal of excitement. She nodded and set him down. There was a smiling light in his eyes as he straightened his shoulders and gave her another formal bow. She curtsied to him and winked, and he gave her a secret smile.

She went to the door, a servant opening it for her before she could reach it. She turned in the open doorway and said, ''I'll see you in the morning, Pietr.'' She looked at the valet with a challenge in her eyes.

The man looked uncomfortable and tugged on his cuffs before saying, ''He will be finished with his prayers at six in the morning. You may have a few moments with him then.''

Kaatje nodded slightly in acknowledgment and left. She followed the stiff-backed servant through the newly renovated wing, but saw little of it. A movement at her right caught her attention, and she turned her head to see the reflection of a bedraggled blond woman in a gilt-framed mirror. Tension bunched her shoulders, and she forced them to relax. She glanced at the glistening marble bust of a Roman goddess in a carved niche, but Kaatje was too weary to envy the perfect coolness of the divine features.

The servant led her down one hallway, then another, then through a gallery into the old part of the castle. They went through a large empty salon with huge, forlorn-looking tapestries on the walls, then another, one room leading off another in a maze. At last the servant stopped and threw open a set of wide double doors, then stood aside for Kaatje to pass.

"A maid will be with you shortly," he said, then bowed and left.

She entered with an uneasy mind. The first room was the sitting room, a pair of gilt and brocade chairs set neatly in front of a large marble fireplace, a chessboard between them. Hand-sized, minutely detailed knights of Charlemagne stood ready to fight the opposing Saracens in a fresh Crusade.

The room was nearly suffocating in its ostentation. Gilt cherubs leered at her from table legs, their chubby fingers grasping the thick marble tabletop. A bombé chest perfectly reflected the flame of a candle glittering in a rare wood sconce that smelled faintly of beeswax. Deep swags of floral brocade draperies looped around the room, making her think someone had turned a ball-gown inside out.

Kaatje slid her fingertips over the glossy surface of a writing desk, her uneasiness turning to bitterness. She spun around, twirling in place until the heavy colors, smells, and textures all wrapped dizzily around her like thick, choking smoke.

All those letters she'd written to Claude. All those

dreams she'd had of her son, here in this castle, claiming his heritage. All those lies she'd told Becket. For this. All for this.

She flattened her palm on the marble tabletop. "Feel that," she whispered to herself. "Feel that cold seeping into your skin. That's the feel of safety. That's what those dreams and letters and lies bought you. This cold safety."

She squeezed her eyes shut. "Becket, forgive me. I only wanted to keep you safe." She scraped her fingernails on the marble. *Safe.*

"That need polishing, ma'am?" a young woman asked from behind her. Kaatje turned. A maid stood there, dressed in a simple blue gown with a white apron, a smile on her spritely face.

"No," Kaatje said, hugging herself tightly.

The maid curtsied. "I'm Cècile, ma'am. Are you cold? I can have a fire laid. A short nap, perhaps? There's a little time 'fore your bath arrives. Then the dressers will be here."

Claude's ball. Kaatje had forgotten. She shook her head and tried to smile. "Don't bother with the dressers. I'm not attending the ball tonight."

The maid looked stricken. "Not attend! Please, ma'am—his highness commanded you." She gestured wildly toward the bedroom. "I've found the prettiest dress! You must go. Oh, my, what can you be thinking?"

Kaatje stood by the chessboard, watching the young woman wring her hands, and remembered Becket saying that Claude was a harsh lord. "I was thinking of . . ." *My lover.* ". . . someone I once knew," she said, picking up the white king. Charlemagne. Legend said he was tall and strong and powerful.

"Please, ma'am. It's such a pretty dress. It's pink with ells and ells of silver lace."

Kaatje picked up the king of the Saracens in her other hand. Cunning and clever and powerful.

The Englishman and the Turk. Becket and El Müzir.

Kaatje squeezed the chess pieces. Two enemies so evenly matched that neither could win. She threw the pieces onto the board, then turned her back on the set, smothering the bleak feeling that both Becket and her son's future were in peril of being destroyed.

But Becket was already lost to her forever.

And her son still needed his medicine. And she still needed Lece to obtain it for her.

"Cècile," Kaatje said, "show me the dress." She would play Claude's game. Whatever had happened to her, Pietr still had his future before him.

Kaatje had to believe that. She had to.

Chapter 13

T he abbey was a ruin. Roofless high walls stood stark against the blue sky, the jagged profile echoing the harsh stone ridge on which it had been built. Becket kneed Acheron up the last rise and headed toward the back, where a room or two looked still intact. The stallion carefully picked his way through the light gray stones that littered the ground.

"Colonel!" Niall Elcot rose from the shadows cast by the tumbled walls, a wide grin of relief on his face. "Colonel! You're here!"

"As you see," Becket answered, dismounting. He kept every movement precise and unhurried; it was the only way for him to keep control of the fury that spumed inside him.

The lieutenant leaped over a short wall and jogged through an overgrown kitchen garden to reach the colonel.

Becket offered his hand and Niall took it. "Welcome, sir," he said, his smile falling when he saw the look in his commanding officer's eyes.

"I take it Oncelus wasn't at Cerfontaine," the lieutenant said. "I'm sorry, sir."

"I did not find Oncelus at Cerfontaine. That does not mean he wasn't there," Becket corrected.

"Was he?"

"I do not know."

"But the widow . . . ?" Niall asked, the question trailing off.

"Indeed," Becket said. " 'But the widow.' " He saw the confused look on his lieutenant's face, but didn't explain.

"Anyway, sir," Niall went on nervously, "it was a throw o' the bones whether the widow would know where her sister and Oncelus had holed up. No need to blame yourself for a bad throw." Niall paused. "It is good to see you again, sir. The last time we saw you, we weren't sure we'd ever see—"

"Thank you, lieutenant," Becket interrupted. He tossed the reins to Niall, who caught them with a flourish. The colonel smacked the stallion affectionately on the neck. "He needs a thorough rubdown—and a bucket of oats. Loyalty should be rewarded."

"Of course, sir," Niall said, leading both Becket and the horse toward the rooms at the back of the abbey.

"Halloo! Harry!" the lieutenant bellowed, waving his arm toward a small window hole set in one of the still-intact walls. "The colonel's here, Harry. He made it!"

Harry Fludd popped his head out of the window and waved excitedly as the two soldiers walked past. He leaned further out, squinting at the colonel's arm. "That's a bullet hole, kern'l," he said accusingly. "That widow give you trouble?"

Becket looked at his servant, his jaw set. Harry glanced nervously at Niall.

"Stop flappin' your gums, man," the lieutenant said with forced good humor. "Can't you see the colonel's bear-hungry?"

"Jus' askin'," Harry mumbled, and ducked back inside.

Silently, Niall led Acheron to a lean-to stable, darting worried looks at the man who walked beside him.

"The boy?" Becket asked, irritated at himself for wanting to know. He hitched his hip onto a half wall and pulled off his gloves as he watched Niall begin to rub down Acheron.

"Little Pietr?" Niall said, flashing a wide grin. "What a great gun, sir. Bravest little tyke. We had some tough spots just on the other side of the border and that firm little Flemish chin of his started to shake, don't you know. Ole Harry thought the game was up, but I whispered to the little guy that it was all right for a soldier to miss his mama, it being cold and rainy and all. One way or another, I told him, we all fight for a woman."

Becket cocked his eyebrow skeptically.

Niall flushed and rubbed Acheron harder, his eyes following his hand with frowning concentration. "I was speaking of her majesty, the queen, colonel," Niall's voice said. "That, and . . ." The lieutenant disappeared on the other side of the war horse.

Becket slapped his gloves against his palm, not liking the tone of the last two words. "And *what*, lieutenant?"

"Well, sir, once we crossed over the border, we slipped past a good three score of French soldiers. Acting like curs, they were, not like regular army. And the little fellow was worried about his mama, so me and Harry kinda told him you was protecting her." Niall glanced at Becket from under Acheron's neck. "It did seem to calm him, sir. She is all right, isn't she?"

Becket stood. "The last time I saw her," he said, "she was entirely in her element." He went to the horse's trough and threw water on his face, then rubbed briskly.

"That's good to hear," Niall said. "She seemed full of pluck when we . . . er, met her on the road outside Odenaarde, but you never—"

"Tell me more of these soldiers, lieutenant." Becket

scraped his hands through his wet hair. "I met a few earlier today. They could be Roulon's men."

"Roulon?" Niall asked, then shook his head. "Don't know, sir. They're settling upriver along the Hespaire. Loud and swaggerin' they are—hard to think the margrave don't know about 'em."

"I'm sure he does, lieutenant. Claude rarely lets anything pass him by."

Niall nodded. "That would explain the extra guards at the castle, then. Harry! Didn't you see new flintlocks being unloaded before we got chased off? Harry!"

Harry planted himself in the middle of the doorway and crossed his arms over his barrel chest. "What ye want? I'm fixin' the kern'l somethin' t' eat."

"Flintlocks. How many of em?"

Harry grunted and spat. "B'ttalion's worth, I'd say."

"Right," Niall said, turning back to the colonel. "An' some of the footmen and such have that checking-over-their-shoulder kind of look."

"Neutrality is not an easy thing to maintain," Becket said. "Claude could just be taking precautions." He looked west, toward the castle, squinting into the late afternoon sun. "Or he might have something he wants to keep all to himself." Becket's gaze snapped to the lieutenant. "Such as a weapon."

"Lucifer's Fire," Niall whispered, eyes wide.

"Have you come across any of Oncelus's usual telltale signs?"

The lieutenant thought for a minute, then shook his head. "None that I've heard of. No disappearances. No unexplained dead bodies."

Becket looked back at the castle, his fingers flexing, then balling into a fist. "He's there all the same."

Bloodlust suffused Niall's face. "In the castle, sir?"

Becket nodded, then frowned. "But it means nothing," he said, gripping the young man's shoulder. "We've been this close before—and good men have paid for our failure to find him with their lives.'' Becket felt the hate bubbling in him like lye in a caldron. He kicked the wall, and a stone cracked out of its mortar.

Denten, Wortley, Meadows . . . all dead. Two and a half years ago, outside Köln, Becket and three others had surrounded a tavern where the Turk had set up shop. Becket drew in his breath with a hiss, remembering how he had savored his imminent victory—until he'd found Denten and the others with their throats cut.

And then, six months ago, he and Segan had run the devil to ground at Chateau d'Agenais. It had been dangerous for them to be so deep in the French countryside during the war, but their orders from Marlborough had made their presence there imperative. And Becket would've been there without orders.

Posing as Italian bankers on a leisurely journey to Paris, they had stayed at a local inn. But Segan had proved too fond of the Chevalier d'Agenais's wife, a dark-haired beauty who claimed her ancient husband left her much too lonely. Becket had discovered Segan's body, unmarked but for the contortions of agony that had made his face almost unrecognizable. He'd been poisoned, and both El Müzir and Lece d'Agenais had disappeared.

"Damn it!" Niall spit out. "You would've had him at d'Agenais if Segan hadn't fallen for that chevalier's wife. I'd never let myself be trapped by a woman like that!''

Becket looked at the red-haired lieutenant, feeling as if the gulf between him and the young man were a thousand leagues wide. He turned his back on Niall and stared at the outline of the castle, black against the setting sun.

Feel a woman's body next to yours and say that, Becket thought bitterly. *Feel her warm and soft and smelling of summer flowers. Feel her caress your brow and murmur lovingly into your ear. Hear her laughter*

*as it lifts away the heavy weight of your black dreams.
And wonder when even her anger touches you and
makes your body and mind sing.*

And when she lies with you . . .

Becket squeezed his eyes shut and shook his head.
"Never be trapped by a woman, lieutenant?" he said
aloud. He opened his eyes, and his gaze held Niall's.
"You don't even feel the net."

The lieutenant was the first to look away.

Harry stomped into the lean-to. He looked puzzled
and out of his depth, his gaze bouncing back and forth
between the two soldiers. "Don't know 'bout no nets,"
he said, holding out a pewter plate to Becket. "A bit
o' venison from his 'ighness, kern'l."

Becket took the proffered food and ate.

"His highness," Niall said with a laugh. "You mean
that bold hussy in his highness's kitchens. Nearly devoured poor ole Harry here, sir."

Harry tugged on his breeches. "Bold enough to fetch
us some meat for our supper."

"Which you *earned,*" Niall added.

Harry grinned. "Leastways I didn't just sit up here
frettin' and worryin'."

"Fretting! Would you listen to that! And after I saved
your arse I don't know how many times. You wasted
half the day in those kitchens."

"I 'ad to get in somehow, didn't I?" Harry jerked
his head toward the castle. "What's a body to do? Ask
for an invitation?"

Becket threw the empty pewter plate onto the stone
floor at Harry's feet. It hit with a clang. "That's exactly
what we'll do. Niall, you'll remain here. Harry will
accompany me as my valet. El Müzir moves fast and
quick through the shadows, but the van Staden sisters
are surrounded by shadows and he's bound to stay too
long in one of them. And I plan on being there when
he does."

Niall's eyes narrowed suspiciously. "You can't just walk up and ask for an invitation. Think of the risk! You're an English colonel."

Becket took a deep steadying breath and held it for a long minute, then blew it out in a gust. "I knew the margrave a long time ago," he said. "And sometimes old acquaintances eclipse new allegiances."

"Now, kern'l," Harry said, "I been wi' ya for nigh on seven years and we ain't never come within a 'undred miles of this place."

Becket held up his hand. "A long time ago." He leaned stiff-armed against the stone wall as if to anchor himself. "In Vienna, Harry. I knew Claude in Vienna."

Becket heard their feet shuffle in the dust and weeds that were strewn across the stable floor.

"Oh," Niall said and swallowed audibly. "Oh."

"We's, ah . . ." Harry began, then broke off and cleared his throat. "We's can find us a way in, kern'l. But first, why not let me take a look at that arm of yours . . ."

Becket raised his head. *Vienna.* The word—all by itself—used to stab him. And the memories it conjured would press on him so heavily that he couldn't breathe. He inhaled deeply, smelling the sharp stable-smell and the heat and dust of the hot summer afternoon. His gaze narrowed on the distant castle.

You have weakened my armor, woman. Weakened the demons that give me power. Was that your plan? Rage and fury billowed through him like thick dark smoke from a deadly fire, but coiling through the smoke was a thin wisp of anticipation. Becket smiled like a wolf. *Your plan did not succeed, madame. You did not weaken the beast—and it* takes *what it needs.*

"Pink!" Lece laughed shrilly, her hands on her waist as she circled her sister in Kaatje's bedroom. "My God,

Kaat. Pink! Only a blond would think she could wear such a color. But at least your nap did your face some good.'' Lece fingered the silver lace that edged the perilously low neckline, and tsked, then spun around and headed for the door.

Kaatje spread the pink satin skirts around her. The image in the mirror looked back at her wide-eyed and unhappy. Until Lece had arrived, she'd thought she'd turned out quite passable. She had even wished Becket might see her and look at her again with that certain light in his eyes. She met her sister's gaze in the mirror and straightened her shoulders.

"Actually, I think the color is closer to a soft damask rose," she said, and risked a deep breath for courage. "Certainly a brunette would not show to advantage in it."

"Oh, hurry up!" Lece said, stalking back into the bedroom. "Auriac's here with his wife—he can't stand her!—and I want to be there when he introduces her to his mistress." Lece saw herself in the glass and frowned. She put her hands to her waist as if to measure it and twisted around to view herself from the back. "Do you think that bumbling half-wit Claude gave me as a maid pulled my stay laces tight enough? I'll be mortified if my waist doesn't look small enough."

Lece laughed again and grabbed Kaatje's wrist and pulled her out of the room. They hurried through a long gallery, and Kaatje heard the music and smelled the scented wax of the candles long before she and Lece arrived at the threshold of the ballroom. Lece waited impatiently for the steward to announce them.

Candlelight shone everywhere, the brightness glittering on the guests' jewels as they made their murmuring and giggling way around the enormous room. Men and women dipped and swayed as they danced in the middle of the room. A ring of columns circled the edge, supporting an open gallery that looked down on the ballroom. They were announced, and Lece stepped in front of Kaatje and glided in ahead of her.

"Damn," Lece muttered. "Auriac's already here. The wretch. He must've known we'd all want to watch."

Kaatje's gaze followed Lece's and she saw a glum-looking young woman with hair the color and, unfortunately, the texture of wet sand standing next to a thin, sharp-nosed man whose face could barely be seen lurking in the shadows of his huge brown periwig. On his other side stood a stunning creature, all glossy brunette hair and creamy skin.

Lece shrugged. "I used to think Auriac wasn't too bad as a lover. And I suppose I might still think so, if I hadn't . . ." Her words trailed off and she looked sharply at Kaatje.

"Missing your lover yet?" Lece asked. "Don't look so shocked. It starts as a tingle in here—" She rubbed her stomach. "And you drink a little more, thinking maybe it's thirst. And you eat a little more, thinking it's hunger. And then your eyes start following a man's hands as he gestures and talks, and your mind starts wondering what those hands would feel like touching you."

"Lece, please!" Kaatje smoothed her skirts, her eyes darting around her at the groups of chatting men and women. She caught a small, carelessly dressed man appraising her, and she turned her back on him.

"No, you're right," Lece said. "You don't want Guillon, little sister. He's as sloppy in bed as he is in his dressing closet."

Kaatje stared straight ahead, clenching her hands together in front of her, and forcing her eyes to follow the dancers in a lively bourrée. Someone walked behind her, and she felt a puff of breeze against her spine, emphasizing the emptiness there.

How she missed having Becket close to her, his

strong arm firm across her back. She gripped her hands together tighter. But he would never be there again. Wherever she looked, in front, to either side, behind her, it would always be empty of Becket.

She could feel Lece's eyes studying her. "Then again, perhaps you don't need to find a *new* lover, little sister. Perhaps the one you had still hovers about?"

"No!"

"The stables, perhaps? Or the attics?"

"Stop this," Kaatje whispered. "I don't know where he is."

"There's Claude over there. See? Talking with that red-faced Spaniard. He might know where your lover is. Shall we go ask him?"

"Why are you doing this?"

"Why are you protecting that Englishman?" Lece dug her fingers into Kaatje's shoulder and shook her, then stopped abruptly as if she'd remembered where she was. She tugged Kaatje by the wrist to the edge of the room and pushed her against a marble column. "You don't think he *loves* you, do you? You can't be such a fool. Letting a man grope you in the dark will hardly make him *love* you."

"Stop talking like that," Kaatje said in an urgent whisper. "Can you think of nothing else? You know I'm here for Pietr!"

"That's not the whole of it. Not anymore." Lece shook Kaatje's shoulder again. "You can be such a little fool. I know who your lover is, little sister. I know your Englishman's name. I know he can kiss you till your knees give way."

Kaatje stared at her sister. Another one of Lece's guesses? "I tire of your bullying, sister."

Lece lowered her voice to a low whisper, so low Kaatje could barely hear it above the noise of the crowd.

"And I know he calls you sylph."

The floor reeled beneath her feet. Kaatje stared at

her sister, not caring who saw the stunned hurt that poured from her face.

Lece hissed and turned away. "You don't have to look so betrayed," she said angrily. "He didn't bed me. But he is a man, little sister. Do you think he doesn't call all his whores sylph?

Kaatje stared into the dozen flames of a nearby candelabrum, breathless with hurt. Her sister talked at her, demanding, then cozening, but Kaatje didn't hear, didn't answer. *Is that true, Becket? Was I just another one of your* . . . She bowed her head, squeezing her eyes shut against the pain.

Long moments later, she straightened and saw that her sister had abandoned her. Of its own accord, her gaze played over the glittering crowd. The music stopped, and the noise of the hundreds of murmurs and whispers buffeted her like the wind on a stark winter day.

She saw the back of a tall, dark-haired man, and her breath caught. Her eyes bored into him as if she were trying to will him to be a certain English colonel. *Sylph*, she heard Becket say in her mind.

The dark-haired man stepped down off the stair and disappeared in the crowd. Kaatje shook her head. *Fool*, she silently chastised herself, *did you really think he would come here for you?*

Her eyes scanned the room one last time. A tall, broad-shouldered man stood with his back to her at the far side of the room, halfway between the light and the darkness. The queue of dark wavy hair and the subtle alertness of his stance seemed achingly familiar.

The people around her ceased to exist, the music and laughter and delicate tinkle of crystal all faded to a distant hum. Could that be he? Even in wine-colored velvet and brocade, the man had the bearing of a soldier. The crowd swelled around her, briefly obscuring her view, and then cleared. He was gone.

She blindly pushed through the crowd to find him. A man grabbed at her: Guillon, his chestnut-colored wig slightly askew. But she yanked out of his grasp and stumbled into a group of men and women clustered around a regal matron seated on an armchair.

Philippe and Claude's Great-aunt Amélie.

"Don't we know you?" the old lady said. "You look familiar."

A squat, middled-aged woman squinted rudely at Kaatje. "No, Amélie, you're thinking of Lavergne's niece. The one who married Brissiaud's son."

"That pale little washed-out thing married Brissiaud's son?" a man standing beside her asked, then harrumphed. "I'd have wagered half my lands that Lavergne would've had that mousy niece of his on his hands forever."

"You *did* wager half your lands, you old satyr," the seated matron said, "and it was on something much less respectable than whether or not Lavergne would marry off his niece. Why do you think you're living here?" The woman pounded her cane on the floor for emphasis. "All of which is of no moment. Come here, girl," she commanded Kaatje.

With a last longing glance across the room, Kaatje stepped forward and curtsied. "Aunt Amélie, ma'am," she said, greeting the Duchesse de Chamboret.

The old woman's neck stiffened at Kaatje's familiarity. "Who are you, girl?"

"Kaatje van Staden de St. Benoit, ma'am."

"St. Benoit? I don't . . . wait a minute. Wasn't St. Benoit that place Claude bought for Philippe?"

"It was in Holland," a voice in the group called out.

"I thought it was in Bavaria," came another.

"It is in Flanders, Aunt Amélie," Kaatje said, her tone firm and distinct.

The duchesse looked thoughtful, her eyes studying Kaatje. "Was I at the wedding?"

"No, Aunt. Philippe and I were married the spring his grandfather became ill."

"Completely and totally popped his cork, you mean. Having the strangest sorts of fits," Amélie snapped. "Claude bustled him off to someplace or other in Italy. Up in the mountains somewhere."

Kaatje blanched. She shivered and started to turn away, but discovered the margrave at her elbow, blocking her escape.

In a whisper that only she could hear, Claude said, "I have another unexpected guest, Catherine. An English lord. An English colonel, in fact. I knew him once, years ago, in Vienna.

"Imagine what a delightful surprise his appearance was after such a long time. Yet here he is, an English lord and army officer traveling through Hespaire-Aube. From where, I wonder. To where, I wonder. With *whom,* I wonder."

Kaatje stood stock still. It *had* been Becket standing there. She stared at the empty place on the other side of the room. Had he seen her? Her flesh tightened along her arms and at the back of her neck. Had he seen her— and turned away?

Please, God, let me talk with him one last time. Let me tell him the truth of things. Let me show him how much I . . .

"You don't dissemble well, do you, my dear?" Claude said idly, as if musing on the weather. "I suppose Philippe must've found the novelty of that amusing at first."

"Claude. Claude!" the duchesse called, pounding her cane. "Stop wasting your time on Philippe's relic. You have yet to dance." She snorted and rocked in her chair. "Really, Claude. It has been nearly three years since little Claude-Denis died and two and a half since his mother died. It is becoming excessive. You need to be seriously considering marrying again. You may have five nephews, all good in their way, but our house has always descended by a direct heir.''

Kaatje flushed and would have turned away, but Claude held her elbow in a pinching grip. ''Indeed, Aunt Amélie, you are right about my nephews. I've seen Philippe's boy, Pierre. He is quite exemplary in every way. With a little polish he will be a perfect son of our house.''

A chill squeezed Kaatje's heart. *A perfect son of the house.* No, no, he's just a little boy, she silently cried out, who desperately needed his medicine.

Panic rippled under her skin like something alive. The room was suddenly much too warm. Dizziness washed over her, and she took a step back to steady herself.

''Yes, it is surprising, isn't it?'' Claude added, his eyes skimming over Kaatje. ''Pierre will soon be perfect. Which is good, of course, because I do not tolerate imperfection.''

By sheer force of will Kaatje kept her wits from skittering away. ''Philippe,'' she began, then took a steadying breath, ''Philippe would be honored by such words, your highness. He was very proud of his son.'' The grip on her elbow lessened, and she twisted away from Claude, at the last minute turning the movement into a curtsy. ''With your permission, Aunt Amélie, and your highness, I'll retire. My trip . . .''

She turned and stumbled away without waiting for them to speak. *Sylph, sylph, sylph. Damn you. Damn your blood.* Kaatje ran through the halls to her rooms, her hands over her ears as if she could block out the voices in her head that taunted her. *Damn your blood,* Becket's voice cursed, then Claude's low, dangerous murmur: *Perfect.*

''Becket, Becket, I am damned,'' she whispered, reaching for the latch to her door. *What will happen to my sweet little son when Claude discovers just how far from perfect he really is?*

Becket stepped back into the shadows at the edge of the ballroom and watched the stunning figure of Kaatje dressed in rose and silver as she made her purposeful way toward the widow of the late Duc de Chamboret. You've come far, madame, he thought bitterly, remembering her that first morning in the doorway of the barn, her rumpled gown twisted tight to her body and her hair still tousled from sleep. She'd looked as if she'd just had a thoroughly enjoyable romp, and it had taken all his self-control not to pick her up and take her back into the straw.

In the glitter of a thousand candles, he saw other men looking at her, their eyes caressing the delicious expanse of her bosom revealed by the too low neckline of her gown. Is that why she had taken such care with her dress? he wondered with jaw clenched. To make herself the object of every man's fantasies?

What man didn't dream of seducing an angel? Becket's skin felt taut across his shoulders, and his vision turned smoky gray. Or had she become a vision of voluptuous innocence for one man—one devil—alone?

The air in the room was suddenly too thin to breathe. He inhaled deeply, steadying himself against a column.

Look at her! his anger commanded him. *Look at the soft, enticing curve of her neck as she curtsies to the duchesse, the same soft neck you kissed only this morning, her pulse still fluttering from her ecstasy. It is all for El Müzir now. Does she smile? Or does she keep that for the devil, too?*

Becket turned his back on her, sucking in a breath against the needles of pain that stabbed him. He'd had hours to let her betrayal seep into his soul. *Bury it,* he told himself, clenching his fist, *bury it deep, next to the marquise's betrayal.* That woman had paid for her schemes, and so would Kaatje. But now was for El Müzir.

He swept his mind clear of everything but his enemy. He studied the dazzling crowd, looking for the Turk.

Two bewigged courtiers bowed gracefully to Becket, their expressions wary. He returned their bow but did not give any sign that he wanted them to stay and chat. They moved on, bowing to a couple who watched the dancing.

It had been a waste of time to attend, he thought. El Müzir would not be here. Cavorting in a ballroom was not his style. Becket raised his gaze to the galleries above. Long sections of them were in deep shadows, where light from the scores of candles in the massive chandeliers couldn't reach; Becket studied the blackness for signs of movement. A faint flicker caught his eye, and he surged toward it, only to see a giggling couple dart into the light and wave to someone down in the ballroom.

His gaze dropped from the gallery and traveled restlessly over the crowd, his eyes dismissing every woman who was not dressed in rose and silver. Noticing that the group around the duchesse had thinned and that Kaatje was not there, he frowned. It was early yet; surely a woman who had put up with the hardships of the Chateau de St. Benoit would linger, reveling in the opulence.

His gaze lit on the couple at the gallery railing, the man nuzzling the neck of the coquettish young woman and laughingly urging her back into the shadows. For a moment, the young woman's light brown hair gleamed golden in the candlelight.

An assignation? Had she gone with one of the men he'd seen gaping at her? His hand felt for his sword and closed around the hilt of a useless dress sword. Unbidden, Roulon's words spoken under the oak came back to him: *The two whores are sisters . . . They've both shared the Turk's bed . . .*

For a long heartbeat, Becket was completely still, his stomach twisting in a savage knot. An instant later, he tore through the crowd. Seething, raw anger pounded through his veins. She had an assignation—but not with a man. With a devil.

Chapter 14

"Cècile," Kaatje cried, surprising the maid who slept in a chair by the unlit fireplace. Kaatje pulled futilely at the laces up her back. "Where's the dress I was wearing when I arrived?"

The maid jumped to her feet and stared at her mistress with terror-filled eyes, wringing her hands. Kaatje stopped in the doorway between the sitting room and the bedroom, her head throbbing. *Sylph*. Hysteria bubbled at the back of her throat. *Damn your blood*.

"Cècile, please get me out of . . ." Kaatje began, then stopped when she saw the maid staring at her blindly, her mouth working without sound.

"Don't beat me, ma'am. Please don't beat me," the girl sobbed.

"Of course I won't beat you, you silly goose," Kaatje said, her tone light and reassuring. "I only want my laces undone."

"Oh, ma'am. What am I to do? Your dress . . ."

"Why are you in such a dither?"

"But when you were sleeping, Madame d'Agenais told me you didn't want it anymore. She told me to burn it."

"She did, did she?" Kaatje said, struggling to keep irritation out of her voice. "Well, from now on, why don't *we* decide what should be done about my pitiful

249

wardrobe. Have you unpacked the cases that arrived with my son?''

The girl lowered her eyes and nodded.

"Don't tell me," Kaatje said with a sigh. "Madame d'Agenais helped you with that, too."

The girl nodded again.

Kaatje looked down at the pink and silver confection that she was nearly spilling out of and said, "Does my sister expect me to wear *this* all the time?"

The maid peeped up at her and giggled. "The gentlemen would be fond of you if you did, ma'am. Though I don't think many of the ladies . . ."

"Well, help me out of this for now," Kaatje said, widening her mouth in what she hoped the maid would take for a smile. "Tomorrow is soon enough to see what my sister has left me to wear."

Kaatje stood like a puppet under the maid's nimble fingers. The morning was not something she wanted to think about. Nor the next morning, nor the one after that . . . With a poof of satin, the skirts fell to the floor, and Kaatje stepped out of them, wishing it were as easy to step out of the morass her life had become.

The maid gathered up the bundle of pink satin and silver lace while Kaatje remained in the middle of the bedroom floor, head aching, dressed in only pink stockings and a borrowed chemise of fine lawn with a low swooping neckline that exactly matched the neckline of the ballgown. The hem of the chemise ended an inch above the tops of the stockings.

A narrow band of delicate lace edged the borrowed undergarment, and she ran a finger over it, remembering her own chemise that she'd worn the night before. The one Becket had torn from her body in passion. Her hand began to shake.

"I think I would like a sleeping draft, Cècile," Kaatje whispered, her fingers clenching closed the neckline of the chemise.

"Are you sure, ma'am? Perhaps Dr. Stephen's water . . ."

"No," Kaatje said, facing the maid. "No." *I don't want to dream* . . . "Just steep rosemary and sage and chamomile in some mulled wine."

The maid curtsied. "Yes, ma'am. But it will take me a while to make it. Are you sure you don't want . . ."

"I'm sure, Cècile."

The maid curtsied again and left by the servants' door, a worried look on her young face.

When she had gone, Kaatje hugged herself in despair. The shadows in the corners flickered, and she frantically lit every candle in the room to keep the darkness at bay. The hot night air soon reeked with the smell of wax.

Kaatje sat at the ornate dressing table and began brushing her hair. Her eyes stared unfocused into the mirror as her mind jumped from Pietr to Lece to Becket.

She thought of Pietr's medicine and realized with a frown that, since their arrival at Hespaire-Aube, Lece had not asked about the clock. It was in Pietr's room. All of her sister's questions had been about Becket.

Where was he now? Kaatje wondered, setting the brush down. In the castle somewhere, Claude had intimated. She remembered the man in the wine-colored coat. What would she have done if that had been Becket and he'd greeted her with all the glittering polish of a courtier?

She would have been expected to curtsy and smile and murmur polite salutations, as if she'd never felt the warmth of his flesh on hers. As if she'd never felt the glory . . . Her hand trembled when she reached for the brush again, but a prickly feeling down her back stopped her. Slowly, she raised her eyes and looked in the mirror.

Becket stood on the other side of the room, watching her.

A scream choked in her throat. Power radiated from him. Strength. Rage, dark and unchecked. He took a step toward her, then another, his pace slow and inexorable, his midnight gaze piercing her.

She jumped to her feet and backed away. "Becket," she said in a hoarse whisper, her hand at her throat. "Becket, what do you want . . ."

He didn't answer. He came closer. He unbuckled his sword belt and threw it aside. It skidded on the marble floor with a metallic hiss. He yanked off his coat and threw it aside, then pulled off his waistcoat, popping the buttons, and let it drop.

"Becket, please . . ." She took another step backward—and her back smacked against the wall. "Becket, please. I had nothing to do with those soldiers. Nothing. Please," she babbled. "Please understand. I had to go with Lece. Pietr . . ."

Becket reached her and put a punishing hand over her mouth. "No more of your lies, madame," he said in a harsh whisper. He pushed into her, using his body to hold her against the wall. "The game is over."

He ran his hand along her curves, feeling the heat of her skin and the tremor of her fear. "Where is he?" Becket demanded. "Where is the devil lover you wait for?"

She tried to rock her head back and forth, screaming her denial against his hand. She struggled under him. The thin chemise twisted and clung to her breasts, making her even more enticing than when he'd seen her sitting at the dressing table brushing her hair. Her stockinged leg kicked out at him, and he remembered when it had once wrapped around his waist. Her hips thrust out to push her body away from the wall, the way they had at the mill to meet his passion.

His anger melted into his rising lust. With a growl,

he snatched his hand away from her mouth and replaced it with his mouth, swallowing her scream. He
took all he could take, forcing her to feed him the sensations they'd shared at the mill. He stroked her tongue
with his, again and again, each time demanding, taking, absorbing the fiery bolts of elemental desire that
fed his animal hunger.

He pressed his hips into her, rocking in an unmistakable rhythm, making her feel the heat and hardness
of his arousal. His hands caressed her breasts, her hips,
fast and rough. He grasped her thigh and lifted it, as if
he could pull her closer to him. He reveled in the soft
pillowing heat of her. He wanted more of her. Closer.
His body demanded, and seemed almost out of his control.

Becket molded Kaatje's body against him as if she
were melted wax. She could feel the twined fury and
lust resonating through him, lunging for her. His hands
rubbed her, taking, not giving. She struggled under
him, knowing every movement was a mockery of their
lovemaking at the mill.

She tore at his shirt and hit at his arms, but they were
solid, unyielding. She pushed on his shoulders, but she
might as well push on the walls of the castle. She
grabbed his hair, and the ribbon tying his queue came
off in her hand. She grabbed again, burying her fingers
deep, and yanked.

His head jerked back and he growled in anger. Kaatje
darted away.

"I am not your whore, Becket Thorne!"

"Then whose are you?" he threw at her. "Are you
like your sister—content to sleep in any man's bed?"

"How many 'sylphs' do you have, Thorne?" She ran
and seized his coat and threw it at him. He caught it in
one hand and tossed it aside. "A German one, Thorne?
A French one? How many English ones pine away at
home for you, dreaming of your cheap endearments?"

She threw his waistcoat at him and he pitched it to the floor. "There's an Italian one, too, I'll wager. But *not* a Flemish one," she cried, grabbing his dress sword, scabbard, belt, and all.

"Do you hear me, Thorne!" She gripped the hilt tightly and slashed out in a wide arc. The scabbard and belt flew off, leaving her pointing the bare blade at him. "Do you hear me, Thorne? *Not a Flemish one!*"

Becket's eyes narrowed, his attention on the blade. His torn shirt hung open in a wide vee, revealing his muscular chest. He took a step toward her. His fingers closed over the thin blade. "You need to remember your lessons, madame." He lowered the blade until it pointed at his hard flat stomach. "Here. Here is where you plunge your weapon." He released it.

She held the hilt steady with a tight two-handed grip. "I do not forget, *anglais.*" He leaned forward, the point beginning to press against his skin.

"Kill me, madame. It is all that will save you now."

Their gazes locked for an instant. She leaped backward, pulling the blade away from his stomach, but she held it steady and pointed at him. "No, Thorne. I will not kill you. I do not play your soldier's games."

"Then you lose, madame." He jumped, feinting to the left. She spun to face him, but he sprang back, his hand snaking in and seizing her wrist. He pulled her to him, face to face, holding her arm out to her side. His grip grew tighter and tighter until her fingers lost their strength and the sword fell to the floor with a clatter.

"I share no woman." He twisted her arm behind her, and she gasped at the pain that shot through her shoulder. She was crushed to him. His free hand held her head immobile as his gaze devoured her face.

"The innocent widow. What a fool I was. Did your husband teach you your tricks? Or have myriad teachers added to your repertoire? The enticing hesitations, the sweet flutterings under your skin, the mewings of just-discovered desire . . .''

He tightened his hold. She grimaced but clamped her jaw shut to keep from crying out.

''Roulon spoke true under that oak, didn't he? The pale—'' Becket broke off and sucked in a deep ragged breath. ''The pale one warmed the devil's bed. I can see you there—'' His voice was a raw growl, as if it were being scraped out of his throat. ''I can see him touch—'' He broke off with a roar and threw her from him. She toppled against the bed.

''God have mercy, woman! Why? Why? Why did you make me—''

''Thorne! I am not El Müzir's lover!'' She stood against the bed, her knees shaking, barely able to support her. ''Believe what you will, Englishman, but—God help me!—I have been with no man but you since my husband died. No man but you.''

A hesitant knock at the servants' door interrupted Kaatje, followed by Cècile tremulously announcing herself. ''A moment,'' Kaatje called out and turned back to Becket. He stood there, chest heaving as he gulped in air, his jaw tensed as he struggled for control. She lowered her voice to a whisper. ''Becket, listen to me! I am not your El Müzir's lover. I swear it on my son's head. What I do, I do to save Pietr. And I'll let no man, Turk or Englishman, get in my way.''

Becket growled his frustration, but his features lost some of their tautness. ''Your son? What has he to do with it? El Müzir would *sell* your son as easily as save him.''

''No,'' Kaatje whispered, shaking her head, ''No, he wouldn't do that.''

''He would do a great many things, madame.''

The maid knocked again. ''Ma'am? Are you all right? I have your sleeping draft.''

A strange pressure tightened around Becket's heart

as he watched Kaatje walk blindly to the servants' door. He tried to hold on to his wrath. He had thought she would lead him to El Müzir, but here she was in such distress that he was nearly suffocating from witnessing it, from having caused it. *Damn you woman. Get out of my blood.*

Kaatje took a pewter mug from the wide-eyed maid and shut the door. She came back to stand by the bed, but looked at the steaming wine, not at him.

His eyes narrowed. Was it all a trick? "What kind of mother are you to bring your son into this? If El Müzir is allowed to live, you risk your son's life along with the lives of countless thousands."

"Bring Pietr into . . . ?" She looked up at him, shocked horror suffusing her face. "No. You don't understand!"

"Don't I? Sweet Jesu, think what you do, woman. Think of the man your son will become—and tell that man his mother dealt with the devil."

"Oh, Becket," she whispered, "what you must think of me to say that." Her words were choppy. She wrapped her arm around her waist. She looked so beautiful and forlorn, standing in front of the lace bedcurtains and thick counterpane, staring at the wine in her hand.

"Rosemary and sage and chamomile," she murmured. "So easy to know what goes in a sleeping draft. But for Pietr—" She broke off, weeping. "I tried, Becket. I tried so hard."

"I do not follow you, madame," he said, fighting not to pull her into his arms and comfort her. "What have you tried?"

He did not trust her distress—and he did not trust himself. Yet something had banked the rage in him. He could still feel it inside, but it burned in the distance, like a night fire on a far mountain.

Kaatje looked at him, tears making her eyes shine

like quicksilver. "At first, I was so full of hope. Each new chirurgeon, each new apothecary meant I might discover—" She shook her head. "I could never figure it out. It's beyond my poor skills. But I thought . . . Oh, my Pietr . . ." She turned her head away and bit her lip to stifle a sob.

He took the mug of mulled wine from her trembling hands and set it on the dressing table. He returned to her and slipped his hands onto her shoulders, his thumbs caressing the soft skin revealed by the low neckline of the chemise.

"Apothecaries?" He squeezed lightly. "Damn it, Kaatje. What does a sleeping draught have to do with your son? Did something happen to Pietr? Niall said he arrived in fine fettle, but perhaps he didn't see—"

"Oh, Becket." She shook her head and tried to wipe away the tears. "You don't understand. You can't . . ."

"I understand you protect El Müzir from me."

"Becket!" She clutched his torn shirt, her fingers curling into the linen. "Oh, Becket, my son, my sweet little boy has the falling sickness."

For an instant, a look of horror flashed across her face, as if the words had slipped out without her willing them to. She took a ragged breath, and her hold on his shirt tightened. "It happened at Chateau d'Agenais. Pietr and I were visiting Lece after Philippe died, and Oncelus . . . Oncelus gave him some medicine to stop the . . . the . . . falling.

"That's why I was going to Cerfontaine. To pay for more medicine." Kaatje released her hold and fell back against the bed. She looked up at him, bleak despair swimming in her eyes. "Don't you see? Only Oncelus can give me his medicine. Please, Becket, no one at the castle must ever know. No one. Promise me. You must never tell."

He pulled back abruptly. *"You betrayed me to El Müzir for a handful of leaves and roots?"* He stepped back. "Sweet God, woman! Any chirurgeon will give you medicine for the boy."

"Becket, no, no. The chirurgeon's medicine only eases the fits. Oncelus's stops them! Don't you see? Claude must never find out!"

"Claude? What does that matter?" Becket forced himself to ask. But inside, the anger, the outrage, the hurt were all shifting, tilting.

Kaatje took a deep steadying breath, and the van Staden composure settled over her face. "Claude locked up his own grandfather, Becket. He put a harmless old man in one of those awful desolate monasteries in the mountains in Italy. One of the ones where half-mad monks used to go to whip themselves in penance." She clutched at the empty air.

"Philippe visited there once, on one of his campaigns, and he said that there was still blood on the walls. Claude would send Pietr there if he knew! Don't you see?"

"Pietr's just a boy," Becket said. "Claude would never—"

"Damn you, Thorne! Why won't you understand? I must go on as I have. Paying Oncelus whatever he asks for my son's medicine."

"Kaatje, you don't know what you say. You can't deal with El Müzir. He will crush both you and your son." Visions of Kaatje in El Müzir's power assaulted him. *El Müzir must be destroyed at whatever cost.*

But what of the little boy who looked so much like his mother? Already, tendrils of evil from that black-souled devil were twining around his innocent life.

Suddenly Becket realized that this woman and her happiness *mattered* to him, mattered deeply. He closed his eyes, fighting clarity of the feeling, trying to bury it. He didn't want to feel . . . anything.

"No one must know, Becket. Swear to me that you'll tell no one. Swear."

Becket brushed a golden tendril from her damp face. "Kaatje . . ." He pulled her to him, and sealed his oath with a kiss, giving, not taking, this time, letting the tenderness in him guide him. He wanted her to taste the gift of caring she'd given him, and to feel the joy that she gave him when he held her in his arms. He wanted her to remember the warmth when all too soon she would discover that the price of her handful of leaves and roots was too high for him to pay.

"Sweet Jesu, woman," he said. "I swear."

There was a sharp crack of laughter from the main door to the suite. Kaatje broke away from Becket and spun to face her sister.

"You really should beat that maid of yours," Lece said, shutting the door behind her and walking across the sitting room to stand in the doorway to the bedroom, arms crossed in front of her, and amusement clearly written on her face.

"She is quite indiscreet, Kaat. She came running to me, babbling of your troubles in front of everyone . . ." Lece's eyes studied Becket from the soles of his shoes to his dark blue eyes.

"Such distress, little sister. Introduce me."

Kaatje felt Becket's hands squeeze her shoulders in warning as he stood behind her. "What are you doing here, Lece?" she asked.

"You're not pleased to see me?" Lece shrugged and came farther into the room. "You're one up on me, sister. Even I wouldn't have dared to defy Claude and run from his ball into my lover's arms." A light of mischief danced in her sister's eyes as she glanced at Becket. "You do not introduce me, Kaat. I wonder why. It doesn't matter, you know. Your Englishman and I are already known to each other."

Kaatje struggled to hide her dismay, but her sister smiled at it.

"Are we not *known* to each other, *anglais?*" Lece

asked, her gaze sliding to him. "Colonel Becket, Lord Thorne, Viscount Thorne of Thornewood and other obscure English lands—all courtesy of his queen. Or would you prefer me to call you Messer Cesare Pallavicino, of one of the great banking houses of Venice?"

Becket released Kaatje's shoulders and stepped to her side. "You may call me enemy," he said.

Lece took a step backward.

"And you may call me *irritated*, sister," Kaatje said, her eyes narrowed. "Your innuendoes are beginning to pall."

Lece's smile hardened. "Don't spit at *me*, little sister. It wasn't an 'innuendo' I witnessed when I came in here. You ran from the ball a bit too quickly, sister dear. That is indiscreet of you."

Kaatje sensed Becket subtly shifting his weight, and a blade of apprehension twisted beneath her ribs.

"Morality from the devil's concubine?" Becket said, taking a step closer to Lece, his hands held slightly away from his body. "You are unfit to criticize Madame de St. Benoit. Do not do so."

"Do you threaten me, Pallavicino?" Lece asked with a biting laugh. "Who are you to talk to *me* of morality, of anything? I remember you from d'Agenais, I remember you well.

"I once thought you a man. I was devastated when you spurned me. What was I to think of myself when this big strapping Italian refused me any kind of comfort? But I watched you, even as Segan drooled his kisses down my neck, and I *saw*. I saw that you are nothing but soot and chalk, a sketch of something that may have once been a man—"

Kaatje leaped at her sister and slapped her, the force of the blow reverberating up her arm. *"No!* It is you who have become so wretched." Lece staggered back in surprise, her hand springing to her face.

"You protect him, little sister? Protect yourself!

There was a great deal of speculation about the hand-some *anglais* at the ball. I said to ask my little sister about him.''

Kaatje gasped as if Lece had slapped her back. "Why would you do such a thing?" Smiling malice lit her sister's eyes.

"It is her nature," Becket said. "Yours is to bind wounds, hers is to make them."

Lece flushed. "You will know of wounds soon enough, *anglais*," she spat out. "When you wake and there is a sword at your throat."

"The devil is ever the coward," he returned.

Lece stumbled backward, as if caught off guard by his intensity.

"He is invincible!" Suddenly, she was wild-eyed, her hands clenching in the air at nothing. "He is no lowly devil. He is more . . . I can see it in his eyes. I can feel it in his hands, his touch. He's a dæmon. Above you. Above all of us."

"You are deluded." Becket balled his hand into a fist. "He is but a dark-souled Turk. Most likely he was born in a pit. Where is he?"

Lece took another step back, and smacked into the wall. She shook her head. "It will be as he wishes. *He* will find *you*. You get nothing from me."

"Where is he?" The command in Becket's voice echoed off the walls.

Lece gulped in a breath and clawed at the paneling behind her. "Oncelus," she whimpered, then regained control as if the name alone calmed her. "You are wasting my time, *anglais*."

The light in Becket's eyes flared with lethal danger. "No!" Kaatje cried, clutching at his arm. "Becket, no!"

"Becket, no," Lece mimicked, but the words were shaky.

"Don't do this, Becket," Kaatje said. "She won't

tell you where Oncelus is. She loves him, Becket. I don't understand why, but she's blind with it.''

He pushed Kaatje's hand from his arm. ''You soil the word for the poets.''

Lece thrust her chin up in defiance, and for the first time Becket saw a resemblance between the two sisters. ''Segan said you were a cold bastard,'' she said. ''He needed consoling as much as I did.''

''So you consoled him into his grave,'' Becket said, his eyes opaque, his face still, his rage a palpable force.

''Grave?'' Lece looked confused. ''What do you mean? When I left—''

''You left him dead.''

''No! I was only to distract him—'' she began, then licked her lips. ''I shared his bed, for God's sake. How can you think I would—''

''And now you sleep in the devil's bed. Where is he?'' Becket's eyes were indigo pinpoints of hate.

''She won't tell you!'' Kaatje cried, grabbing at his wrist. ''Don't you understand? She won't betray him.'' Kaatje looked at her sister. ''She loves him.''

Lece turned her head away.

Kaatje hid her hands behind her to keep him from seeing them tremble, but she kept her gaze steady with his. ''A woman does not betray the man she loves,'' she said quietly.

With infinite sadness, she felt Becket withdraw into himself. He stepped away from both of them.

''So, madame, you have not left off protecting him,'' he said, his face a haggard mask. ''For Pietr, you would betray me still.''

''No—'' Kaatje gasped.

''I have my duty, madame.'' His eyes had turned unreadable, but she saw a flash of contempt in them when he glanced at Lece before returning his gaze to her. ''And you, you and your son have the devil.''

Becket snatched his coat and waistcoat from the floor, then looped his sword belt over his shoulder.

He strode to the main door, threw it open, and walked out.

Kaatje put a trembling hand over her mouth and slumped against the high bed. She looked out the window. It was nearly dawn. "Get out, Lece."

"Come now, little sis—"

"I don't want to talk with you now. Perhaps later, in the morning." She rose and went to the dressing table and picked up the sleeping draft she'd had Cècile make. It was cold. "Or perhaps not."

"Kaat—"

"Go, Lece."

Her sister shook out her skirts in indignation. "Well, well. Little Kaat is in a pique. I'm all a-tremble." When Kaatje didn't rise to the bait, Lece snorted and rolled her eyes. "Oh, all right. I'll go. But you have a lot to learn about lovers, little sister. Especially dangerous ones."

Kaatje turned her back to her sister. She didn't even flinch when Lece slammed the door closed so hard it rattled the hinges.

Becket returned to the room the margrave had provided him in the castle and quickly dressed in a dark gray velvet coat and breeches that Harry had scrounged. Then he brusquely pulled on his boots. *El Müzir,* he chanted silently. *Kaatje will lead me to El Müzir. And that will end it.* There was a stabbing pain in his chest as he thought it, but he gritted his teeth and headed toward the stables.

He quickly saddled Acheron, then guided the stallion out the castle's southern gate, the guards saluting as he passed. The sun was just cresting the eastern hills.

"Now," Becket rasped out to the horse as soon as they were out of sight. He gave the stallion its head and

they were soon hurtling through the air, as if without
touching ground. The gray velvet coat billowed behind
him as he leaned over the horse's neck and rode.

Battle memories careened through his mind. Blenheim, Ramillies, Odenaarde . . . Horses screaming,
dying, men grunting and cursing and crying out as they
fought, and as they fell. Breathing the reek of other
men's blood and other men's fear. And his own. Deadly
whirlpools and eddies of battle battering at him, catching at him, pushing, pulling, stronger than a river at
full flood. Fighting on, he and Acheron and his sword
becoming a single being roaring through the maelstrom.

Now, the horse moved under him, with him, at a
dead run up a dry streambed. Instinctively, Becket
ducked and swerved from low-slung branches as they
flashed by in the early morning mist. He was pushing
his body to the limit, his lungs burning, his muscles
protesting, his heart pounding with exertion—

But it wasn't enough.

A trickle of water appeared in the streambed as they
rode farther south. The trickle grew to a brook, then a
stream. Acheron and Becket splashed on, slower now,
until he brought the stallion to a halt in the cool water.

Becket leaped off and staggered into the water until
it reached his knees. He scooped up double handfuls
and dowsed himself again and again until the sweat-
stained gray velvet coat dripped.

And it wasn't enough.

Kaatje.

He straightened, drinking in deep gulps of air. He
closed his eyes and shook his head, sending water droplets arcing out from his unconfined hair.

"Why you, Kaatje?" he roared to the small empty
valley around him. "Why couldn't it have been an ordinary woman on that road from Odenaarde? With no
van Staden spirit in her gray eyes, no soft sunlit hair . . ."

He broke off, his voice hoarse, then added in a whisper, "with no *caring*, Kaatje.

"And with no son to give over to the devil."

In his head, his duty was clear. Find El Müzir and kill him. And with that duty came his fate. He and the Turk were evenly matched, strength for strength, skill for skill. They would both go down together.

But in his heart . . . *No!* He shook his head, breaking the dangerous thread of his thoughts. There was nothing more than duty.

But he had brought Kaatje into this and it was his duty to aid her, whether she wished that aid or not.

He slogged back through the water to Acheron. He was being a fool. He should ignore Kaatje and her woman's fears. She would betray him again, if she had to. The thought cut into him like a lash across his back.

He clenched his jaw. What was a tale of a mad grandfather next to the real madness of El Müzir? But he remembered the anguish in her eyes . . .

She would fight him, of course, with every dram of her courage and spirit. He walked faster.

Becket mounted Acheron and headed back down the valley toward the city. He had come far in his wild run, and the sun was hot when he turned the stallion toward the ruined abbey.

A light morning breeze cooled him, its scent promising a storm a day or so away.

An image of Kaatje and her blond-haired son, so like her, came to his mind. Did Pietr know what a precious thing his mother's love was? Children seldom did. But the boy had his mother's pluck and courage, and the thought of him in El Müzir's hands made Becket's stomach twist.

Kaatje was wrong about what would happen to the child if the margrave learned of his illness. And it was his duty to prove that to her.

Niall stood waiting for him outside the stable, talking

with three other men. The men backed away as Becket approached, eyeing him and his stallion warily.

"Lieutenant," Becket said. He dismounted and let the reins fall to the ground. Niall's horse stood silent in the stall.

"Colonel, good to . . . ah, see you, sir," Niall said, taking in the state of his colonel's clothes. When Becket said nothing, he went on. "I was just sending these stout fellows out to see the sights on the Hes, so to speak. See what the French are up to, and all."

Becket crossed his arms and leaned a hip against the stone wall. "Carry on, Niall."

The lieutenant nodded and turned back to the men. In a few minutes, one after the other trotted off down the hill toward the city. When they were alone, Niall turned his attention back to Becket.

Becket uncrossed his arms. "What do you know of Italian monasteries, lieutenant?"

"Sir?"

"Monasteries, Niall. Italian ones, specifically. I suspect they may even have Italian monks in them." Becket watched Niall mulling it over.

"Does this have to do with the French rabble up the river, sir?"

"No, Niall, it does not."

"Ah," the lieutenant said, clearly not understanding. "With El Müzir? Has he escaped to—"

"No."

Niall swallowed. "I know nothing of Italian monasteries, colonel." He headed for his horse. "I expect you'll want me to find out, though. It'll take some time. Italy's a stretch o' road south o' here." The lieutenant put one hand on his saddle, then paused, a puzzled look on his face. "Isn't it, sir?"

Becket clapped Niall on the shoulder. "No need to travel so far. I want you to ask around here. I have heard a tale that the margrave's grandfather was shut up

in a monastery in the Italian mountains. I want specif-
ics. When. Where. How long. Everything you can
scrape up.''

"Yes sir, colonel." Niall mounted and rode out.

Becket pushed away from the wall. He went to Acheron and swung into the saddle, then kneed the stallion
down the hill toward the castle.

He cursed the coat across his shoulders. It had been
a long time since he had worn velvets and brocades
instead of his uniform. Could he ever go back to being
a gentleman? Foolish question. There was no going
back. It would end with El Müzir, end with nothing but
oblivion or hell. He would discover which one soon
enough.

At least now he could get on with his duty. It was
time to set a trap for a devil. But the Turk could see
through any trickery. That had been the problem at Köln
and at the inn outside d'Agenais—so it had to be set
carefully.

With the right bait.

Himself.

Chapter 15

"I won't ask if you slept well," Lece said, standing next to Kaatje's chair at breakfast. "I can see that you didn't."

A caprice of Claude's had led him to have breakfast set up in the gardens, and now Kaatje sat staring at a plate of eggs drenched in butter, and greasy sausages. The smell of fennel was nauseating.

"For God's sake, stop chattering!" Kaatje pushed the plate away and closed her eyes, trying to will her sister to leave her in peace.

Monsieur Guillon sauntered up and bowed to Kaatje, his wig still askew and one lace cuff still tucked up his coat sleeve. He began to pull out a chair next to her, but Lece sat down in it instead.

"Thank you, Guillon." Lece waved him away. "No, no, go away. My sister doesn't want to talk with you. And do something about that cuff."

Kaatje rose. "And I don't want to talk with *you,* Lece," she said, and began walking toward the castle.

Lece caught up with her and grabbed her elbow. "Don't ever do that to me in public again," Lece warned in a deadly whisper. "Never forget that I always return insult for insult, little sister." Kaatje wrenched out of her hold and kept walking.

Her emotions were in turmoil as she entered the castle with Lece just behind her. Her sister reminded

268

Kaatje of everything she wanted to forget. She didn't want to think about what had been said the night before, or that Becket had walked away from her, leaving her feeling as if she had stood too close to thunder.

Lece stifled a yawn. "The next time you want me to save you from an assignation, have the courtesy to pick a more civilized time! I already need a nap."

"Stop it, Lece," Kaatje said sharply, walking on through the hallways of the new wing. "You haven't yet learned that there's more to life than . . . carnal gratification."

Lece stopped at the door to her rooms and looked at her sister with cynical amusement. "I've *seen* your lover, Kaat," she said, twisting the latch. "Tell me you dream of planting herbs instead of receiving carnal gratification in his arms."

Kaatje flushed. Lece snickered and opened the door. "I always suspected you were a pious little hypocrite." She started to close the door on her sister.

"No, Lece," Kaatje said, and stopped the door with her splayed hand. "You didn't *always* suspect that. We used to be sisters. *Real* sisters, Lece. Don't you remember?"

Lece's eyes narrowed in bitterness. She grabbed Kaatje's hand from the door and pulled her into the room, slamming it behind her. She spun Kaatje around and pushed her into a chair.

Kaatje's eyes followed Lece as she paced, her footfalls silent on the carpet. "Lece, what of all those times we spent together learning about herbs and such from Mother? You enjoyed that, I know you did. And we used to laugh and play in the caves, remember?"

"I don't remember, Kaat," Lece said harshly, turning away.

Kaatje squeezed the back of the chair, willing her sister to remember. "Those bright stones in the caverns—remember? You'd roll them around in your hands, saying they were good luck. You used to tell me that someday a man would give you diamonds as big as those stones.''

''Worthless pink crystal.''

''They were our treasures, Lece.''

''They were children's games.'' Lece glanced at her sister, then looked away. ''And we are no longer children.''

''And are we no longer sisters as well?'' Kaatje waited, watching Lece hug herself and rub her arms.

''Don't talk like a fool. We merely went different ways.''

''But why, Lece? Why do you . . .''

Lece looked at her, unbelieving. ''Now it is you who doesn't remember, is that it? Let me refresh your memory, little sister. Stepfather came home.''

''Stepfather?'' Kaatje asked, surprised. ''What has he to do with us? At first he made a fuss, but then he—''

Lece laughed bitterly, pacing faster, her skirts brushing Kaatje's as she walked past. ''We rusticated while he went to Versailles, for what—three, four years? But then he came home.

''I was twelve, Kaat. Starting to become a woman. And he was all elegant manners and exquisite clothes. And I wanted him to notice me.

''But it was you he noticed, *you* his eyes watched instead of me whenever we came into the room, *you* he would hug too long and kiss goodbye on the lips—while I barely got a touch on the cheek.''

Kaatje shuddered, remembering her stepfather's unwanted attentions with distaste. ''*He* didn't matter, Lece. And he stopped soon enough. I was only ten, for God's sake! What can you be thinking?''

''What can I be thinking? I wanted him to like *me!* You should thank me for turning his attentions from you. What he gave you so freely, I had to work hard for. I had to earn."

"Lece! What are you saying?" Kaatje said, twisting sideways in the chair to follow her sister's frantic pacing. "You were his stepdaughter!"

"What did that matter? Men were noticing me. And I liked it. I wanted more. One of Cerfontaine's nephews showed me what I wanted—and Cerfontaine himself taught me the rest."

"My God, Lece." Kaatje stood up, not knowing what to do. Her eyes darted from the carpet, to the elaborately carved stone mantle, to the gilt chairs and marble tables, everywhere but to her sister. She rubbed her palms against her skirts.

"And then it was *me* he would visit in the night," Lece said. "*My* sheets he would slip between. Not yours . . ." Lece's voice faltered. "Not Mother's."

Kaatje rubbed her arms as if suddenly too cold. "My God, Lece. Why didn't you tell anyone? My God, someone could've stopped him!"

Lece squeezed her eyes closed. "Don't you realize, Kaat? I didn't want him to stop. *I didn't want him to stop.*"

Kaatje stared at her sister. "How could you want to do anything so monstrous?"

"He stopped bothering you, didn't he?" Kaatje gasped, but her sister waved it away. "Haven't you figured it out, Kaat? That's all a man wants from a woman. How else to get a man to pay attention to me but to let him kiss me and fondle me? When Stepfather stopped—

"Then I knew that was the thrill of it. Let a man seduce me and he may smile or he may leave. I craved the anticipation of it. The excitement of the uncertainty. Sometimes that was all that let me know I was alive."

Kaatje's head was spinning as if she'd drunk too much wine. "You *wanted* them to leave you?"

Lece hugged herself again, and for a brief moment

she looked like a small, frightened child. "They all leave. That's what men do. Father did. Father left us and never came back."

"Father died, Lece. He was killed in battle." Kaatje reached out toward her sister, but a chill had entered her sister's eyes, and Kaatje pulled back.

"*They all leave,* Kaat. I thought with Stepfather . . ." Lece shook her head. "It didn't matter. I *did* want them to leave me. After Stepfather, it all became much easier. Cousins, servants, once a peasant I saw loading hay . . . then, when I was older, the courtiers. Even Philippe, you know. Claude stole me from him. That's why they married him off to you, so he wouldn't make such a fuss."

"But you married. Your vows. Didn't you even try to be faithful?"

"Why would marriage change anything? I still wanted attention."

"How can you still—"

"Oh, not 'still,' little sister. It all stopped when I met Oncelus." Lece fell into the chair opposite her sister, her skirts billowing out around her.

"I'd gone to this inn near Chateau d'Agenais to meet someone, a German, I think. I remember walking down the hallway, the whisper of my slippers on the wooden floor. A door to my right opened just as I came to it— and there he stood, wrapped in his black robes."

Lece sighed, a dreamy look on her face. "I completely forgot the German. I was intrigued. I couldn't see anything of the man in his robes. I stepped into his room, not caring what I might find. I thought he might kiss me, but he offered to draw up my star chart. I laughed and asked him to come to the chateau and draw it up there. In the evening.

"He arrived that night, and did not leave. For six months I watched him build his laboratory in an unused wing of the chateau.

"He demanded gold, and I would take a trip into the city to sell one of the jewels Constantin had given me. Eventually, of course, I ran out of jewels I could sell without getting caught. But Oncelus demanded more gold." Lece shivered and hugged herself, a smile of sensuous memory on her lips.

"I told him there was none. He grabbed me. His robes fell back. And I saw him, the dæmon. He kissed me. Handled me roughly. Touched me quickly, deftly . . . and he brought me to an ecstasy I'd never known. I'd had scores of lovers, Kaat, and had *never* felt anything like that.

"When I came out of my swoon, I saw that Oncelus had returned to his work, but this time without his robe. He stood there, in the candlelight, his muscles gleaming, his long white hair glowing like a nimbus of divinity around him.

" 'More gold,' he demanded. And I found it for him."

A long silence stretched between them. Lece's eyes were overbright and held a fervor that made Kaatje afraid for her. So much separated them now. They were sisters, but they were also strangers.

Lece cocked her head as if listening for something. Was that light in her sister's eyes love? Kaatje wondered with a shiver. Or obsession? She cleared her throat, and the noise made her jump. "Is he here with you? El Mü—Oncelus?" she asked.

Lece erupted in laughter. "Did your Englishman tell you to ask me that?" She leaned forward, took Kaatje's hand, and turned it over. "Your hand is empty, sister. This is what he'll leave you with when he goes away. An empty hand." A leer flashed across her face. "Be careful that he leaves your belly empty, too. An English bastard would be hard to explain away. I can show you ways to prevent it."

Kaatje pulled her hand back, curling it closed. "Is

Kaatje pulled her hand back, curling it closed. "Is Oncelus here? I need Pietr's medicine.

Lece's attention faded, her eyes focusing through the door to her bedroom. "Hmmm?" she murmured, standing abruptly.

Unsure, Kaatje rose slowly to her feet. Lece absently patted her shoulder. "You'll get it, Kaat. You'll get it. Don't worry so." She bustled her sister toward the door with a few more mumbled assurances.

"Lece—" Kaatje protested.

"Anon, little sister," Lece said, looking over her shoulder into her bedroom. "You have plenty of time."

Kaatje returned from Lece's rooms drowning in shock and confusion. Could all of what Lece had said be true? She unsteadily clicked the latch to her door and stumbled inside.

Once she was out of the stares of the courtiers, her control over her nerves broke down and she could go no farther than one of the chairs in the sitting room. She fell into it and rubbed her arms, feeling unclean.

Dull-eyed, her gaze rested unseeing on the chess set that Cècile had reassembled. But the girl did not understand the game, for she'd placed the white queen next to the Saracen king. Kaatje kicked the table, sending the pieces tumbling.

She shot to her feet and paced in front of the unlit fireplace. "Did I ever know you, Lece?" she said into the empty room. "I once thought you everything I ever wanted to be. But now . . . My god, Stepfather! Why, Lece? Why?" She stopped, biting her lip to keep from crying.

To feed her own needs, Lece had hurt so many people: Mother, Constantin, the unnamed wives of her married lovers . . . But what did that matter now? Kaatje asked herself, thinking of her son and Becket.

"No, I won't let you hurt them," she vowed. "I had

thought to save you, Lece, but I can't save you from yourself. You will give me Pietr's medicine and I will do my damnedest to keep your devil lover from Becket.''

You would betray me still, a voice in her head taunted.

"No, Becket, no," she whispered.

Kaatje heard a rustle coming from her bedroom, and she looked up. Cècile stumbled into the doorway, nearly hidden behind a cloud of pale pink lace.

"Oh, ma'am," the maid cried. "I heard you talking with someone . . ." The girl lowered her arms a bit and peered into the sitting room over the top of the lace, her eyes widening when she saw that Kaatje was alone. "Do you need anything, ma'am?" Cècile asked in a small, wary voice.

Kaatje smiled a ragged smile. "I need a great deal, Cècile. But it is all out of reach.'' She followed the maid into the bedroom and went and sat by the tall narrow window, opened against the heat of the summer day. "Have you ever noticed, Cècile, that a hundred little concerns will seem overwhelming, then something storms into your life and turns it upside down, and blows all those little concerns away. Suddenly you remember those simple hardships with a certain longing.''

"I guess so, ma'am."

Kaatje smiled, watching the girl bustle about with a surprisingly diverse selection of gowns. Cècile had piled most of them on the bed and was smoothing them out one after another.

Kaatje picked up one made of a cheery-red silk. "Where did all these gowns come from?" she asked.

The maid's hands stopped working. "Madame d'Agenais's maid brought them just a little while ago—''

"They're from my sister?" The maid nodded, and

Kaatje turned away, her hand clenching into the red silk. "Get rid of them," she ordered.

"All of them, ma'am? But what will you wear?"

"I'll wear what I brought from St. Benoit, Cècile." The maid stared at her in disbelief. Kaatje ignored it. "And then I'd like a bath," she added.

The girl's stare went from disbelief to shock. "You just had one yesterday! Ma'am, your health! Let me send for the court physician, ma'am. He'll tell you."

"Please, Cècile, just do as I ask."

"Y-y-yes, ma'am," the girl said, twisting the plain blue cotton of her skirts in her fingers. "If you're sure?"

Kaatje nodded, and Cècile slipped out of the room.

Kaatje threw the red silk gown onto the floor, cursing her sister and the fate that tied her to Lece. She poured rose water on a handkerchief and dabbed it on her neck and wrists to cool her anger-heated skin. If only Pietr . . . *No, not my little boy. He's the only innocent one in this chaos.* She would never put Pietr in jeopardy.

Sylph.

Becket, how can I make you understand? I would not betray you. I do not choose between you and El Müzir. Only between life and a kind of death for my son. Kaatje drew the damp handkerchief along the neckline of her gown, remembering Becket's kisses that had trailed along the same path. The memory was vivid and potent, and the strength of it unsettled her.

There was a scratching on the servants' door, and a pair of husky footmen entered at Kaatje's command, struggling with an ornate brass tub. She soaked until the hot water had turned cold, then wrapped herself in a voluminous dressing gown and ate a plain supper of partridge pie.

In the heat of the late afternoon, she drowsed on top of the counterpane, a book open and unread at her side, her mind drifting from one farfetched solution to another.

But it was all for naught. Her heart had already chosen its destiny—and fate had already chosen to keep her from it. A tear slipped onto her pillow, and she slept.

As soon as she'd bundled Kaatje out the door, Lece picked up her skirts and ran into her bedroom. The room was silent but for the rasp of her breathing that had quickened with anticipation. On her dressing table was a flask that hadn't been there before. Lucifer's Fire. She trembled.

"Oncelus? Are you here?" she whispered to the room.

A black shadow moved away from the darkness of the bed curtains and glided toward her. Oncelus was enveloped in his robes. "It has been so long," she murmured, her hand reaching out to him.

He brushed her fingertips with his and walked past to stand in the open doorway between the two rooms. "She knows," he said to himself.

Lece twirled to face him, her smile of welcome faltering. "Kaat? What does Kaat know?"

"He has told her more than I expected. She knows of . . . me."

"Do you speak of your colonel? He is here, Oncelus. In the castle."

"Of course he is, my dear. I trained him well." Oncelus spanned the doorway with his hands, gripping the doorframe. He snapped his head to one side and looked at Lece over his shoulder, his long white hair whispering over the silk. "What is she to him?"

"What is Kaatje to Thorne?" Lece shrugged, a frown marring her forehead. She didn't want to talk of her sister; she didn't want to *talk* at all. "I know he's bedded her. More than once, I'd wager."

"Does she love him?"

"Probably. She's that kind."

"Is there any more you haven't told me about him?"

Lece folded her arms across her chest. "When that stupid maid told me Kaat was distressed, I rushed to her room. And there he was, *kissing* her. From what the maid had said, I'd gotten the impression that Kaat had become distraught. Perhaps Thorne rushed to help her. He looked like he'd been comforting her."

"So, my *esir* hastened to her side." He released the doorframe and turned to face Lece. "That is a weakness in him." His nostrils flared as he drew in a deep breath. "I am fond of weaknesses, my pet."

He rubbed his fingertips with his thumb. "I could rape her and wait for him to come running. The outrage of that would certainly put him off his balance."

"No! I told you when you brought her into this that she wasn't to be hurt."

"You *told* me, my dear?" Oncelus said slowly, with a dangerous gleam in his eyes. He lowered his eyelids and shrugged. "A simple rape then. No . . . refinements."

"Nothing!"

"You still think of others, my pet. I am not pleased."

Lece turned away. "She is my sister."

"She is nothing," he said flatly. "You are to think of no one but me. Do not displease me again."

He studied her for a long while, and she smoothed her skirts nervously. "For that, my pet, you may tell your sister that the price of her brat's medicine has changed. I no longer need her gold. Now I covet something in scarlet. *English* scarlet. If Kaatje wants the medicine, she must deliver up her colonel. The medicine for the man."

"You are cruel," Lece said, and turned away from him. He laughed, and she looked back at him.

"Cruelty is one of the great pleasures of being a man," he said and let his robe slither down his bare arms to pool on the floor. He strode to her dressed only in his black silk trousers and slippers.

He grabbed her by her throat and lifted her up so she had to balance on her toes to keep from choking. "I have rutted as I watched a man being beaten to death, the whipmaster matching his lashes to my thrusts. I would become delirious with pleasure, paying no heed to the woman on whom I spent myself. I would have her buried with the whipped man in the same grave. Such delicious irony."

He lowered Lece to her feet and released her. "But it is not in my plans to kill you," he said and pulled a small black-bladed knife from the waistband of his trousers.

She stood poised to run, watching the knife warily, not at all sure of his mood.

"As usual, my dear, you are overdressed," he said and began cutting the laces of her bodice one by one. "Discard it," he ordered when he was done, and she clawed the heavy satin off her shoulders and let the bodice fall to the floor.

Her breasts swelled over the tightly laced stays, and he stroked the quivering flesh with the flat of the blade as if he were sharpening the knife on a strop. The flat of the blade slid upward and came to rest on the rapid pulse at her neck. "Red is such an arousing sight against fair Christian skin."

His brown-black eyes were half closed and his lips had molded into a smile of remembered depravity. He removed the knife blade from her throat and plunged it into the cleavage between her breasts, slicing off her stays. Her breasts swayed free as he wrenched the material off and tossed it aside. "Your skirts, my dear," he said, tucking the knife back into his trousers.

She fumbled with the ties, then hurriedly stepped out of them. "Oncel—"

He put two fingers in her mouth and wrapped his

other arm around her neck, pinning her to him. "Shhh," he said, and drew his fingers out to the first knuckle. "A woman's tongue has more useful tasks than speech. Remember your training." He pushed his fingers back into her mouth. He stroked her tongue, coaxing it, drawing his hand in and out. "Yes, yes," he murmured, as she began sucking on his fingers. "Harder," he commanded, his movements becoming faster.

Without warning, he pulled his fingers from her mouth and wiped them on her breasts, leaving a wet, glistening trail. He plucked her aroused nipples with his slippery fingers. "A woman should be naked except for her stockings." He stroked her neck. "Were we in Temesvár, I would have a golden chain around your neck. You would sit at my feet dressed as you are now . . ." He tugged the soft brown fur at the vee of her thighs. ". . . ever ready for my pleasure."

His fingers slipped inside her, to stroke the inner dampness, then he pulled them out and thrust them back into her mouth. "Harder," he said. She winced, but obeyed him. "Yes, yes. You trained well." He pulled the fingers out of her mouth and pointedly licked them.

"Kneel," he ordered and she slowly went to her knees in front of him, the marble floor cold on her overhot skin. She smiled, her head falling back and her eyes closing. She flattened her palms against his engorged phallus, rubbing it through the taut black silk. He untied his trousers and she pulled them down. He dug his hand into her hair and pushed her face into his loins.

"Yes, yes," he hissed as her lips closed over his hard flesh. He rocked into her mouth, holding her head against him. "Ah, yes. You learned well." He drew in a sudden breath. "Exquisitely well.

"Did your husband ever suspect you were beneath my shrouded table that night he came to see me? Yes,

yes. He talked endlessly. Ah, again, again. Such a delicious trick it was. To watch his mouth move, and his tongue flick against his teeth as he spoke, knowing his bitch knelt in front of my chair and moved her mouth and flicked her tongue to much better effect. My pleasure was long that night.

"Yes, yes. Harder. Ah, yes." He tightened his grip on her hair and held her still as he rocked hard into her mouth. "And I shall leave you . . . even better . . . tutored . . . than when—"

He sucked in his breath. "Aiy, aiy," he snarled and spewed out a stream of Turkish words, his body shuddering . . . then he was still.

Oncelus pulled her off him and dragged her to her feet by her hair. He squeezed her jaw and kissed her savagely.

Lece tried to push away, but he held her tight until he was done. She stumbled away, falling against the high mattress of the bed. "What do you mean, 'leave me'?" she gasped out, and wiped at her mouth with the back of her hand.

He stepped out of his trousers and slippers and came at her brazenly naked. With one hand, he grabbed her around the throat and bent her backward onto the bed. "I mean what I say."

He plunged two fingers between her legs and up inside her, working them in and out.

"No, no," she cried and tried to crawl away, but he held her too firmly. His fingers flicked against the tiny potent source of her ecstasy and she heard the slippery telltale sounds of her excitement. *"No,"* she whispered, trying to deny the desire that burned where his hand worked.

"This is what you hunger for under your pale European skin." He flicked again and she jerked in response.

"Ah," she sighed, squeezing her eyes shut as her hips began moving against his intruding hand.

"You crave the betrayal of your body. The humiliation of the last moments of frantic rutting with a lover who has discarded you." He rubbed her harder.

"Yes, yes," she screamed, grabbing his hand and holding his fingers inside her as she rocked against it. "Ah, ah, ah—" She shuddered uncontrollably.

He released her and she rolled onto her side, tears falling onto the counterpane as she quivered for long minutes with the aftershocks of her passion.

Oncelus turned his back on her and went to the window. "Now *esir,* it is time for my other pet to return to me," he said. "You will soon be a colonel no longer. I know your weakness. And I have saved your chains."

Chapter 16

⁀◟◜◞◟

"Kern'l," Harry Fludd said, a disgusted look
on his face as he stood firmly between his
master and the door, "ye gots to get some rest. Ye been
in the saddle for days 'n' ye didn't even sleep a-t'all
last night. Now we ain't had no soft beds since last
winter and we prob'ly won't again till *next* winter—so's
how come yer not *in* it? Any one o' us could search the
d'Agenais piece's room fer ya."

Becket had spent the day wrestling with the problem
of trapping the Turk, seeing to it that Lece and Kaatje's
chambers were being watched. He had to search Lece's
room, to flush out El Müzir—though the devil was elusive and never where he was expected to be. But in
truth, Becket wanted nothing better than to get some
sleep. Meeting El Müzir at less than peak strength
would be foolhardy.

Early that afternoon his informants had told him of
Kaatje's talk with her sister in Lece's suite. He'd barely
been able to control himself from bursting into the
d'Agenais's room and demanding El Müzir, pulling
the paneling from the wall and the marble from the
floor to search for him.

It ate at him that Kaatje still protected that devil. He
knew why now, yet—

"Have you heard anything more?" Becket asked
Harry now.

The long-suffering servant sighed, and his look of disgust deepened. "Same as afore, kern'l. The widow ain't come out o' her rooms. No doubt *she's* catchin' up on her sleep while yer spendin' all her time frettin' about 'er."

"One does not 'fret' about an adversary."

"An adver—Is that why she takes so many baths?"

"An opponent, Harry."

"Nah, sir. She be a good woman. Raised a fine boy, she 'as. Bright as a new penny and full o' pluck."

"Enough," Becket said, chopping the air with his hand to dismiss the subject. "Her sister. What is the report?"

Harry's eyes narrowed knowingly, but he only answered the colonel's question. "The d'Agenais piece is still in 'er rooms. 'Er maid'll come runnin' if'n things change, kern'l, but last I 'eard, the d'Agenais was curled up tighter than a bug in the middle o' 'er bed and 'ad been fer hours."

"Damn." Becket hit one of the bedposts with his fists, making the whole bed shudder. "I want to know the minute she stirs. I want her out of there, Harry. I'm too close now to lose that devil if his whore calls Claude's guards."

Harry shook his head. "I'd wager my second-best breeches that she ain't budgin' for the rest o' the night." He went to the bed and flung back the counterpane. " 'Ere now, kern'l, have yourself a little rest. I'll let yer know if she toddles out." He patted down a pillow.

Becket snatched the pillow from under Harry's hand. He threw himself into a chair, his scabbard clattering against the ornate gilded chair leg, and stuffed the pillow behind his head. He hooked a booted foot around the leg of a facing chair and pulled it closer, then put his feet on the seat and stretched out as comfortably as he could.

Sleep immediately tugged at his body, and he crossed

his arms in front of him to fight it off. He was more
tired than he'd thought. A golden image flickered at the
edge of his suddenly sluggish mind. "You say she took
another bath."

Harry bit back a smile. "Yes sir, kern'l. Your pretty
Flemish widow sure's a clean one."

Becket's arms relaxed against his chest and his head
fell slightly to one side as his eyelids drooped closed.
"She's not my . . ." he began, but his words trailed
off into sleep.

"No, sir, kern'l," Harry whispered to his slumber-
ing master. "I can see that. That explains why yer
payin' two stout footmen t' guard 'er little boy's door.
An' why the man watching 'er has t' report twice as
often as the rest o' us." Harry shook his head. "No,
sir, kern'l, she ain't yorn a-tall," he said, and quietly
slipped out the servants' door.

Becket dreamed he was back in his cell, alone. Where
were the others, the nameless damned men with whom
he had shared this hell? Faint light from the sun stole
under the door. It must be early in his captivity; El
Müzir had had that blocked up after a year or so had
passed. The door opened, flooding the tiny room with
light.

His arm went up to protect his eyes and he blinked
against the glare. "You are hurt," a woman's soft voice
said. He lowered his arm and saw a golden-haired
beauty poised in the doorway, naked but for a transparent wrap of gauze.

"No!" he cried out, twisting and turning in his sleep.
"Not you. Not here . . ." *Not Kaatje, not* his *Kaatje,
in the hands of El Müzir.*

She glided over to him, the door closing silently behind her, but still the light followed her. "I am here to
heal you," she said, brushing her fingers over his forehead, the feather touch soothing him. She caressed his

bruised and whipped body with tender caring hands. His body trembled with want, with need for her. Long-dead responses kindled to life.

He reached to embrace her, but she began to fade into nothingness, sadly shaking her head, and whispering, "I will do anything to save my son. Anything."

She faded completely, only her words lingering in the darkness of his cell, her words and the subtle scent of her hair. "Sylph," he cried out. "Sylph! You don't know what you do . . ."

Dark masculine laughter filled the blackness.

Becket wrenched himself out of his dream. He grabbed at his sword hilt and bounded to his feet, the pillow falling from the chair. It had been torn in half, its down spilling white and pure onto the carpet from the gaping rent.

"You will soon be done with laughter, El Müzir," he grated out to the dark shadow laughing in his head. "You will soon be done with *life*. There will be an end to this." He shook his head to rid himself of the echo of that hated laughter.

"Harry!" he bellowed. "Harry, *now!*" It was late in the night and the candles had burned low. Becket paced the length of his room to let the air of the summer night dry his sweat-dampened skin, and to banish the foreboding and regret that the dream-Kaatje's words had left him with.

Why hadn't she told him of her son earlier, when they still traveled, when they still had time to . . . *What? What has changed?* Nothing. The resolutions he'd made during his mad morning ride seemed paltry now. It had been foolhardy to send Niall off tracking the tale of Claude's grandfather, imprisoned in an Italian monastery. In truth, there was little he could do to help her.

A tiny fluff of down had stuck to his breeches, and when he brushed it off, it clung to his fingers. "You

gave me hope, Kaatje. Your caring, your softness . . ."
He rubbed the delicate strands into a tiny ball, then
watched it expand, returning to its full shape. "But
there is no returning, is there Kaatje? Dealing with the
devil is no way out for you, for your son. Make your
peace with Claude. It is the only hope you have." The
softness of the down reminded Becket of her dream-
touch, and he flicked it away. "El Müzir will die,
Kaatje. He will die." And so would he.

He slammed open the servants' door and roared,
"Harry!"

"I hear yer, kern'l. I hear yer," Harry said, setting
his foot on the last step of the servants' round stone
stairway. "It's me bones that's old, not me ears."

Harry came into the room, and Becket threw the door
shut behind him. The servant snorted at the mess of
down on the carpet. "Slept well, I see. 'Is 'ighness
asked about yer, kern'l, an' I says yer a tad under the
weather." Becket snarled at the intimation of infirmity,
but Harry chuckled and went on. "An' 'is 'ighness
says, 'Under the weather? I don't recall any maid named
'weather.' "

"Report."

Harry shrugged with a sigh. "They's all still sleepin', kern'l. Both the widow an' the wanton." He
tucked his thumbs over his belt and stared at the muddy
landscape painting hanging behind Becket's left shoulder.

"The widow ate a bit o' partridge pie," he said, "a
chestnut salat, and sipped 'alf a glass o' canary wine,
then sat by the winder fer a bit, read a bit, then retired.
The wanton skipped the pie, and the salat, and went
straight t' bed wit' a bottle o' canary. No winder. No
book. On 'er second bottle, she is, curled up 'round it
like a baby wit' a rag doll."

Becket turned away to face the unlit fireplace. "And

the boy?'' he asked, looking back at Harry, who grinned.

"Sleepin' like a angel,'' Harry said, then lowered his eyes and shuffled his feet. "I . . . uh, I looked in on 'im myself a bit ago. Thought he'd like to see an old face. What a game 'un, kern'l. Beamed at me like I was the cap'n-general hisself, and 'e fell o'sleep listenin' to . . . uh, some old story er other.'' Harry wouldn't meet Becket's eyes.

"You didn't boast of Ramillies, Harry? The boy lost his father in that battle.''

"Nay, nay, kern'l, I knows that. I's tellin' 'im about yer scatterin' the whole left wing of the French cavalry wit' yer sword a-flashin' and that black hell horse o' yorn jes' plowin' clean through 'em like it was judgment day!''

"That's enough, Harry. His mother wouldn't like it if she knew you'd been feeding him bedtime battle stories.''

"Yes sir, kern'l,'' the servant said reluctantly, and turned to go.

"Harry,'' Becket began, then stopped.

The older man looked back at him. "Yes sir?''

"If anything should happen . . . If the boy ever appeared to be in danger . . .'' Becket turned back to the fireplace, not letting his servant see his face. "Mothers can be so unpredictable when their children are in danger. Madame de St. Benoit might do something that would interfere with the performance of our duty.''

Becket hit the mantel with his fist. "Harry, if anything happens, just get the boy out of here. Get him to safety. Take him to the captain-general if you have to. His mother, too.''

"Get 'im outta . . . 'Is 'ighness's nephew, kern'l?'' Harry's eyes were wide with disbelief. " 'Is 'ighness'll 'ave yer 'ead! Takin' a margrave's nephew! Even the cap'n-general couldn't save yer, kern'l.''

"That's an order, Fludd. Do what you have to do, but I want Pietr de St. Benoit and his mother safe."

"Yes sir, kern'l," Harry mumbled, and opened the servants' door. He slowly walked out of the room, shaking his head. "But the margrave'll 'ave yer 'ead."

"He's welcome to it," Becket told the empty room. "By the time he will have caught up with me it will be the head of a corpse."

The next morning, Kaatje woke feeling nervous and unsettled. She wanted to see her son, to hold him and reassure herself. She gulped her morning chocolate and could hardly hold still for the fumbling maid to pull her laces tight.

When Kaatje finally broke free of Cècile's tucking, tugging fingers, she hurried to Pietr's room. Two hulking men stood outside it. She stumbled to a halt.

The men challenged her, but Pietr's valet opened the door and looked out with his face pinched. "What is the meaning of all this noise? Oh, it is you, madame."

"Who are these men?" Kaatje asked.

The valet shrugged. "They appeared. I never question his highness, madame. What do you want? Monsieur Pierre is at his riding lesson."

"Oh. I wish to see Grette."

"The old woman?" the valet asked with a sniff. He opened the door wider and gestured to the servants' door behind him. "She is through there."

Kaatje brushed past him and then slowed as her eyes swept Pietr's room. There was a small sky-blue velvet coat laid out on the bed, brushed and ready for him when he returned from his riding lesson. She smiled shakily, wanting to touch it, smooth it, the way she had for so long.

The room, the valet, the riding lessons—they were all what she wanted for her son, and yet . . . she missed seeing him run in to show her a new treasure, watching him wolf down freshly baked bread dripping with jam. And most of all she missed just being with him. Well-bred sons did not spend much time with their mothers.

She went to see Grette. The old servant assured her Pietr was doing well and, under her breath, told her that he took his cordial every morning without a murmur. Relieved, Kaatje impulsively hugged her. She went back through the room, stopping to pick up one of Pietr's new silver hairbrushes. A few golden strands were caught in the bristles. A treasure indeed. She put the brush down and left, her throat tight.

She returned to her rooms and spent the next few hours almost convincing herself the tangle of their lives could be undone. Word came that Claude insisted she participate in an afternoon of card playing. Kaatje hated piquet.

Cècile appeared, and Kaatje tried not to squirm as the girl tightly laced her into yet another gown, this one of green silk. Storm clouds were racing in from the northwest, obscuring the sun, and the damp, heavy air made the silk cling uncomfortably to her skin. The gold lace across her bosom scratched.

"Where did this come from?" she asked the maid, not at all comfortable with the elaborate costume.

The maid looked taken aback. "His highness, of course, ma'am."

Kaatje frowned, studying herself in the mirror. Claude? She grimaced. She wanted the old Kaatje back, the one whose plain cloth cap didn't have ruffles sticking out from her head like rays of the sun and four long lace pinners fluttering down her back. The one whose petticoats had been under her skirts, not covered in tiers of ruffles with the sides of her skirts pulled back to show it.

The one whose heart was her own. She looked away from the image of herself.

There was a knock on the door, and Lece burst in.

Kaatje gasped in surprise. Dark circles were smudged under her sister's lackluster brown eyes.

"My God, Lece!" Kaatje whispered urgently. "Are you ill?" She put a hand on her sister's arm, and Lece patted it, then pushed it away, surprisingly gently.

"No, little sister." Lece's movements were abrupt and jerky as she looked around her. "This room is stifling. Open the window," she ordered Cécile.

She stepped back, hands on hips, scrutinizing Kaatje. "So Claude finally told that lazy *dame d'atour* to do up some clothes for you. Someone must have mentioned to him that you were dressing in castoffs." Lece chuckled. "I'll bet that old witch hasn't been so busy in years!"

Kaatje turned to the maid, snapping the train of green silk behind her. "Please tell the mistress of the robes that in the future—" She broke off the words, her stomach in a knot tighter than the lacing had been. The *future*.

"Ma'am?"

"I-I prefer simpler gowns," Kaatje said unsteadily. She watched Lece—the only source of her son's medicine—moving frenetically around the bedroom, picking up hairbrushes, one by one, then setting them down, then fingering the lace ruffles of the bedcurtains. The silk of her sister's gown rustled luxuriously, but Kaatje saw the troubled look in Lece's eyes.

"Is anything wrong, Lece?" Kaatje asked.

Her sister shot a look at the maid. "Leave us," she ordered. The girl gave a quick curtsy and obeyed.

Unnerved, Kaatje closed her eyes and made her lungs draw in air to speak. "Lece . . ." She opened her eyes.

Lece was inspecting a small figurine from the bedside table.

"What's this?" she asked. "It looks like a chess king."

Kaatje took the carved Charlemagne from her sister

and set it back on the table. "What is it, Lece? Has El Mü—Has Oncelus not come with Pietr's medicine?"

"That's twice you've done that," Lece said, looking speculatively at her sister out of the corners of her eyes. "Start to call him something else. Is it a trick your Englishman taught you?"

Kaatje turned away, refusing to let herself be baited. "Is he here, Lece? Does he have Pietr's medicine?"

Her sister remained silent and Kaatje faced her, an alarm starting to jangle in her head. "Lece, he must have it! Please . . ."

Lece shrugged, her overbright eyes darting around her to the walls, the bed, the floor, everywhere but Kaatje. "Oncelus wants to meet with you," she said, her voice scarcely above a mumble.

"Thank God!" Kaatje expelled, her hand on her chest. "Oh, Lece, thank you!" She impetuously hugged her sister, for a brief moment closing the chasm between them. "Finally an end to this waiting."

Lece rubbed her eyes as if she were immeasurably tired. "I must go," she said.

"No, wait!" Kaatje said, putting out a hand to stay her sister. "Oncelus—where do I meet him? And when? The clock! I must get it from—"

Lece snatched her arm out of Kaatje's reach. "I'll send word."

Kaatje put her hands to her flushed cheeks. "Lece, the clock . . . I don't know what to do. It was broken. The French searched St. Benoit and—"

"What does it matter?" Lece cried, hysteria wavering at the edge of her words. "What does the price matter?" She spun around and darted toward the door.

Kaatje ran after her. "Lece! For God's sake—" she began, but her sister threw open the door and left, slamming it closed behind her.

Face burning, Kaatje leaned against the door with a

sigh. This was what she'd waited for, hoped for, fought for. But now . . .

Becket.

You can't deal with El Müzir, his voice said in her mind. *He will crush both you and your son.*

She closed her eyes and put her hand over her mouth. Sweet God, just moments ago, the ending—their ending—had not seemed so near. He would hate her, despise her weakness.

But it had to be.

"Becket, forgive me. I have no choice."

There was a knock on the servants' door. "Ma'am?" the maid asked as she pushed it ajar, then stepped into the room and curtsied when she saw Kaatje by the main door. "Ma'am, his highness sent word that you're expected in the Green Salon. The Duchesse de Chamboret is waiting to play piquet."

Kaatje straightened. "Thank you. I shall be there shortly."

Cécile curtsied again and departed.

The clock—what was left of it, anyway—was still in Pietr's room in one of his trunks. She wanted to have it with her when she met with El Müzir. Kaatje glanced at the window. It was only late afternoon, but already the coming storm had darkened the sky to the dimness of twilight. She couldn't defy Claude, as much as she wanted to, so she would have to get the clock later tonight. She shook out her skirts, then left her rooms, heading for the Green Salon.

As Kaatje entered the room, music drifted from the gallery in a taunting counterpoint to her mood. And as she passed the gaming tables, she heard the provocative giggles and low suggestive murmurs of men and women flirting.

Heat made her back prickle. All the sconces were lit

to chase away the gloom, and candlelight reflected off the castle windows, making the glazing sparkle.

The steward led her to the table where Aunt Amélie, the Duchesse de Chamboret, already sat, the margrave nodding absently as Kaatje passed. A stick of a man called Georges sat mute next to the grand dame. There was a deck of cards in the middle of the table. She sat down.

"Deal, my dear," the older woman said. Kaatje dealt.

"There!" the duchesse said in the middle of the hand. "Isn't that your Englishman?" She fluttered her cards toward someone standing behind Kaatje.

The pips on her cards blurred. She forced herself to look behind her at the man standing in front of a painting of three cavorting nudes, ostensibly the Three Graces. He was flirting with a lady who bore a remarkable resemblance to one of the women in the painting.

The man bowed toward them, his long dark wig falling forward. Annoyance flashed across his companion's face. Kaatje looked back at her cards. "The Englishman is not mine, Aunt Amélie. And that is not he."

The man shrugged when Kaatje did not return his notice. The duchesse laughed and returned to her cards.

The heat of the room suddenly increased, radiating against Kaatje's back. A spasm of panic squeezed her throat shut.

Becket leaned over her shoulder and plucked the cards from her hand. He threw them on the table, face up. "The game is ended, I'm afraid, Madame la Duchesse."

The duchesse frowned at him and opened her mouth to reply, but she only smacked Georges on the knee and said, "Philippe's relic is leaving. Play out her hand."

"But you've seen it!" he complained.

"That's why I know I'm winning. Play."

Becket squeezed Kaatje's elbow and pulled her to her feet. He was dressed in deep burgundy velvet, embroidered with gold. It still startled her to see him in courtier's clothes; she missed the scarlet.

"Lord Thorne," she began.

"This way, madame." He escorted her to the painting of the Three Graces. Gentlemen and ladies nodded as they passed, then returned to their play.

"Why are you doing this?" she asked, keeping her voice low. "You made it clear you'd done with me when you walked away after the ball."

He stood next to her, watching her. They were alone here, the crowd a mere hum behind them. The women in the picture above her seemed to be laughing at her, and spinning about all by themselves, faster and faster—

"Your sister visited you earlier," he said. "What did she say?"

She looked at him, willing her stomach to unknot. He couldn't know El Müzir was here, wanted to see her. Not so soon. "The Graces are very beautiful," she said.

"They are not to my taste."

Kaatje swallowed. "But their skin is like ivory. And their—"

"I prefer skin like alabaster," he murmured. "By moonlight."

She flushed and lowered her eyes. He did not touch her, yet she could feel his warmth against her side.

"Your sister's rooms yielded hints of"—he glanced around him—"a recent guest, but nothing—"

"The m-music is lovely," she stammered.

"I have heard sounds a thousand times more lovely, Kaatje." His voice caressed her, the timbre resonating through the air to settle against her skin like an embrace. Her flush deepened.

He lifted her chin with a finger, then removed his touch. "Tell me what I wish to know."

She could still feel the impression of his touch on her skin. Her throat contracted. "I don't know where he is. Lece didn't tell—"

"Why would your sister not tell you where he conceals himself?" Becket asked, disbelief clear in his tone. "It is you who have chosen not to tell me."

"Becket . . ." A chill washed over her, and her eyes darted to the window, expecting to see that the storm had hit. But the storm was at her side.

"Do what you will," he said. "I shall stop you."

She licked her lips, reluctant to move her gaze from the window. "What is it like to survive a battle, Becket?" she asked in a whisper. "Do you catch your reflection and think, that is not the man who came this way in the morning? Do you mourn what you've lost, or do you rejoice in merely being alive?"

She let her gaze slowly travel to him.

"Do the days and months that follow seem pallid? Dull waking dreams filled with dim candlelight and distant laughter, as if your life had ended on that battlefield and the memories are the only part of you that remain alive?"

"You do not need an answer from me, madame," he said, his eyes hard. He studied her intently. "What does your reflection tell you? What do you mourn that you have lost—or are about to lose?" He stepped back from her and bowed, ready to depart. "As for the memories, you will soon know for yourself."

Chapter 17

L ate that night, Kaatje sat in front of the unlit fireplace, the carving of Charlemagne clutched in her hand, and the green silk bodice of her gown stained black with undried tears. Twice he'd walked away from her.

She set the chess piece back in its proper place. The wind buffeted the windows, and she glanced up. It was time. She could put it off no longer. She rose and untied the long train from her skirts with clumsy fingers and laid it over the back of the chair, then pulled the ruffled cap from her hair.

Kaatje unlatched the door and went out, walking softly through the night-quiet old wing of the castle to Pietr's room. This late, everything was eerily silent and dim, with only an occasional candle to illuminate the shadows.

As she neared the nursery, the walls became starker, made of bare stone or simple planed wood, no gilded cherubs or costly tapestries of cavorting nymphs. It reminded Kaatje of the root cellar at St. Benoit.

With a start, she realized that that's what children were to Claude. Unripened fruit which one kept in some out-of-the-way place until they could be of use.

She rounded the last corner, and her steps slowed. Candlelight blazed from a fully lit seven-candle sconce. In the center of the brightness the two bulky footmen she'd seen that morning stood in front of Pietr's door, silent and menacing in their ill-fitting livery. Why was Claude having Pietr guarded?

She lifted her chin and approached them cautiously, telling herself they would not deny entrance to the boy's mother.

"Sorry, mum," one of the footmen said, holding out a massive arm to bar her from unlatching the door. "The boy is sleepin'."

"I should hope so, at this hour," she said calmly, hiding her damp palms in the fullness of her skirts. "He is my son. I . . . I understand he had a difficult riding lesson this morning and I wish to make sure he is unhurt."

The two footmen glanced at each other. "You're his ma?" the other one asked, frowning.

Kaatje sighed. "He is my son. That makes me his mother." They glanced at each other again. "Let me enter!" she demanded in a harsh whisper. "Or do you wish me to recite his entire blood line?"

"No, mum," one of them said.

The other unlatched the door for her, then stepped aside. He put his finger to his lips in a surprisingly gentle gesture.

She entered the room with her heart in her throat, her eyes riveted to the picture of her sleeping son. A single candle burned on the night table. For a long time, she stood unmoving at the foot of his bed and watched him, cherishing the gentle rise and fall of his chest and the tangle of his soft blond curls on the pillow. He was a vision of perfection.

Claude's words rushed in on her. *I do not tolerate imperfection.* She shivered and put a steadying hand on the bedpost, telling herself over and over that the margrave would never learn of his nephew's "imperfection."

She searched through the large wardrobe that held

Pietr's clothes, then a high chest scuffed with age before she found the worn brown velvet bag that held the broken clock. The tinkle of precious metal sounded loud in the quiet room when she picked up the heavy bag, and she silently cursed the French and Roulon and their careless searching of St. Benoit.

A rumble of subdued voices came through the door. A certain inflection, a certain familiar resonance made her alert. *Becket.* Her breaths became shallow as she strained to hear.

"How long has she been?" the colonel's voice said. Kaatje clutched the clock bag tighter and ran to the servants' door. Gentle snoring greeted her, and she discovered Grette sleeping on a cot in the tiny room.

Kaatje spared a smile for the old servant's faithfulness as she slipped past the sleeping woman and entered the servants' stairs.

Darkness smothered her, smelling of rancid oil and damp. She walked on, letting her hand guide her along the rough stone wall until her eyes adjusted to the light from the single oil lamp that burned on a crooked high wooden ledge, creating more shadows than illumination.

Kaatje swallowed the lump of panic that had settled in her throat. She turned down one narrow hall, then hesitated and stepped back into the main corridor. She held the bag closer to her, then jumped at the tinkling it made and almost dropped it. Her heart thumped in her chest. What was that sound behind her?

She spun around, her eyes frantically searching the way she'd come. Empty. She stepped into another hallway and peered into the thick shadows. The blackness repelled her. She took a step back . . .

. . . and bumped into a solid unmoving barrier that hadn't been there a moment before.

She swallowed a scream. Hands clamped on her

shoulders. Her breathing stopped. The hands pulled her around.

Becket. He loomed before her, the light behind him casting his shadow over her. Energy pulsed from him. He stood there, alert, battle-ready, his hair unbound, his shirt undone under his scarlet coat and waistcoat, a soldier roused from sleep by a call to war.

"I gave you fair warning, madame," he said, his voice flat and cold.

"It is but a clock!" she said. "What aid can that be?" Her hands reached out to him. "Becket, I pay him for medicine—nothing more."

"Ask yourself what payment he will demand after the clock," he told her, taking the bag and tying it to his belt as if it were but a money pouch.

"You will pay him nothing," Becket said, grabbing her wrist and pulling her to him. Eyes dark as the night storm bored down into hers. "Nothing now. Nothing ever."

He turned and dragged her, stumbling, into a stair-well that led down into darkness.

"Becket, I must," she gasped, her slippers skidding over the uneven stone. "Release me!" She struggled to pull out of the iron hold on her wrist. "This solves nothing, you damned Englishman!"

"Damned, indeed, madame," he growled. "But you come with me." Turning and twisting, they descended the dark labyrinth of the servants' stairs. He stopped abruptly in front of a barred door. She bumped into him, his back seeming more solid and unmovable than the stone wall.

He slammed back the bar. There was a shriek of rusted iron. He kicked the door open, and the blustery night wind swirled in around her.

The door led to one of the castle's gardens. Torches had been set out for the earlier party; most had been blown out, but a few still burned, their flames roaring sideways in the wind. Becket pulled her outside, his hair whipping madly around his face.

"Becket, stop this! What are you doing?" Kaatje cried, struggling against his pull. The wind blew her words away. "Where are you taking me?" Her skirts billowed and puffed around her.

"Away from the castle," Becket told her, his deep voice cutting clear and strong through the wind. "Away from the devil."

He dragged her farther into the garden. The wind slackened for a brief moment, and Kaatje heard a sobbing cry just ahead of them. Becket pulled her into the deep shadows of a tall yew hedge.

Cècile ran past them, tightly holding the shreds of her gown to her, blind with tears. Leaves and tiny sticks were tangled in her hair and she cried with deep wracking sobs. Stunned, Kaatje stepped out of the shadows to run after her, but Becket's fingers slid into the waistband of her skirts and grabbed hard.

She staggered back a step—and that was all that kept her from colliding with Claude. He strolled after the maid, looking both sated and pleased with himself.

Kaatje recoiled, but the margrave stopped and ran his gaze over her windblown hair and tousled skirts. The touch of Becket's fingers burned into her back, but he remained still and hidden in the shadows.

"You are certainly *busy*, my dear," Claude said. "You arrive here with your reputation barely intact, and now—an assignation in the gardens." He ran his fingertips down her neck and shoulder. "Hmmm. I may have underestimated you. 'Tis a pity you're not my style, but I suppose I could compromise."

Behind her, Kaatje heard the hiss of a knife being drawn.

Claude's eyes narrowed, and he studied her speculatively. "Would your lover really try to kill me if I wanted to take you? Would he risk so much?"

Kaatje was terrified, knowing Becket was capable of killing anyone.

Claude nodded and rubbed his thumb at the outer corner of her eye, then dropped his hand. "Yes, I believe he would." He gave her a mocking smile. "My dear, as inviting as your curves are, you are hardly worth dying for. But perhaps I'll compromise about that too . . ."

He began to stroll off, then stopped and turned back to her. "I shall, of course, have to order Pierre's tutor to be more strict with the boy. His mother has such loose morals. A pity, but there it is.

"But at least you don't have that pinched look so many females have when they don't have a man to satisfy them." He continued on, smiling to himself, then disappeared beyond a hedge.

Becket yanked on her waistband, and she fell backward. He caught her and scooped her into his arms. The knife was gone.

"We tarry," he said, and strode to the castle's south gate. The bag with the clock jangled as he walked, sounding like spurs.

"Release me, damn you," she cried, hitting his shoulder and trying to kick out of his hold. She struggled harder, but he rolled her into him, using her own body to trap her arms against his chest.

"Fight me, chatelaine," he said, his voice low. Kaatje went still.

Acheron was just past the wall. Becket set her on the stallion, then mounted behind her. The familiarity of his arm pressed across her back was dangerously welcoming. She tried to jump off, but his arm locked around her waist. His muscles moved beneath her in a command to the horse, and they surged forward.

She hit at his shoulders again. "Why are you doing this?" she demanded. "Damn you." Her blows were growing weaker and weaker. She choked on a sob of frustrated anger. "Damn you, Becket. Why won't you let me save my son?"

"You are misguided."

"*I? I* am misguided? You almost killed the Margrave of Hespaire-Aube!"

"Yes."

The word swirled around her in the wind, then blew away. The first spitting drops of the coming storm fell, adding new stains to her gown. Ahead of them, the deserted abbey was a darker shadow against the storm clouds.

Becket kneed Acheron up the last hill and into the stable lean-to. The rain grew harder, the sound of the individual drops blurring into a din.

He dismounted, then pulled Kaatje off the horse. "In there," he ordered, shouting over the rain and pointing to the nearest doorway.

She hesitated, not wanting to obey him. He undid the saddle and threw it over a railing. He strode toward her.

She took a step back. Then another. Then turned and dashed into the room. He followed a heartbeat later.

"Niall is on the other side of the city tonight," he said, lighting a lantern. The glow revealed the old stones of the room's wall and a blanket thrown over a pile of straw in one corner.

The summer night was wet and violent, but not cold, and the sound of the rain enclosed them.

"All I want to do is save my son," she said, "but everything is such a tangled knot."

He pulled his knife from his boot. Her breath caught. Light from the lantern's low flame caressed the knife edge and reflected the dark smile in his night blue eyes.

"Any knot may be undone, madame." He slid the blade under the cord that held the clock bag to his belt and sliced upward.

He pulled at the bag, breaking the last threads of the

cord, and threw the bag against the wall. The crash was louder than the rain. Small pieces of gold and enamel spilled out, scattering onto the dirt floor like precious seeds. "You go to meet him. Tell me where."

She knelt to gather the strewn fragments.

Becket caught at her arm. *"Tell me where he is."*

She glanced at the knife in his other hand, then looked him full in the face. "Do you threaten me, Colonel Thorne?"

He flung the knife to the ground, the blade piercing the earth at his feet. His hands clamped around her arms and he lifted her bodily from the dirt. "No! You will not grovel for *him.*"

He set her on her feet, his hands still tight around her. "How can you keep silent! Haven't you smelled him in the castle? Haven't you felt the cold of his evil seeping into the stones under your feet? There are so many shadows."

He released her. He went and stood in front of the window, his hands reaching up and pressing against the top of the stone frame. "But the shadows of hell are the only domain fit for El Müzir."

Kaatje watched him, her hands clenched at her sides. "You have your duty and I have mine. My little boy is all I have. You saw Claude tonight. The medicine at least gives me time."

Lightning speared the ridge across the small valley, throwing the outline of Becket into sharp relief. Thunder cracked a heartbeat later.

"How can you think your son will be safe when his life hangs on the whim of a devil?" Becket breathed in deeply as if he were trying to inhale the power of the storm. He gripped the stone harder and crumbling mortar dusted the ground. "Why won't you see?"

"See what?" she asked bitterly. "See that my son will become a victim of your war as surely as his father did?" He dropped his arms and turned to face her.

"What are you asking of me? That I sacrifice my son for a king? A queen? An emperor? For the life of one soldier? A thousand?" She locked her gaze with his. "Or are you asking me to sacrifice my son—for you?"

He looked away, spitting out a curse. "I want you to *save* your son . . ." He scraped his fingers through his hair. "Sweet Jesu, woman, what must I do to convince you of your folly?"

"Folly? What would you have me do?" She paced in front of him, hugging herself. "I choose only to save my son. Nothing more."

"Here, madame," he said, ripping off his coat and waistcoat and tearing his shirt over his head. He came to her and grabbed her hand, pressing it against the vicious scar above his heart. He dragged her palm down the scars on his naked chest. "Here, madame, here is your choice. The man who did *this*."

Kaatje stared at her hand, feeling the warmth of his flesh and the strong beat of his heart, not the scars.

"Don't do this to me," she grated, pulling her hand out of his grasp. "Leave me alone! Leave me and my son alone."

"No!" He grabbed her shoulders and shook her. "I will not let you go to that devil. Tell Claude, damn you!"

"No!" she shouted.

"Woman," Becket roared, "he's a goddamned *angel* next to El Müzir. You can't even comprehend what the Turk would do to your son."

"Stop it stop it stop it!" She put her hands over her ears and bent over as if to curl up against his words. "I'm sick of these nameless terrors of yours. You were a prisoner of war! Pietr's just a little boy."

"Stop being so goddamned blind." He grabbed her arms and lifted her from the floor. She struggled frantically and he pressed her back against the wall. "Kaatje! Kaatje, listen to me. Damn it, listen!"

"I will not tell Claude!" She shook her head back and forth, her hair spilling down over her shoulders. "I know what that place is like," she shouted at him, her voice hoarse. "I've seen it over and over and over in my dreams. Not my Pietr. Not my son."

"Do you think that's the only hell in this world? Do you think you're the only one who dreams dark dreams?" she spit out. "All I want from El Müzir is a handful of roots and herbs. Why don't you want me to get it? *Why?*"

He pulled her away from the wall and held her face in front of his. *"Stop being so goddamned blind,"* he growled. "Because then he would get *you.*"

He kissed her. Long and hard and deep. She struggled, but he could feel the subtle growing arousal of her body. Her hands curled into his hair, not softly but demanding. Her mouth, her tongue began answering his kiss, as if her anger had suddenly spilled over a dike and flooded into desire.

He knew her every response, and there was a rumble of satisfaction deep in his throat. He let himself sink into the bliss of it, into the bliss of the knowing.

She wrenched her lips from his. "No," she rasped, gulping in breaths.

"Yes," he said, and kissed her again. He crushed her to him, her feet dangling above the floor. He pressed her back against the wall. He let her body slide down until his hips were even with hers. Then he pinned her there with his loins.

"Oh, God," Kaatje cried, feeling his arousal through her skirts. Her eyes half closed, she used the wall to support her and moved her hips against his. "Oh, God, yes."

He nipped her neck. His fingers tore her bodice lacings free, his open mouth sliding over her breasts swelling above her stays. He pulled them out of their confinement, his fingers stroking, pulling, plucking the rosy nipples.

Kaatje moaned, her back arching out from the wall. "Oh, God. Oh, God." Her head rolled back and forth. She whimpered. Her hands dragged over his naked chest, reveling in the heat and the hardness, like forged steel just taken from the fire.

She grabbed his shoulders for support and wrapped her legs around his thighs. She rocked her hips harder against his.

"Sweet *Jesu*," Becket gasped. He swept his hands under her skirts, pushing them out of the way. She whimpered deliciously.

He unbuttoned his breeches with fingers that shook with the drumming insistent fire that roared in his blood. He grasped her thighs and pulled her higher.

"Oh, God, yes, yes," she moaned, locking her legs around his waist, her woman-flesh soft, hot, and wet against his phallus.

A groan rumbled through him at the contact. She rocked again and again, opening herself for him. He grasped her behind, holding her, matching her rocking. He thrust in.

"Ahhhhh—," she shouted, throwing her hips harder against him. Her nails dug into his back. She was tight, exquisitely tight. He worked into her, exerting every thread of his unraveling control to not hurt her.

"Becket," she gasped, "oh, Becket, I want you. I want . . . Oh, yes, more, more . . ." With a hard thrust, he filled her completely, and her words trailed off with a moan. He plunged into her over and over, nearly delirious with the sweet hot pleasure. She met his thrusts—fully.

Kaatje moaned and squeezed her legs tighter around him. The glory . . . So close. So close. He pounded into her. "Sweet God sweet God sweet God." So close.

The crest grew. So close. Swelling, swelling, swelling—"Ah. Ah . . . *Becket!*"

He felt her ecstasy and it pushed him over the edge. He plunged one last time and held himself tight inside her. *"Kaatje,"* he said with a groan, and shuddered with release.

For long minutes they remained there, Becket supporting her against the wall. They panted from their exertion, nearly mindless with the after-pleasure.

"Sylph," Becket whispered, kissing her neck.

Kaatje slowly came back to awareness. Her body still pulsed with the heat of her ecstasy. It was luxuriously wanton to feel his weight pressed on her, his touch on the bare flesh of her behind, the steel hard velvet of him inside her. He slid his hands down her legs to resettle her.

"No," she murmured. "Don't . . . go."

She felt his soft laugh as he nuzzled the delicate flesh under her ear. He drew his hands slowly back up her thighs to cup her hips. "Sweet sylph . . ."

She kept her eyes closed, memorizing the feel of him inside her, the pressure of his body holding her against the wall, the feather touch of his hair falling across her face, the moist warmth of his mouth on her flesh . . . She stroked his back, letting her fingers feed her memory with the solid feel of the long hard straps of muscle.

"You're a fever in me, Kaatje," he said, kissing her cheekbone, her temple, her forehead.

"Becket," she whispered, gazing into his indigo eyes. They weren't opaque. "I feel a wanton, staying like this." She drew her thumb along his high cheekbone. "Wanting to."

"Not a wanton, Kaatje. A *woman.*" He bit at her earlobe and drew it through his teeth. She gasped. "A woman of passion."

"For you," she murmured.

Becket watched her as she caressed him, her eyes dreamy and unfocused, as if all her senses were in her fingertips. The sight of her was irresistibly erotic. Her head lounged against the wall, her golden hair picking up pinpoints of lantern light, her opened bodice hanging free at her sides, framing her breasts mounding full above the stays he'd pulled down in his desire.

"Oh!" she said in surprise, her eyes wide. He smiled provocatively and moved his hips. "Ohhh," she said again, her eyes lowering as she focused on the sensations inside her. "I didn't know you could . . ." Her hips began moving with small delicious movements as his arousal swelled inside her. Her head lolled against the wall. "Oh, Becket."

He bent and swirled his tongue around a swollen nipple. He took tasting licks in the valley between her breasts, then kissed the hollow at the base of her throat. "I need to carry you to the bed, sweet sylph," he told her.

She nodded absently, her hands roaming over his body. She unlocked her legs, and he held her tight against him as she lowered them.

She shook her head, as if coming out of a daze. "How could I have done such a th—" she began, but he kissed her swoony all over again. She melted against him, and he lifted her into his arms and carried her to the soft mound of blanket-covered straw.

He loved her a second time, and a third, their passion slow and easy as they ascended twice more into glory. And when they finally rested, Becket dreamed dreams of golden hair and alabaster skin and a cherished, matchless spirit.

But Kaatje did not dream.

She woke in the early hours of the summer morning. The storm had passed, and in the east was the faint glow of the coming dawn. Becket slept next to her, his breaths deep and steady. His warmth kept the chill of the morning at bay, his arm across her waist. She carefully squirmed out from under it. He stirred but did not wake.

Clammy dampness enveloped her, dissipating the last wisps of well-being that had suffused her from Becket's lovemaking. She fumbled with her clothes, then picked up the clock bag as quietly as she could.

She neared the door, then stopped. Kaatje closed her eyes, not wanting to turn around, not wanting to look at Becket, knowing it would be for the last time.

She turned. Her gaze caressed the long muscular length of him, trying to memorize the beloved sight. He was stretched out on the bed of straw they'd shared, his body curved as if she still slept beside him. His touch, his loving had awakened her body—and the woman inside it. It was a gift he'd given her with his passion.

She felt as if all the glazing in the castle's windows had shattered inside her. It was hard, so hard, to keep all the shards of pain from spilling out.

"I love you, Englishman," she whispered to the sleeping man, her voice almost inaudible. "I love you, Becket." She turned and walked out the door.

Outside, the heavy rains had gouged deep gullies in the path through the garden, the footholds nothing but slippery, silty mud. The remains of the clock she carried were heavy, throwing her off balance. The roofless abbey ruins loomed to her right, and she made her way there.

Inside, high, freestanding stone walls towered above her, blocking the breeze and the glow of the eastern sky. The hushed stillness settled into her bones as she walked down the ruined nave and headed toward the massive opening in the abbey's walls where huge doors once stood.

From behind her came the scrape of stone against

stone. She froze for a heartbeat, then spun to face the sound. The massive branch of an ancient oak had been blown down by the storm, ramming it onto the western abbey wall. A stone had broken free of its mortar and rested precariously against the branch.

"Don't fall," she whispered into the stillness. "Don't fall. Let me believe it's possible to balance on the edge of a precipice."

Pebbles of mortar dribbled down in answer. Kaatje hurried out, stumbling as she ran down the path toward the castle—leaving the man she loved behind.

Becket woke to the squealing protest of stone against stone. In an instant, he was on his feet, sword in hand. He was alone. The bag was gone.

She'd left him.

It cut through him like a sword thrust. Sweet Jesu. Last night there'd been light in his soul, and she had given it to him. Even in his youth—before Vienna—he had never felt anything so heady. But now . . .

The black ice inside him solidified.

He stamped into his boots and ran outside. Her footprints were clear in the mud leading down the path through the garden. He followed them. She'd slipped here, stumbled there, and here, she'd turned toward the abbey. He rushed inside, sword at the ready.

"Madame!" he roared. Silence. Then a creak of wood. A crumble of pebbles. "Did you think it would be this easy?" he shouted, mimicking words she'd said to him long ago beside the pony cart on the Odenaarde road.

A loud splintering scream of oak answered him. A stone that had teetered on a precipice crashed to the floor, cracking a block of the foundation. Another fell, then another, until the entire middle of the abbey's west wall collapsed in a loud rumble of rock and dust. Becket leaped out of the way, a limb of the oak branch as thick as a man's thigh falling inches from him. He sliced his sword out in fury, shattering the limb with one stroke of the blade.

Chapter 18

W here was Oncelus? Lece figdeted with the ruch-
ing on her bodice as she sat in the darkest corner of the music room and listened to *Le beau Berger
Tircis* being played on the harpsichord. It was late, and
she was almost all alone.

Was he angry with her? It had been three days since
she'd left him and gone to see Kaatje. When she'd returned to her rooms, he'd been gone and he hadn't yet
come back to her.

He couldn't know that she hadn't yet told her sister
about his new terms, that what he now wanted in ex-
change for Pietr's medicine was the English colonel.
She hadn't wanted to defy Oncelus, but he didn't understand about Kaatje. *Lece* didn't understand. She
thought of her sister's many frantic notes requesting to
see her; notes she'd left unanswered.

The Englishman meant nothing to Lece; she'd serve
him up with a chine of mutton if Oncelus asked it of
her. But with Kaatje . . . Lece shrugged. Perhaps it
was because once, long ago, before Stepfather, before
the burning inside her had begun—they *had* been sisters.

*Ah, you make me suffer! Little by little I feel myself
ensnared . . .* The musician had a fine voice, but the
song's lyrics made Lece smile bitterly. She rearranged
herself in the overstuffed chair and thought of Once-

313

lus, of what he could do to her. Lece remembered his power and shuddered with rising hunger. Between her legs, the unquenchable itching was beginning again, and she crossed them to shut it out, but the movement only made the sensation intensify. In her mind, she saw nothing but Oncelus, heard nothing but Oncelus, felt . . . *Mon Dieu.* Her body craved what he did to her. There was a scratching at the door, and a footman entered. He went to Lece and bowed, extending a silver salver with a sealed note on it.

"Madame d'Agenais?" he asked.

Lece snatched the note, broke it open and read it. Her breath quickened, and she impatiently waved the servant away.

With a rustle of satin and petticoats, she rushed out of the music room in answer to Oncelus's summons, the strains of *Le beau Berger Tircis* following her. Cherubs leered at her from the sconces in the wide halls as if they knew her secret as she hurried past. The desire that burned between her legs was carnal and hot. Her eyes scanned every man she passed. She silently cursed their long coats, hiding what she wanted most. *Aiiy, what do they matter,* she thought, *they are all soft and weak and . . . unskilled.* Only Oncelus knew her. Only Oncelus loved her. No, Constantin loved her, even now, but . . .

Her foot caught on a loose piece of lace from her petticoat, and she stumbled. She gasped and bit her lip, her eyes fluttering closed for an instant. Behind her, she heard muffled laughter, but it didn't matter. Lece picked up her skirts and fled. Nothing mattered, no one mattered, no one but Oncelus.

She yanked the latch to her door open and pushed. "Oncelus," she called, breathless. She saw him standing by the cold hearth, his face and hair obscured by his robes. "Oncelus. I came as soon as I—"

He moved, revealing the Comte de Roulon rising from a chair behind him.

"Roulon," Lece said, gagging on the name. A shroud of apprehension settled on her shoulders. Oncelus had obviously welcomed him. A glass of wine sat on the low table in front of him, next to a bowl of raspberries. "What is he doing here?" she asked.

"Ah, the ever *supine* Madame d'Agenais," Roulon said, bowing to her with a mocking flourish.

"Enough," Oncelus said, the power of his voice jarring them both into silence. A hand slid out from the black silk and grasped Roulon's shoulder, forcing him down until the Frenchman's knees buckled and he collapsed back into his chair. "Ignore the woman. She is of no concern. Tell me again of your men on the Hespaire. I require more than your usual rabble."

Oncelus's callous words sliced into Lece and she turned her back on him. Jealousy ate at her. She cursed Roulon, spitefully savoring all his remembered inadequacies when he'd been her lover. Hurt made her squirm. Humiliation made her cheeks burn. Her hands went to her stomach. There was a delicious weakness there. She rubbed downward with the heel of her hand.

From behind her, she heard Roulon objecting to something Oncelus had said, but the pitiful flame of his resistance was instantly quenched by a command from the Turk. She wanted the Frenchman to leave.

She heard Oncelus's words of dismissal to the comte, followed by the whisper of velvet as Roulon stood. Lece turned in time to see him bowing deeply to Oncelus.

Roulon passed her on the way to the door. "You have risen high on your back, I see," he murmured to her.

"And you are where you always have been," Lece answered, not looking at him. "On your knees."

"Putain," he said. Whore. He walked out, slamming the door behind him.

"Why are you dealing with that misbegotten wretch?" Lece asked Oncelus. He let his hood fall back into a cowl on his shoulders, but said nothing. His black eyes watched her, and she burned all the more.

"You can destroy an army!" she said. "What can you possibly want with that pitiful group of deserters Roulon attracts like flies to carrion."

"Why have you not told your sister the price of her brat's medicine? I want my *esir.*" His robes slid from his shoulders and fell to the floor. He came toward her with his black-bladed knife held before him. She ran into the bedroom. He followed.

She backed up, her hand at her throat, until she smacked into her dressing table. Oncelus undid his trousers as he reached her and let them fall to the floor. He sliced her out of her clothes and threw them aside. He forced her backward onto the table, pots of powder and flasks of perfume crashing to the floor.

He penetrated her in one stroke.

"My *esir* shall be betrayed and broken. He shall beg for death—and I shall deny him, deny him escape into that silent dark solace. Your sister kept me from him once. Now I will make her betray him."

The table scraped against the floor with each of his quick thrusts. "No," she whispered frantically, grabbing at his shoulders. Her hips began moving with his, the demanding heat inside her building. "Ah, ah," she moaned, her head lolling on the wood.

His rocking increased its tempo against her. "I shall lead him back to Cerfontaine, where only I will hear him begging for mercy. I want to savor his defeat and drink in his anguish like the . . . blood . . . of a sacrifice."

His rhythm changed, faster, more urgent. "I shall not kill him. I shall *destroy* him, flesh and mind and soul."

It was too soon. "No," she gasped. Too soon. She had so far to go . . . His fingers dug into her hips and he slammed her to him, then held her there, tight. "No, no," she cried. His indrawn breath was the only sound of his passion spilling into her.

He backed away, leaving her slumped on the table. "I don't understand," she whimpered, her legs weak. The soft flesh inside her rippled with unfulfilled desire.

"Don't you? That is what you are *for*, my pet."

She rubbed the flat of her hands low on her stomach. "But you left me . . ."

"Pleasure yourself."

Lece turned her head away from him, her hands clenching in the air. "You are cruel."

"I am lenient beyond measure." Naked, Oncelus went into the sitting room and dug his hand into the bowl of raspberries. He drew out a handful, red juice oozing through his fingers and down his arm.

He kicked two chair cushions onto the floor and sat on them, cross-legged. "You have greatly displeased me," he said, holding the raspberries to his face. "You deserve to be flayed." He bit into the mass of red fruit.

Lece stood in the doorway, her arms crossed in front of her, her gaze riveted to the red juice dripping down his hand. "W-what can you mean?"

"Your sister." He took another bite.

"I . . . I have not seen her."

"You lie. I have been much too indulgent with you." He finished the raspberries and licked his palm. "Tell her. Tell her, or I shall show you what it means to incur my wrath."

"I should never have let you bring Kaatje into this,"

Lece said, burying her face in her hands. "She's right. I am no sister to her."

"You are nothing but what I say you are," Oncelus said, watching her from his cushions on the floor. He held out his stained hand to her. "Come to me, my pet."

She slowly crossed the room, unable to keep each foot from placing itself in front of the other. The air was heavy against her naked skin.

"On your knees," he told her, his black eyes locked with hers.

Lece knelt. She cupped his sticky hand in hers and bent forward, lowering her mouth to his wrist, sucking and licking the sweetened flesh.

"Perhaps I shall put a chain around your neck after all." With his free hand, he measured the span of the delicate bones that encircled the base of her neck. "A gold one. Made from the gifts your Constantin gave me."

He put his hand over her face and she began licking his palm. "You see, my pet? I have honed my . . . talents since my *esir* left me." His fingers clenched and she cried out. "Flick your tongue between my fingers. Yes, yes. It is one of your more accomplished skills.

"I have gained subtlety in those years. Before, I would have had you hanged the moment I realized you'd disobeyed me. I would have enjoyed watching your feet flutter like the wings of a dying butterfly as my ropemaster dangled you from the walls of my citadel. But now, now I have a more refined punishment for you."

"Are you discarding me?" she asked in a whisper. His arousal had swollen again, full and tall against his loins.

Oncelus seized her wrist and pulled her staggering

off the floor, purposely keeping her off balance. He dragged her into the bedroom.

"What are you doing?" she gasped, stumbling. He tore a length of lace from the bedcurtains in answer.

"No, no, please," she cried. "What are you—"

Oncelus flung her over a low-backed upholstered chair, the back of it pressing into her stomach. With his teeth, he ripped the piece of lace into two and tied her wrists to the front legs of the chair.

She squirmed, trying to get free. "No! Untie me. Oncelus, please." He tore two more lengths from the bedcurtains and tied her ankles to the back legs.

"You struggle provocatively, my dear," he said, kneading the globes of her bottom, thrust out so lewdly over the back of the chair. He smacked her hard, then moved away. She gasped and twisted her head, watching him stand regally naked a few feet away as he inspected his handiwork. He circled around her, looking.

"Oncelus, please," she whispered, writhing under his intense gaze.

"Excellent." He encircled his engorged phallus with his own hand and stroked it slowly. "Myriad are the ways of pleasuring," he murmured, his eyelids lowering until he focused on what he was doing to himself. He smiled and removed his hand.

"Ah, but now is not the time for the idle spilling of seed." He ran his hand up her back to her neck and tugged on her hair, forcing her to lift her head a few inches. "I have kept track of your moon cycles and now is the time I have waited for."

"Wh-what do you mean?"

He chuckled. "You have been clever, haven't you my dear? So many tricks you have for not conceiving one of your lovers' brats. Did they ever guess that your diverse ways of mating were devised not to excite them, but to keep them from planting a bastard in your belly?"

He leaned down to her ear and circled his tongue around it. "I guessed, my dear. But I let you play your game with me, so I could see how much more you had to learn. And now is to be your final lesson." He released her hair.

Genuine fear fluttered in her stomach. "Why are you doing this?" she choked out, twisting her head, trying to keep him in view as he walked around her again. He ripped off a strip of her petticoat and returned to her, calmly gagging her.

"It shall be sublime. I am content in knowing that you will grow big with my child and that no man will desire you. You will be alone, with only placid Constantin for company. He will accept you back as his wife. And you are clever enough to convince him the brat in your belly will be an honorable addition to the house of d'Agenais."

He put his hand under her and rubbed her stomach. "Could that be fright that makes you quiver? Delightful."

He squeezed her breast and rolled the hardened nipple between his thumb and forefinger. "But fear isn't enough, my dear. You must feel all the sensations that matter. Fear, pain, then ecstasy. You see? Already the muscles of your bottom are beginning to tremble. Your body betrays you, as always."

He went behind her and stood between her spread legs. The back of the chair held her womanhood at a perfect level for his work.

He cupped the down-covered plumpness revealed to him. "Such a well-used little nest," he said, testing the moistness inside with his finger. "There is not a part of your body I have not known intimately." With one hand, he cupped her bottom, while with the other he used his fingernail to scratch down the back of her thigh. She flinched. "Yes, yes," he said, squeezing her bottom. "Again," he ordered, and scratched her once more.

She gasped against the gag and tightened her muscles to try and move away, but she was held too firmly. Out of the corner of her eye she saw him retrieve a riding crop.

"No!" she screamed, but it was muffled against the material he'd stuffed into her mouth. She shook her head violently. "No, no, no . . . Not that. Please not that!" she screamed again, but the words only came out as incoherent sound. She tensed every muscle she could, the chair scraping an inch along on the floor.

The crop was hard and barely flexible, with an inch of looped flat leather attached to the end. He lightly skated it over the bare flesh of her thigh and she jerked.

"You must peak an instant before I spew my seed into your womb." He sliced the crop across her bottom.

He hit her again, the crop leaving an angry red line. "You live in an uncivilized country, my dear. At home, you would be chained in my bedroom, your leash always near my hand." Another blow stung her bare flesh. "I would fill your nest whenever I felt the heat in my loins. Whip you when I wished. Then grab your hips and pull you onto me, with none of your wriggling tricks." *Whack.*

"And I would watch as a young man, barely fledged, would plunge into you hard and fast—for the last time in his life—and spill much too quickly." *Whack.* "That was always a favorite of mine."

A haze of heat and pain enveloped her below her waist. Her mind melted away. *He* commanded her every feeling, her every spark of passion; *he* transformed her into the nothingness that she was.

"This is your final lesson, bitch. *Power* is the ultimate ecstasy. The power to inflict fear and pain and make sure it is never forgotten." *Whack.*

An instant later the blows stopped, and an instant after that he plunged into her. He dug his fingers into her hips and frantically rocked in and out. "Yes," he hissed. "The whip has stirred your blood. I can feel it. Your body betrays you. Yes, yes."

Through the haze, Lece could barely hear the slippery sounds of her arousal, but she knew they were there. She had no control over her body, no power. He commanded her every response. She was nothing now, nothing except a channel for his lust.

The chair scraped fast and steady against the floor. Tears ran from her eyes. The spasms began in her knees and leaped up her thighs like a growing chain of lightning. A hot wave of ecstatic oblivion followed. She welcomed it, her body shuddering.

Oncelus rocked one last time and held her tightly to him. "Aiy, aiy, aiiiiiy . . ." He collapsed onto her, a smile of satisfaction curling his lips. "Good, good. The bitch has taken."

He pulled away and went to retrieve his knife. He sliced the bindings at her wrists and ankles. She staggered to her feet, her knees scarcely able to support her to the bed.

"Leave me," he commanded.

"Oncelus," she whispered raggedly.

"Go! It is nearly dawn. Go to your sister, my little *putain,* she is waiting to hear from you."

Kaatje was numb inside. It had been three days since she'd left Becket in the abbey. Three days she'd been alone. She lay in bed, early in the morning, writing yet another note to her sister. Another note Lece wouldn't answer.

The quill scratched loudly on the paper. She tried to remember the light in Becket's eyes when he'd looked at her in the abbey, the indigo bright with his passion, but it was no use. His dark blue eyes would only look at her in anger now.

The threads of her life were all falling from her fingers. Claude allowed her glimpses of her son; at Pietr's music lesson, or his dancing lesson, she was allowed to watch from the edge of the room. But she was not allowed to watch him being instructed in sword fighting or riding.

Her hand shook, and a drop of ink blotched her words. She crumpled the paper in her fist and fell back against the pillows, hot angry tears falling down her face.

Damn you, Lece. Why won't you answer my notes? What more can you ask of me?

Someone scratched at her door. Kaatje glanced at the pale predawn light beginning to fade the night's darkness. She set the lap desk on her night table and got out of bed, wrapping her batiste dressing gown tightly around her.

"Who is it?" she asked at the closed door. She heard a feeble mumble in response.

Kaatje frowned and opened the door an inch. Lece slumped against the doorframe, carelessly wrapped in a simple dressing gown.

"*My God*, Lece," Kaatje cried, throwing the door open and helping her sister into the sitting room. Lece collapsed onto one of the chairs. She cried out and winced as if in pain, then huddled over, her arms around her waist.

Kaatje knelt beside her, stroking her shoulder. "Lece, what happened? You're hurt. Where? How?"

Lece turned her face away from Kaatje. "It's nothing I didn't deserve," she said in a shaky whisper.

"Lece—"

Her sister waved her silent. "Kaat," she began, then stopped to swallow. The corners of her mouth were torn and she spoke carefully as if it hurt to form the words.

"Little sister, forgive me. Oncelus doesn't want the clock anymore."

Kaatje went cold. She sat back on her heels, looking up at Lece. "What do you mean? He wants something, doesn't he? Lece, I must have that medicine! I'll pay anything. What does he want?"

Lece's gaze met hers. Kaatje gasped at the bewilderment there, the confusion, all mixed in with despair that was almost palpable. Lece's eyes slid from her sister to the chess table. She slowly reached out and picked up the white king.

"Here," she whispered, holding out the carved Charlemagne to Kaatje. "This is what Oncelus wants in payment for Pietr's medicine. Your Englishman. The medicine for the man."

"No." Kaatje knocked the chess piece out of Lece's hand. It hit the marble fireplace and shattered. *"No,"* she screamed and leaped to her feet, backing away from her sister. "I won't pay! I won't—" She backed into the bedroom and stumbled against the dressing table. "Get out! Get out! I don't know you." She swept off the bottles and jars and flasks with one angry swipe, and they crashed to the floor.

"Get out!" She threw the lap desk toward the door of the sitting room. The ink pot splintered into a thousand glass shards against the doorframe. Black ink dripped down the wood like a wound.

"Kaat!" Lece cried, standing unsteadily. She had to balance against the chair.

"You are no sister to me! You are nothing to me! Go back to your devil. Get out!" She threw the silver candlestick from her night table. It clanged against the leg of the chess table.

Lece hurried as best she could to the door. "Kaat, I—"

"Get out." Lece opened the door and walked out.

Kaatje stood alone in her bedroom, her lungs heaving

as she gulped in air. Her vision shimmered, grayed. Her breaths turned into sobs.

''No no no.'' She wailed the single word over and over as she collapsed to the floor. She curled into a ball, her fingers mindlessly grasping at her nightgown, her tears mixing with the dust. ''My Becket, my Becket,'' she sobbed. ''I am lost.''

Chapter 19

*S*t. *Benoit*. Kaatje slowly awakened, the image of home swirling in the gray mists that clouded her mind. *St. Benoit*. She had fallen asleep on her bedroom floor.

She raised her head and wiped at her wet face. Dust and grit had mixed with her tears, as abrasive as the regret and anger and self-loathing that scoured her heart.

Becket had known the price she would be asked to pay. Why had she kept hoping there was a chance for Pietr's future when it was held in the hands of a madman? She'd seen what the Turk was at Cerfontaine. Yet she'd chosen blind hope over her Englishman.

Still shaky, she rose, letting her crumpled nightgown drift down to the floor. It would be hard to go back. The farmers' crops would have been destroyed by the battle, trampled or burned or cut for forage. Livestock would have been stolen or butchered on the spot. Wood might be scarce in the winter. But she had no choice.

She sat down hard on the chair in front of the dressing table and leaned forward, staring at the reflection in the mirror. The woman who stared back bore no resemblance to the woman who'd left St. Benoit in a pony cart with her son at her side.

The sorrow of an impossible love haunted her gray

eyes, and the remnants of madness. Perhaps it was the same thing—love and madness. She traced the sad mouth, and the lips that had known such kisses . . .

"The devil wants you, Becket."

Anything, she'd told Lece. She'd pay anything for Pietr's medicine. It had been the truth at the time—until the devil had asked for the one thing she wouldn't pay.

The life she'd dreamed of for Pietr was gone. But she could get chirurgeon's herbs to ease his sickness. And they would get through the seasons, somehow. They had before.

Her van Staden spirit stirred.

She glanced out the window. Midmorning. Pietr would be at his riding lesson. She smiled unsteadily, the urge to see him overwhelming. She summoned the maid to dress.

"Ma'am?" Cècile said, slipping in the servants' door.

"I want to go riding—Cècile! You shouldn't be here." Kaatje said. "Claude hurt—"

"Please, ma'am, don't tell anyone," Cècile pleaded. "I'm to go with the duchesse when she returns to Chamboret. If she heard, she'd think I was a flirt and wouldn't take me.

"And he didn't hurt me much. I-I just caught his notice, is all. It's what happens."

"No!" Kaatje cried, grabbing the girl's shoulders and shaking her. *"Never say that. Never!"*

The girl cringed and shock hit Kaatje at what she'd done. She embraced the maid, stroking her hair. "Oh, Cècile, I'm so sorry. I didn't mean it. I'm just not feeling well."

"I understand, ma'am." The girl pulled out of Kaatje's hold and patted her mistress on the arm. "I know how you been fretting over your little boy."

Kaatje shook her head. "No, it was wrong of me."

She wiped the dampness from her eyes with the heels of her hands. "You should still be in bed, after what Claude did to you."

The maid shrugged. " 'Tain't the first time, ma'am. I'm just a bit sore is all. Cook boiled me up some new milk and rose oil to ease it."

"Sweet God," Kaatje said, and put a hand over her mouth to keep from trembling. *This is my son's heritage.* "Pietr, forgive me."

"Oh, ma'am, I was to deliver this to you this morning," the girl said, digging into an apron pocket. She held out a folded square of parchment, the words "little sister" scrawled across it in a strange spidery script that looked nothing like Lece's.

Kaatje stared at it. *No! I will not pay what you ask.* She took it from the maid's hand and threw it aside, not wanting to touch it any longer than she had to. The parchment slid on the floor till it came to rest against the leg of the dressing table.

"Oh, ma'am. What's wrong? I'm sorry, I—"

"Don't blame yourself, Cècile. I am at fault. I trusted blindly when I should not have trusted at all." Kaatje swallowed hard. "Sometimes we just want too much."

Cècile glanced at the note on the floor, then nodded hesitantly. "Yes, ma'am," she said, going to the wardrobe.

Kaatje was quickly dressed in a comtesse's old riding habit, the long green coat buttoning like a man's over the skirts. It was snug across her breasts, but it wasn't the too-tight fit which made her breathing difficult.

She walked to the stables with the cautious steps of someone not sure of her footing. For all her resolve, her muscles had not stopped their trembling.

She entered the stables, and the head groom bent from the waist in a carefully calculated bow that exactly matched her station—poor relation, but a relation to the margrave nevertheless.

Kaatje drew herself up. "I wish to watch my son's riding lesson."

The stout man straightened and crossed burly arms over his chest, then shook his head slowly, as if he were exerting all the patience in the world. "Ain't no females allowed."

"He is my son!"

The man uncrossed his arms. "Highness's orders," he said, then added as an afterthought, "ma'am." He moved away, busying himself with a bridle.

She heard a chorus of nervous boyish laughter, quickly stifled by a gruff scold, and she ran outside. On the other side of the stables, she could see Pietr and his four cousins being led toward a trail that went into a shallow valley east of the castle. The boys rode with their backs ramrod straight, rigidly gripping the reins, and their legs sticking out from the sides of horses that were much too large for them. The riding master was a stern-faced man.

"Why aren't they on ponies?" she called from the open doorway "Those horses should only be ridden by grown men."

The head groom gave her a look of tried patience. "They's too old for ponies. Ma'am. Once they been breeched, *gentlemen's* sons don't ride ponies."

Anger warred with her sense of loss. She had to see Pietr. She had to. She studied the valley where the boys were headed. It formed one side of a giant W; the other side was the valley where the abbey was. In the middle was a ridge that overlooked both valleys. It was scattered with outcroppings of boulders large enough to conceal a mother wanting a glimpse of her young son.

Her heart tripped in her chest at the thought of being so close to the abbey, to where she and Becket had . . .

She clenched her hand into a fist, letting her nails bite into the palm.

"I wish to go riding."

"The riding master'll send ya back with a burr under your saddle."

"Have a horse saddled for me."

He raised his bushy eyebrows and pointedly studied her. She lifted her chin.

"Pasc'l," the head groom called, and a tall lanky stable boy popped up beside her in the doorway. "Saddle Gênant for the lady."

The boy shrugged and started walking toward the other end of the stables, his movements so loose it looked as if someone had forgotten to tie his joints tight enough. In minutes though, he saddled a pretty little chestnut mare and helped Kaatje mount sidesaddle, arranging her voluminous skirts and petticoats without a murmur.

She rode out, conscious of the head groom watching her, and she headed toward the abbey, away from the boys. After the power and grace of Acheron, riding the mare was like sitting atop a trundling cart of bones. But when she arrived at the abbey, she forgot everything but the old building and what had happened there.

It stood mute, deserted. She remembered the stone balanced on the precipice above the nave, and as she rode by, she looked at where it had been. She sucked in her breath. The entire middle section of the western wall had collapsed.

Kaatje pushed her mind away from the omen. Her fingers shook when she tethered the mare in the shade of an apple tree gone wild near a pool of rainwater. The room that overlooked the ruined garden stood silent, and she turned away.

She set out walking up the steep rocky slope that overlooked the other valley, and reached the top of the ridge a half hour later. Pietr and the other boys were below her, tiny figures at that distance, but she could see her son. She hid in a group of boulders and watched them, their horses moving in an occasional symmetry that seemed more accidental than skilled.

The riding master was strict and demanding, but Pietr performed flawlessly. Her heart swelled with love and bittersweet pride to see her little boy. He was growing up so fast. The thought clawed at her precarious control.

The sun was an hour past its zenith when the man led the weary boys back to the stables. Kaatje rose, her throat tight with both heartache and pride. Pietr would have been the finest gentleman in Hespaire-Aube.

Kaatje brushed the dirt from her skirts and headed back down the hillside toward the abbey. In a year or two, perhaps she could afford to get Pietr a genuine riding master and let Marten return to his other duties. Were all riding masters as harsh as this one appeared to be?

Was this what Becket's riding master had been like? She imagined him performing his lessons as flawlessly as Pietr, seated on a feisty black pony, his dark blue eyes intense with concentration.

A smile came unbidden to her lips. Had his eyes been intense even then? What would his children . . .

She staggered and steadied herself on a boulder, feeling light-headed from the midday sun. She squeezed her eyes closed to shut out the glare and the images in her mind. *It will pass,* she told herself. *The time will get longer and longer between the memories. You know it will.* She looked around her, trying to focus.

She tried to think of St. Benoit, of keeping busy managing their meager lives. Then she wouldn't have so much time to think of Becket, and to remember . . .

A sigh of despair escaped her. What was the use? It would be an eternity before a day—an hour—would pass when she didn't think of the black-haired Englishman.

No, no, it's the sun, the heat. She shook her head and looked about her more closely, then realized that none of the rocks looked familiar. She twirled around, trying to find her original path.

"You're acting the simpleton," she scolded herself. The abbey was down the hill, and it was easy enough to tell which way was down. She put a foot in front of her to go on.

The clang of sword against sword stopped her. She froze, breathless with panic. Her heart pounding, she ducked behind a boulder, and reached for a rock. It was a long moment before her mind would even consider what might be going on.

Keeping still and alert, she listened. From the sounds of the fighting, and the accompanying grunts and curses, she guessed that there were only two swordsmen. But she sensed no rage or bloodlust. The clanging stopped for a moment.

"Again," a man's voice commanded. Becket. Her heart thudded.

The ringing of steel against steel resumed, and for the first time, Kaatje became fully conscious of the stone in her hand. She stared at it. When had she changed so? A short while ago the chatelaine of St. Benoit would have stumbled right into the midst of the fight, risking her life in ignorance and naïveté.

She hefted the rock in her hand, then tossed it away. She had indeed changed from the woman who had begun this terrible journey by screaming at Roulon for making a shambles of her kitchen.

"The devil be there, right enough, kern'l. Right

where yer said. Can't get close, is all," said a voice
which Kaatje recognized as that of Becket's servant,
Harry Fludd.

"Indeed," Becket said. "What of the sisters?"

"The d'Agenais piece still be in her rooms."

"And the other," Becket said.

Lieutenant Elcot answered. "Rode off to see the little fellow's riding lesson. He's going to be a damned
fine horseman, colonel." Kaatje gave a start, and listened more closely.

"You are certain that's where she is?"

"As certain as a gulden'll make me. That head
groom would sell his soul for a stiver." She heard
Niall give a bark of laughter. "The horses'd be dearer,
though. They're worth more to him than his soul."

"And the rest?"

"Found an old nurse in that business you asked me
about. Harry and me are headin' upriver soon's we leave
here," Niall told him. "The French rabble up the Hes
are starting to stir."

"This nurse," Becket said, "is she near that rabble?"

"Not so far south."

"Keep your head up if they move. I need you alive."

"Yes sir, colonel."

Kaatje heard the splashing of water in a pond, and
the rumble of the men's voices became indistinguishable. She waited against the rock, her heart hammering
in her chest.

I've just heard the true Becket, she thought, her
knees weak. *No,* she corrected, *the true Colonel
Becket, Lord Thorne.* The soldier, the English officer,
the *man.*

He was keeping track of every player in this sordid
masque of El Müzir's.

The splashing of the water stopped, and she heard
the unmistakable sounds of departure.

"Kern'l, now, ye'll wait till we comes back, won't ye?" Harry said, his voice sounding worried.

"An hour before sunset, Harry, no later."

"Colonel," Niall said unsteadily. He stopped and cleared his throat.

"You have your orders, lieutenant," Becket said. "See that all of them are carried out."

"My word on it, sir," the lieutenant said, his voice full of emotion.

"I'm counting on that, Niall." The sounds of their leaving slowly faded.

She waited a few more minutes, then rose and walked into the level clearing where Becket and the others had been.

Kaatje wrapped her arms around her and bleakly studied the grasses trampled in the practice sword fight, the soft murmur of water in the pond lapping behind her.

The sun was hot, making her head ache. The sound of the water stilled. There was a glade under the spreading branches of a group of beeches, and she walked into the refreshing coolness of the shade. She unbuttoned the top of her habit and knelt by the pool, dipping her handkerchief into the cool water.

The stillness broke in on her mind. Her heart beat faster. She slowly raised her head.

Becket glided silently through the water toward her. With one powerful stroke he propelled himself to the edge of the pond and rose from the water, like a god rising from the sea.

Water ran from his naked chest and over his buff leather breeches in sparkling rivulets as he sat on a flat rock in the sun. The sunlight played over the wet landscape of his body, highlighting each glistening drop. Kaatje remained unmoving, staring, suddenly aware of her thirst.

"You are on my battlefield, madame," he said, making no move to cover his naked chest, or the wet breeches that had molded so tightly to his form that he might as well have been unclothed. "I do not advise you to stay." He rested an arm on his bent knee and watched her.

"Becket. I . . ."

"Your fate is in Claude's hands or the devil's—not mine." There was little in the way he looked at her to hint that his hands had once, with exquisite slowness and patience, brought her unawakened body so much pleasure.

She wrenched her gaze from him and sat back on her heels. "You are harsh," she said. "Were he your son . . ." Her voice failed her, her throat as tight as if she'd swallowed alum. She heard his indrawn breath and looked up.

"Were he my son," Becket ground out, "he would know that honor is not something his nurse crumbles into his milk." He leaned forward, his power latent in the fluid movement.

"Were he my son, he would know that the price of being a gentleman is not dishonor and treachery." He locked her gaze with his.

"Were he *my son,* madame, he would know that his father was proud of the boy he is. He would know I was not ashamed of him for so small a flaw."

"Ashamed!" Kaatje reeled as if she'd been knocked breathless. *"Ashamed.* Of Pietr? How can you say that of me? How can you *think* it?" She leaped to her feet, her fingers clawing at the empty air. "Pietr is *not* your son. He is mine." She grabbed her skirts and whirled to leave the glade.

He was behind her, his hands on her shoulders, stopping her. She wrenched away, not turning to face him. "I've done with your devil, Becket. *And I've done with you.* Don't demand that I tell you where he is. I do not know. You will have to discover that for yourself.''

"I have.''

Becket heard her gasp. She spun to face him, her gray eyes wide with shock.

"How?'' Emotions flickered across her beautiful face like firelight. Fear, dismay, confusion.

"This morning, there was a certain note—''

"The one Cècile brought! No, oh, no. How could I have been so unthinking! Why didn't I burn it?'' Her hand reached out to touch him. "It seems I have led you to your devil after all.''

That was part of her, to reach out, to touch. Her fingertips brushed his chest, and he stepped back.

"I will meet him, Kaatje,'' he said. "But you must return to the castle. Tell Claude of Pietr's sickness. It is your only hope.''

"No, you're wrong,'' she whispered. She bent her head, rubbing her forehead. She looked dazed. "I'm all confused, Becket. I-I—'' She swayed and he caught her, and lowered her to the soft moss-covered ground. Honeysuckle grew nearby, and he settled her where she would smell it.

He started to unbutton her habit, but her hand closed around his wrist to stop him. "I didn't swoon,'' she said. "I was in the sun too long, that's all, and felt a bit unsteady.'' She rose to her elbow and looked up at him kneeling over her, her eyes studying his face intently. "I can't tell Claude, Becket.''

He gently removed her hand from his wrist. "Think what you do, Kaatje.'' He stood. "Rest awhile. There is time before I have to . . . go.''

He tore his gaze from her and retrieved his sword belt. He wanted to leave, to walk out of the glade and not smell the honeysuckle and not see her luminous eyes wide with concern and not hear the soft sounds of her breathing.

"Becket . . . ?"

He didn't answer. He snapped open a pouch on his sword belt and removed a sharpening stone, a small vial of oil, and a cloth, then sat down against the trunk of a tree and pulled his sword from its scabbard.

"Why are you here?" he asked, his question punctuated by the rasp of the sharpening stone on the sword's blade. He wanted her gone. Letting her stay was a weakness in him. His blood should be surging with hate, with bloodlust, not—

"I came to watch Pietr's riding lesson," she said, her eyes following his hands as he worked. "I wasn't allowed to be close to him, so I watched from the ridge.

"Do you hate me, Becket?"

Becket stopped his hand. The edges of the stone bit into his fingers. "El Müzir was at Cerfontaine," he said. He began sharpening again. "Where?"

She closed her eyes and turned her head away as if in sudden pain. "There's a room—a bolt hole, you called it—off the old library. One of the fireplace caryatids has a button in its mouth to open the panel door."

"Why did you lie to me?"

"I was a coward, Becket," she said, meeting his gaze. "And terrified. All I could remember were the stories you'd told me about your El Müzir.

"I swear to you—when I visited my sister at Chateau d'Agenais, he looked a harmless old astrologer wrapped in his robes. But at Cerfontaine . . . at Cerfontaine, he was neither old nor harmless. He knew you, Becket. He knew you. He wants to *kill* you."

"And not quickly," Becket said, the rasp of the stone suddenly louder. "What of it? What *he* wants matters little to me."

"I'm not a soldier, Becket. I panicked. What was I to do? Tell this . . . devil . . . that the man he wanted to kill was camped on the other side of the north ridge? How could I do that to you? You had . . .'' She flushed and looked at the ground.

The glade fell silent. Becket held the sharpening stone unmoving in his hand. "Kaatje—"

"You had kissed me, Becket," she whispered unsteadily as if forcing the words out. "And . . . and . . . made me feel things I had never felt before. You had told me of the demons that haunt your soul. However you felt about me deserting you while you slept near the campfire, I could not lead your enemy to you."

She dug her fingers into the honeysuckle, and the stems snapped off in her hand. "So I lied to him, Becket. *I lied to El Müzir.*" Her gaze returned to his. "He threatened to stop Pietr's medicine if I stood in his way—but I couldn't tell him where you were. I couldn't . . .''

"But why did you lie to *me,* Kaatje?" Becket asked, his eyes darkening to indigo.

"His threat," she began, then stopped and shook her head. "No. I was afraid. He seemed so powerful. In that room, he *smelled* of assurance the way you smelled of gunpowder. I was afraid he would kill you." She couldn't keep the tremor out of her voice. "Please, Becket. I lied to keep you safe. I do not want you to die."

"Kaatje . . .'' Her words created a tumult inside of him. *I do not want you to die.* He gripped the sword hilt and leaned back against the tree, squeezing his eyes closed. His heart cried out, urgent, insistent. The sound was hoarse and cracked from disuse, but unmistakable.

He rammed the sword home in its scabbard. "You should not have done that, Kaatje. Things . . . things would have been so much simpler if you hadn't.'' *I*

*would never have come to know the woman you are,
the woman I . . . must lose.*

She came to him, and touched him, her hand smelling of honeysuckle. "Becket, don't hate me. I only did
what I thought I must. I was afraid for you. I didn't
want you to die."

But I will die, sweet sylph. He knew his enemy well.
They were too evenly matched. But what was the death
of one more Englishman in this war?

He rose to his knees and wrapped his arms tightly
around her and buried his face in her hair. "So much
simpler, Kaatje. My sweet sylph, you don't understand."

Becket could feel her face pressed against his chest,
her breath warm on his wet flesh, and the soft sensation
of her hands stroking his back as if to ease the pain that
wracked him. He felt a sense of wonder at her abundant
undemanding empathy that let her feel his pain and try
to soothe it.

Did she know how deeply she was touching him?
Did she know that her hands were stroking not just his
flesh, but down into the darkness that had shadowed his
soul for so long? Did she know she had brought a dead
man to life?

He had thought her lies self-serving, but he had been
wrong. She did not follow the cold, strict soldier's honor
he was used to; she followed her own honor. It was
warm, and soft, and caring.

"Kaatje," he whispered, holding on to her as if once
she left his arms he would never again feel her warmth.
He would rid the world of El Müzir—that was in the
stars, fixed and immutable—but never had he thought
the price he would have to pay would be so high.

"I want to understand," she whispered, her hands
stroking the back of his wide shoulders. She brushed
his wet hair away from his face with a tender caress.
"I want to know that there is hope—"

He stopped her words with a kiss. His fingers slid into her glorious golden hair as his tongue slid into the deep warmth of her mouth. Jesu, but she was a weakness in him.

He cupped her face in his hands and kissed her again and again, tasting both the sweetness of her lips and the sweetness of her caring. "You should go," he murmured against her mouth.

"Yes," she whispered in answer. He kissed the soft flesh beneath her ear.

"I do not want you here," he said, nipping at her earlobe.

"No," she agreed. He kissed the rapid pulse at the base of her neck.

"This cannot be," he said. Her hands, her exquisite hands, explored his body, stroking, pressing, rubbing each contour of his muscles. "It is before a battle, and I must—" Her fevered tongue licked a droplet of water from his chest. "I must—"

He sucked in his breath as a luxurious tension tightened in his loins. He put his hands on her shoulders and gently pushed her away. "Kaatje, I must not. I must prepare for the coming fight. I've dreamed and planned of this day for long dark years. I cannot—"

She looked up at him with eyes half dreamy from his kisses. Her coat was partially unbuttoned and his hands on her shoulders had parted the front, revealing her breasts swelling above her stays.

"My Englishman," she murmured, kissing his hand on her shoulder. "For but an hour, there could be no colonel, no chatelaine. A man. A woman."

He said nothing, and dropped his hands.

Without sound, she stood. A sense of loss stabbed him. She started to walk away. This would be the last afternoon he would see her. The last time he would see the sunlight in her hair or the spirit in her eyes, feel the—

"*Kaatje,*" he cried out. She turned. "Come to me, sweet sylph." He held out his arms. "Make me think of nothing but now."

She ran back to him. He crushed her to him. He kissed her slowly, deeply, relishing the taste of her as if she were the last sip of a rare wine. It was a gift she was giving him. His mind pushed aside the soldier, pushed aside the darkness and the rage—and freed the man.

"Would we were in a soft bed with the fullness of the night ahead."

Kaatje felt his strong arm across her back. "What does the place matter?" she murmured against his neck. "I see only you."

"Madame," he said in that way he had, making the word a long slow caress, "the honeysuckle is easier on the eyes."

She traced his profile with the pad of her finger, slowing as she passed over his lips. "Not to me."

He kissed the tip of her finger, flicking it with his tongue. She started at the sensation that sparked through her, then gently rubbed his lips. Her own lips parted in anticipation.

He drew his open mouth down over her soft flesh, and tasted the scented valley between her breasts. With deft fingers, he finished unbuttoning the coat and slid his hands down her neck and shoulders, pushing the coat off as he went. It fell to the ground.

He hungered for her. But it was a hunger spiced with the knowing anticipation of a lover. He wanted to love her slowly and savor the fullness of each touch, each kiss, each taste. The tension in his loins intensified.

He lowered her to the soft verdant moss and kneeled over her, kissing her, his fingers unlacing her stays. He freed her breasts, and with his thumbs he rubbed the soft pink circles around her taut nipples, teasing her, coaxing her.

"Oh, please," she begged, her back arching to meet his touch. He flicked the nipples, and her sigh caught in her throat, then slid out as a long low moan. "Ah, ah . . ."

Sensation lapped at her everywhere. She writhed beneath his insistent touch. Her fingers tingled and her toes curled and uncurled. An urgent heat spread through her, glowing and pulsing each time she felt the contact of his touch on her body.

Becket kissed the base of her neck, her skin damp from where he'd held her. He stole quick licking kisses up the swell of her breast, then swirled his tongue around the taut peak. Kaatje gasped and arched her back higher. His blood thrummed at the voluptuous response.

He was hard with passion, and he unbuttoned his breeches and peeled them down his legs. He wanted to feel all of her next to him. Each shimmer beneath her skin, each tiny whimper of overwhelming sensation, each sensuously slow movement of her body welcoming him. Every response held out the promise of still greater passion, greater fulfillment. A promise he knew her body would keep. His breaths quickened.

He swept off her skirts, his lips kissing the soft inner flesh of her thighs. He caressed her and kissed her and tasted her, exploring with his mouth and his fingertips every enthralling curve of her body. He was lost in her, and time drifted like a morning mist toward the sun.

"Becket . . ." she whispered, ending his name with one drawn-out thread of longing. Her knee rose, revealing her secret places to his exploring mouth. The arousing female scent of her nearly maddened him, and he kissed her deeply, intimately.

He heard her moans, the soft catches of her breath, and the sounds became a part of him, seeping through his fevered skin, echoing through his blood like achingly sweet music. She was the essence of life to him, his life, all life.

His fingers buried themselves in the soft golden fur that warmed her womanhood. "My beautiful sylph . . . all warm and golden . . ." With the pad of his finger, he dipped inside her and gently rubbed the slippery swollen bud. He heard, he *felt* her gasp, and his body shook with desire.

Sweet Jesu. A field of sensation surrounded him, surrounded her. He trembled. Her hips rose to meet his touch. He sucked in a breath. Her movements melded with his flesh as if their bodies were already joined.

He breathed in deep. *Sweet Jesu, the scent of her.* He breathed in again, drawing that maddening perfume deep into his body. No, no, he had to control . . . no, he had to try to control . . . no, no, *Sweet Jesu, she makes me mad.* Becket drew his body over hers, anchoring himself with his arms at her side.

"Becket . . . Oh, God, come to me . . . Now, now . . ." Kaatje cried, her hands rubbing up his sides to urge him closer. The pale skin above her golden fur fluttered with her approaching ecstasy.

"Kaatje. Sweet Kaatje." He plunged into her, her name ascending into a wordless cry torn from his throat. She wrapped her legs around his waist, sending him deeper into her, filling her completely. He was nearly mindless then, his hips thrusting in and out with a primal urgency and Kaatje meeting his driving body.

He gasped and threw his head back. *The bliss of her.* A long slow groan rolled out from deep within him. *The bliss of her. The hot velvet bliss of her.* He groaned again, the indescribably sweet-sharp pleasure-pain of ecstasy rising in his loins.

"Oh, God, oh, God," Kaatje cried, her hands clutching at his shoulders, rocking with him. "Oh, yes, yes, yes . . ." Her head fell slack and her eyelids fluttered rapidly. "Oh, God, oh, God, ohhh . . ."

He drove into her and her body shuddered with spasm after spasm of rapture. The last thread of his control burned away. With a hoarse cry, he followed her into the oblivion of paradise.

Kaatje woke with a smile, feeling Becket's arms still around her. She stretched luxuriously against him and felt his chuckle. She opened her eyes to the drowsy dappled sunlight of midafternoon and saw him propped on one elbow, watching her.

"You entrance me," Becket said, drawing his fingertip in a straight line from her neck, through the valley between her breasts, to the fluff of her golden down. "Your beautiful golden hair. Your fair skin all flushed rosy from passion. Your gray eyes as soft and gentle as a swan's wing in shadow."

She leaned over and kissed the scar on his chest so near his heart. His breathing hesitated for the briefest moment. "A poet and a soldier," she said, then trailed tiny sucking kisses along the hard contour of his chest.

He growled and rolled onto his back, pulling her on top of him. "You could make a man forget his duty, sylph." He paused then, as if remembering something.

She nipped at his neck. "What I could do," she said, wriggling her hips against his loins, "is lay here entwined with you forever."

He dragged her up him and his mouth took hers. She moaned into him and answered his passion with her own.

He broke off the kiss. "This is forever," he said, his voice thick with renewed desire. He slid her down his body, his engorged phallus slipping into her.

"Becket!" she gasped and tried to sit up. He grabbed her hips and began lifting her up and down. "Becket, oh! Oh! Oh, yes . . ." Her knees took over the work of his hands and he ran his hands up her body to gently knead her full proud breasts. He flicked her taut nipples with his thumbs, and her body gave a start of pleasure.

She rubbed his hard flat stomach and chest, the rhythm of her strokes matching her more intimate rhythm. "Oh, I had no idea . . . Oh . . ." The sound trailed off in a low moan. Her eyes closed and her head fell back in the ultimate pose of sensuous pleasure.

Becket watched her, his own eyes slightly glazed with the slow steaming heat that she was sending through his veins. He drifted in heaven, wrapped in the most exquisite sensations he'd ever known. The sight of her completely caught up in her pleasure, the incense of her woman-scent filling him with every breath, the music of her tiny moans and cries, the taste of her still on his tongue . . .

His hips began rocking to match her movements and she mewed her pleasure at it. He smiled a slow lazy smile. Dreams drifted in and out of his mind, dreams heated from his arousal, dreams thick with sensual visions of Kaatje.

He wanted to sit by a fire, his eyes on her sitting next to him, and feel the sweet-sharp stirrings of anticipation in his loins. She would be in his bed that night. She would be *his* that night, every night.

He groaned. She bounced down on him, ending with a tiny tug that nearly sent his control careening. "God, woman, what are you . . ." He sucked in his breath. *"Sweet Jesu . . ."*

Kaatje gave him another deep intimate caress and shook her head wildly, feeling intoxicated with pleasure. She tingled everywhere. Desire sluiced through her, hot and insistent. She was joined with him. They were one. And at their joining was the most insistent desire of all. A demanding, sweet, sweet tyrant.

Becket drove into her, pushing her closer, closer with each hard masculine thrust. The hot tension, pushing,

pushing, demanding . . . Tears fell unheeded down her face. Oh, God, she burned.

Becket rammed her hips down onto him, madness seizing him. He was joined with her so fully, so completely . . . He gasped, panted, every muscle straining, every drop of his soul focused on that self that she enveloped.

"Becket, Becket, Oh, God." She whimpered, her head shaking from side to side. "Oh, Becket, I can't . . . It's too . . ." She was crying. "No, oh, no, no. Oh, God. Becke-e-e-e- . . ." She shuddered hard and long, her last wordless cry trilling as if her soul were leaving her body.

"Kaatje. Sweet God . . . Ahhhhh . . ." The sound turned into a roar. His body jerked off the ground, arching up as if to fling itself into the heavens. Silent thunder rolled through him till his mind left his body in one last blinding shock.

Chapter 20

In the coolness of the glade, Kaatje slipped into dreams, gathering up all the sights of him in her memory, all the times she had felt the warmth of his flesh on hers, all his myriad masculine scents . . . gathering them all to her into a tumbling armful of memories as if she could tie them up in ribbon and lace and lay them in her heart like a posy in a drawer of linen.

Her sleep deepened and other memories came, of seeing the torment in his eyes, his restless power, his rage that could only be released when El Müzir was dead. She whimpered in her sleep, and his hands gentled her back into a peaceful slumber.

When she finally woke, Kaatje lay quietly beside Becket, listening to the regular breathing of his deep slumber. Her mind tumbled with what they'd done, with what had happened to her, with her dreams.

She slipped from his side, alarmed at the weakness in her limbs. Slowly, she stood and gathered her scattered clothes and tried to dress. Petticoats tangled in her feet, laces knotted in her fingers . . . She stopped and took a deep breath, then painstakingly threaded the laces of her stays and pulled them tight.

"A man should always wake to such a sight," she heard Becket say. Her head snapped up, eyes wide. He rose to his feet, stepping back to steady himself. With

347

a look of surprise, he shook his head and ran his hands through his hair. "I shouldn't have slept."

The words hung in the glade. There had been no choice in the matter for either of them, and it was clear he knew it. Silently, he picked up his breeches and put them on.

"I must return," she said, her voice husky. She buttoned the top button of her coat.

He nodded and looked up, meeting her eyes. "As must I, Kaatje." He retrieved his shirt, coat, boots, sword, and put them on piece by piece, becoming her familiar red-coated colonel.

With a devastating smile, he gave her a proper bow and held out his arm to her, as a gentleman to a lady. "Madame."

"My lord colonel," she said, and started to curtsy, but had to settle for a shallow dip when her legs threatened to betray her. She put her hand on his arm, but even that touch was too potent, and she snatched it back. "I-I—" Kaatje started, but had to stop, struggling against the sudden urge to cry. "I'm sorry," she whispered, "I-I've never . . . I didn't know it was possible to feel that way."

His face was troubled, but he gently grasped her fingertips and lifted them to his lips. "Neither did I," he said against her skin. He breathed in deeply, and his eyes looked suddenly drowsy. He kissed her fingers, the back of her hand, her wrist, his tongue hot and wet on her flesh. He held her hand to his open mouth and closed his eyes, breathing in again, as if smelling the scent of her.

Kaatje stood still, her heart racing. His touch, his kisses, drew her in, and she leaned toward him, her lips parted.

"Kaatje," he said, caressing her with the word. He nipped the fleshy part of her palm. "Kaatje . . .

"Sweet God." He dropped her hand and stepped away from her, shaking his head.

Becket straightened and bowed to her again, then walked beside her without touching. He had wanted to be with her one last time, to have something to hold on to in that last heartbeat . . . But she had given him a gift, a wondrous gift few men ever know—she had given him life.

All too late.

She had given him life just as he was about to lose his. He walked on, putting what he felt for her away in his heart. It was his rage he needed now, and his hate, his duty, his oath.

The abbey came into view. She saw the collapsed wall and knew that she, too, had fallen from a precipice.

Their pace instinctively slowed, as if each was reluctant to end their time together. But still they reached the wild apple tree and the little chestnut mare.

Kaatje patted the horse's neck and toyed with the reins. "You go to meet El Müzir. I don't want to know when. I don't—" she said in a ragged whisper. She bent her head, closing her eyes against the truth. "Yes. Tell me."

"I meet the devil when the sun sets. He is a creature of shadows and he shall die in shadows."

She felt all loose inside, as if she were a wooden doll being taken apart. She would never see him again. He would kill his El Müzir and return to his duty. "How can I say goodbye?" she asked.

Becket lifted a golden strand that had fallen from her hastily pinned hair and kissed it. "You already have," he said, tucking the strand back up. He stepped back.

"I-I will miss you, Becket," she said. She squeezed her eyes to keep from crying. "Would I had never known you—" *No, when he returns to Marlborough, I will have my memories and I will think myself blessed.*

"No." She shook her head and looked at him, smiling shakily. "Every time I travel the Odenaarde road, I will remember the Englishman in his scarlet coat." *And in every other place and time.*

Becket flicked her chin. "You will have little reason to travel the Odenaarde road, sylph."

"Once a sennight—on market day," she told him. "Pietr and I are returning to St. Benoit. I am leaving Hespaire-Aube."

"Kaatje—" he began, then stopped. She met his gaze and was surprised to see a struggle going on in the blue depths. "You can't go back, Kaatje. I thought you knew. The chateau at St. Benoit is—"

"Is what?" she cried, dread rising at his tone.

He reached out to touch her, then pulled back. "In the last hours of battle, St. Benoit was hit with a cannonade."

Kaatje stared at him, gray madness fluttering at the edge of her mind. *"No,"* she whispered. "No! How can this be? My sister is lost to me, my dreams for Pietr gone, my home . . . And you—" she broke off and grabbed the facings of his coat. "And you will soon be back with your Marlborough and your army. There is nothing left for me and my son. Nothing but an uncle who would lock him away for his imperfection."

He caught one of her trembling hands. "My sweet sylph, you are young and beautiful, and your life will be full of new summers. Don't spend them in fear. The margrave will accept the boy. Your only hope of peace is to tell Claude of Pietr's sickness."

"Then there is no hope!" She pulled away. "You didn't hear Claude speaking of how 'perfect' Pietr was. Of how he cannot tolerate imperfection. Or how they laughed at the stories of Philippe's grandfather!"

"Kaatje, you must. Philippe's grandfather was an old man with an old man's madness. You cannot think the margrave would treat his six-year-old nephew that way.''

''How can you know that? You think he would act as you would. That he would not be ashamed of Pietr for so small a flaw.'' She turned to the horse and fumbled with the saddle trappings, tears burning her eyes. ''You don't understand him.''

''I understand too well,'' he said. ''But you must tell Claude.'' He lifted her onto the sidesaddle, and she arranged her skirts with trembling hands. He covered them with his own.

''I never meant for what is between us to happen. Sweet sylph, I had thought the man inside me dead, but you— Forgive me, Kaatje. Would I didn't have to leave you so. But the course I take is fixed and unchangeable. It was charted years ago. I am but playing it out.''

His words stabbed her. ''But you *are* leaving,'' she said, yanking her hand out of his hold. ''Play it out! Go to your devil, Englishman. Between the two of you, you've pulled down my life, stone by stone, till there's nothing left!

''I'll tell Claude, damn you. But if anything happens to my son, I'll curse your soul to hell every day of my life.''

She dug her heels into the mare's flanks and rode away—from his words. From him.

Kaatje stared at Claude lounging in a gold brocade chair in the Green Salon. The tables had been taken away, leaving the carpets and the groups of chairs around the walls. He watched workmen removing the painting of the Three Graces.

She straightened her skirts as best she could. In torment and hurt anger, she'd ridden back to the castle and demanded to see Claude, not trusting her courage to last the hour.

"You are becoming an embarrassment, Catherine," Claude said, rising to stand before her.

"I need to speak with you," she said. She glanced at the workmen. "Privately."

"Tell me who you rode out to meet. The lover in the garden?"

Kaatje averted her face, her flush accentuated by the light of the late afternoon. Claude grasped her chin and forced her to face him.

"Gossip says you are consorting with the Englishman. Is that true? Is Thorne bedding you? *Tell me,* you pale little mouse." He slid his open hand around her neck and slipped his fingers into her hair.

"But perhaps you are not a pale little mouse. Thorne is a wild man. I knew him more than ten years ago, in Vienna. He was but a boy, but how I envied him his lust for living. Women rushed to him like little rivulets running to join a raging river. But he proved too full of rapids for most of the delicate creatures. I would have thought you one of them."

He tugged at her hair, making it sting. "Can you truly satisfy a wild man? Perhaps Philippe shouldn't have been pitied so much."

Inside, Kaatje was cold and shaking, her stomach queasy with apprehension. "Claude, please," she said, choking the words out. "Why are you doing this? I just came here to talk to you."

"Later, Catherine." He released her hair. "Confessions are so tiresome before one has had one's supper."

Kaatje swallowed to settle her stomach. "Claude, really I must—"

Claude gestured sharply to a footman. "Escort Madame de St. Benoit to her rooms and see that she does not leave them."

Kaatje was taken aback. "What? Why are you—"

"As you wish, your highness." The man waited stiffly for her to follow, arms crossed, face impassive.

"My supper waits, Catherine." She hesitated, and his gaze raked her with impatience.

Her courage was dissolving. "Claude, don't do this! I need to—''

He looked disgusted. "I can do anything I wish, my dear. *Anything*, Catherine. You would do well to remember that. You may be my sister in the law, but even priests can be paid off if I wish to transgress. Paid off, or destroyed, like the abbot of St. Crispin's. Even God's custodians think twice about crossing the Margraves of Hespaire-Aube. As should *you.*"

"Claude—''

"I haven't time now," Claude said, pausing to let his gaze travel over her rumpled riding habit. "And do tend to your ablutions, my dear. At the moment you are a *dirty* little mouse. I shall come to you later and you may unburden yourself then. And when I arrive, Catherine, I wish to find a *woman,* not a mouse." Claude turned his back to her and walked away.

Kaatje clenched her teeth to keep the words that choked her from spilling out, words of disgust and anger and contempt. She stared at her brother-in-law as he walked away from her. The man who had embodied her son's heritage. The man in whom she had to confide Pietr's imperfection. She turned abruptly to the footman and followed him to her rooms.

The sun neared the horizon. At the abbey, Becket let the sharpening stone whisper its deadly promise along the sword blade one last time. He oiled and wiped it down.

He was ready. His battle fury beckoned, rising with each sharp movement as he put on his scarlet waistcoat and coat. He buckled on his sword belt and slid the sharpened blade home with a crack. He strode to Acheron and mounted.

The beast inside him lunged. And he smiled. Soon

now, it could be unleashed. His hand curled as if it already held a sword hilt, and he could feel the impact in his arm of blade hitting blade.

He signaled the stallion, and Acheron moved out toward the castle.

Halfway there, a dust cloud rose from the south. He did not slow his pace. The horse and red-coated rider came straight at him at a dead run. Harry Fludd.

Harry pulled up his horse hard and matched Becket's fast trotting gait. "All's to 'ell, kern'l. Niall's holed up wi' the ol' nurse, and it looks like that French rabble is moving out. Said to tell ya som'thin about there ain't just monks in th' monast'ry."

The castle lured Becket on. The shadows on the ramparts taunted him. But the shadows would wait until sunset. They had to. Now another duty summoned him.

"Kern'l?"

His breaths were controlled, a calculated bellows fanning the fury inside him.

"We ride to the lieutenant, Fludd," Becket said. Acheron swerved to the south, toward Niall—and his one last duty to Kaatje.

Kaatje paced in her bedroom, her emotions careening between despair and fury and hopelessness. She had kept sending word to Claude that she needed to speak to him, but he had not come, and her resolve was crumbling. No, she had to tell him. She'd promised Becket.

She glanced out her window. Nigh on sunset. Her throat choked closed. Had Becket caught up with El Müzir?

She clenched her hands together in a desperate prayer. *"Pater noster, qui es in caelis . . ."* Our father who art in heaven . . . She broke off with a sob. "God, please God, keep him safe. His sins are not so great as mine."

There was a scratching on the servants' door, then Cècile came in, a bundle of gold silk billowing out of her arms.

"Ma'am," the girl said with a brief curtsy. She held out a folded note from under the silk. "This is for you."

Kaatje took the note. It was written in the same spidery scrawl as before. Her hands shook as she unfolded it.

"You did not come, little sister. I am displeased. One way or another, you shall give me the Englishman." She gasped and threw it onto the night table.

El Müzir. What would he do? Kaatje stared at the crumpled paper. No! She had to tell Claude.

Kaatje forced the tension from her shoulders. "Cècile, I need you to pass on two messages for me. Tell Madame d'Agenais that I must see her immediately. And tell his highness . . . *Ask* his highness to please remember his appointment with me."

The maid curtsied. "Don't know if I can, ma'am. Least not the one. Madame d'Agenais left all sudden like.'Twas quite a flurry. I'm surprised you didn't hear the noise."

"Left?" Shaken, Kaatje turned away. "See that his highness receives the other message, then. I know he, at least, has not left."

Cècile giggled and Kaatje turned sharply. The young woman picked up a length of gold lace and draped it over her arm with a flourish. It was a petticoat. *"These are from his highness, ma'am."*

Kaatje flushed and turned away. "The clothes can wait."

"Sorry, ma'am, but you must—"

"The clothes can wait. See that his highness receives my message *now!"* Wide-eyed, the maid stumbled into a deep curtsy and hastened away.

A few minutes later, the servants' door burst open

and a half dozen maids scurried in followed by a dour
middle-aged female.

"His highness commands you to be dressed at
once," the woman announced to the room at large.
With excited chatter, the maids scooped up the clothes
from the bed and began laying out each piece. There
were clouds of gold lace and delicate silk, and a red
velvet cloak.

Why was he doing this? Kaatje's stomach knotted at
the implications. Was *she* to be the price of her son's
safety? "I don't want . . ." she began.

The female tsked. "Pray, madame, what has that to
do with anything? His highness will arrive shortly."
She issued sharp orders, directing each maid by name,
and soon Kaatje found herself in the middle of a lace
and silk storm.

Anxiety gnawed at her. She tried to push away the
awareness of the maids slipping off her dressing gown
and tugging on the stockings.

Claude would be there soon. What if Pietr never has
another spell? Was this course wrong too? She swallowed hard. Becket was right—she couldn't deal with
the devil. She would have to deal with Claude.

Two maids tugged on her stay laces, pulling them
stiflingly tight. Kaatje looked in the mirror. A golden-
haired vision stared back at her. Her breasts were the
color of new cream and rose full and round from a froth
of silken lace. Stockings peeked through a nearly transparent petticoat.

The maids lowered the silk gown over her head.
When she emerged, she saw sadness in the wide gray
eyes that stared back from the looking glass. If Becket
had seen her as she was now, would he have chosen to
stay with her instead of chasing his mad Turk?

You are beautiful. Kaatje closed her eyes and ran her
hands over the silk sleeves. Underneath the elegant
gown, her body ached for his touch and her heart

yearned for his presence. If only he would come back . . . She shook her head, knowing it wasn't to be. He would return to the battles and the gunpowder, not to her. Perhaps Lece was right. Perhaps love does always leave.

The door to her room crashed open. "Claude, I . . ." Kaatje began, turning around.

A road-weary Becket filled the doorway. His boots and uniform were covered with dried mud and dust.

"Becket," Kaatje gasped.

The maids squealed and scampered behind the furniture.

"Get out. All of you," he ordered the maids. They screamed and darted through the servants' door.

"Madame!" the older woman said, taking a step backward, her mouth pursed.

Becket glared at her. "Out." He slammed the servants' door open against the wall. "Now."

The woman's bravado crumbled and she fled. He threw the door closed with a crash, the great wood slab cracking at its hinges.

Kaatje jumped and put her hand over her mouth to keep from crying out. It was the soldier who'd come back, not her lover. She was shaking, her throat tight with sudden unshed tears.

He turned to her, his legs spread wide, his knees slightly bent, his weight balanced on the balls of his feet. "Have you told Claude?"

She was too shocked to speak.

He lunged at her, grabbed her by the arms, and lifted her off the floor, dangling in front of him. He looked her straight in the eyes. *"Have you told him?"*

"No, damn you!" she cried out, squirming in his numbing hold. She had thought him mortally wounded, dead, but his vitality swirled around her like the current of a deep river. "God knows I've tried! He promised to meet me. I sent him a message to remind him—and he sends a silk gown and that cackling flock of hens to dress me!''

Becket set her on her feet and released her. Fury blew through him like a hot summer wind. It scorched him as he dragged in a deep steadying breath. El Müzir had bolted. Becket had learned it as he'd ridden past the castle gates.

Damn her blood! The devil would be dead by now, if it were not for her. If not for his own caring. *Jesu!* He didn't want to care.

''Don't glower at me!'' she said, walking back and forth in front of the window, his eyes following her as she moved. ''Is that why you came back? To hold me to my promise?''

''Damn you, woman,'' he roared, coming at her. She gasped and sidled away from the window, her gray eyes wide with shock. She stumbled against the bed. He kicked a chair out of his way, sending it splintering into the wall. ''I was almost free of him. I was ready for that dark oblivion his death would cost me . . .''

Jesu, but he was weak with her. He raised his fists upright in front of him, shaking his cuffs back to expose the scars at his wrists. ''Damn you, woman. Do you see the shackles? Do you see the new chains I wear? Damn *me!* For they are chains of my *own* making, they are chains of my weakness. And I would have them off.''

''Becket, I swear to you I'll tell him!'' She grabbed the bedpost for support. ''I promised you I would tell Claude, and I will.''

''Tell me what, my dear?'' the margrave asked from the doorway. Startled, she spun around to face him, her back to Becket. Claude stood in the doorway, hands on hips, his gaze traveling over her appreciatively, then around the room. He studied the shattered chair for a long moment.

''Quite the domestic scene, Catherine,'' he said,

crossing his arms. He glanced at Becket and raised an eyebrow. "Thorne. It is you she's been with. I'm glad indeed I didn't challenge your ardor that night in the garden."

"Claude, I must—" Kaatje began, but Becket grabbed her upper arms and pulled her back to his chest, kissing her shoulder. She gasped, startled, and tried to protest. "Becket! Colonel Thorne!"

He didn't release her. His warm lover's kisses traveled up her neck. "What are you—"

"Say nothing," he whispered urgently. He kissed the soft flesh in front of her ear. *"Nothing."*

Claude looked piqued. "Pardon me for interrupting your amusements, Thorne, but I shall be making an announcement at dinner that Catherine may perhaps be interested in. You will no longer have to concern yourself about your son's welfare, my dear. I have decided to adopt Pierre as my son and heir."

"No!" Kaatje cried. She tried to leap out at the margrave, but Becket held her fast. "No, you can't do this!"

Claude shook his head regretfully, as if her want of understanding was a great burden. "Of course I can, my dear. I should love to stay and watch, but I'm afraid I'm expected elsewhere." He turned to go, then paused. "Take your time. I trust your confession will keep. And if you're late to dinner, I'll explain all about the Englishman to the others." He studied Becket for a moment. "By the by, Catherine, do you prefer him with his spurs or without?" Claude walked out, the door snapping shut on his laughter.

Becket released her and his breath at the same time. Kaatje whirled on him.

"What are you do—" she began, but he took her head in his hands and kissed her soundly. He savored the taste of her, the feel of the soft wet warmth, the touch of her fingers uncurling and stroking his hair as, even in her anger, she responded to him.

It was a kiss only of the present—no pounding insistent memories of their shared desire, no shadows of future regret when he must leave her again to search for El Müzir, and face the same inevitable end.

Kaatje twisted away, her lips darkened from his kiss. "Are you mad? First you insist I tell Claude and now you won't let me."

He sat down wearily on the bed and rubbed his face.

"Kaatje, you cannot tell Claude about Pietr," Becket told her, watching her gray eyes grow shadowed with bewilderment.

Her gaze crisscrossed over his face. "I thought that's what you wanted."

"Niall—" Becket broke off. He shot to his feet and strode to the wall, hitting the paneling with the flat of his hands. "Close! I was so close."

He pushed off the wall and faced her again. "But there was one more surprise in store for me. One more twist of the knife."

"Surprise?" Kaatje said. Her lips parted with a sudden fearful thought. "About Pietr? About his sickness?"

"It's about . . ." Becket slid his hands over her shoulders, wanting desperately to protect her, wanting—needing—to touch her. "Claude's son."

She stepped out of his hold, shaking her head, denying the words he had not yet spoken. "He's dead. Claude-Denis is dead. He died three years ago. In a hunting accident."

Becket clenched his jaw for a long moment. Regret settled over him like a heavy cloak. He squeezed her shoulders. "The boy did not die. He was only injured, a blow to the head. But he began having fits, Kaatje. And now Claude-Denis is in the care of the Brothers of the Holy Cross of Montefeltro."

"No." She backed away from him, hugging herself as if the summer evening had turned bitterly cold. "No. He's dead. Dead, I tell you! Philippe went to the funeral. You said Claude wouldn't do that to a little boy! You said—"

He caught her and forced her struggling body into his fierce embrace. He could feel her pain. "Kaatje—"

"No, I tell you. Claude's son is dead." She pounded his chest again and again. "Who told you this? I don't believe it!"

He crushed her to him. "You believe it, Kaatje."

"No," she choked out, trying to shake her head, but he held her too tightly. She sobbed, and he felt her body shudder. Her strength left her and she collapsed into a sudden dead weight in his arms.

He stroked her hair to comfort her as she cried out her fear and her horror and her terrible weariness. He murmured endearments, as if the litany of sounds could keep the chaos and the clamor of the world at bay.

She stirred in his arms, her quicksilver eyes brimming with sadness. "What do I do, Becket? I can't let Pietr remain here. What is left to me?" She looked deep into his eyes. "You will leave again, won't you? I can see it in your eyes, that dark shadowed pain. You didn't kill your devil, Becket."

He went still.

She pushed out of his hold and he let her go. "It's starting all over again, only now I have nowhere to go."

"Niall has orders to see you and your son to safety."

"Safety? Where is that, Becket? Tell me, *anglais,* where?" She stumbled to the marble night table, splaying her hands against the cold stone, her fingers on El Müzir's note.

"Do you plan on sending me to your duke, your captain-general? For what? Would your Englishmen try to ransom me back to Claude, the way the English ransomed the French officers' women at Blenheim? I would have a long wait, colonel. Who would pay ransom for a French officer's widow and her oh-so-imperfect son!''

"You dishonor me, Kaatje," Becket said. "I have given my word as an English army officer. Marlborough will honor it, even when I'm dead.''

"Damn you," she screamed, his words tearing across her mind. "What would he honor?'' A sob escaped her. "That I'm the widow of one dead man and the mistress of another?"

"Kaatje—"

"I don't want you to die! I tried so hard." She stared at her empty palms. "I lied. To you. To El Müzir. And I am left with nothing. Lece was right.

"Leave me, Becket. Ride to your devil."

A woman's scream pierced the air. Kaatje jumped. A crack of musket fire resounded, then more screams. Becket leaped to the window.

"Roulon and his rabble from upriver," he growled. He hit the sill with the flat of his hands, his eyes intense with concentration, then pushed off. "El Müzir's lackey is attacking to cover the devil's escape."

Becket strode to her in two long strides. He swept up her cloak and wrapped it around her, pinning her arms inside. In a heartbeat, she was thrown over his shoulder like a sack of millet.

"Becket!"

"I may have left you with nothing but your life, madame, but by God, you're going to keep that.''

Chapter 21

B ecket sprinted across Kaatje's sitting room and threw open the door. He drew his sword and ran into the hallway.

Energy pumped through him; Kaatje's weight on his shoulder was as nothing. Screams bounced off the richly paneled walls as women darted back and forth in a panicked frenzy, slowing Becket down. Men, dress swords drawn, ran toward the sounds of the fighting, merely glancing at him and his silken burden as they passed.

"Where's your pistol?" Kaatje asked, frantic, her hands searching his waist. She felt it tucked into the back of his breeches. She scrambled to pull up the skirt of his coat. Her fingers curled around the butt of the pistol, the etched Thorne crest pressing against her palm. She squeezed the handle as if to imprint it into her flesh.

They rounded a corner. Two filthy French foot soldiers waited. Becket raised his sword.

At the end of the hall, another soldier aimed the barrel of a matchlock at Becket's head. "Becket! Behind you!" Kaatje screamed, thumping on his back.

She straightened as best she could and took aim. Both hands gripped the handle. The man sneered at her. Two stubby fingers wiggled the slow burning match cord, then lowered it to the flashpan. She squeezed the pistol trigger.

A shot rent the air and the pistol butt kicked in her hand. The Frenchman toppled sideways.

Two of Claude's hard-eyed footmen ran around the corner. Two more shots rang out, and the men facing Becket fell.

One of the footmen turned to them, a gleaming new flintlock in his hand. His face was impassive as he faced the Englishman with a woman slung over his shoulder. "Monsieur, madame," he said with a slight bow. "Sorry to take your fight from you, but his highness's orders are to clear the dogs out fast. The east end is clear."

"The children's wing," Becket said, his tone commanding.

The servant shrugged. "Ain't heard. His highness ordered us to protect only the important parts of the castle." He began to reload his gun.

"Pietr," Kaatje cried out. Becket slid her down his body and set her on her feet. He took the empty pistol and shoved it back into his breeches.

"Come," he said, pulling her down the hall after him. They ran to the older section of the castle, careful to check each room before they dashed through it. When they finally came to the nursery corridor, they heard loud arguing voices coming from in front of Pietr's room. Becket peered around the corner and saw the two footmen he'd hired trying to convince Harry that they should be allowed to go join the fighting. His sword lowered.

Becket tugged on Kaatje's hand and spun her into his tight hold. "Madame," he whispered into her ear, "pray hold your curses till after we are free of this place. Whatever you think of me, your fate at Marlborough's hands is preferable to a lead ball. He will honor my bond, Kaatje." He looked down into her gray eyes, full of unanswered questions and wariness. "As will my father."

"Your fa—"

The arguing grew louder around the corner and they heard Harry bark a curse of exasperation. "Aw right, aw right! Get yer arses outta 'ere." Before he had even finished speaking, their heavy boots were thumping down the corridor. They ran past Becket and Kaatje, and scrambled to a sudden halt. In unison, they jerked a bow in Becket's direction, then continued on their way.

Becket led Kaatje around the corner and she broke into a run to Pietr's room.

"Good t' see ya, kern'l," Harry said, opening the door for Kaatje. "Been waitin fer ya. T' others are—"

A scream of despair escaped her, and she turned on Harry. "Where's Pietr? Where's my son?"

"Been tryin to tell ya, ma'am. The lieutenant took t' others to the abbey to saddle up."

"We go, Kaatje," Becket said, heading out the servants' door.

All three of them made their way to the garden door. Becket raised his sword and Harry drew a pistol from his breeches. Becket nodded to him and threw back the bolt.

The garden was a horror. Kaatje gasped. A light supper had been set out for the guests just before the attack. Now chairs and tables were overturned and smashed into rubble. A half-dozen bodies sprawled on the ground.

Becket led her carefully through the destruction, his hold on her hand firm and steady. The dead proved to be mostly Frenchmen, one's hand still clutching a streamer of torn lace much like the lace around Kaatje's neckline. She swallowed hard and looked away.

They rounded the yew hedge and surprised a Frenchman methodically stripping a dead courtier.

Roulon.

Kaatje screamed. Becket pushed her behind him.

The comte stuffed the rings he'd just pulled off into his pocket and jumped to his feet. He assumed a fighting stance, his sword held before him.

Becket shifted his weight to the balls of his feet.

Roulon kicked the body in front of him. "Guillon was sloppy enough to forget his sword."

"Don't shoot, Harry," Becket called behind him.

The older man spit on the ground. "Not to worry, kern'l. I ain't gonna waste good lead on a dog."

Roulon snarled. "So the brave Colonel Thorne deserts the fight. What tales I'll have of how you turned coward, and ran."

"You'll have no tales, Roulon."

Two foot soldiers ran out of the hedge to stand beside the comte. "Attack, you bastards!" Roulon screamed. With a blood-freezing yell, the soldiers leaped toward the Englishman.

Becket's sword carved quick arcs through air and flesh, and both men fell.

He closed with Roulon. "Your battle is lost," Becket grated, his muscles taut with readiness. He slashed out.

With a protest of steel against steel, the comte met Becket's blade. "The Turk would have paid a great deal for you alive," Roulon gasped out. "I'll have to see what he'll give for you dead."

The comte was skilled, but had little discipline, and he couldn't hope to match Becket's strength. Again and again, the Englishman sliced under the comte's guard.

Roulon's arms shook with the effort of holding back Becket's powerful cuts and thrusts.

Becket slid his blade free with a hiss. "You are debris in my path, Roulon." The comte's sword slashed out. Becket parried it. The Frenchman's blade slid past Becket's arm.

There was the opening he needed. *"Adieu,* count of

the dogs,'' Becket said, and drove his blade into Roulon's heart.

Becket yanked his sword out of the Frenchman's body
and let it topple on top of Guillon's. Rings tumbled onto
the ground.

Kaatje stood rooted to the place Becket had pushed
her, the din of her terror beating in her ears. She
wrenched herself into motion, following Becket. Harry
trotted after her.

They continued on, hurrying past the deserted guard-
house at the gate. Once past the castle walls, Becket
urged them all to a run. They rounded a small hillock
and Kaatje saw three horses waiting under a wide
spreading oak. An inert form lay on the ground near
the black stallion's hooves.

Acheron stamped the ground and snorted, his reins
dangling. Harry ran up to the body, his pistol aimed at
the head. He booted it in the side, then tucked the pistol
back in his breeches. '' 'Ead's been kicked in,'' he said,
sliding a glance at the colonel's horse. ''Never did take
t' bein' rode by strangers, did ya, Atchie.''

Harry dragged the body out of their way as Becket
lifted Kaatje onto the gelding. He mounted Acheron.
''We ride, Mr. Fludd,'' he said, and headed out for the
abbey.

Kaatje saw nothing of their short ride, not the shiny
leaves of the beeches nor the rain-washed gullies cutting like wounds into the earth—only the scarlet soldier
on the midnight horse riding ahead of her.

Becket led them up to the stable lean-to where Niall
waited. Becket kicked out of his stirrups and dropped
to the ground. He helped Kaatje dismount. She had a
hand on his chest to steady herself. She pulled back
and wrapped her red cloak around her.

Niall rushed to them. ''Good to see you, colonel,
ma'am,'' the lieutenant said. ''We were startin' to get
a bit—''

Kaatje stared at the open doorway to the room where she and Becket had made love. A scrambling noise came from inside, then Pietr appeared framed in the opening.

"Mama!" he shrieked, his child-sized arms stretched wide. She ran to him and scooped him up, enveloping him in a hug.

"Oh, my baby, my baby," she murmured into his hair, spinning around, oblivious to everything but the precious wiggling little boy she held in her arms. She carried him inside.

"We heard shots, Mama! Pop, pop, pop," he said, his eyes lit with a feverish excitement. He glanced at his old nurse sitting in the corner mumbling her prayers. "Grette was scared, but I held her hand tight, Mama, and told her not to be afraid."

From behind them, Niall cleared his throat. Pietr looked abashed, his rosy cheeks deepening with a flush. "I guess . . . I guess maybe she held my hand a little too."

He pushed back in his mother's arms to look at her face. "Kern Torn won't think me bad, will he? I mean, 'cause I was a little afraid and all?"

Kaatje heard a sound behind her. She turned with Pietr still in her arms to see Becket watching them from the doorway. A perplexing range of emotions flashed through his eyes, making them darker and more enigmatic than ever.

"No, my lord chevalier," Becket said, bowing slightly and coming into the room. "Courage is never to be despised."

Pietr straightened his shoulders. "Courage, Kern Torn?" the boy asked, his eyes wide with hope and expectation. "But I was afraid!"

Becket squeezed the boy's shoulder. "Courage, Pietr. What else is courage but being afraid, yet going on?"

Kaatje smiled shakily at him, and Becket's chest

tightened with a bittersweet ache. He touched the boy's golden hair, so like his mother's. Death had once meant only an end to the anger that choked him. But now, for the first time in seven years, he wanted to live. Sweet God, he wanted to live. He forced his gaze away from Kaatje and met Niall's understanding eyes.

"Aye, sir," Niall said, " 'tis courage indeed not to listen to everything inside you shouting not to go on, to take what you've got and run. 'Tis a courage of the finest sort, sir."

"That it is, kern'l," Harry said from behind him.

"The horses, Mr. Fludd," Becket said.

"At the ready, sir." Becket nodded, and went to Niall and began talking with him in low urgent tones.

Kaatje hugged Pietr tighter. She felt as if she were continually holding her breath, not knowing what each minute would bring.

Becket seemed suddenly to materialize in front of her. "It's time," he said. She set her son on his feet.

Becket took her hand and led her out to the horses, Niall and Pietr following behind them. She looked at her Englishman, the large mass of his war horse dark behind him, framing him with massive power. They were both creatures of war, trained for battle, trained to plunge through thick gunpowder smoke and the deadly rain of musket fire, trained to fulfill their duty.

He cupped her face in his hands. "Stay with Niall till you reach England. He'll see you settled."

"No, I—" She looked deep into his indigo eyes.

"El Müzir has bolted," he told her. "I must follow him to Cerfontaine."

She closed her eyes tight, not wanting him to see her tears. His battle was nearly done. There would be no rallying cries, no urgent drums beating out the signal to march on—and no victors.

"Becket—"

He dropped his hands and swung into Acheron's saddle. "Lieutenant," Becket called, going alongside Niall. "Take the northeast road you came in on. No reckless heroics. Niall, get them out safely. That's the only thing that matters." He looked at Pietr standing next to Niall. "My lord chevalier, take care of your mother." The boy's chin trembled, but he nodded and straightened his shoulders.

"The papers, Niall?" Becket radiated intense, barely controlled power.

Niall smacked his coat pocket. "All right here, colonel. Letters to the captain-general—" He broke off and glanced at Kaatje. "And to your father."

"Remember, lieutenant. Your obligation to me does not end until madame and the boy are safely under my family's protection."

Niall swallowed hard and nodded. "Yes sir."

Becket held out his hand and Niall gripped it firmly. "My regards, lieutenant."

"Kern'l, sir," Harry said, coming up to Becket.

The colonel clapped him on the shoulder. "She'll need your help, Harry. It won't be easy for her. Serve her as well as you've served me. I couldn't ask more of any man."

"Yes sir, kern'l."

Becket looked at Kaatje one last time, his eyes crisscrossing her face as if to burn her features into his memory. Then he turned Acheron and dug in his heels, the man and beast riding out of the abbey grounds without looking back.

Pietr untied a soft leather pouch at his belt and held out a shiny stone to show her. "See what Aunt Lece gave me, Mama, when she came to say goodbye."

Kaatje gasped. With a shaking hand, she cupped her son's outstretched palm in hers. Kaatje knew exactly what the stones meant. They'd come from El Müzir, not Lece, and they told her where the devil would be waiting.

Pietr looked at the rock in his hand. "Is it bad, Mama? She gave me more." He shook the bag, and it rattled.

"No, sweetheart. No, they're not bad. Mama played with stones just like this when she was a girl. In the caves at Cerfontaine."

"Do you want this one, Mama?" Pietr asked. "I have plenty."

"Yes . . . Yes, thank you, sweeting." She took the small pink rock from her son's hand and tucked it into the front of her bodice.

Niall came up behind her. "We must go, ma'am."

She said nothing, her eyes straining to see where Becket had ridden away from her, to the north, toward Cerfontaine. The rock hidden between her breasts dug into her flesh. She frowned. How will he know where to find El Müzir?

The Turk was hiding in the caverns. Becket would never find him there. She had to— *No, no.* She was fragmenting inside, the mortar that held everything she loved crumbling away. *What do I do? What do I do?*

"Lieutenant, how safe is the ride out of here?" Kaatje asked, shaking with the battle going on inside her. How could she leave Pietr again? *No, no,* she couldn't.

Becket will die if you don't.

Niall's hand gripped and ungripped his sword hilt. "The only danger is here, madame. Once we're past the city, the way is clear. We . . . The Allies control the road from the border. Now, ma'am, we—"

"Where do you go, lieutenant?"

"*We* go to the Hague! The duke's quarters. Then to England."

"Could you keep my little boy safe without me?" *How can I even say the words?*

"Ma'am! You must come with us! The colonel's orders—"

Kaatje faced him, her eyes stinging. "I have to go after him, lieutenant. He needs me."

"He'd have my head if I let you go!" he said, clearly appalled. "We must leave, *now!*"

"And El Müzir will have *his* if I don't go!" She pulled the rock from her bodice and held it out to him. "This is from my sister. When we were children, we used these to mark our way in the caverns near Cerfontaine. Have you ever been lost inside solid rock, lieutenant? Scores of passages leading off everywhere. El Müzir has my sister to guide him. The colonel has no one.

"Think, Niall! Who catches whom then? The devil will track him like an animal and put him back in his chains."

The lieutenant's eyes were wide with understanding. "Lord have mercy on my soul, ma'am. I have my orders. I can't let—"

"You must! She whirled and knelt to hug Pietr tightly.

"My little soldier," she whispered. "Colonel Thorne still needs me, sweeting. Do you understand that?"

He looked at her with eyes wide with apprehension. "Kern Torn needs you?" he asked, then added in a small voice, "You're leaving me?"

She rubbed her little boy's arms. *How can I do this?* She brushed a gold lock of hair out of his face. "My precious chevalier, you're so young." She swallowed unshed tears. "When you've grown big and tall and somebody needs your help very very much, will you help them?"

He nodded, looking at the ground.

"Even if it meant you'd have to leave behind the dearest thing in the world? For at least a little while?" *Please God that it's just a little while. Please God that I come back.*

He straightened his shoulders and raised his eyes to

hers. He nodded. "Yes, Mama. It'd be my duty." He sniffled. "Mama, do you have a duty to Kern Torn?"

"Yes, sweetheart, I do." She hugged him. "I made a mistake, Pietr. And this is the only way I have of making it right. Can you ride with Lieutenant Elcot and keep Grette safe?"

"Yes, Mama."

She wrapped Pietr tight in her arms one last time. "I love you, sweeting."

His arms went around her neck. "Me, too, Mama." His chin looked unsteady, but he straightened his shoulders. He looked at Niall, his eyes shining with both pride and unshed tears. "Kern Torn needs my mama," he told the lieutenant.

Niall shuffled his feet. "Ma'am—"

"Do you stop me, lieutenant?"

He remained silent.

Kaatje took the gelding's reins from a startled Harry Fludd. " 'Tain't wise, ma'am," he said, shaking his head.

"Wise be damned, Mr. Fludd," she said. "Lift me up." Harry grunted and threw her onto the horse with a thump. She leaned over and kissed him on the cheek. "Maybe I can help him, Harry. I have to try."

Niall scraped his hands through his red hair. "Ma'am! I gave my word I'd see you and the boy safe—"

She met his eyes and held them. "Your bond still holds. Keep my son safe, lieutenant—or you will never be safe from me."

Niall scooped up Pietr and plopped the boy on his horse's saddle. The lieutenant leaped into the saddle behind him. Harry helped Grette mount his smaller horse.

"Ma'am," the lieutenant began, his hand hovering near his sword hilt.

Kaatje swallowed. "I can catch up to him, Niall. I'm his only chance."

Niall dropped his hand. "Not much light left, ma'am. You'll have to ride at a dead run to catch him."

"Thank you." She kissed her son goodbye one last time, then dug in her heels and headed toward Becket.

Kaatje ignored her billowing cloak as she raced down the north road. The gelding couldn't match Acheron's strength or power, but it was fast. The image of her little golden-haired chevalier tore at her. *My sweet baby, I have to do this.*

Even if she'd stayed with him, her son's safety was in the hands of others. Becket's safety was in hers.

She gave the castle and the city a wide berth, her heart pounding in her chest at the thought of the attacking Frenchmen coming after her. None did. Claude's men must be giving them a good fight.

Ahead, as she neared the fateful inn of the ambush, she could see Becket on the black stallion, riding with a smooth, ground-eating gait. The darkness of the forest spilled out over the hills ahead of him.

"Becket!" she shouted. He pulled Acheron up sharply.

"Jesu," she heard him say as she rode up.

Becket grabbed the gelding's bridle. "My God, I'll see Niall hang for letting you go."

"No, it wasn't his fault," she said, trying to quell the uneasiness inside her. Becket's eyes were opaque. "Don't be angry. I had to come." He started to turn the gelding back the way it'd come. "What are you doing? We have to go to Cerfontaine!"

"We go east until we meet up with Niall. After I kill him, he can take you on to England."

"No, I must—" she put a hand on his arm to stop him.

"Your place is with your son, Kaatje."

She dropped her hand. "I know. I know. My heart is already breaking. But I have . . ."

Kaatje pulled out the small pink rock from her bodice and held it up for him to see. "I have this. Lece gave it to Pietr to give to me. It is from El Müzir."

Becket tugged off his glove and took the rock from her, his fingers closing over it. It radiated the warmth from her breasts into his skin, and he held it tight.

"Lece and I used them to mark our way through the caverns when we were little. Becket, that rock is a message to me from El Müzir. It tells you where he is." Her voice faltered.

Acheron grew suddenly restive until Becket settled him with his hand. "Explain yourself, madame."

"El Müzir isn't in the chateau, Becket. He's in the caverns. That's what this rock means. But you would never find him there. *He* would find you. He knows that. I must go with you, to guide you."

"No."

"I must!"

"Damn you, woman—*I don't want you with me.*" He threw the rock to the ground and thrust his hand back into his glove.

"I must, Becket. You will never find El Müzir without me," she answered.

"Kaatje. Kaatje. You weaken me. If I falter, if El Müzir—"

She reached out and put her hand to his lips to stop the words. "I know, Becket." *What if Becket should die and El Müzir yet live?* Kaatje's throat closed with sudden pain. Her eyes stung. She felt suddenly empty inside like a burned-out tree that by a freak of nature had been left standing. The pain of it seared her.

"I don't want to lead you to El Müzir. If I thought he would not find you in that labyrinth, I would leave with my next breath. But he has Lece to guide him."

"I do not want you with me."

"I know," she said unevenly. Her eyes squeezed shut. "Please. It is a bitter gift for me to give. Accept it. It is all I have."

She heard his weary indrawn breath. His lips were a feather touch on her forehead. "We ride to Cerfontaine," he said, and turned Acheron to the north.

They spent the next three days riding side by side. The nights they spent in each other's arms, two lovers murmuring a lifetime's worth of dreams in the few hours left them. Sleep would steal over them, and Kaatje would slumber with Becket's heartbeat strong and sure beneath her head.

On the third day, well before dawn, Becket woke sitting at the base of a giant oak, Kaatje cradled in his arms. He let his head fall back against the trunk, his eyes closed, cherishing the beloved pressure of her body.

She stirred. "No," she said sleepily, "I don't want the day to begin."

"Neither do I, sweet sylph. But we cannot stay the sun."

They prepared to leave. Kaatje went to the gelding, but Becket swept her into his arms and set her on Acheron. He rubbed the stallion's nose and looked up at her, his eyes shadowed in the dim light before dawn. "Take Acheron for your son's horse, Kaatje. He and his get are worthy of such a brave chevalier."

She choked on a sob as Becket mounted behind her.

They arrived at Cerfontaine in the hour before dawn and rode up to the kitchen door, Becket leading the riderless gelding. The sun would soon rise from behind the eastern ridge.

Kaatje made a move to dismount, but he put a hand on her shoulder. He dropped to the ground. Listening, sensing, he studied the darkness around them.

"I don't trust the quiet," he said, his voice low.

"El Müzir is hidden deep in the caverns," Kaatje said. "He won't know we're here."

"He knows, Kaatje."

She looked into his shadowed face. The details of his beloved features were murky in the darkness, but her mind filled in the indigo of his eyes, the planes and angles that made up the face she had come to love.

"Afterward," he said, "ride to the nearest village. Take refuge in the church and send for Niall."

"I'm the daughter of Kapitein Pietr van Staden, remember?" She sat up straighter in the saddle. "I shall not hide."

"I want you safe, hussar's daughter. You ride." He pressed her hand to emphasize his words, then he faded into the shadows that surrounded the kitchen door.

She inhaled to call out after him, to bring him back, but then closed her mouth and let the words go unsaid. The whisper of leather hinges told her he'd entered the kitchen, though the door made no sound.

An owl hooted and leaves whispered in the breeze of a passing animal. Kaatje's skin prickled, making her feel as if she'd walked through a spider's web. At that moment, the darkness began fading with the first light of morning, bringing that breath of stillness that settles over the land when the creatures of night cease their rustlings and the creatures of day have not yet ventured forth. The shroud of night lifted.

A twig broke under a footfall. She gasped. A hand clamped her wrist in an iron grip.

"Kaatje," Becket said, then released her hand. "You were right. He is in the caverns. The bolt hole in the kitchen has been cleared."

He lifted her off the horse and she stumbled. He caught her, and the warmth of his hands chased the morning chill from her arms.

Don't take your touch away. Hold me. Hold me that

I may forever remember . . . He gently pushed her away.

He strode to the well in the garden and brought back a dipper of fresh water. "This will quench your thirst, if not your sadness," he said.

She met his eyes. "How can we walk through this morning as if it were any other? Becket . . ." Her hands went to the dipper, touching the uneven wood with her fingertips. "No, I'm sorry. It is this place, I think, that makes it all so much worse.

"It seems that here is where I am destined to lose those I . . . cherish. I lost my mother here, and my sister—without even knowing it." Kaatje's throat tightened. "And now—"

She put the rim to her lips and drank a cool swallow. She held the dipper out to him. He put his hands over hers and drew the wooden bowl to his mouth.

Her hands were warm under his, and he could feel the small nervous movements of her fingers. Her lips had parted with a quick indrawn breath. He drank deeply, wanting to say words that would soothe the sadness from her eyes of cloud-shadow gray.

Long curling tendrils of golden hair had been tousled from their pins during their ride. A single tear fell from the corner of her eye and slipped down a strand like a diamond being strung on a chain of gold.

Becket threw down the dipper and cupped her face, pressing his forehead to hers. "God help me," he said, his voice unsteady. "God help me . . ."

"Becket, let other soldiers do this," she begged. "Let others die. I love you. I can't bear—"

"I gave my oath, sweet sylph. An oath to a dying man."

Kaatje covered her mouth with her hand to stop the trembling.

"That man was my brother, Kaatje."

He held her close. He had known her, had loved her

body, had come to love her soul. She had made him more than he had been. He could not curse the fates, for they had given her to him if only for so short a time.

He was no longer a cursed man. He was a man who— once in his life—had been blessed.

"Becket—" With shaking hands, she smoothed the facings of his scarlet coat. She looked up at him. "I love you."

He looked shaken, as if caught off guard, then he took her mouth in a quick deep kiss. "Sweet sylph," he said, his lips touching hers as he spoke. He kissed her again, then stepped back.

"The sun has risen, Kaatje," he told her, wanting to tell her so much more. "It is time."

The chateau was eerily quiet as she stepped into the passage behind the panel door in the kitchen. He was close at her back, holding a kitchen lantern, its light spilling into a feeble pool before her. He filled the narrow tunnel behind her, scarcely able to walk upright.

They headed downward. Rough wooden walls quickly gave way to damp, musty-smelling stone as they entered the labyrinth of the caverns. Kaatje strained to bring back the memory of her childhood games. Black tunnels beckoned to the right, then the left; their path would branch off and she would close her eyes to recall her footsteps from so long ago. Breathing seemed to get more difficult, but she knew it was just her mind imagining the pressure of the rock above her head.

The energy at her back condensed, like wine distilling into potent brandy. The intensity built, making her feel as if a hungry stalking animal were at her heels. There came a steady, near-silent *click, click, click,* and she knew Becket's hand was on his sword hilt. She fought the urge to hurry, halting at intervals to listen in the dim lantern light.

Ahead a breath of sound caught at her and she

stopped. The tunnel curved away. Kaatje could see the flickering shadows of torchlight. Panic ate at her.

She turned to face him. With the thread of a whisper, she said, "Around the corner, the tunnel opens up into a cavern as big as one of Claude's rooms." She struggled to see him clearly in the murky light. "Becket—"

He pulled her into his arms and held her close one last time, as if letting the battle fury slide away if only for a moment. He kissed her golden hair. His arms were strong and warm, and her heart fluttered like the wings of a startled bird.

She squeezed her eyes closed. *No! Sweet God, it hurts.*

"All the words to say—" he began.

"No," she whispered, "no, say nothing. Let me lie to myself. Let me go on believing that one day you'll come to me again."

"I cannot stay my fate, Kaatje." He caressed her cheek with a feather-light touch. "My sweet and honorable lady," he whispered, "tell your son of me. Tell him how you brought a dead man to life with your love."

He struggled with something inside himself for a long silent moment, then he kissed her.

"I love you," he breathed against her lips. She drew his breath inside her as if that alone would keep him alive. He pulled back and smoothed her hair with his gloved hand.

"Becket—" Her words choked her.

"I must go," he whispered into her hair.

A woman's shriek came from the cavern. Lece.

Becket's battle fury slid seamlessly back into place. He moved Kaatje aside.

"Go back to Acheron," Becket commanded. "Kaatje, for God's sake, *go.*" She took a step away from him.

He drew his sword. With long powerful strides, he went to the cavern entrance.

El Müzir stood on the other side of the cavern, his image wavering in the torchlight, dressed in black silk trousers, a scimitar in one hand and a rope in the other. The rope was around Lece's neck.

"The world has grown weary of you, Turk," Becket said, his voice ringing out across the cavern. "As have I."

The Turk put his fists on his hips, his wide muscular chest heaving with irritation. "Welcome home to your master, *esir,*" he said. He jerked on the rope, then threw Lece from him. "You are early. Perhaps the little sister was too impatient to betray you."

"Did you think to catch me, Turk? She told me of your schemes."

"Indeed." El Müzir kicked at a pile of shackles at his feet, and they rattled. "And did she tell you I saved your chains?"

Hate made Becket's vision shimmer at the edges. He took a step toward El Müzir. He stopped, forcing himself to shoot an appraising glance around the cavern. Torches were stuck at intervals in cracks in the rock. Ledges thrust out from the stone wall of the cavern like small platforms. On one stood a small onion-shaped flask.

"Yes, yes, come to me, *esir.* Feel what it is like to walk free for the last time."

Becket's balance imperceptibly shifted to the balls of his feet. "Come to *me,* Turk."

El Müzir frowned. His dark gaze slid to the flask near his shoulder. He raised his scimitar and rocked it with the point of the blade. And laughed. "Did you come for this, *esir?*" He rocked it again. "I may give it to you. At the end. Perhaps your Kester would not have babbled so long if I'd used this to end his suffering instead of a whip."

A low level thrumming came from deep in Becket's chest like the rumble of a warning predator. He advanced.

El Müzir laughed and crouched to meet him.

Kaatje watched from the tunnel, a hand jammed into her mouth to keep from screaming. Power from the two men radiated out like heat from a smith's forge. There was something terrifying between them that went beyond the meeting of two adversaries. Becket closed on El Müzir with the deliberate steps of a man closing on his mortal enemy.

Their swords met, steel on steel, again and again, the deadly clang reverberating through the cavern till her bones were ringing with it. She barely noticed Lece crawling toward her along the wall.

Hate consumed Becket. Dark passion surged through his blood, the pounding rhythm like Acheron's hooves thundering on the road.

Vengeance throbbed at his temples. Exultant fury commanded the muscles of his shoulder, arm, wrist. The coppery taste of his imminent revenge was sweet on his tongue.

Becket's sword matched the Turk's blow for blow, slash for slash. Black silk caught on Becket's blade, then fell away in two halves. The scimitar's blade skimmed across his arm, and scarlet wool parted.

"Hate me, *esir*," El Müzir said with a gleam in his dark eyes. He deflected a powerful cut from Becket's sword, and blade slid on blade with a loud undulating moan. The deadly curved edge of the scimitar sliced a button from Becket's coat. "Remember your brother, *esir*."

Kester! Becket *became* the fury inside him, the hate, the rage that he had carried with him for so long. Years of dark avenging dreams were dry tinder to the flames that fed his bloodlust and turned his vision red.

El Müzir's blade veered at the last moment, sending

it slicing toward him. Becket twisted. His arm shot out,
extending the full length of his reach. The scimitar collided with Becket's sword near the point of the blade.
With a two-handed grip, the Turk used the full force of
his body to drive his blade down. Becket's muscles
strained against the powerful stroke.

A low rumble came from Becket's throat. His muscles burned with the effort to keep the scimitar from
gouging into him. The yell grew louder, stronger. He
felt El Müzir's blade give a hair's breadth. The sound
resonated in Becket's chest, down his arm. It formed
itself into a single drawn-out sound of defiance.

"Hür adam," he roared, and threw off the Turk's
blade. El Müzir swayed, then leaped out of Becket's
reach.

Becket shook his head, trying to clear the red haze
from his vision. Both men stood back, dragging in deep
gulps of air, their keen eyes watching each other. The
devil grinned at him.

Grinned. With the impact of a cannonball, Becket
realized he was fighting the way El Müzir wanted him
to fight. Hate, not skill, was guiding his blade. And
hate made a man stupid.

Becket struggled with the dreams, the fury. He faced
his enemy. He met the cold black eyes that had tor-
mented him. Devil's eyes that had glinted with laughter
when Kester died.

He's just a man, Becket, Kaatje had told him. *A man,
not a devil.*

"Do you think you can best your master?" El Müzir
called to him with a sneer. "Think how well you will
fight shackled in the darkness. I'll have you whipped
and dragged through the dust. Not even dreams of your
Flemish whore will sustain you."

Becket's vision cleared. He straightened and shifted
his weight. Colonel Becket, Lord Thorne faced the

once-powerful sultan of Temesvár. Enemy to enemy.
Man to man.

"She is your weakness, *esir.*"

Becket raised his sword. "She is my strength."

The gleam left El Müzir's eyes and the grin died.
"Attack me!" the Turk snarled. "Why do you hesitate?
Is your courage faltering? Is cowardice freezing your
bones? *Attack!*"

El Müzir charged. Becket met him, their swords
crossing with a resounding clang. The impact jarred
Becket's arm, almost numbing it, but he countered immediately. He sliced through the Turk's shoulder. Red
spilled out on the dark skin.

"Dog!" El Müzir slashed out. Becket twisted, and
turned it aside. A gold uniform button flew off, cracking against the stone.

Kaatje collapsed against the wall, her heart in her
throat, Becket's words resounding in her head. Lece
crawled to her and dragged herself upright against the
wall, a pistol dangling from her fingers.

"Forgive me, little sister," she gasped out. Livid
bruises marked her face. She laughed bitterly, then
groaned, grabbing her ribs. She coughed.

"My 'great love' is done with me, Kaat. And there
is no . . . thrill in it. It was all a—" Lece broke off,
flinching with a spasm of pain. "Oh, Constantin, forgive me." Kaatje reached out to touch her, to comfort
her, but her sister waved her away. "No, keep your
comfort for your *anglais.*"

Lece straightened a little and looked at the pistol in
her hand. "I could go back to my husband. Constantin
always takes me back, no matter what." She sobbed
and put a hand on her stomach. "No matter what."

She clawed at Kaatje's arm. "It was all a lie, little
sister. From the first. We were so easily led by his
handful of tricks. Even little Pierre . . . Pietr."

Kaatje squeezed Lece's fingers on her arm. "What about Pietr. What tricks?"

Lece looked away, her brown eyes blearily focused on the end of the pistol barrel. "It would be so easy," she murmured. Her thumb played with the hammer.

Kaatje wrapped her fingers around the barrel and pulled the pistol from Lece's slack grasp. "What tricks, Lece?"

"Pietr has no falling sickness, Kaat. Oncelus needed more gold for that filthy Lucifer's Fire of his than I could get for him. So he gave Pietr a potion to make him sick."

A trick.

"Easy then to drain the St. Benoit coffers of gold." Lece pushed off from the wall. "We've both been fooled, little sister. He got to your purse through your son, and to my purse through my . . ." She broke off, running her hands down her body, her hands stopping at her stomach. "Constantin always takes me back," she said, and staggered away down the tunnel.

A trick. The pistol was heavy in Kaatje's hand, the hammer stiff against her thumb. Her vision dimmed. *A trick.* Her little boy. She raised the barrel. The fear. The anguish. The lost dreams.

Kaatje gripped the pistol with both hands and aimed.

Becket's uniform was in shreds, a score of shallow, bleeding cuts on his arms, his chest, one across his forehead. Lines of red crisscrossed the Turk's bare arms and chest. Both men were rasping harsh and fast.

Becket parried a deadly blow and sliced a long arc of red down the Turk's chest. El Müzir snarled and leaped back. Becket followed. Their swords collided with a vicious clang.

Kaatje watched them down the barrel of the pistol, her body frozen. Hilt to hilt, Becket and El Müzir faced each other, every muscle straining against the other's strength.

"Shoot, little sister," the Turk hissed out.

El Müzir pushed, and Becket fell back, glancing at her. Mad laughter boomed out. "You see, *esir,* you cannot win."

"Kaatje—" The word came out in a quick burst as he gulped in air.

"It was a trick, Becket," she cried, her throat nearly choked closed from her hate for the Turk. "Pietr has no falling sickness! *All a trick.*" The pistol shook.

The Turk jumped onto a low ledge, then scooped up the flask of Lucifer's Fire and dangled it in front of him. "Shoot me, little sister, and this falls on your *anglais.*"

El Müzir strutted back and forth on the ledge. "You are mine again, *esir.*" Stones dribbled down the side of the cavern. He threw his scimitar at Becket, who struck it aside. It clattered to the stone floor. The Turk laughed. "I shall be long in thanking the little sister for distracting you, *esir.* Shall I let you watch?"

He swung his arms out in wide gesture, one hand firmly gripping the flask. "Yes! How I shall savor—" The ledge slipped. El Müzir scrambled to keep his footing.

The flask shattered against the stone. The silvery contents splattered onto the Turk's hair. In a frenzy, he tried to get it off. He jostled a torch. And burst into flame.

"Aiiiy," he shrieked, the sound rising to a piercing blade of sound as flame enveloped him.

Becket sprinted to Kaatje. She stared at the pillar of fire on the crumbling ledge, the pistol inert in her hands. He grabbed it, twisted—and shot El Müzir in the heart. The keening ended.

Becket stood motionless. With an act of mercy, he had fulfilled his oath to his brother. The devil—the *man*—was dead.

And he was alive.

The pistol dropped. His senses returned to him. The sound. The smell.

Kaatje. Becket whirled and lifted her into his arms. He rushed into the tunnel, crouching over to shield her body with his as he sped out of the darkness, following her whispered directions. Daylight streamed in through the open panel door. He was through in an instant. He kicked open the kitchen door and carried her into the sunlight.

He held her close, and spun around and around in the bright midday light. Laughter bubbled out of him.

"My sylph! My sweet, sweet, Kaatje." He set her on her feet, cupping her face in his hands. "No more battlefields. The darkness is ended."

She reached up a shaking hand and drew it over his face as if not believing it was real. He closed his eyes and kissed the palm. "Be with me, Kaatje. Always." He looked into her great gray eyes and smiled. "Sweet sylph."

He kissed her softly. "Sweet wife."

"Becket," she whispered. "Oh, my Englishman. Always."

He carried her to Acheron. The gelding was gone.

"Lece must have taken—" Kaatje began, but he stopped her with another kiss. She smiled up at him, and Becket knew his love would be ever new and ever in the sun. With a laugh such as he had not laughed in years, he twirled her around again.

He sat her on Acheron's back and looked up at her, glorying in the sight. "Sweet sylph, will you mind your little golden-haired chevalier growing up to be an English gentleman?"

She put her hand to his cheek and shook her head, her eyes telling of the fullness of her emotions. "How could I mind if he grows up with the honor and goodness and strength of his Kern Torn?"

He swept her down off the horse and kissed her thoroughly. "I love you, Kaatje van Staden de St. Benoit. You are my strength. My strength, Kaatje. Forever."

Becket kissed her again, then set her on Acheron. He mounted behind her and they rode into the sunlight, his arm strong and sure across her back.

Avon Romances—
the best in exceptional authors and unforgettable novels!

DEVIL'S MOON   Suzannah Davis
76127-0/$3.95 US/$4.95 Can

ROUGH AND TENDER   Selina MacPherson
76322-2/$3.95 US/$4.95 Can

CAPTIVE ROSE   Miriam Minger
76311-7/$3.95 US/$4.95 Can

RUGGED SPLENDOR   Robin Leigh
76318-4/$3.95 US/$4.95 Can

CHEROKEE NIGHTS   Genell Dellin
76014-2/$4.50 US/$5.50 Can

SCANDAL'S DARLING   Anne Caldwell
76110-6/$4.50 US/$5.50 Can

LAVENDER FLAME   Karen Stratford
76267-6/$4.50 US/$5.50 Can

FOOL FOR LOVE   DeLoras Scott
76342-7/$4.50 US/$5.50 Can

OUTLAW BRIDE   Katherine Compton
76411-3/$4.50 US/$5.50 Can

DEFIANT ANGEL   Stephanie Stevens
76449-0/$4.50 US/$5.50 Can

The WONDER of WOODIWISS

continues with the publication of
her newest novel in rack-size paperback—

SO WORTHY MY LOVE

☐ #76148-3
$5.95 U.S. ($6.95 Canada)

THE FLAME AND THE FLOWER
☐ #00525-5
$5.50 U.S. ($6.50 Canada)

THE WOLF AND THE DOVE
☐ #00778-9
$5.50 U.S. ($6.50 Canada)

SHANNA
☐ #38588-0
$5.50 U.S. ($6.50 Canada)

ASHES IN THE WIND
☐ #76984-0
$5.50 U.S. ($6.50 Canada)

A ROSE IN WINTER
☐ #84400-1
$5.50 U.S. ($6.50 Canada)

COME LOVE A STRANGER
☐ #89936-1
$5.50 U.S. ($6.50 Canada)

THE COMPLETE COLLECTION AVAILABLE FROM AVON BOOKS WHEREVER PAPERBACKS ARE SOLD

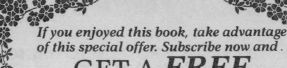